"Are all deities so insane?" he grumbled.

Yes. But... "Call me after you've lived seventy thousand years without anyone to share it with," she snapped. She had her brethren, but they were all just as miserable as she was, for the most part. "Sorry—I didn't come here to pick another fight. I came to apologize for my lack of compassion toward you. And now I'm offering my help, if you want it."

He lowered his head and let out a sigh. "I don't know. I don't know anything anymore. It feels like my life..." His voice trailed off into deep contemplation.

Ixtab moved behind him and pressed her body and cheek against his bare back. "I am sorry," she said quietly, placing her hands around his waist.

Antonio sucked in a sharp breath and jerked his spine straight. "Why do you keep touching me?" he said in a low, deep voice.

She sighed. "I don't know." Then she inhaled his scent, fully expecting him to pull away, but he didn't. Several moments ticked by and she noticed that his heaviness began to lift, replaced with a heat that sieved through his skin and into her body. Her own heart began to thump in time with his.

Gods, what was happening to her? She instantly knew she would never get enough of this, of him. She was addicted...

READERS LOVE
THE ACCIDENTALLY YOURS SERIES!

The following humans have been spared from the apocalypse (and will get one free ride on Cimil's unicorn):

"A thrill ride of *epic* proportions...and that is just the guy in the book."
—Jean B.

"Mimi, girl, your books made me PMP (pee in my pants)."
—Name removed to protect reader's social life

"Mimi Jean, your books got me into a lot of trouble with my husband...and I loved every minute of it!"   —Kassie B.

"Mimi's books sizzle; they make me laugh and fall in love with love every time I read them."   —Ashley Swartz

"Incredible book! I was up all night reading and laughing my buttocks off!! Keep them coming, Mimi!"
—Kimberly DiNino-DeCenso

"You keep me up all night wanting to reread each book over and over. I think your writing is addicting and I love it."
—Ashlee R.

"The gods will have you saying *Fifty Shades* of what?"
—C. B. Wells

"Give me some black jade and a god for the weekend. No Payals or Maaskab need apply. P.S. Someone please find Cimil a garage sale and something pink to keep her out of trouble. Maybe."
—Dy

"Who needs a man, when you can have a god!"   —Ally K.

VAMPIRES NEED NOT...APPLY?

MIMI JEAN PAMFILOFF

FOREVER

NEW YORK   BOSTON

Forever
Hachette Book Group
237 Park Avenue
New York, NY 10017

www.HachetteBookGroup.com

Printed in the United States of America

Originally published as an ebook

First mass-market edition: March 2013
10 9 8 7 6 5 4 3 2 1

OPM

Forever is an imprint of Grand Central Publishing.
The Forever name and logo are trademarks of Hachette Book Group, Inc.

The Hachette Speakers Bureau provides a wide range of authors for speaking events. To find out more, go to www.hachettespeakersbureau.com or call (866) 376-6591.

The publisher is not responsible for websites (or their content) that are not owned by the publisher.

To my readers. Your endless smiles, funny notes, and cheering make this world such a godsdamned happy place to live in. Thank you! (You also get a WOO!)

Acknowledgments
(aka "Woos!")

Javi! I wrote another book, and you still love me! WOO!!

Seb and Stef...you guys rock for pitching in while I worked like a madwoman so...woo! (And I love you.)

Accidental Beta Readers: Many WOO-HOOS for you ladies! Thank you for taking time out of your busy schedules to provide feedback. Vicki Randall, Kim McNicholl, Karen Schwartz, Ute Carlin, Naughty Nana, and Ashlee Randall.

Latoya and Team Forever! Woo! (That transition was a lot of dang work, but we made it...so that gets an extra WOO!)

Warning

This book contains very naughty words (in two languages, no less!), sexual content (yes, I know . . . not nearly enough. You ladies are such horndogs! Seriously . . . ☺), hot men with unrealistically large man-goodies, silliness, snark, sarcasm, and blatant abuse of the Engleesh language. (Cir..il would be proud.)

Match the Quote

Which Deity Said What?

1. "There's a method to my madness. Yes, that method might be a teensy bit evil and seemingly random, but someone's gotta make life interesting."
   A. Cimil, ex–Goddess of the Underworld
   B. Acan, God of Intoxication and Wine
   C. Zac Cimi, God of (TBD)

2. "Living for seventy thousand years without love is a fate I would not wish on my worst enemies."
   A. Máax, the One No One Speaks Of
   B. Camaxtli, Goddess of the Hunt
   C. K'ak, just... K'ak.

3. "A happy ending awaits us all, but only if we are brave enough to risk everything and have faith it will come."
   A. Ixtab, Goddess of Suicide
   B. Camaxtli, Goddess of the Hunt
   C. Akna, Goddess of Fertility

4. "Don't touch the unicorn. Never, ever touch the unicorn."
   A. Cimil, ex-Goddess of the Underworld
   B. The clowns (Cimil thinks they are deities, so that counts)
   C. Cimil's unicorn

SEE ANSWERS IN BACK

VAMPIRES NEED NOT...APPLY?

Prologue

New Year's Day. Near Sedona, Arizona. Estate of Kinich Ahau, ex–God of the Sun

Teetering on the very edge of a long white sofa, Penelope stared up at the oversized, round clock mounted on the wall. In ten minutes, the sun would set and the man they once knew as the God of the Sun would awake. Changed. She hoped.

Sadly, there'd been a hell of a lot of hoping lately and little good it did her or her two friends, Emma and Helena, sitting patiently at her side. Like Penelope, the other two women had been thrust into this new world—filled with gods, vampires, and other immortal combinations in between—by means of the men they'd fallen in love with.

Bottom line? Not going so great.

Helena, the blonde who held two bags of blood in her

lap, reached for Penelope and smoothed down her frizzy hair. "Don't worry. Kinich will wake up. He will."

Pen nodded. She must look like a mess. Why hadn't she taken the time to at least run a brush through her hair for him? He loved her dark hair. Maybe because she didn't truly believe he'd come back to life. "I don't know what's worse, thinking I've lost him forever or knowing if he wakes up, he'll be something he hates."

Emma chimed in, "He doesn't hate vampires. He hates being immortal."

Pen shrugged. "Guess it really doesn't matter now what he hates." Kinich would either wake up or he wouldn't. If he didn't, she might not have the will to go on without him. Too much had happened. She needed him. She loved him. And most of all, she wanted him to know she was sorry for ever doubting him. He'd given his life to save them all.

Tick.

Another move of the hand.

Tock.

And another.

Nine more minutes.

The doorbell jolted the three women.

"Dammit." Emma, who wore her combat-ready outfit—black cargos and a black tee that made her red hair look like the flame on the tip of a match—marched to the door. "I told everyone not to disturb us."

Penelope knew that would never happen. A few hundred soldiers lurked outside and a handful of deities waited in the kitchen, snacking on cookies; new vampires weren't known to be friendly. But Penelope insisted on having only her closest friends by her side for the moment of truth. Besides, Helena was a new vampire herself—a long story—and knew what to do.

Emma unlocked the dead bolt. "Some idiot probably forgot my orders. I'll send him away—" The door flew open with a cold gust of desert wind and debris. It took a moment for the three women to register who stood in the doorway.

The creature, with long, matted dreads beaded with human teeth, wore nothing more than a loincloth over her soot-covered body.

Christ almighty, it can't be, thought Pen, as the smell of Maaskab—good old-fashioned, supernatural, pre-Hispanic death and darkness—entered her nose.

Before Emma could drop a single f-bomb, the dark priestess raised her hand and blew Emma across the large, open living room, slamming her against the wall.

Helena screamed and rushed to Emma's side.

Paralyzed with fear, Penelope watched helplessly as the Maaskab woman glided into the living room and stood before her, a mere two yards away.

The woman raised her gaunt, grimy finger, complete with overgrown grime-caked fingernail, and pointed directly at Penelope. "Youuuu."

Holy wheat toast. Penelope instinctively stepped back. The woman's voice felt like razor blades inside her ears. Penelope had to think fast. Not only did she fear for her life and for those of her friends, but both she and Emma were pregnant. Helena had a baby daughter. *Think, dammit. Think.*

Penelope considered drawing the power of the sun, an ability she'd recently gained when she had become the interim Sun God—another long story—but releasing that much heat into the room might fry everyone in it.

Grab the monster's arm. Channel it directly into her.

"Youuuu," the Maaskab woman said once again.

"Damn, lady." Penelope covered her ears. "Did you swallow a bucket of rusty nails? That voice ... gaaaahh."

The monster grunted. "I come with a message."

"For me?" Penelope took a step forward.

The woman nodded, and her eyes, pits of blackness framed with cherry red, clawed at Penelope's very soul. "It is for you I bring ... the message."

Jeez. I get it. You have a message. Penelope took another cautious step toward the treacherous woman. "So what are you waiting for?"

"Pen, get away from her," she heard Emma grumble from behind.

Not on your life. Pen moved another inch. "I'm waiting, old woman. Wow me."

The Maaskab growled.

Another step.

"Don't hurt my grandmother," Emma pleaded.

Grandma? Oh, for Pete's sake. *This* was Emma's grandmother? The one who'd been taken by the Maaskab and turned into their evil leader? They all thought she'd been killed.

Fabulous. Granny's back.

For a fraction of a moment, the woman glanced over Pen's shoulder at Emma.

Another step.

Penelope couldn't let Emma's feelings cloud the situation. Granny was dangerous. Granny was evil. Granny was going down.

"We wish"—the old Maaskab woman ground out her words—"to make an exchange."

Penelope froze. "An exchange?"

The woman nodded slowly. "You will free our king, and we will return your prisoners."

Shit. Free Chaam? The most evil deity ever known? He'd murdered hundreds, perhaps thousands of women, many his own daughters. His sole purpose in life was to destroy every last living creature, except for the Maaskab and his love slaves.

No. They could never let that bastard out.

But what about the prisoners? She debated with herself. In the last battle, the Maaskab had trapped forty of their most loyal vampire soldiers, the God of Death and War, aka Emma's fiancé, and the General of the Vampire Army, aka Helena's husband.

Dammit. Dammit. Crispy-fried dammit! Penelope had to at least consider Granny's proposal. "Why in the world would we agree to let Chaam go?"

"A bunch of pathetic ... little ... girls ... cannot triumph against us," the Maaskab woman hissed. "*You* need the vampires and your precious God of Death and War."

Penelope's brain ran a multitude of scenarios, trying to guess the angle. Apparently, the Maaskab needed Chaam back. But they were willing to give up Niccolo and Guy? Both were powerful warriors, perfectly equipped to kick the Maaskab's asses for good.

No. Something wasn't quite right. "Tell me why you want Chaam," Penelope said.

Another step.

"Because"—Granny flashed an odious grin—"the victory of defeating you will be meaningless without our beloved king to see it. All we do, we do for him."

Ew. Okay.

"You, on the other hand..." She lowered her gravelly voice one octave. "...Do not have a chance without your men. We offer a fair fight in exchange for our king's freedom."

Okay. She could be lying. Perhaps not. Anyone with a brain could see they were three inexperienced young women—yes, filled with passion and purpose and a love of shoes and all things shopping, in the case of Helena and Emma—but they didn't know the first thing about fighting wars. Especially ones that might end in a big hairy apocalypse prophesied to be just eight months away.

Sure, they had powerful, slightly insane, dysfunctional deities and battalions of beefy vampires and human soldiers on their side. However, that was like giving a tank to a kindergartner. Sort of funny in a Sunday comics *Beetle Bailey* kinda way, but not in real life.

"Don't agree to it," Helena pleaded from the flank. "We'll find another way to free them."

"She's right, Pen," Emma whimpered, clearly in pain.

Penelope took another step. They were right; they'd have to find some other way to get the prisoners back. Chaam was too dang dangerous. "And if we refuse?"

The Maaskab woman laughed into the air above, her teeth solid black and the inside of her mouth bright red.

Yum. Nothing like gargling with blood to really freshen your breath.

"Then," Granny said, "we shall kill both men—yes, even your precious Votan; we have the means—and the end of days will begin. It is what Chaam would have wanted."

Granny had conveniently left out the part about killing her and her friends before she departed this room. Why else would the evil Maaskab woman have come in person when an evil note would have done the evil job? Or how about an evil text?

No. Emma's grandmother would kill them if the offer was rejected. She knew it in her gut.

Penelope didn't blink. *No fear. No fear.* The powerful light tingled on the tips of her fingers. She was ready.

"Then you leave us no choice. We agree." Penelope held out her hand. "Shake on it."

The Maaskab woman glanced down at Pen's hand. Pen lunged, grabbed the woman's soot-covered forearm, and opened the floodgates of heat. Evil Granny dropped to her knees, screaming like a witch drowning in a hot, bubbling cauldron.

"No! No!" Emma screamed. "Don't kill her! Don't, Pen!"

Crackers! Penelope released the woman who fell face forward onto the cold Saltillo tile. Steam rose from her naked back and dreadlock-covered skull.

"Grandma? Oh, God, no. Please don't be dead." Emma dropped to her knees beside the eau-de-charred roadkill. "She's still breathing."

The room suddenly filled with Penelope's private guards. They looked like they'd been chewed up and spit out by a large Maaskab blender—tattered, dirty clothes and bloody faces.

That explained what had taken so long; they must've been outside fighting more Maaskab.

The men pointed their rifles at Emma's unconscious grandmother. Zac, God of Who the Hell Knew and Penelope's right hand since she'd been appointed the interim leader of the gods—yes, yes, another long story—blazed into the room, barking orders. "Someone get the Maaskab chained up."

Zac, dressed in his usual black leather pants and tee combo that matched his raven-black hair, turned to Penelope and gazed down at her with his nearly translucent, aquamarine eyes. "Are you all right?"

Penelope nodded. It was the first time in days she'd felt glad to see him. He'd been suffocating her ever since Kinich—

"Oh, gods!" They'd completely forgotten about Kinich! Her eyes flashed up at the clock.

Tick.

Sundown.

A gut-wrenching howl exploded from the other room. Everyone stiffened.

"He's alive!" Pen turned to rush off but felt a hard pull on her arm.

"No. You've had enough danger for one day. I will go." Zac wasn't asking.

Penelope jerked her arm away. "He won't hurt me. I'll be fine. Just stay here and help Emma with her grandmother." She snatched up the two bags of blood from the floor where Helena had dropped them.

"Penelope, I will not tell you again." Zac's eyes filled with anger. Though he was her right hand, he was still a deity and not used to being disobeyed.

"Enough." Penelope held up her finger. "I don't answer to you."

Zac's jealous eyes narrowed for a brief moment before he stiffly dipped his head and then quietly watched her disappear through the doorway.

She rushed down the hallway and paused outside the

bedroom with her palms flat against the hand-carved double doors. The screams had not stopped.

Thank the gods that Kinich, the ex–God of the Sun, was alive. Now they would have a chance to put their lives back together, to undo what never should have been— such as putting her in charge of his brothers and sisters— and she would finally get the chance to tell him how much she loved him, how grateful she was that he'd sacrificed everything to save them, about their baby.

This was their second chance.

She only needed to get him through these first days as a vampire. *And orchestrate a rescue mission for the God of Death and War and the General of the Vampire Army. And deal with the return of Emma's evil granny. And figure out how to stop an impending apocalypse set to occur in eight—yes, eight!—months. And deal with a few hundred women with amnesia they'd rescued from the Maaskab. And manage a herd of insane egocentric, accident-prone deities, with ADHD. And carry a baby. And don't forget squeezing in some time at the gym. Your thighs are getting flabby!*

"See? This Kinich vampire thing should be easy," she assured herself.

She pushed open the door to find Kinich shirtless, writhing on the bed. His muscular legs and arms strained against the silver chains attached to the deity-reinforced frame. He was a large, beautiful man, almost seven feet in height, with shoulders that spanned a distance equal to two widths of her body.

"Kinich!" She rushed to his side. "Are you okay?" She attempted to brush his gold-streaked locks from his face, but he flailed and twisted in agony.

"It burns!" he wailed. "The metal burns."

"I know, honey. I know. But Helena says you need to drink before we can let you go. Full tummy. Happy vamp—"

"Aaahh! Remove them. They burn. Please," he begged.

Oh, saints.

He would never hurt her. Would he? Of course not.

"Try to hold still." She went to the dresser, pulled open the top drawer, and grabbed the keys.

She rushed to his ankle and undid one leg, then the other.

Kinich stopped moving. He lay there, eyes closed, breathing.

Without hesitation she undid his right arm and then ran to the other side to release the final cuff.

"Are you okay? Kinich?"

Without opening his eyes, he said, "I can smell and hear everything."

Helena had said that blocking out the noise was one of the hardest things a new vampire had to learn. That and curbing their hunger for innocent humans who, she was told, tasted the yummiest. Helena also mentioned to always make sure he was well fed. Full tummy, happy vampire. Just like a normal guy except for the blood obviously.

Penelope deposited herself on the bed next to Kinich with a bag of blood in her hands. "You'll get used to it. I promise. In the meantime, let's get you fed. I have so much to—"

Kinich threw her down, and she landed on her back with a hard thump and the air whooshed from her lungs.

Straddling her, Kinich pinned her wrists to the floor.

His turquoise eyes shifted to hungry black, and fangs protruded from his mouth. "You smell delicious. Like sweet sunshine."

Such a beautiful face, she thought, mesmerized by Kinich's eyes. Once upon a time his skin had glowed golden almost, a vision of elegant masculinity with full lips and sharp cheekbones. But now, now he was refined with an exotic, dangerous male beauty too exquisite for words.

Ex-deity turned mortal, turned vampire. *Hypnotic. He is...hypnotic.*

He lowered his head toward her neck, and her will suddenly snapped back into place. "No! Kinich, no!" She squirmed under his grasp. Without her hands free, she couldn't defend herself. "I'm pregnant."

He stilled and peered into her eyes.

Pain. So much pain. That was all she saw.

"A baby?" he asked.

She nodded cautiously.

Then something cold and deadly flickered in his eyes. His head plunged for her neck, and she braced for the pain of having her neck ripped out.

"Penelope!" Zac sacked Kinich, knocking him to the floor. "Go!" he commanded.

Penelope rolled onto her hands and knees and crawled from the room as it was overrun with several more of Kinich's brethren: the perpetually drunk Acan; the Goddess of the Hunt they called Camaxtli; and the Mistress of Bees they called—oh, who the hell could remember her weird Mayan name?

"Penelope! Penelope!" she heard Kinich scream. "I want to drink her! I must drink her!"

Penelope curled into a ball on the floor in the hallway, unable to stop herself from crying. *This isn't how it's supposed to be. This isn't how it's supposed to be.*

Helena appeared at her side. "Oh, Pen. I'm so sorry. I promise he'll be okay after a few days. He just needs to eat." She helped Penelope sit up. "Let's move you somewhere safe."

Penelope wiped away the streaks of tears from her cheeks and took her friend's hand to stand.

The grunts and screams continued in the other room.

"I can't believe he attacked me, even after I told him." Tears continued to trickle from Penelope's eyes. Why hadn't he stopped? Didn't he love her?

"In his defense, you really do smell yummy. Kind of like Tang."

"Not funny," Penelope responded.

"Sorry." Helena braced Penelope with an arm around her waist and guided her to a bedroom in the other wing of the house.

Helena deposited Penelope on the large bed and turned toward the bathroom. "I'll get you a warm washcloth."

Ironically, Penelope's mind dove straight for a safe haven—that meant away from Kinich and toward her job, which generally provided many meaty distractions, such as impending doom and/or anything having to do with Cimil, the ex–Goddess of the Underworld.

"Wait." Penelope looked up at Helena, who'd become her steady rock of reason these last few weeks. "What happens next?"

Helena paused for a moment. "Like I told you, Kinich needs time to adjust."

Penelope shook her head. "No. I mean, you heard

Emma's grandmother; without Niccolo and Guy, we can't defeat the Maaskab. We have to free our men."

"Well—"

"I know what you're going to say," Pen interrupted. "We can't release Chaam, but—"

"Actually," Helena broke in. "I've been meaning to tell you something."

"What?"

"We've been looking for another way to free them, and I think we found it."

"Found what?" Penelope asked.

"A tablet."

Uno

New Year's Day. New York City

"Save me. Please save me."

"Dammit. Where are you?" Thirty-four-year-old Antonio Acero frantically searched the dark, empty, cavernous room, helplessly listening to the woman's cries.

"Time is running out. You must work faster," she wailed.

"I am doing everything I can," he called out, his voice bouncing off the bare, smooth walls. "But I can't get to you. If you just tell me..." Two catlike eyes punched through the darkness, sucking the words from his mind. He wanted to see more of her, to touch her. He felt like he might become the one who needed saving if he did not.

"Save me. Please save me," the woman repeated. "Time is running out. I have the answers you need, but you must work faster. Destiny—"

Antonio catapulted from his deep slumber, dripping in cold sweat. "*Puta madre*," he whispered and flipped on his stainless steel reading lamp. It had been the same damned nightmare every night for the last month. Ever since he'd found that fucking tablet in Mexico. Or had it found him?

Doesn't matter. It's what you were looking for, the answer to your prayers.

"Everything all right, baby?" A silky arm slipped out from beneath the steel-gray satin sheets and rubbed his bare thigh.

"Uh...yeah. Sure." He looked down at the mop of brown hair. Her face was as obscure as her name.

Mierda. What was he doing? It didn't matter how many women he brought home, he couldn't wash her—the woman in his dreams—from his mind.

He slid from bed and plucked his discarded tee and boxer briefs from the floor. On his way to the kitchen, he slipped them on and tried not to punch something.

Dammit. The dreams were only getting worse, more vivid, more frantic with every passing night.

He yanked open the fridge, pushed past the Odwallas and beer, and grabbed the soy milk. He knew this madness didn't make sense, but what the hell did that matter? The dreams kept coming. Scotch—the good stuff—sex, hypnosis didn't matter. Every night she came. Every night he woke. Every day he worked and didn't stop until his mind reached exhaustion. And even then, he couldn't stop thinking about the tablet.

Or her...

Shit. What was happening to him?

He went to his lab, a room at the back of his sparsely decorated apartment, and flipped on the phosphorescent lights, stopping briefly to remove the black stone tablet from a rat-filled cage. He carefully unwrapped it from the plastic sleeve and shook his head. The damned thing was like a goddamned Mayan Rubik's Cube.

"You think you can win, don't you?" No fucking chance, *pinche jodida* tablet. He laid it down and stroked its rough surface. "You and I, we finish this tonight."

Yes. He was close to unlocking its secrets. And when he did...then what? Would she be there? The woman with the haunting eyes? The woman he knew in his soul he was destined to meet?

Goddammit, he fucking hoped so.

He placed a welder's mask on his face and leaned over the tablet, a pair of long tweezers in hand. He reached up and adjusted the overhead light, focusing the powerful beam on the corner of the object. This had to be it, his last test to prove out his theory.

"Steady hand, *coño*. Steady hand." He carefully scraped off a tiny particle and placed it on a glass slide. He removed the mask and wiped his brow.

"Coming back to bed, baby?" a silken voice purred from behind. A soft pair of arms reached around his waist and a set of full breasts pushed against his back.

Is she still here? Doesn't she have her own bed to sleep in? He placed the slide under his microscope. "Yeah. Be right there."

Yes. Just as he suspected. The black jade had again transformed. He'd left it encased for ten hours with his two most aggressive rats. The day before that, he'd exposed it to his goldenzelle orchid. The day before that, frogs. Each life-form, plant or animal, rearranged the configuration of the microscopic crystals and the hieroglyphs.

"It's like the damned thing is alive," he muttered to himself. And now he knew for certain his hypothesis held water. Subjecting the tablet to the right combination of elements would unlock its power and, hopefully, open the portal. A portal that could access any dimension at any point in time.

"I'm alive, baby. And if you come back to bed, I'll show you how much," Betsy—or was she Brenda?—whined. He hated whiny women. They were so . . . whiny.

"Look, Bre— *Señorita*." He turned and stared down at the attractive brunette wearing too much mascara and his favorite polo shirt. "I have work to do. If you need to cuddle, my cat Simon is around somewhere."

Fury flickered in her brown eyes, and she stomped off, mumbling some profanity about Don Juans. "And my name is Belinda!" she screamed from somewhere inside the spacious apartment.

"Mujeres!" He shook his head. Why did women always behave that way? So damned irrational and needy. It wasn't as if he hid his true colors, either. In fact, he made it a rule to be transparent. "I don't date anyone but my work, and she and I are happy together. Alone," he'd say.

Couldn't get much clearer than that. Yet they always came home with him. They always wanted more. They always left angry.

Well, too damned bad. He knew what mattered: cracking this code, saving his brother from a terrible fate, and if he were lucky . . . ? He would finally meet this woman.

An image of her flashed in his mind. He saw himself in a dimly lit bedroom, the light from a fireplace flickering over the walls as he thrust himself between her thighs and stared at her obscured face.

A loud crackle suddenly came from the microscope. *What the...?*

He bent his head and looked through the lens. The molecules shifted again, but this time they moved with such fluidity that he could swear it was a liquid, not solid. *"Qué diablos?"*

The black crystals swirled on the plate and a tiny black hole opened up as if the center had disintegrated completely.

"Caray. It's amazing," he mumbled as an earsplitting snap cracked through the air. The tablet vibrated on the table and jumped as if hooked up to a lowrider suspension system.

"Coño!" He lunged as it reached the edge and fell to the floor with a crash. An explosion threw him across the room, the wall breaking his momentum.

Antonio felt his body slide down the wall, the air sucked from his lungs. The room flickered from bright white to red to darkness. But he wasn't unconscious. No. Not at all. The pain he felt was not a dream.

And he could not see.

Dos

January 3. Time: 6:00 p.m. Rec Room of Valley Hills Elementary, Sedona, Arizona

"Hi, everyone. I'm Ixtab. My friends call me...well, I don't really have any friends, so it's just Ixtab, I guess."

"Hi, Ixtab," said the middle-aged group of twelve men and women sitting on foldout chairs in a circle.

Ixtab stared through her black veil, down at her feet. "And it's been twenty-two days since I caused the death of an innocent mortal."

Applause.

"Thank you." She took a deep breath. That had been easier than she'd thought. Normally, she wouldn't stop to join in a wishy-washy human gathering, but she'd happened to be in the neighborhood on a job and suddenly felt the urge to share.

Of course, it was normal for Ixtab to go with the flow;

that's how the Universe directed her toward the humans most in need. Though sharing like this was a definite first, and she enjoyed it in some weird way, even though she'd compelled them all.

Ixtab sat and took a sip from her foam cup. The coffee was bitter and cold. Good. She didn't deserve anything warm and comforting. "It hasn't been easy steering clear of accident-prone men; though, I have been improving. But even with the extra effort, I still can't avoid them completely. Last month, for example, I went to the fabric store—spring is coming, so I thought I'd make a new dress—pink linen or pale yellow cotton with white daisies."

The crowd stared with perplexed faces.

Ixtab looked down at her shapeless, flowing black dress through her black lace veil. "Oh. I like to wear summery things underneath." Why? That was a very long, emotional detour of a story.

The group nodded and murmured a collective "Aha."

Ixtab sighed and then placed the cup at her flip-flop-clad feet. "Even though I waited until just before closing time, and I swear there was no one left in the store besides the clerk, boom!" She clapped her hands together. "I rounded the corner near the pattern section, and the man ran right into me."

What came next was always the hard part: watching them die after they touched her. Why? Simple. She was poison. Dark, bitter poison—most of the time, anyway.

"Go on," urged one of the women wearing a red sweater and name tag that said Anne. She had a bright, soothing smile. "What happened next?"

Ixtab held back the urge to cry. "Before you could say

'Singer' he shoved an entire McCall's M6466—a really nice off-the-shoulder dress pattern—right down his throat." She shook her head and sighed. "Such a shame. Such a shame. He was so good-looking, too. The accidental kills always are. Always hot. Always men. Why do you think that is?" she asked the group.

The crowd shook their heads. They didn't have a clue, either.

"It's not right. Why do I have to be so...deadly?" Ixtab reached under her veil and whisked away a tear. "Is it too much to ask? To touch a handsome man without killing him? I mean, really. Just once. Just one damned time, I'd like to bump into a nonevil guy and have him smile at me, maybe give me his number. But noooo. Their eyes haze over like a week-old fish, and then they find the nearest deadly object."

Anne reached for Ixtab's shoulder to comfort her, but then snapped her hand back. "It's not your fault, Ixtab. And remember our first rule? Acceptance. We must accept the things we cannot change. And sometimes we can't change the fate of others. Sometimes, their time is simply up."

Ixtab shrank on the inside. That's what Francisco used to tell her. *Don't think about him. Don't think about him. You promised yourself you wouldn't do this anymore.* Surely two hundred years of suffering for accidentally causing the death of one's soul mate had to be long enough. Wasn't it?

Ixtab didn't know, but she desperately wanted to move on. It was time. Maybe that's why she was here tonight, trying to take a step forward.

Or maybe she was there for another reason: justice.

Ixtab cleared her throat. "The only thing that really keeps me going is that in between the accidents, I really do save lives." With the right amount of concentration and a little help from the Universe, she had the ability to extract the darkness from a good soul. "Just this afternoon, for example, the Universe led me to a very sad girl—sweet as a bag of kettle corn. She'd obviously been feeling down lately—lots of bad energy buildup around her heart—and thought it would be fun to try these pills her boyfriend gave her." Ixtab opened her hand and showed everyone the pills. "She would've died and not gone on to fulfill her destiny of being a pediatric surgeon."

Murmurs of approval erupted.

"See, Ixtab. There's always a ray of sunshine to be found in every situation," said the other woman to her left named Jess.

Ixtab smiled appreciatively at the two young ladies. "Yunno, I'm really glad I found you guys. It's nice to have someone to talk to for once. And, yes. You're right. There's always a silver lining." Ixtab got up, walked across the circle, and stood before a shabby looking man in his early thirties. His head was too small for his body and his bulging brown eyes matched the stain on his wrinkled T-shirt.

"What the hell are you looking at, freak?" he said.

"Jerry, right?" Ixtab's heart tingled with giddiness.

He shifted in his chair. "Yeah. That's right. Jerry's the name."

Ixtab slid off her veil.

The man jerked his head back and then flashed a lusty grin. "But hey, baby, you can call me anything you want."

Ixtab leaned down, putting them at a breath's distance, and stared into his pupils. *Ah, the eyes. They never lie.*

Sometimes they showed an image of what one might become later in life, but this guy? *Nada*. The only thing to gaze upon was his bleak soul and the reflection of her own turquoise eyes.

"Baby, huh? Aren't you sweet?" She smiled and placed her index finger on the tip of his chin. The man's mouth dropped open and she popped the pills inside. He instantly convulsed and frothed from the mouth.

"How about I call *you* dead?" she seethed.

The man leaned forward, pulled a knife from his boot, and stabbed himself in the heart. He dropped to the floor.

"That'll teach you to sell drugs to children, you shit." Ixtab turned toward the crowd who sat motionless in their chairs. "Wow. I really do feel better! Thanks for letting me crash your Road Ragers Anonymous meeting. Same time next week?"

The group nodded.

"Excellent." Ixtab turned to leave. "Oh. Everyone will be kind to their fellow drivers from now on. You'll also forget you ever saw me. And Jerry there? He flipped out and ended his life after taking his own smack. 'Kay?"

The crowd nodded with an absent gaze.

Yes, being the Goddess of Suicide wasn't all shits and giggles—it was mostly shits—but it did have its moments.

Tres

⌒

Ixtab looked at her pastel yellow watch and frowned. Dammit. She was ten minutes late to the gods' summit meeting and would be left with cleanup duty. Again. She only hoped her brother Belch, God of Intoxication and Wine, hadn't brought his keg this time. Or the donkey with the sombrero. And that he'd remembered to wear pants.

As Ixtab hurried through the modern, southwestern-style estate toward the summit room, she wondered what would become of the place. With its large skylights, indoor cactus gardens, and warm desert colors, Kinich, her brother, would likely want to move. But where would he go? He'd always loved the desert and the tropics.

Ixtab shivered imagining him living in a gloomy, depressing vampire lair, which made her wonder, *How*

*can humans like vampires so much? They're so... icky—
except for Kinich, of course. Poor guy. But surely if
humans knew how horribly morbid vampires were, they'd
come to their senses!* Maybe she should start a list and
publish it.

*Vampires are icky, reason number one: they hate
sunshine.*

Reason number two: they're not really alive.

Reason number three: they drink blood.

*Yes, but many creatures live on blood: mosquitos,
flees, Cimil's unicorn...*

Okay, skip that reason.

New reason number three: vampires are violent.

Speaking of violent, she paused outside the hand-
carved double doors adorned with the Mayan sun on
one side and the Mayan calendar on the other. *Phew, no
screaming. Not yet, anyway.* Her brethren were such an
unruly lot.

Ixtab pushed open the doors of the giant Mayan-esque
meeting chamber decorated with hieroglyphs, a big screen
TV, and fourteen thrones seated around a large stone slab
table. Eight frowns immediately greeted her, the only
smile coming from Penelope who, like usual, wore a plain
tee and a pair of jeans with her dark hair pulled back into
a sleek bun. "Hey, Suicide. We're just getting started."

"Ixtab. The name is Ixtab." She curled her fists and took
the throne baring her Mayan glyph toward the middle of
the table. Damn, she hated this chair. It depicted her with
giant, pointy nipples, a noose around her neck, and decay-
ing cheeks.

Stupid Mayans, nooses are so last baktun. "And my
nipples are cute and perky," she grumbled.

"Um. Thanks for sharing?" Penelope looked around the room. "Anyone else like to share a description of their nipples before we get started?" Penelope shot a glance toward the end of the table. "It's a rhetorical question, Belch. Put your hand down."

He slowly removed his greasy palm from the air and wiped it down the front of his green Puma sweatshirt. As usual, he had his dark brown hair styled with a nonflattering bedhead look. "I wore pantsss today," he slurred proudly.

"Actually," Ixtab pointed out, "those are called under-wear. And they're not even men's underwear."

"But they *are* spectacular," Mistress of Bees added. "Who knew they made thongsss in transparent plastic?"

As usual, Bees wore a large living hive atop her head and something beeish. Today, it was a tight yellow bodysuit that hugged the curves of her tall, athletic body.

Belch glanced around the chamber. "When did I leavvve the costume party?" He shrugged and then took a swig from his supersized Playboy tankard.

"Okeydokey, then." Penelope picked up her official Ruler of the House of Gods writing tablet—now an iPad instead of stone since she'd insisted the gods start upgrad-ing their technology—and took roll call. Present were Acan, God of Intoxication and Wine (aka Belch); Ah-Ciliz, God of Solar Eclipses (aka A.C.); Akna, Goddess of Fertil-ity; Camaxtli, Goddess of the Hunt (aka Fate); Colel Cab, Mistress of Bees; K'ak and Zac Cimi, who had yet to find their special gifts, but were quite powerful physically and very popular with the ladies; and last but not least, the God-dess of Forgetfulness. Sadly, no one ever remembered her name and Penelope forgot to count her, as usual.

Missing were Chaam, the God of Male Virility;

Kinich, ex–God of the Sun and recently turned vampire; Votan, God of Death and War (aka Guy); Cimil, the ex–Goddess of the Underworld; and the One No One Spoke Of, more affectionately referred to as Máax, which meant "Who?" in Mayan. Ixtab really missed the stubborn bastard, but what was done was done.

Penelope then moved to setting the agenda. Unanimous votes passed to discuss the news of this mysterious tablet and some physicist named Antonio Acero. The topic of Emma's evil Maaskab grandmother would be postponed until later; her survival after Penelope's Maaskab BBQ special was uncertain.

"I wish to discuss the fate of Kinich," Zac said acrimoniously.

Penelope glared at him. "What's to discuss?"

Ixtab felt the negative energy spike through the thinning ozone. *Here we go.* Everyone knew that Zac loved Penelope, and though she tried to hide it—no doubt because of her deep love for Kinich—Penelope felt some attraction for Zac, too. Like the other gods, Zac was tall, recklessly handsome (by mortal standards, not Ixtab standards), well built, and quite sharp. His only shortcoming was that he hadn't discovered his gift. Yet. Although Ixtab and the others suspected he was the God of Love.

Lucky bastard.

"He attacked you—our leader," Zac said. "This is an offense punishable by death or permanent banishment in the case of a deity."

Penelope gasped, and the other gods protested vehemently. Point being, Kinich was no longer a deity so that meant death.

Zac's icy blue-green eyes swept the room. "Are you

denying Kinich has broken the law? Or that he is a danger to Penelope?" He looked straight at Ixtab. "What say you, sister?"

That's an easy one, you lame ass. "We should discuss Kinich," Ixtab replied. "But how to help, not how to punish him."

Zac scowled and took his seat while voting concluded. Death or punishment of any sort would be off the table, but Kinich's fate would be reviewed.

"All right." Penelope clicked her pen and flashed an annoyed look at Zac. "I bring the first topic to order: Dr. Antonio Acero and the tablet."

An Uchben soldier entered the room and passed a folder to Penelope. She nodded and placed it on the table. "Thank you."

"What is that?" Zac asked.

Penelope shook her head but wouldn't make eye contact. "We'll discuss it in a minute. And stop stepping out of protocol."

Zac's eyes narrowed at Penelope. "Is this the response you would give to Kinich? If he were here, that is, instead of our jail for trying to murder you?"

Ixtab sighed. This situation was a ticking love triangle waiting to explode. She wished a male would love her enough to behave like a complete ass. Or not die when she touched him by accident. Either-or.

Ixtab mentally right hooked herself. *Dammit! Get over it.* But that was easier said than done. Perhaps because time hadn't dulled the effects of murdering her soul mate.

You don't know that Francisco was your soul mate. And you promised not to think about him anymore. It's a new baktun, it's a new you...

"Where was I?" Penelope said. "Oh yeah. The Maas-kab tablet discovered by Helena and her vampires. Has anyone heard of it?"

Fate was the first to speak. "The Mayan had many sacred tablets. They recorded their most valuable secrets on them."

Penelope pulled out copies of several ancient texts from a folder on the table. "Well, supposedly this one is made from black jade and had more than just secrets. I've been researching our records; it's believed to have the power to open a portal to any dimension. If that's true, then we could free Votan, Niccolo, and our men."

Interesting… How had this tablet existed without the gods' knowledge? Ixtab wondered.

"You are not getting anywhere near it," Zac stated coldly. "So do not think of proposing to do so."

Pen glared at him and then looked at Ixtab. "That's where you come in."

Me? They need me? Ixtab felt her spine straighten a little. "How?"

Penelope threw down the file. "Meet Dr. Antonio Acero. World-renowned physicist from MIT, heir to Spain's wealthiest family, current owner of the tablet, and the only being on the planet capable of unlocking it. That we know of."

"Why does he possessss the tablet?" Bees asked, blowing kisses to a tiny bee on the tip of her finger.

Penelope's mouth twisted with disgust as she watched. "We don't know how he got it, but we think he's trying to make a name for himself in the scientific community. Unfortunately, he refuses to work with us and money won't entice him. Neither will threats. Everyone who's attempted contact says he's stubborn, arrogant, and rude. Anyway, Helena and her vampires have been keeping close tabs on him. They were about to resort to glamouring him, but something happened during an experiment and he triggered an explosion. The good news is he'll live. Bad news is he lost his sight."

All heads swiveled toward Ixtab.

"Why are you looking at me? I can't cure blindness," she said.

"Mr. Acero's physician," Penelope explained, "is one of our undercover Uchben. She suspects his condition has something to do with the tablet's dark energy and may be reversible. In the meantime, he's extremely ... unhappy and refusing to continue his work."

"So you want me to fix him?" Ixtab asked, wondering if he deserved saving. Accident aside, he didn't sound like a very nice person. In fact, he sounded like a snobby, rich playboy who might deserve the hand he'd gotten.

"Can you do it, Ixtab?" Penelope asked.

Ixtab scratched her forehead through the itchy veil. She hated toying with anything Maaskab. Their power was based on dark energy, which was highly unstable and unpredictable. Yet absorbing bad juju and saving humans was her gift. Yes, yes, she also dished the bad juju, but curing those in need was always her first priority.

"Ixtab? Can you?" Penelope asked again.

"Of course, she cannn! She'sss like a giant rrrechargeable battery," Belch slurred.

"Ixtab, if you'd like my two cents"—Fate spoke with a casualness that insinuated some sort of authority—"it is too dangerous. And we all know you are not brave or useful in situations of peril. You should not risk it."

Ixtab glared at Fate. Even her outfit—a little white pleated dress and white knee-high moccasins—was annoyingly prissy. *Damned goody-goody, always trying to put everyone down.*

Ixtab lifted her chin. "I'm game."

"So am I. Wanna see?" Belch stood and stretched his seven feet of inebriated male mass, showing everyone his thong, which now looked like a little transparent tent. He was clearly having a special, special moment with himself.

"You're disgusting," Bees hissed and fired her yellow samurai at his exposed butt cheeks.

"Deities! Please focus!" Penelope barked.

Belch plopped back into his seat, too drunk to notice the bees plunging their stingers into his body.

Penelope winced. "Uh…Thank you, Suici— I mean Ixtab. That's very generous."

Ixtab bowed her head. It was the first time she could ever remember being asked to do something important like this.

"Thank you. Here's the information you'll need." Penelope slid the folder toward Ixtab.

Ixtab opened it and felt her insides curl into a heavy knot. *No. It can't be. He looks like…Francisco.* The entire room wobbled beneath her. The man had the same dark hair—though the short, mussed style was quite different—olive-green eyes, and deep, deliciously tanned Mediterranean skin. And like Francisco, he was the most exquisite mortal she'd ever laid eyes on.

But it wasn't Francisco, because Francisco died long ago. Yes, she'd seen to that, hadn't she? This…*Antonio* was simply a look-alike. A genetic anomaly. Those happened, right? Yes. Come to think of it, she'd once seen a dead ringer for Elvis walking down the street. A dead ringer. So close, in fact, that if she hadn't had firsthand knowledge of Elvis's fate, she would have asked for his autograph or an imprint of his sideburns.

"He sure izzzz delicious," Bees said, staring at the headshot.

"He kinda looks like an older, tanned Zac Efron," Penelope blurted.

"I'd make him my lucky one," added Fate.

Ixtab swallowed the sticky glob of dread and centuries of baggage stuck in her throat. *I can't breathe. I can't feel my body. I can't be in the same room as that picture.*

"I-I can't do this. I'm sorry. I have to go." Ixtab bolted for the door. Why wouldn't the Universe let her forget Francisco? Hadn't she suffered enough?

Living this way was simply too much to bear.

"Was that a no?" Fate asked with a suspicious grin.

One of these days, Penelope was going to find out what the deal was between her and Ixtab. However, for the time being... *Christ! Why is everything with these deities so damned dramatic? They're like Jan and Marcia. On steroids. During an orange polyester shortage.*

"I think so." Penelope's head fell forward. "Dammit. She has to change her mind. We need that physicist back to work, especially now that he's so close."

"How do we know he's close?" Fate asked.

"Because he unleashed the tablet's power and knocked out the electricity in Helena's building," Penelope replied.

"Pleazzz explain," Bees asked.

"That's the irony; Antonio Acero is renting an apartment in Helena's building—for the time being, anyway," Penelope said. "She just bought the building last month to turn it into a luxury halfway house for new vampires. That is, as soon as she has any vampires to rent to since they're all on vacation."

The gods stared at Penelope and crickets ensued.

Dammit, she'd hoped to slide that one in without notice; the last thing she wanted was to worry them further. In the end, it wouldn't make their already dire situation resolve any faster.

Penelope sighed. "Apparently there's a law, enacted centuries ago by the prior queen. Now that the evil vampires have been exterminated, all good vampires are to indulge in a mandatory yearlong celebration." She shrugged. "Of course, they're really only getting eight months, unless we find a way to stop the apocalypse."

"Deities almighty!" Zac exclaimed. "We won't be stopping anything without the aid of the vampire army. We're outgunned against the Maaskab. If they attack, it's over."

"What about our Uchben?" Penelope asked. "Don't we have enough human soldiers to defend against an attack?"

"No," he replied coldly.

"Really? Our Uchben kick ass. It's not like they're just regular old humans," she argued. The Uchben were highly skilled warriors, trained by the gods and their fiercest vampire allies. In some cases, they were given the light of the gods, making them immortal, too. They also oversaw everything for the gods in the mortal world, including flying their planes, maintaining an army, and managing their assets.

"The point is, they are easier to kill than a vampire; we'd only be able to hold out for so long."

She hadn't thought they were that vulnerable, but she supposed if anyone knew the really-really, it would be Zac.

"Can't Helena command the vampires back?" Fate asked Penelope.

"She tried. It's some obscure vampire law that no one knew about. Once word got out, the army took it to heart; they believe their laws are the only thing keeping them from turning into savages."

"Then she should change the law." Fate waved her hand through the air as if it were that easy. But it wasn't. Didn't they know by now that nothing was easy in this world?

"That's why we need Niccolo rescued," Penelope explained. "Helena is only the interim leader—she can't change anything. He can."

"So where'd they all go?" Zac asked.

"Euro Disney," Penelope responded.

The deities stared.

"Yeah. I know," she said. "And I'm just gonna say it: Doesn't anyone think this all a little weird? Our vampire army at Disneyland? Niccolo being the only one to change that? The tablet being right under our noses?"

The gods looked at each other and simply shrugged.

"Oh, come on! This reeks of a Cimil master plot," Penelope barked.

Again the gods simply shrugged, only this time, they did it as if she'd stated the obvious and mundane. *(The sky is blue! Ducks quack!)*

"See," Penelope griped, "this is what drives me bonkers about you guys! Now would be a great time for you to react or make some sort of drama, but I get nothing."

The gods didn't make the slightest reaction.

Maybe they're just drama-tarded. "All righty. And moving on...So what do we do?" Penelope asked.

"The only thing we can. Ixtab must visit the physicist and get him back to work," Bees stated blandly and looked at Penelope.

"Agreed," Penelope said. "I'll go talk to her—"

"After we discuss the next topic, Penelope." Zac's voice was cold and commanding.

"Why are you doing this?" Penelope whispered. Couldn't they just forget the Kinich topic and leave him alone?

Zac didn't blink. "Because *he* is no good for you."

"I'll decide what's good for me, Zac." *Which might be spiking a fireball down your leather pants.*

"When it comes to Kinich, nothing good can ever come of him. Not anymore. If you opened your eyes, you would see that." He handed her a letter. "Read it; then tell me what's *good* for you."

Cuatro

Ixtab quickly gathered her belongings from the guest room. She needed to get out of there before one of her brethren came demanding an explanation. Telling anyone about what happened long ago with Francisco, besides Kinich, was out of the question. The pain of what she'd done was bad enough without having her entire brethren know.

"Where are you going?" Fate stood in the doorway with a joyous expression.

Right on cue. And how did I know they'd send Miss Rubitinyournose? "I've got to go to Denver," Ixtab replied. "There's been an outbreak of depression due to a snowed-out romance convention."

Fate removed her quiver, walked over to the bed, and plunked down. "We both know that's an excuse; romance fans are a hearty, resilient breed. They'd never need *your* help for something so trivial."

True. And…true. In any case, at least she could get in some good skiing and get far, far away from the other gods. And yes, for the record, she skied with her veil on because she never took it off except to shower. The veil was her penance, a reminder to always be careful of whom she touched.

"Well, is there anything I can say to change your mind about going?" Fate asked cheerfully.

"No."

"Figures. You always were the most cowardly of us all." Fate buffed her nails on the hem of her white dress. "I guess I'll have to go to New York and see if I can't help the cute physicist myself. I've been itching for a new boy toy." She sighed with contentment. "Perhaps it's time for me to take my new black jade necklace for a test-drive. After all, Cimil did say we were to use her gift immediately."

Black jade, though first discovered by the Maaskab, wasn't entirely evil. In fact, it was an inert substance that absorbed supernatural energy. Expose it to something bad, it was bad. Good, good. In the case of gods? Well, for the first time ever, they could use the jade to blunt their energy to have intimate relations with a human— something previously impossible due to a god's over-whelming power that essentially fried the poor human's brain.

"And something tells me," Fate added, "that bad boy Spaniard could go all night."

She wants him? Ixtab's jealously ran across the court in squeaky sneakers, jumped, and spiked a ball through her possessive hoop. The thought of Fate getting any-where near the physicist made her blood boil. Why? She had no clue. This man wasn't Ixtab's Francisco; he just looked a lot like him. Nevertheless, the words "But I'll be going to New York right after Denver" burst from Ixtab's mouth.

Why? Why had she said that?

Fate's eyes narrowed. "I thought you were too busy?"

Ixtab answered with her own narrowed eyes and added a Dirty Harry, one-eyed twitch for good measure. If only Fate could see it. "Not too busy to save the world." *Bitch.*

"Fine."

"Fine."

Fate stood and smoothed down the front of her pleated, short dress. "By the way, we'd like you to visit Penelope before you leave."

"What's wrong with her?"

Fate cocked one sassy, golden brow. "You should've stuck around for the rest of the meeting."

Fate turned to leave but Ixtab sprinted to the door and slammed it shut. She knew Fate wouldn't touch her. No one touched her; they were simply too afraid. "Dish, you dirty pig whore, or I'll hug you."

Fate rolled her eyes. "You think you're so much better than the rest of us, don't you?"

Me? She's accusing me of being a snob? The nerve! "Oh, Fate. I know I'm better than you because I actually have a working heart. Now dish or I'll take those arrows of yours and make a Fate-kabob."

Ixtab paused outside Penelope's bedroom door. The sobs could be heard from the other side of Arizona, but who could blame her, really? According to Fate, the rest of the summit meeting had not gone well thanks to Zac who arranged to have Kinich sent away. Worst of all, Kinich himself had agreed. He'd written a letter to his brethren, confessing his urge to kill Penelope and asked that she stay away from him. Indefinitely.

Ixtab knocked lightly. "Penelope?"

"Hold on." Sniffle, sniffle. "Be right there." Blow, blow. "Come in."

Ixtab popped her veiled head through the doorway. "You okay?"

Penelope stood at the other end of Kinich's spacious bedroom—complete with indoor waterfall and trickling stream—gazing out the large window overlooking the moonlit hills of the surrounding desert.

"I was just watching Cimil on the live YouTube cam," said Penelope with a dreary voice. "She's ironing that vampire's capes—did you know he's got over a thousand?"

Ixtab glanced at the flat screen on mute. Sure enough, there was Cimil, ex–Goddess of the Underworld, ironing and disco dancing in a sparkling pink bikini while eating glazed doughnuts as Roberto the Ancient One watched with a giant hungry grin.

Ixtab shuddered. "I find that extremely disturbing."

"Yet, it's impossible to look away."

Yes, probably because there was a certain poetic justice to it all. Given Cimil's treachery and lies—too many to count—Ixtab couldn't imagine a more just punishment than being slave to a very ancient vampire who had a lover's bone to pick. Nevertheless, the whole situation didn't taste right. Before being taken away, Cimil confessed to having lied to everyone. All these millennia, she'd only pretended to see the future? It didn't make sense. Not when there was no shame in the truth—Cimil's real gift was speaking to the dead, who existed in a place beyond the confines of time, an equally powerful gift. Simply put, her lie made no sense.

Perhaps she's finally gone off the deep end.

"You know, I tried to cure Cimil of her insanity once," Ixtab stated quietly.

"What happened?" Penelope asked.

"I failed. It was about five hundred years ago, but I can still taste Cimil's darkness. I never did find out what caused her so much pain, but her misery branded itself in my mind right before putting me in a two-hundred-year coma."

"That must've felt awful," Penelope said.

"I was asleep the entire time, so it didn't feel like anything even though my brothers and sisters had to find over ten thousand country-club members."

"Country-club members?" Pen asked.

"When I absorb dark energy from others, I must expel it somewhere. Preferably into a worthy victim—I prefer to call them country-club members. Sounds more pleasant. But until I find them, whatever ailments and darkness I absorb stays within me. If I don't cleanse the darkness, I eventually reach capacity and shut down."

"So you're the anti–Robin Hood?" Penelope asked. "You steal from the good and give to the evil?"

"Or the innocent," Ixtab mumbled regrettably. "I can't help it; sometimes they're drawn to me. Sometimes the dark energy has a mind of its own...like in the case of Cimil. The darkness didn't want to leave her."

Penelope's eyes flashed toward the screen. "I thought watching Cimil be punished would cheer me up, but now

I only feel sorry for her." Penelope made a pathetic little shrug and sat down on the unmade bed. "Ixtab?" Penelope looked up at her with her large green eyes. "Do you believe Kinich would hurt me?"

He'd eat you up like a vampire Pop-Tart. "Penelope, I wasn't there, but the other deities went to see Kinich again and witnessed him going crazy after smelling a few drops of your blood. Sending him away is best for you and the baby."

"I know. You're right. But why does a part of me refuse to believe he'd actually hurt me? It's ridiculous, right?"

"Sometimes believing the truth isn't easy. Like the time Cimil brought Bigfoot to my apartment in Italy riding on her unicorn."

"Huh?"

Oh. I think that was supposed to be a secret. "Uh—nothing. I said Kinich is going to stay in an apartment in Helena's building for now so I can keep a close eye on him—"

"You're going? To New York?"

Ixtab nodded.

"Thank gods. I know if anyone can fix all this and help Kinich, you can."

The vote of confidence felt so good that Ixtab almost believed in herself. Almost. "I'll call the moment he gets himself under control."

Penelope's gaze suddenly fell empty.

"Penelope? You do want me to call, don't you?" Ixtab asked.

Penelope stood and walked over to the window again. "I-I wonder if he'll ever love me the way I love him. Maybe it's just not meant to be, like Zac said."

Zac? That he-brat? "Don't listen to him."

"Zac asked me to marry him," Penelope blurted out.

Oh. That was so wrong. And so Zac. He always took whatever he wanted. He'd once taken Ixtab's favorite island, but that was Tahitian water under the bridge. In all fairness, the gods tended to be greedy when it came to material things. It was a deity thing.

"How did you respond?" Ixtab asked.

"Said I'd think about it." She looked down at her stomach. "How can I not? Kinich's only interest in me is for blood, and I'm not strong enough to do this on my own." She rubbed her face and groaned. "And I have to admit, there is something about Zac I can't pinpoint. I feel drawn to him."

That sounds fishy. Though no one knew for certain, everyone believed Zac was the God of Love. However, except under very specific circumstances, it was prohibited for a god to use his or her powers on another of their brethren without permission. This was one of their most sacred laws, right up there with time travel. A big, giant no-no. So had Zac been using his powers on Penelope?

"Look at me." Penelope did, and Ixtab gazed deeply into her eyes.

Hmmm... She didn't see any odd-looking colors or residuals that might indicate foul play, but this wasn't her area of expertise. She did note, however, a gray tint coating Penelope's aura. So much sadness. "I'm going to help you feel better."

Penelope bobbed her head slowly.

Ixtab took a deep breath and visualized the empty cells inside her body. She willed them to open their arms to Penelope's darkness. Ixtab gripped Penelope's shoulder.

"Teen uk'al k'iinam. Teen uk'al yah." I drink your ache. I drink your pain.

Penelope's body stiffened and then collapsed as it released the darkness enveloping her spirit. Ixtab scooped her up, carried her to the bed, and laid her down as the transfer completed.

"What did you do to me?" Penelope gazed up at Ixtab with wide eyes.

Such a lovely soul.

Ixtab smiled beneath her curtain of black lace. "That was my gift to help you through the next few days." She turned to leave. "Oh, and Penelope?"

"Yes?"

"You should know...I felt your baby's light, and it is pure love. That means Kinich is your true soul mate. Now you have no reason to doubt that everything will work out."

Ixtab left before Penelope saw the sadness overtake her. Penelope's despair, now circulating inside Ixtab's body, was profound, the type only encountered when true love was in jeopardy. How had Penelope been functioning with such heaviness in her heart?

Such a brave creature.

Ixtab headed straight for the garage. She'd need to find at least three country-club members tonight.

Cinco

Roberto the Ancient One's Secret Lair

"Wow, baby. I'm lovin' this glazed doughnut. Ummm…" Swinging her hips, Cimil took a large bite in front of the camera as she ironed cape number 520.

Sitting on his burgundy velvet love seat just a few feet away, Roberto's eyes widened into ravenous orbs.

"Oh, you like that, huh?" She smiled. "Or is it *this* that you like?" She turned to show him the skimpy backside of her shiny pink bikini.

He nodded like a hungry dog.

"Thought so," she said. "Well, Cimil's got a big, yummy treat for you, my little, tasty vamp—"

The alarm on Roberto's watch buzzed.

"Okay," Cimil said. "That's a wrap."

Roberto stared.

"Oh, come on," she said. "Shut the camera off. We're done."

Roberto stared.

"No. We are not having sex on camera."

Roberto stared.

"Because the last time I did that, the video went viral, and I didn't even get a damned penny! Now turn that thing off, we have work to do. There are only a few days left before our next big move."

Roberto sighed and flipped the switch on the camera mounted to a tripod in the corner of the room.

"Hey, watch your language," Cimil barked. "This You-Tube thing was your idea. And I have to admit, a very good one. The others don't suspect a thing, but seriously? How can anyone believe I could be *your* prisoner?"

Roberto shrugged his brows.

"Yes, yes. Because you're brilliant," she said. "And convincing all the vampires they needed to go to Euro Disney was a stroke of genius. Now the pressure's really on Ixtab to open that portal. By the way, your ability to forge the dead queen's hand is phenomenal. What other hidden talents do you have?"

Roberto stood next to the camera and eyed her body like a vampire lollipop.

"Oh, really . . . ? Okay, we can have sex, but I get to be anchor on the trapeze this time."

Roberto nodded.

"Gods, you rock, though not as much as me." Cimil snickered and headed for the door. "Turn the iron off, would ya? Don't want to burn down the place."

Roberto did as he was told.

Cimil's cell phone vibrated on the nightstand. "Oh!

That must be the incubus!" She picked up the cell and read the text. "Oh, it's actually our friends, the Maaskab! They say they've received my message and agree to the trade."

She began typing: Fabulous! I'll meet you at the incubus's estate as planned. The tablet will be yours. Can't wait. Hugs. Kisses. Many evil thoughts.

She put the phone down and Roberto grunted.

"Yep!" she replied. "It's all going like clockwork. Now, where were we? Ah, yes! Let's swing."

Seis

⌒

January 5. Two Days Later

Heart pounding, palms sweating, Ixtab cracked open the door of the physicist's apartment unsure of what she might find.

"Hello? Is anyone here?" The place was supposedly unoccupied at the moment, but with her luck, there'd be some random, hot best friend apartment sitting, waiting to accidentally bump into her.

"Hello?"

No reply.

Ixtab stepped inside and closed the door. What the hell was she doing there? She didn't really know, but after the four-hour flight, she'd found herself telling the driver to head straight for Helena's building near Central Park, instead of the hospital to help Mr. Acero. Perhaps she wasn't ready to see the man who so closely resembled

Francisco—the man she once loved. Perhaps a part of her wondered if her demons might chase her for eternity. But perhaps, just perhaps, she'd come to his apartment for another reason altogether: hope.

She slid off her veil, draped it on the coat hook, and inspected the living room. Nothing much to see there: gleaming hardwood floors, large flat screen, glass coffee table, and a navy-blue leather couch. Aside from the air being a bit stale and the decorum seriously lacking a woman's touch, the place was nondescript. And remarkably tidy for a single male.

She passed by a large beveled mirror mounted to the wall and caught her reflection. She looked...awful. No, her overall appearance never changed, not really, but her long, chocolate-brown hair, turquoise eyes, and bronzed skin seemed noticeably duller, as if she'd been soaked in chlorine or left to fade in the sun. Her lack of enthusiasm for life was finally catching up to her.

She'd have to pay a visit to the Goddess of Forgetfulness soon; maybe that would help her to move on. *If only I could remember how to find her...*

Ixtab went over to the window and pushed it open, stopping to admire the early morning sun climbing up over the cityscape. The air outside was crisp and cold, but even this many stories up, it smelled thick with winter pollution. Funny how after all these decades, the unnatural odors of industrialized man still bothered her. Give her mountains, trees, and sunshine any day over this.

Ixtab wandered into the sparkling-clean kitchen also finding it with little personality—gray glass tile, another television, and a glass breakfast table. She tugged open the stainless steel fridge and crinkled her nose at its contents. *Yuck. Healthy stuff.*

Now that's where she drew the line with nature. Didn't he have any junk food? *Fruit, yogurt, soy cheese—ick, and...hmmm, okay. Beer.* She grabbed one and popped off the top.

Ummm. At least he had good taste in something.

She chugged the rich, creamy contents and dumped the bottle into the stainless steel sink. She wandered down the hallway, also bare of any personal effects—not a painting, photo, or tchotchke to be found in the entire place. She found his bedroom and stood in the doorway, staring longingly at the empty, unmade bed. She imagined Francisco lying there, beckoning her to come to him.

Dammit! You're being ridiculous. You know this man is not your departed soul mate. Nevertheless, as ludicrous as it might be, she couldn't help but want proof, anything to cement her squarely in the jaws of reality and smother her ridiculous fantasy that this man might actually be his reincarnation. *A second chance...*

Ixtab sat down on the bed and ran her hand over the soft, gray satin pillow. The man's head had rested there. Would he smell like Francisco? That sweet, spicy, masculine smell she'd become addicted to? That she missed so much?

She lifted the pillow to her nose. "Cheap perfume," Ixtab growled and threw it down. She pulled open the top nightstand drawer and stared in bewilderment at the pile of condoms inside. "XXL. For the all-night lover?" she said. *A whole drawer full of them? Manhooker!*

Dammit! Why had she come here instead of going straight to the hospital to get this over with? There was nothing in this apartment that would tell her what she didn't already know: Francisco was dead. She killed him, and he wasn't coming back. Period. End of story.

Ixtab stood and felt something brush her leg. "Oh, shit!" The large orange cat shrieked and then dove back under the bed.

"Oh no! Kitty." Ixtab got down on all fours. "Come here, kitty. Come to Ixtaaaab." The cat's golden eyes, wide and full of fear, told her the dang critter wasn't coming anywhere near her. "Dammit, kitty. Why did you touch me? Why?"

Ixtab swiped for the cat, but it was out of reach. *Shit.* She had to do something fast before the cat choked itself on its own tail or . . .

The cat bolted from underneath the bed and out into the hall. Ixtab froze. *Hell. The window!*

Ixtab ran to the living room just in time to see the tail disappear outside.

"No!" She stopped at the sill and looked down, but there was nothing she could do. The cat was gone. And dead. Very dead.

Ixtab slid down onto the floor, gripping the sides of her head. *Why? Why? Why?* How could she have killed the guy's cat? No, she didn't actually pick the poor little creature up and chuck it out the window, but she felt just as responsible. *Poor, poor kitty . . .*

Gods, she was so fed up with this! So sick and tired of being the bringer of self-imposed death. It wasn't fair. She didn't want to kill—well, not unintentionally, anyway. But hell! The Universe had a sick, sick sense of humor.

A small blinking light and a beep from underneath the sofa caught her attention. Sniffling, she crawled over and found a cell phone. It was on its last legs and needed a charge.

One hundred and fifteen messages? She wiped her nose on her black lace sleeve and pressed play. "Antonio, this is Vanessa. Where you been, baby? Call me back." "I gotta itch tonight, Dr. Acero, wanna scratch it? Call me." "Meowww, Antonio. Want to play with my puss—"

What the . . . ? I guess he's not going to miss the damned cat. He's got backups all ready to go!

As each message played, Ixtab felt the rage build and the fantasy of him being something more than just a Francisco look-alike slip further and further away until it died with a gruesome twitch right then and there. This Antonio Acero was a womanizer, a man whore, and clearly inconsiderate of anyone's feelings. The messages, which became more and more desperate as the women concluded Antonio would not be calling them back, were a testament to his lack of respect for them or their feelings.

Ixtab slowly picked herself up, still crying. "Well, I guess you got what you came for. This is not Francisco, and now you have proof." The man she once knew was the most caring, compassionate being on the planet. He'd never use women in such a way.

Now she could truly put the past behind her. Francisco was gone. And she needed to forgive herself. *You've just taken the first step.*

Then why was she so damned angry? Shouldn't she feel liberated?

Maybe because *someone* needed to pay this Antonio man a visit and let him know that treating women like single-serve coffee cups wasn't okay.

Ixtab smiled. "I so love it when I get to be *someone*."

"But Mr. Acero," the nurse pleaded, "he's your brother. Why don't you want to see—"

"*Coño!* I said *no*. And if you haven't noticed, I am unable to *see* anything or anyone. My goddamned life is over." Why was everyone trying to convince him that everything would be all right? *Caray*. Nothing would be all right. Not one goddamned thing because he blew it.

The nurse sighed. "You and I both know you hit your head. The doctor thinks it could be reversible."

Right. He knew how this game was played. They'd fill him full of hope only to deliver the bad news later. "I don't give a shit what the doctor says. I do not want to see anyone. And I do not want to eat; I'm not hungry. Just get the fuck out! Let me die!"

Antonio knew his brother remained camped outside in the waiting area, but he couldn't bear to face him. Not after this. Without sight, his work would have to stop and there would be no hope in changing their fates. And, as if to torment him further, the nightmares only worsened. Day and night, those turquoise eyes clawed at the inner sanctum of his mind, the mysterious woman frantically pleading for salvation. A salvation he would never deliver. Not to her. Not to anyone.

"You're not dying, Mr. Acero—"

"*Puta madre*. Leave me the hell alone!"

The nurse sighed. "I'll send the counselor. Maybe she can talk some sense into you."

"I don't need a *pinche* headshrink!" he screamed at the disappearing footsteps. "And don't come back!"

"Hi there," said a soft female voice.

"Who the *hell* are you?"

"Has anyone ever told you it's not nice to talk to people like that? I suppose to someone like you, it doesn't matter."

Though she spoke sharply with an unrecognizable accent, her voice was actually quite lovely.

Mierda. Probably beautiful, too. The kind of woman who wouldn't dare give him the time of day now unless it was to help him cross the goddamned street.

"You people don't give up," he grumbled. "I said I don't want a psychiatrist."

A long, awkward moment passed with complete and utter silence. A breath, sweet and gentle, touched his lips, causing him to shrink back and slam his head against the headboard. "Ow. For fuck sake! What are you doing?"

Had she tried to kiss him?

Silence.

"Hello?" he said.

Silence.

"I know you're there. This isn't funny." He felt her presence vibrate through the room.

A loud sigh gave away her location.

"Who the hell are you?" he asked.

"Do Spaniards always swear so much? Tsk, tsk. So ungentlemanly. As for me? You could say I'm a friend. And by friend, I mean someone who finds your existence repulsive but chooses to take pity on you regardless. You're kind of like a little bug with a broken leg that gets put outside to live another day instead of being squashed on the spot."

"Is this some idiotic American reverse psychology bull

crap? You tell crippled people they're disgusting? Well, guess what? I agree with you. I'm useless!"

"What an idiot," the woman growled. "By the way, there's nothing wrong with the package—you still have your gorgeous face. And that body. Hell, you're a crime against female nature and should be shot on the spot for being so beautiful. Sadly, I can't say the same for what's on the inside. In fact, you're disgusting."

"What the ... ?"

"Don't act surprised," she said. "I know how you use women, then throw them away. And I'm here to warn you: if you continue your cheap man-whoring ways, I will hunt you down and pluck out your gonads. Got it?"

Man whore? Gonads? He had no clue how to respond.

"Let's get on with the show, shall we, Romeo?" she said.

Who was this woman? She sounded crazier than he did. "And what show would that be?" he asked.

"Does that pathetic brain of yours still work? Because I heard you're supposed to be smart. You don't sound so smart to me."

Santa Maria. She was ruthless. No way was she a doctor or psychologist; she was *pinche loca.* "Who the hell are you?"

"Shut up before I change my mind. *Teen uk'al k'iinam. Teen uk'al yah.*" A pair of hands hit his chest, jolting him like a defibrillator.

His back painfully arched and each muscle in his body went rigid with the blistering heat. The air filled with the scent of fresh-cut daisies and fragrant vanilla, and the heaviness lifted from his chest. It was as though a dark cloud had been sieved from his soul. Clean air entered his lungs, giving him quarter to breathe again. Memories, happy ones, flooded his heart—playing hide-and-seek with his brother in the Spanish vineyards during summer, scuba diving in the Mediterranean, the paella at his favorite little restaurant in the town near his home in Penedès.

"What did you do?" he whispered into the abyss.

"I saved your sorry ass, but not so you can continue your dude-slutting. Got it? You will take this chance I've given you to do bigger and better things—one of which will be going back to work on that tablet."

"How do you know about the tablet?" It was a secret.

"I'm a spy for the government. We know everything," she said as though she was overwhelmed by boredom.

"Here." She shoved a card in his hand. "Once you're home, call this number. They'll send you a tutor and an assistant. And yes, Einstein, the number is written in braille. I'm also having the landlord install a braille phone and set up your computer. The tutor will come to reteach you to read. And before you thank me, you should know that I accidentally killed your cat. I'm really sorry but it…"

Antonio's mind whirled as the woman apologized pro-fusely for murdering his cat—something about it getting loose and jumping out a window?—and then proceeded to hurl endless, demeaning insults, peppered with every swear word in the English language along with a few choice words in Spanish, too. She was so…*damned hor-rible and bitter*! The sourest, most cantankerous female he'd ever met. A thousand sailors could not compete with her sharp edges and unfiltered mouth. And yet, she was strangely alluring.

"So"—she took a breath—"you got it? *Comprende*, Señor Acero?"

"Uh...yes?"

"Good. My work here is done. Have a happy life, assho— I mean, Antonio."

"Wait! You're leaving?" He sat up in bed.

"Sorry. Gotta get back to saving lives and all. And by the way, Tony, we'd all appreciate it if you'd get back to work on the tablet before the world blows up."

"You're going to use it to fight terrorists?" he asked.

"Sorry, I can't divulge that information. It's a matter of national security. See ya."

The moment Ixtab left the room and fell out of earshot, she found the nearest wall and leaned in to prevent herself from having a good, old-fashioned heart attack. She didn't know what came over her, but the moment she saw that man, she'd lost it. Completely lost it. Had it something to do with the fact that as soon as she set eyes on him, every painful memory of Francisco came crashing down? Or had it more to do with her knowing he slept with all those women?

Ixtab clawed at the black lace fabric over her heart, trying to catch her breath. Dammit, the man even frowned like Francisco and had done that little scrunching thing with his beautiful sable eyebrows when he'd felt confused.

Ixtab sank with her back against the wall, panting and trembling. No. This man wasn't Francisco, she knew that now, but he *was* her punishment—karma for all her sins. And she hated him for it.

Why, oh, gods, why?

Worse of all, seeing the man callously revived those dormant feelings she'd thought dead. Useless feelings. Gritty, raw, needy feelings.

Ixtab's overloaded mind replayed taunting images of Antonio. Yes, that man was pure sex. Not that Ixtab had ever had sex. Or ever would. Even with black jade— a fairly new discovery that blunted a deity's energy and allowed him or her intimacy with humans—at her disposal, that sort of physical contact was simply not in the cards. Not for her, anyway. The dark energy channeled through her touch was simply too potent. Didn't stop her from wanting, though. This man, with his deep olive skin and strong lips, was built like a champion stallion. Had he known his robe was open at the bottom?

Ixtab sighed.

With such an enormous distraction, how had she even performed the cleansing ritual and managed to keep her cells polarized in the right direction?

"Are you all right, ma'am?" A young nurse reached for Ixtab to aid her, but Ixtab scrambled away and then sprang to her feet.

"Don't touch me. I'm fine." She scurried down the hall into the stairwell. She needed to get the hell out of there and off-load quickly. Antonio's darkness and self-loathing swirled in her head. What had the man done to hate himself so profusely? Not even she disliked herself that much, and she'd done some pretty outrageously heinous things worthy of hatred—on accident, of course. Always on accident.

Gods, I can't think straight. She needed to shed this physicist's energy fast. It felt like it had wrapped itself around her heart in a stranglehold. She'd never experienced such an alarmingly intense sensation.

Ixtab bolted outside to the pedestrian-filled street, careful to steer clear of any humans, and headed for the subway. There was always someone worthy of a little death on the subway.

Yes, all she needed was to cleanse and everything would be fine. Wouldn't it?

Siete

Five deserving victims later, Ixtab returned to Helena and Niccolo's building. It was quite a nice place actually. The communal areas, including the lobby, were decorated with modern furniture, mostly reds and whites, with a few richly upholstered, overstuffed chairs and velvety pillows. Kind of an *Alice in Wonderland* meets Target look. Of course, Helena was bunkered down with her man-nanny and daughter at Kinich's, so she'd offered up the unoccupied penthouse, which Niccolo had decorated in classic vampire chic (top-of-the-line, spare-no-expense, modern everything).

But first, a stop. Ixtab got off the elevator on the nineteenth floor and knocked on the first door. Ironically, the physicist's apartment was only one door down. What would Dr. Acero think if he knew his neighbor was a vampire?

"Go the fuck away!"

A very cranky vampire. Ixtab rolled her eyes and pushed open the door. "Sure. I'd love to come in."

Though dusk had already made its appearance, Kinich's blinds remained drawn and he sat in the darkest corner of the living room, staring at a wall.

It pained her to see her favorite brother like this. He truly had been dealt a nasty hand.

"Hi. I'm looking for Kinich. He's about yea tall. Master of all things sunny. Thinks he's king of the Universe. Recently turned undead. Have you seen him?"

Kinich didn't budge.

"Okay. I'm not getting the funny bone award, but cut me some slack; I'm the Goddess of Suicide." She reached into her bag and popped an orange Tic Tac into her mouth. She still tasted that damned physicist on her tongue. She'd have to cleanse again later and see if she could dispel the lingering residue.

"Go the fuck away," Kinich grumbled.

Ixtab flipped on the lights and cringed. *This is seriously depressing.* Black-and-white prints of necks hung on gray walls, and most of the furniture was black.

She took a seat on the black leather couch and continued to inspect the room. Yes, clearly Helena had furnished the apartment expecting the usual vampire tenant. She'd bet her favorite red flip-flops that the bedroom had a four-poster bed with black bed curtains and red satin sheets.

She leaned forward and glanced through the doorway leading to the bedroom.

Yup. Kind of a surprise, too, because Helena and Niccolo—a vampire and ex-vampire—had excellent taste in furnishings for their private homes. But this? She made a sour face. *Icky.*

Ooh! New reason! Vampires are icky, number four: their homes look like an after-hours strip club minus the pole.

To be clear, the pole would be an improvement—liven up the place a little.

"Are you still here? I said get the fuck out!" Kinich screamed.

And while she was adding to her icky list, she should also note that vampires were in a constant state of irritability. So. Annoying. She'd yet to meet a male vampire who didn't trigger an urge in her to kick him in the man taters. Exception being Kinich, of course. Poor guy. He lived for sunshine. And now he was anti-sunshine.

Mr. Cloud?

"Kinich, I know things are rough, but Penelope needs you. She calls every day, crying and asking to come see you—"

His head snapped up. Those eyes, which were usually a stunning turquoise like hers, turned coal-mine black. "I tried to kill her. Fucking kill her, Ixtab! What she needs is nothing to do with me."

She wanted to reach out and provide comfort, but she'd yet to ever touch a vampire. Who knew what might happen? Probably not the best time to find out.

"You're still adjusting," she argued. "Give it time—"

"I've had sixty-five! Sixty-fucking-five bags of fucking blood and can think of nothing but drinking her! She's carrying my baby, for fuck sake."

"Jeez. I wasn't aware vampires were so into naughty words." *Reminds me of the physicist actually.* "I love naughty words by the way, but only when used sparingly and in witty, creative context. So can I buy a non-f-word, please, Alex? I'll take Tormented Vampires and Their Stranded Pregnant Mortals for two hundred dollars."

Kinich didn't laugh.

Dammit. She was only trying to make him feel better.

"Okay. I need to work on my jokes," she said. "I feel like that damned android from *Star Trek*—Info? Or... Megabit?" She scratched her temple. What was his name? *Well, I guess I know what I'm doing tonight: reruns!*

"Seriously, Kinich, you're going to have to find a way to get over this—whatever the hell it is—and go to her. Otherwise, you'll lose her."

He laughed into the air like a madman.

"What's so funny?" Sporadic, inappropriately timed laughter always put Ixtab on edge. It reminded her of Belch right before something bad happened.

Kinich's laughter died with a little sputter. "The irony. That's what's so goddamned funny." He rubbed his forehead. "There was a time—not too long ago, in fact— that I would have given anything, anything at all, to be a vampire."

Eww... "Why?" she asked.

"Right after I met Penelope, she was attacked by the Maaskab in her apartment and I happened to be on the phone with her." He paused and swallowed. "The torture of listening to her screams was unbearable, and I said to myself, 'I'm a deity. A goddamned deity! And I can't save her. But a vampire could. A vampire could simply sift to her and always be there to protect her.' "

"You're saying that you really wanted to become a vampire? Just to protect her?" Ixtab couldn't believe that a god, *the* most powerful god in the Universe, would want such a thing.

"I suppose I did. Now, that doesn't matter. Not only am I unable to sift because the Maaskab barricaded that dimension, I'm Penelope's biggest threat. In fact, thank gods I can't sift; there'd be no way to keep her safe from me."

Wow. In some ways, he was right. Vampires being unable to sift was a hidden blessing. *Funny how things sorta work out that way sometimes.*

"She's fucking better off without me," he added.

"Ahhh. Spoken like a clueless dipshit. Because with the sort of despair she's enduring, she will end up with someone, and that someone will be Zac."

Kinich's nostrils flared. "Zac?"

"Yes, brother. She has the weight of the world on her shoulders and a baby on the way. If she fails..." Ixtab couldn't bear to finish the dreary, apocalyptic thought. "Everything is at stake, and she needs someone to stand by her side. Friends aren't enough. The gods aren't enough. She needs...you. And if she can't have you, then eventually she will cave. Zac is quite determined."

Kinich snarled.

Ixtab nodded. "Good. I'm glad you understand. I'll be back to check on you tomorrow. In the meantime, I suggest you take this." She slipped a small, insulated pouch from her enormous floral handbag. "It's a vial of Penelope's blood from her doctor. Start desensitizing yourself."

Kinich's eyes fixated on the pouch. Saliva dribbled from the corner of his mouth.

Oh, sweet gods. "Get a hold of yourself. It's only blood."

"It smells..." He sniffed the air. "Delicious."

It was going to be a very, very long week. "Just don't drink the stuff. I had Belch put a drop of his ball sweat in the vial."

Kinich dropped his head. "You are too cruel."

It was the only way to keep him from gulping it down, given Ixtab couldn't very well keep running back to the well now, could she?

"Perrrty much." Ixtab headed for the door. "And by the way, brother, I met your baby. It is beautiful. I've never felt a more pure and happy soul. I suggest you remember that when you say you cannot cure yourself of this desire for Penelope's blood."

Kinich didn't blink, didn't move, didn't breathe. "Is it a boy or a girl?"

Ixtab shrugged. "If you wanna know, you'll have to get your act together and help Penelope save the world."

She slammed the door behind her and smiled. She'd seen his aura shift from a deep gray to a light brown. Yes, there was hope for him yet.

Eighteen saves, twenty-five cleanses, and one accidental death later, Ixtab stood before a group of unfamiliar faces. "Hi. My name is Ixtab. My friends call me..." *Darn, I really need to get some friends so I can have a nickname.* "...Ixtab."

"Hi, Ixtab."

"It's been"—she looked at her pastel yellow watch—"ten minutes and seventeen seconds since I last killed an innocent mortal."

Applause.

Why are they clapping? It's awful!

Because you compelled them to be attentive and polite perhaps?

"Well, the reason I'm here is because something

strange is happening. Take today, for example. I'd just removed the darkness from this poor woman who spends her days feeding the homeless and had fallen into a horrible slump; simply saw too much suffering is my guess. Anyway, I cleansed her, found a few thugs hanging out in front of the liquor store. Cleansed. Went on my merry way. I didn't make it two blocks until my body filled up with dark energy again."

The group of elderly women exchanged glances.

"I know, it's weird. Right?" Ixtab said. "And the strangest part is that it started after I helped that physicist. I can't get his damned taste out of my mouth." Ixtab smacked her lips. "His darkness is kind of nutty." Ixtab snorted. "Oh! Get it? *Nutty Professor*. I'm on fire today."

Crickets.

She rolled her eyes. "Cut me some slack. I'm the Goddess of Suicide. Comedy doesn't come naturally. Neither does not lopping people's heads off when they don't laugh at my jokes." She paused. "*Seeee?* That was a joke. I really suck at this. Almost as badly as I suck at smiling. I once went an entire century without smiling—not that anyone would ever notice since I wear a veil."

Someone chuckled under their breath.

"*That* wasn't a joke." She shook her head. Why was her suffering always funny? That just didn't seem right.

Ixtab sighed. "As I was saying…now I'm unsure what to do. I cleansed twice this afternoon—a sweet score: bagged a murderer and a pimp. But I keep filling up again. Any ideas what to do?"

"Have you tried praying?" The slightly plump woman, wearing a gray sweater garnished with white cat hair, pointed toward the chapel in the other room.

Ixtab shook her head. "My prayers don't get a lot of traction with the whole killing innocent people and all. Even if it's by accident."

"How about knitting?" asked one woman who sat farthest away in the circle. She had deep smile lines etched into her kind, wrinkly face. "When I have trouble finding an answer, I knit. Then the answer just pops in my head."

Ixtab bobbed her head. "Sure. Why not? What are we knitting today?"

"Baby bootees."

"Oh, perfect. I can make some for Penelope and Kinich." She grabbed a pair of needles from a basket in the center of the circle and plopped down in an open seat. Gods, her hair was itchy. "Mind if I take this off?"

No one objected, so she did.

The women gasped.

"Dear," said the woman with the cat hair garnish, "you *are* exquisite. And those eyes, they're   stunning."

Ixtab squirmed in her chair. She didn't like it when people looked at her that way, with admiration. Simply put, she didn't deserve to be revered. Yes, it was true that being worshipped was one of the perks of being a god or goddess. In fact, many deities thrived on it. Fate, for example, wouldn't last a day without having someone light a candle in her honor. But Ixtab didn't want to be adored; she wanted to be good. "You're only complimenting me because I've compelled everyone here. If you knew the real me, you and your walker would be ten blocks away already. I am about as ugly as they come." *On the inside, anyway.*

Her mind quickly flipped to her beloved Francisco. Perhaps that is why she'd loved him so much. He made her feel beautiful on the inside and worthy for the first time in her existence. It was a feeling she missed more than she cared to admit. *If only second chances truly existed.*

Ixtab suddenly felt the urge to see that physicist again.

No. Didn't you learn your lesson? Stay away from him—you'll only end up killing the guy, and we need him to stay alive and work on the tablet. Not to mention… he's the Latin lover poster boy!

"Does anyone have yellow yarn?" Ixtab asked. "I don't want to give away the baby's sex. Better if it's a surprise."

That's right. Stick to knitting and your work. No physicist.

Yet somehow she knew the situation with Antonio Acero was just getting started. Because that's how the Universe rolled.

Ocho

⌒

January 13

Despite missing his cat and being unable to see, Antonio's arrival home one week earlier hadn't been nearly as difficult as he'd thought. After the visit from the mysterious woman in the hospital, his dismal outlook on the world had shifted. He knew he could tackle any obstacle despite the impossibility of this situation. Yes, he was happy. Genuinely happy.

Perhaps she was an angel? *A really, really mean angel.*

Antonio slipped on his favorite black sweater and black jeans. At least he thought they were black. He hadn't had time to work with his new assistant to organize his closet since they'd been spending every waking hour learning basic braille—mostly numbers.

In any case, he decided he'd go out for his first walk today. Just around the block to clear his head. Although the woman from his dreams continued haunting him every hour of the day and he still believed she was his destiny, the key to everything, he couldn't stop obsessing over that cruel, yet mesmerizing banshee from the hospital. He fantasized what she might look like. Was she a leggy blonde with the slim frame of a runway model? Or a curvy Latina with full breasts, the sort of breasts a man could lose himself in? No matter. If that voice were any indication, she had to be the most gorgeous creature to walk the planet. The mere thought of seeing her again created a sense of bliss until he wondered if she would want him. A blind man.

Forget about her. The woman from your dreams is your destiny. You must focus on that.

This fantasy woman had appeared with the tablet, and the tablet had been the answer to his prayers. Yes. It was true; he was a man of science, but his faith…that was what carried him. Perhaps it had something to do with being brought up in Spain, perhaps it was that he and his brother were raised by Kirstie the maid, an overly superstitious gypsy woman with an addiction to borscht, but the likely answer was that science couldn't guarantee salvation from his problems or deliver freedom. Faith was all he truly had.

So you have faith the woman from your dreams will help you. But shouldn't you at least attempt to find the woman from the hospital first? She saved your life.

Yes. That would be exactly what he would do. He would find her and thank her.

And bed her.

Dammit, coño. *Do you ever stop?*

But what was there to say? His cock moved into a state of high alert each time he thought of the cruel woman.

Of course, that had nothing to do with why he wanted to find her. No, *señor*. Not. At. All.

⌒

"Kinich, you have to keep trying!" Ixtab watched her brother pace back and forth across his living room.

"I cannot break the urge," he growled. "It doesn't matter what I do. Each time I open that vial, I drool like a rabid dog. Belch's ball sweat has no deterring effect whatsoever."

"You didn't actually drink any, did you?" Ixtab asked.

"No. But I wanted to. If Penelope walked into this room right now, I'd tear out her throat. I wouldn't be able to stop myself."

"How are you around other humans?" she asked.

He shrugged. "No issues. Not even the innocent who smell of cotton candy tempt me. I've been sticking to a steady diet of bagged blood without issue."

Hmmm. It was normal for a vampire to become crazed for blood when they first woke, as he had with Penelope, but this was different; he continued to lose control only for her. Vampires didn't have person-specific cravings. They were either in control or they weren't.

Something about this situation didn't feel right.

Dammit all to hell! She wished the vampires would come back from holiday so she could consult with one of them. Maybe they'd know what to do? And how exactly did an entire race simply up and take a vacay—to frigging Euro Disney, no less!—when they knew how critical they were to the line of defense? But no! Mickey, Goofy, and vampire law were clearly more important than saving the world. Adding insult to injury, they weren't even carrying cell phones! Oh no, because according to Helena—who'd texted her—they were spending their days on the Pirates of the Caribbean ride. Wouldn't want to get their phones wet. Gods forbid. Because they were all *so* broke and would never be able to afford new ones.

Cheap bastards.

Oh! Vampires are icky number five: they are too obsessed with managing their money.

Well, they do live a really, really, realllly long time.

Okay. Fair nuff. Strike that last one.

"Well," she offered, "Penelope sent a few Uchben to hunt down Viktor—maybe he'll have a few suggestions." Viktor, a thousand-year-old Viking vampire, had just about seen it all. That included Cimil's bed. It was a miracle he survived actually, and lucky he did because he'd very recently found his mate. Ironically, she was Penelope's mother. Confusing? Oh yeah. Throw in the fact that Penelope's mother was a fallen angel—well, they had themselves a regular paranormal *telenovela*. Univision had nothing on them.

Kinich crossed his meaty arms and stared out the window. "I cannot lose Penelope. I cannot. But I am not making progress." He paused for a long moment, clenching his jaw. "How is she?" he finally asked. His eyes remained fixed on the skyline.

Funny how Penelope had done the same thing, as if she and Kinich were staring from across the country at one another, longing. Ixtab knew the feeling—the ache of missing someone you love. That's why she had to do something to get the two back together.

Should she tell Kinich about Zac? The entire truth about his pursuit of Penelope? On one hand, it might send

Kinich over the edge. On the other, maybe he needed to hear the truth. Perhaps it would provide the added motivation for him to overcome his obsession with drinking Penelope.

"You want to know how she is?" Ixtab grumbled. "She's spending a lot of time with Zac. He brings baby books and reads to her. And when she can't sleep, he rubs her back and hunts down exotic snacks at two a.m.— baklava, Pop-Tarts, anchovy pizza, anything she wants. And when she awakens, he is there to hold her hair out of the toilet—the typical things mortal men do for their mates."

Kinich's fingers dug deeply into his biceps and tiny drops of blood hit the floor. "I see."

"But she misses you, brother. Every day she calls and asks to see you. And every day she cries when I tell her you are not ready."

Kinich's jaw muscles pulsed once again, and his chest heaved rapidly. "Leave. I need some time alone."

"I have to make my rounds, anyway; I'm all filled up again—the dumnedest thing because I haven't helped anyone." Ixtab scratched her veiled forehead and told him she'd return in the morning. Not that it would do much good because Kinich wasn't making any progress. It was as if he'd been programmed or cursed. *Something's just not right.*

"Get some rest, brother."

"You ought to stop calling me that, you know."

"Why?" she asked.

"We are not related, and now I am a shame to both my old and new species. I am so...weak."

Idiot. "Kinich, I don't care if we are not blood—none

of us are—but you will always be my brother, and I'm proud to call you so. This will all pass, I promise. Just have...patience."

She wanted to say *faith*, but not even she had that.

"See you in the morning, brother."

Kinich didn't say a word as she left. *Poor guy...*

Ixtab reached for the elevator call button, but the doors pinged and out stepped Antonio. "Christ!" She jumped out of the way. "Watch where the hell you're going."

Antonio, who wore stylish sunglasses, a thick off-white sweater, and soft, worn jeans, looked like a giant, warm slice of man heaven. She knew without a doubt that his sturdy frame didn't have an ounce of fat and his height, though not as tall as her brothers, was well above six feet. Somewhere near the six-and-a-half range perhaps. Who cared? All that mattered was Ixtab enjoyed the view from down there in five-foot-eight land. He was all man. All mortal. All delicious.

Stop that! Remember, he's just some...player. Some serial defiler of the female heart.

"Funny," he said and then started to chuckle.

"What's so funny?"

He chuckled a few more times and caught his breath. "You said, 'Watch it.' That's the funniest damned thing I've heard all day." He tapped his walking cane in front of him to make his point.

Ixtab growled and then offered him a few choice words in Spanish.

"Dios mío!" he said. "It *is* you! The agency you went through to get me that assistant didn't know anything about you."

"Yes. It's me." Once again, Ixtab found herself being

inundated with unwelcome emotions. Gods, this man was frigging hot.

Is it getting warm in here? Why do I feel so warm? "Nice to see you again, but I gotta run." She poked the call button again.

"Please. Don't leave. I only want to speak for a moment about what happened in the hospital." He stepped in front of the elevator, blocking her from the doors.

"I can't," she said coldly and stepped back.

Gods, I need to get away from him. She felt like her body might launch into orbit, combust, and become a second sun.

Why is it so hot? She tugged at her collar.

He frowned and his lips made a hard line. "Why not?"

Why? Why? Because you're doing something unholy to my body! Gods ... I want to grrrrab you and maul you with my lips. Maybe rip off your pants and have a very deep conversation with that giant penis of yours.

What? Did you just say you want to talk to his penis?

Yes. Yes, I did. I need to get the hell out of here!

"We can't talk because ... I'm a superspy. Remember?" she said.

"Doubtful. Please. Tell me who you are." He stepped toward her and reached for her shoulder. She found herself wanting to lean in and let him make contact, but caught herself and jumped back.

"Shit! Buddy, do you have a death wish or something? Don't touch me!"

His expression turned bleak. "Do I disgust you that much?"

Oh, gods, no. I want to strip you naked, cover you in chocolate sauce, and swab you with a doughnut. "Yes. People like you always do. So ... back off!"

Gods, that was a mean thing to say, but it worked. He backed away and his expression turned to one of sheer outrage.

Suddenly, she felt strangely weak. She looked at her hands. Gray. She was filled to the brim with despair, and if she didn't cleanse quickly, she'd fall into a coma. "Oh, hell..."

The elevator beeped. She stepped in and sank to her knees. What the hell was happening to her?

Nueve

The small sapling of hope blossoming in the depths of Antonio's soul shriveled up and died a gruesome death on the spot. He'd finally found the mysterious woman from the hospital only to be told he disgusted her.

Of course, you disgust her, coño, you're nothing but a pathetic useless—

A loud crash followed by a man's painful scream startled him. It came from the doorway directly in front of the elevator, one door down from his. It was his new neighbor, the one who paced day and night and never slept. Perhaps the man had finally passed out from exhaustion. *Or something worse...*

Antonio cautiously approached the door and listened. All was quiet.

He knocked. "Hello? Is everything all right?"

A muffled moan filtered through the door. *Caray.* Had

the man been injured? Antonio turned the doorknob and pushed open the door. "Do you need help?"

Dammit. He couldn't see shit. The man might be a foot away, bleeding to death, and Antonio wouldn't even know.

"Hello?" He stepped inside and tried to listen for any sound.

Nothing, dammit. When would his Spidey hearing kick in? Wasn't his body supposed to compensate for his lost sight? *Dios*, he sucked at everything, didn't he?

The door slammed shut behind him. "Who the fuck are you?" asked a deep, ominous voice.

Antonio's heart pounded furiously inside his chest. "I'm your neighbor. I heard a crash and..." *Santa Maria!* "It smells like blood."

"I punched the wall and cut open my hand." The voice had moved in front of him.

This guy sounded crazier than he was. "*Bueno*, I see you are alive and breathing, so I'll be on my way."

A firm hand pushed him away from the door.

"What the fuck?" Antonio extended his hands defensively, but the man seemed to be everywhere all at once.

"Listen, *coño*," Antonio said, dropping his arms, "if you want to kill me, you'd probably be doing me a favor, but make it quick."

He felt the man's hot breath on his face right before his sunglasses were torn away. Antonio knew he had no use of his eyes, yet he couldn't break the urge to open them and strain to see what was happening.

"Your aura is too bright," said the man. "I can't kill you. Guess it's your lucky day."

Right. Lucky. My day has been a giant pinche *shamrock.* "I would not call it that."

"Mine neither," the man grumbled.

"Sorry to hear that." *You* pinche *psychopath*. "If you're not going to kill me and you're not dying, I'm going back to my apartment to drink myself into a stupor."

"Stay. I will pour you a scotch."

"No, *gracias*. I think—"

"I said, 'Stay.' *Relax*. This is what you want." Something in the man's voice compelled him to obey. Ironically, the sensation felt far more unnerving than being threatened physically.

"If you insist," Antonio replied reluctantly. *What the hell is going on?*

The man grabbed him by the arm and dragged him across the room. *Caray*, what a fucking grip this man had.

"Sit," the man commanded. "I will return in a moment."

Antonio's body obeyed, but his mind clicked back and forth between caged-animal panic and an artificial complacency.

Keep your cool. Get him to let his guard down and then run for the door...

The man returned promptly with a cool-to-the-touch, smooth glass tumbler.

Antonio took a whiff. Single malt scotch. Very fine. "Macallan 1926?" Antonio asked.

"You have a good nose."

"I learned to drink scotch in my late teens; wanted to piss off my father, who happens to be a vintner." *And possibly the most vile son of a bitch on the face of the planet.*

The man laughed. "A very expensive rebellion."

Scotch had only been the beginning of a lifelong pursuit to reject everything his father stood for. If it was the last thing Antonio did, he'd beat his father—and by beat, he meant kill.

"These days my tastes have humbled," Antonio said. "I'm a big fan of Belgian whites. In fact, I have a six-pack in the fridge if you'd like to try—"

"You will stay and relax," the man commanded.

The anxiety instantly drained from Antonio's body. "Yes, I'd like that." *I think.*

Again the man laughed. "Good. So, you are my neighbor," he said.

"Yes. I am Antonio Acero."

"Kinich. Nice to meet you. So, tell me more about this bad luck," Kinich said.

"Why?" Antonio never discussed his problems with anyone. What good would it fucking do? They'd either think him crazy or . . . well, fucking crazy. Nor could anyone help him. So no fucking thanks.

"If it's worse than mine," Kinich replied, "it might make me feel better." He added in that strange, deep voice, "I insist."

Antonio took a large swallow of the smooth, smoky liquid. Oddly, he felt the gripping urge to tell the crazy man everything.

But will he believe you? Antonio's situation exceeded the boundaries of sanity and defied every law of the universe. It was the reason he'd left home at his first chance. It was the reason he'd studied quantum physics. It was the reason nothing mattered more than proving alternate dimensions existed.

Of course, proof seemed like the illusive pot of gold at the end of a rainbow until two months ago when a colleague—as a joke—sent him an article about the

Mayans and time travel. The legends spoke of a sacred tablet, and with it, they'd traveled the stars, saw the future, and eventually returned home to share their wealth of knowledge. The Mayans then constructed pyramids, complex irrigation systems, and a calendar more accurate than what was used today.

However, the Mayan holy men, knowing the danger of time travel and dimensional exploration, kept this knowledge close to the vest. Only their high priests and kings ever knew of the existence of the tablets. And it was said that when the Spanish arrived, it was Fray Diego de Landa who discovered their secrets and witnessed their powers firsthand. Yes, *the* Fray Diego de Landa. Infamous Franciscan monk who led the Mexican inquisition and subjected the indigenous population to violent forms of torture in the name of Christianity. He burnt every shred of paper, including the sacred codices, and destroyed every tablet he could get his "holy" hands on. No one understood his violent, bloody rampage of destruction, but if he had indeed seen the tablets open a portal to another world, one could easily guess why a monk of that day and age would believe it to be the devil's magic.

Luckily, however, not everything had been destroyed. A few precious historical documents survived along with the record of one remaining tablet that had been hidden from the Spaniards, kept safe all these centuries somewhere near the border of Belize.

"I am waiting," said Kinich.

Antonio felt an odd pressure inside his head, compelling him to speak. "It all started when I went to Mexico to find an artifact I'd been searching for. A tablet. I didn't believe it would be there, but the fucking thing practically hopped in my lap—as if it was looking for me," Antonio said.

"You do not truly believe the tablet sought you out, do you?" Kinich asked.

Antonio took another sip. "I've thought to myself many times, *Puta madre! I have lost my mind.* But I cannot deny what I saw.

"I'd been in Tulum, Mexico, for a week with my companion, a lovely German woman named...*caray.* I cannot remember—Ute. *Sí,* Ute was her name. She was built like a swimsuit model and insatiable, but her incessant whining drove me mad. 'Make love to me again, Antonio. You work too much, Antonio. You never spend enough time with me, Antonio.' *Caray.* It was too much; a man's got to have a few hours of downtime. I grabbed my gear, took my map, and headed out in my Jeep. However, I think I already knew where I was going—to a dirt road in the middle of the jungle. That is when the engine died."

"Let me guess. A strange redhead wearing pink appeared to you."

Antonio felt the pressure in his head pull back. "How did you know?"

"Lucky guess," Kinich said.

Lucky guess my *pinche* foot. "How did you know?"

Kinich cleared his throat. "That redheaded woman is my sister. She has a way of popping up like that."

"Your sister?"

"Yes," Kinich said, "and I'm going to bet she spoke of clowns, talked to a bug, and then directed you to the tablet?"

Sí. That is exactly right. How did he know? "I thought

I'd dreamt the entire thing. The scuba diving, finding the tablet inside a cenote, the Jeep starting on its own. But when I woke up in my bed back in New York, I knew. It had been fate."

Kinich chuckled. "Not Fate. Cimil. Fate doesn't usually get her hands dirty with overly complicated jungle-based plots. This has Cimil written all over it."

"How do you know all this?"

"I suppose"—Kinich paused—"there's no harm in telling you. I'm going to have to wipe your memory before you leave anyway."

"Excuse me?"

"I am a god," the man said casually. "Well, I was a god."

Yes. Of course you are . . . The man was clearly insane. Actually, this entire conversation had taken a trip to Salvador Dalí Land. *Care for a fucking melted pocket watch anyone?*

Antonio stood. It was time to get the hell out of there.

"Where are you going?" Kinich asked.

"My assistant is coming to help me translate notes. She's probably waiting outside right now," Antonio lied.

"Bullshit. She comes in the morning, and it's eight o'clock at night," Kinich said. "Tell me what Cimil said and then you may leave."

Once again, Antonio felt an odd sensation pressing against his mind, pushing him to talk. "The redhead said that I was to study the tablet, decipher it, and unlock its secrets. If I did so, my destiny would be fulfilled." He left out the part about finding his true love and happiness. Men simply didn't say that sort of crap to other men.

"I see." Antonio heard the man scratch his chin. From the sound of it, he hadn't shaved in weeks.

"Then I believe this is what you must do—unlock the tablet's secrets. Quickly."

"How do you propose I accomplish this?" Antonio asked. "My most important tool happens to be out of commission, and it's impossible to teach someone else to translate what they see in a meaningful way for me."

"You still have your brain; you'll figure it out. And if you do not, you will die."

Santa Maria! He turned to leave, only to find two cold hands pushing him back into his seat.

"Relax. I told you that I am not going to kill you, it is forbidden to kill mortals who are not evil—kill them on purpose, anyway. But my brother and a very good friend are trapped inside another dimension. If they are not released, the Maaskab are prophesied to make the planet their personal playground of death and destruction."

Maaskab? What the hell is that? And his brother is trapped? End of the world? "You are mad."

"I speak the truth," Kinich said with a low hypnotic voice.

"*Sí.* And my *huevos* are magical coconuts."

"Your eggs?" the man questioned.

"Balls. My balls!"

"And you say I am insane? At least I do not believe my testicles are magical," Kinich said.

What the . . . ? "I've answered your questions. I'm leaving now." He stood and beelined for the door, instantly slamming into a table. His body toppled over and his face smashed into a pile of whatever had been on top, including something made of glass. Something sharp.

"Puta madre!" Blood gushed from his cheek as his body tumbled.

A feral growl seeped into his ears. "You broke the vial. It smells so...so..."

Antonio felt the cool tickle of air move across his face as two sharp knives sank into his throat.

Diez

⌒

Two blocks from Helena's building, Ixtab sighed with relief. She'd staggered into the alley and had found a worthy country-club member. He'd been passed out behind a Dumpster with one eye cracked open. That was enough for her to see his soul. *Ah. Black aura. Bingo!*

A few seconds longer and Ixtab would have been down for the count. But why had she filled up without touching anyone? And that damned taste in her mouth wouldn't go away.

As she strolled down the sidewalk bustling with people heading out for their evening fun, her cell vibrated and then played the Death March. She dug it out from her enormous straw handbag—the one with plastic daisies on the outside and stuffed to the gills with Tic Tacs, a spare veil, and the knitted bootees she planned to gift wrap later.

"Hey, Penelope."

"Any news?"

What should she say? If this situation was heartbreaking to watch from the sidelines, it had to be a thousand times worse for the stars of this drama. Gods, she wished she could simply fix Kinich. But she couldn't. "I'm sorry. He's still working on it. Just give him a few more days."

"That's what you said yesterday, and the day before, and the day before that."

"That's because he still goes monkey balls every time he smells your blood," Ixtab explained.

"He won't kill me, Ixtab. I know he won't. He loves me too much. Maybe if we let him have a nibble?"

Patience, patience...

Oh, hell. I can't hold it! "Would you like a wooden or a plastic barrel for your trip down Niagara Falls, today, Miss Evel Knievel?"

"What does that mean?"

"Nothing. I just think it's amazing. For most humans, elevated pregnancy hormones make them more cautious and protective. But you, you turn into a goddamned daredevil!" Ixtab said.

Awkward silence.

"Evel Knievel rode a motorcycle, not a barrel," Penelope said quietly.

"Oh. What. Ever! The point is you have more than yourself to think about now."

"I know. That's why I'm here in New York. I need to see him. I need to fix this. Not for me, but for the baby, too. It deserves a chance to have its real father."

"No! Dammit. It deserves to live, which it won't if you go anywhere near Kinich. Besides, you're forgetting that he doesn't want to see you. He doesn't want to risk hurting you and the baby."

Long pause. "You're right," she said with a heavy sigh. "I know you're right." Long pause. "Can't I talk to him on the phone? Can't he at least say it to my face? Or ear. Crap. Whatever!"

I tried that. He said hearing your voice would send him into a frenzy. "What's the point? He's only going to tell you what I've already said. Give him time, Penelope, and I'm sure—" Sobs broke out on the other end of the phone.

Normally, crying humans didn't bother Ixtab much, but for some reason, it really got under her skin when Penelope did it.

Maybe you really care for her?

What? Me?

Ha. Never.

Okay. Maybe a little. Ixtab tapped her foot on the cold concrete. *Okay. A lot.* "Fine. I'll go to his apartment and get him on the phone, but don't come near his place."

"I'm staying upstairs with you at Helena's," Penelope said.

"That's too close."

"Ixtab, stop. You're not my mother."

Clearly not. Ixtab was far from being an angel. "You're absolutely right. If she were here now, she'd..." *What kind of punishment would an angel dole out?* "She'd... poke you in the eye! Uh-huh! That's right."

Penelope made a little *caah* "whatever" sound.

"You know, Penelope, I consider you like a sister. Only a less annoying, mortal-ish version with a heart. And a conscience. But clearly the Creator didn't pluck you from the brainy branch. Did he? Kinich. Is. A. Vampire. One who would like nothing more than to gobble you up like a ten-year-old holding a hand-dipped waffle cone filled with birthday cake, M&M's, and topped with vanilla ice cream. And video game tokens. Well, maybe they wouldn't eat the tokens, but you get the gist."

"Ixtab, I can't help it. My brain says stay away, but everything else says to go to him, that it will all work out if I trust him, if I trust our love. I didn't do that before when I should have, and it only made things worse."

"Getting anywhere near my brother is a death sentence, Penelope. I'm seventy thousand years old, and you'll simply need to trust that I know what I'm talking about."

"Ixtab, you don't under—"

"But I do. I do— Wait. Why are we even having this conversation? You know, I could never understand people with a death wish. Seriously. You'd never see other animals pulling this crap, but you humans ... *oy vey.* Would a dog BASE jump off the Empire State Building? How about a chipmunk? You'd never see those furry little bastards doing stupid crap like free climbing El Capitan, and they're goddamned nuts. And evil. Oh yes, evil. Which makes Alvin and his sweater-wearing, pop-star buddies all the more disturbing. I digress. Point is, humans who don't value the gift of life really irk me."

"I know I'm being an idiot," Penelope said, "but I can't think of anything other than Kinich. It's driving me insane. And in my heart, I know he wouldn't kill me. It—it doesn't make sense, Ixy."

Ixy? Did she just give me my first nickname? Ixtab suddenly felt warm and gooey inside.

"Why would the universe," Penelope continued, "and fate go through so much to bring us together only for him to kill me? We're meant to do this—this saving-the-world thing together. Two parts of one soul, Ixtab. You said so yourself. We are mates. And..." She sighed deeply. "I can't breathe without him. I'm afraid that one day soon, I won't be able to get out of bed. Or see this through for me or the baby. My soul can't keep going like this—all broken."

Dammit. Failure wasn't an option. Ixtab would have to put Penelope on life support, aka daily cleansing.

"Please, Ixtab. Will you get him to call me?"

"Yes. I'll go to him now. But stay away from his apartment. Go straight to Helena's."

She pressed End and headed back.

Five minutes later, Ixtab stepped off the elevator and heard a wail that turned into a nasty gurgle. The noise came straight from Kinich's apartment. "Oh, fancy fudge."

She bolted through the door and found Kinich hunched over a pair of twitching legs. "Kinich! No!"

She tackled him to the floor and felt a spark of pent-up, evil energy release from her body. *Christ almighty!*

Kinich's eyes blackened and his lower lip quivered as he stared straight up at her. He seemed just as shocked as she was.

She looked over her shoulder, horrified to see the victim. *Antonio? Oh, gods. Please no.* He was unconscious and bleeding from the neck.

She launched off of Kinich and scrambled to Antonio. "No. No. No!" She ripped off her veil and reached for his neck, pausing for a moment. Dammit, she had to stop the bleeding, but if she touched him without getting her mind straight, he'd likely die anyway.

She closed her eyes and urged her cells to open, to pull the flow of energy inward instead of readying to release.

Nothing.

Antonio's breathing shallowed, and his blood ran freely onto the floor.

"Oh, hell." Maybe she'd be able to pull the bad energy back out before he woke up.

Good fucking luck with that. Once transplanted, dark energy always seemed to stick better to its new home and was ten times harder to pull out.

Doesn't matter; there is no other choice.

She compressed the wound with the veil. Ixtab gasped and felt her entire body surge with a powerful light that circulated between them. In and out. In and out. It was as if...

Our lights are dancing together.

What the ... ?

She looked over at Kinich. "Dammit, sunshine. Get your ass on the phone and call that vampy doctor."

"What doctor?" he grumbled, still immobile on the floor.

"There's a magnet on your fridge. Didn't you see it?" Helena had mentioned in their last phone call that she'd put them in all the apartments for the newly undead. "Move!"

She looked back down at Antonio, feeling mesmerized by the intertwining of their souls and by his exquisite male beauty. She brushed back his dark brown hair. "Don't die on me, Klaus Van Mad Scientist. Don't you dare die on me." Gods be damned she didn't know what was happening, but she'd never touched a mortal like this. She wasn't draining his darkness or killing him. They were simply ... touching.

She sighed and soaked him in. His eyelashes—so

thick and dark—the masculine dip in his chin, the strong stubble-covered jaw. "You need to help us save the world," she whispered in his ear. *Perhaps you will save me, too...*

Again she glanced over her shoulder. Kinich wasn't in the kitchen. He was standing in the open window, readying to jump.

No! Dammit! She'd dosed him with darkness. He was trying to kill himself.

She bolted across the room just as Kinich launched.

"Nooo!" She leaped forward and caught him by one thick ankle. Her entire body jerked violently outside with Kinich's weight. She caught the ledge with her shellacked pink fingernails and dug in hard, her body dangling precariously from the frosty ledge. Damn, her brother was heavy.

Ixtab grunted as a few onlookers from the street below screamed. Thank the gods it was nighttime and the building had few exterior lights or the entire city would be able to see him.

"Let me go." He fought and squirmed.

Oh, hell. This was not happening. She clenched her eyes shut. *Reverse for fuck sake. Reverse!* She needed Kinich to want to live. Antonio was bleeding to death, and if forced to choose between him or her brother, it would be Antonio. Didn't matter that her brother meant everything to her, that besides Francisco, Kinich was the only being on the planet who'd treated her like someone important or that Kinich had never turned his back on her. Not even after she nearly lost her mind from killing the man she'd loved so deeply that it had left her soul twisted and mangled.

But that water had flowed past the dreary-goddess

bridge thousands of moons ago. This water had yet to pass and was coming fast and furious and its name was Antonio Acero, the keystone to opening the portal. And her bond with the Universe would always dictate she put humanity first.

Goddammit. The tears squeezed from her body like a lemon in a press as her muscles strained under his weight. She'd been given many gifts, but the gift of strength? Not a chance.

I hate you, Universe! Don't do this to me! Don't you dare make me choose! she mentally scorned with every flicker of her immortal soul. *Please, please, reverse.*

"Aaah!! *Teen uk'al k'iinam. Teen uk'al yah. Teen uk'al k'iinam. Teen uk'al yah. Teen uk'al k'iinam. Teen uk'al yah...*"

Kinich's body went limp. Had it worked?

Ixtab gritted her teeth and pulled up, but two hundred and fifty–plus pounds of pure ex–Sun God was more than her frame could support.

His heel slipped a centimeter. She flexed her nails and penetrated his skin, but she was losing her grip. How long could she hold on? And every second lost was another ounce of blood loss closer to death for Antonio.

Her eyes flipped down. Would a vampire survive the fall? She had seen them survive far worse over thousands of years. She'd also seen a few die from lesser injuries.

"Kinich, can you hear me? Goddammit, you have to grab on to something." There was a small ledge below that led to a window in the downstairs apartment.

Kinich didn't respond.

She yanked one more time, but it was useless, too heavy. "Kinich, I don't know if you can hear me, brother, but I love you. You're the only family I've ever had, and for this I will never forget you. But if I don't save Antonio, the portal will not open, Guy and Niccolo will remain trapped, and the Maaskab will exterminate us all—your precious Penelope and baby included. I have to choose. I have to. And my heart chooses you, but my duty chooses..."

Sobbing, she clenched her eyes shut and released his ankle.

"Nooo!"

At that exact moment, Ixtab looked up only to see Penelope's face witness Kinich's fall to earth.

Oh, gods. No. No...

There simply weren't enough souls, evil or good, to cleanse the pain and darkness she witnessed in Penelope's eyes.

Once

⌒

"Please, Viktor." Ixtab paced across Kinich's living room. "Don't tell me this is a cluster. I know it—"

"Well, it is," he replied. "The biggest cluster I've ever seen." Seven feet of pure angry Nordic vampire crossed his leather-clad arms over his chest. He wore a deep blue turtleneck sweater and black leather pants that matched his black leather duster. His long blond hair was elaborately braided down his back with strips of brown leather woven in.

"Honey, don't dwell on the things we cannot change," said the petite blonde woman with wide hazel eyes at his side, better known as Julie, Penelope's mother and—well, fallen angel recently turned vampire. Confusing? Oh yeah. Someone might have even written a book about it.

Viktor beamed down at Julie with his cobalt-blue eyes and then patted her cheek. "Yes, my angel. As usual, you are right."

Pacing frantically across Kinich's living room, Penelope

glanced at them both with a directness that emphasized this was the end of her rope. "Please, Mom. Viktor. Do something fast. Please? For me?"

"What a cluster." Viktor turned toward the heap of twisted muscles and broken bones on the couch. "Fine. I will give Kinich my blood to keep him alive, but he will require massive amounts of human blood to heal—if he's going to heal. Unfortunately, he's unable to feed so I suggest we start an IV." He looked at Penelope. "Please retrieve the blood bags from the refrigerator and bring me the emergency kit from Helena's kitchen upstairs."

"Thank you, Viktor. Thank you," Penelope said and scrambled out the door.

"And keep him out of the sun! It will weaken him!" Viktor yelled toward the door.

"What about the physicist?" Ixtab asked.

Viktor gave her a stern look. "Turning a mortal into a vampire isn't something we do simply because the person is dying."

Ixtab was about to go kamikaze on this crowd. "This isn't a normal mortal. If he dies, we all die. Just do it and get it over with."

Viktor's eyes flipped her the middle finger.

Like she cared. She'd been "blessed" with the "gift" of suicide, which pretty much meant she'd been given the middle finger by life itself.

"And are you going to take personal accountability? Are you?" Viktor asked Ixtab. "Will you teach him about the Pact and how not to kill innocent mortals, Ixtab? We just got rid of evil vampires. I don't want to be responsible for making new ones. I like my neighborhood Obscuro-free."

Ixtab rolled her eyes. "Why do all vampires have to be on vacay, and I get stuck with Mr. Vampy Rogers who wants a beautiful neighborhood?"

"Yes or no, Ixtab?" he prodded.

Ixtab nodded. "Yes! Yes! You idiot! Save him!"

Viktor's attention moved to Antonio who lay on the floor with a bandage wrapped around his neck. The bleeding had slowed, but the wound was severe, and to Ixtab's estimation, he wouldn't last much longer. "He needs to drink my blood before his heart stops."

"No. I do not want to be like him. I don't want to be a monster," a low voice mumbled.

All eyes moved to Antonio.

Trapped in a nightmare of pain, Antonio's mind flickered on and off again like a waning lightbulb dangling from the ceiling of a third world interrogation room. Each time his awareness illuminated, the ugliness of his reality— the pain of having his throat ripped open—was more-terrifying than death.

Vampires were real? This was what the voices said. *No. A dream. A crazy dream.*

"Antonio," a soft voice cut through the darkness, "you can't give up; we need you." A soft and soothing warm hand stroked his wrist, and the feeling of pure levity embraced him. The scent of vanilla and daisies filled the air. "That's right. Let go of those thoughts of death. Give them to me."

The woman then spoke to someone else in the room— a man with a deep voice and a European accent. "Turn him now, he's slipping away," she begged.

"He does not want to be a vampire. You heard him. He called me a monster," the accented man replied.

"My father . . . I . . ." *I don't want to be a monster like my father*, Antonio thought, but could not manage to say the words.

"See! He's trying to say he doesn't want to die. He wants to see his father."

"That's not what he said," the man argued.

"Oh. Crapola!" she hissed. "Can we just get this over with? It's for the greater good."

God, he loved this woman's voice. It was like sweet, warm nectar dribbled in his ears.

"Spoken like a deity," the man said. "You're a bunch of sick bastards, you know that don't you? The man does not want immortality, so find another way to open the portal."

"Please," the woman whispered in Antonio's ear, stroking his cheek. "Do it for me."

"No compelling!" The strange man scowled.

"I'm not!" she barked and then returned to touching Antonio's cheek—it felt so heavenly, soothing.

"Antonio, this is important," she said. "You must say yes."

Antonio suddenly wanted to. And just like that first time he'd heard her voice in the hospital, he didn't want to separate from her. She was like a drug.

His mind whirled and sputtered, dancing in and out of conscious thought. Dream and reality mingled into an inseparable murky soup. "I wish I could see you. Just once," he mumbled. "Are you as beautiful as you sound?"

She snickered. "Entire armies have fallen to their deaths for a peek."

"And you will not leave me? Ever?" he whispered.

Emptiness filled a long stretch of time, and then, "I will not leave you."

The word *yes* bubbled from his lips.

"Ha! You heard him! Do it!" the woman cheered.

The strange man groaned. "All right, I hope you know what you're in for." Hot, salty liquid poured into Antonio's mouth and slid down his throat. It spread like a raging wildfire through his veins. Antonio peered through the lavalike pain scalding his throat into the haze. A pair of luminescent eyes gazed back.

"Relax, mad scientist. Let go. I'll be waiting for you on the other side," she whispered.

Antonio felt the life slip from his body and hurtle toward the stars. It was as if gravity had relinquished the claim on his soul and sent it to unite with the cosmos. He let out one final breath and slid into oblivion.

Doce

After two days of sitting beside Antonio's dead body, Ixtab had reached her threshold of despair and went out to cleanse the negative energy flowing in her veins. Not every vampire transformation ended successfully, and the thought of Antonio dying brought her right back to the night of Francisco's deathbed when she'd helplessly watched his body succumb to the poison he'd ingested. It had been too much to bear then, and it was too much watching a near replica die once more. Ixtab's cells burst at the seams with sadness, and unfortunately, she couldn't find sufficient country-club members at that hour, so she had to go after a few less-charismatic creatures. Park services were going to have about one hundred trees to replant in the spring.

Exhausted and needing to lie down, Ixtab made her way to the penthouse. Voices poured into the hallway, bantering back and forth as she stepped off the elevator.

Zac. It was Zac. *What the hell is he doing here?* she wondered, listening through the door.

"Penelope," he said, "you are being ridiculous. Kinich does not care for you like I do. I would never toss you aside like that."

"I love Kinich, and that's not going to change."

"Did he tell you his bond broke?"

"What are you talking about?" she asked.

"When he was in Sedona, that night he became a vampire, I spent hours with him. He told me his bond with the Universe had broken. He has been free for some time now, no longer a slave to humanity's well-being."

"So, what are you saying?" Penelope asked.

"I'm saying that again and again, even before he became a vampire, he had the choice to stay with you, to put you first, but he didn't. He tossed you aside."

"Yes. It's true; he put humankind first before his own wants and needs, but that makes him a hero," she argued.

"No. It makes him selfish. He can't stand the thought of letting someone else save the day because he wants the glory all for himself."

Silence.

"I would have found a way," Zac said, "not to hurt you and to do my job. My brother is a blind fool for letting you go. And regardless of if he wakes up, he will always hurt you again because he will never put you first."

Ouch. He's going for Penelope's jugular, Ixtab thought, unable to believe Zac's cruelty.

"I can't help how I feel, Zac. I just can't."

"Yes, you can. Look at me," Zac commanded.

Uh-oh...

"What are you doing, Zac?" Penelope whimpered.

"You will forget him, Penelope. You want to be with m—"

Ixtab burst through the door. "Zac, stop."

Zac's turquoise eyes broke with Penelope's absent gaze and then fixed on Ixtab.

"What the hell are you doing?" Ixtab growled.

He looked at Penelope and released her. "We were talking."

"Like hell you were." Ixtab stormed between the two, careful not to touch Penelope. She removed her veil to stare up into her brother's irate face. "You were using your gift on her, weren't you?"

"No. It's okay, Ixtab," Penelope said from behind.

Zac was a good foot taller and infinitely stronger, but Ixtab had other gifts. Ones her brothers and sisters knew not to mess with. And she didn't mean knitting.

Ignoring Penelope, Ixtab stood on her tiptoes. "You weren't *just* talking, and we both know it."

Zac made a little shrug and crossed his arms over his chest.

"How long have you known your gift?" Ixtab asked.

He smiled and his eyes twinkled. No wonder Penelope couldn't resist him. His smell. His body. He was like honey and human women were like bees. How could they, the gods, have missed it? Zac's attractiveness and magnetism were ten times that of any normal deity, which said a lot considering how humans threw themselves at the gods. But Zac, he had an extra helping of irresistibility.

"Zac, go home. Now!" Ixtab commanded.

"I'm not leaving without Penelope. I love her, and she's mine," he said.

"No. You want to possess her. That's not love. And if

you try to take her, then you'll have to go through me, and it won't be pretty." Ixtab raised her hands, and Zac backed away.

"Then you'll go down with me if you use your powers against my will," he said smugly.

Ixtab shrugged. "Ask me if I give a rat's ass. Remember, I've got nothing to lose, and I hate my role. Let them banish me and take away my powers. It would be the vacay I've been praying for."

To prove her point, she swiped at Zac's chest.

Zac jumped back and growled as he turned for the front door. "This isn't over, Ixtab." He slammed the door behind him.

Ixtab swiped her veil and covered her head before turning to Penelope. "You okay?"

Penelope shook her head and placed her hand over her stomach. "I don't know. I don't feel...right."

"It'll wear off in a few hours." Ixtab turned and glared at the front door.

Idiot. She'd have to bring this up at the next summit. Zac had gone too far. Not only had he known his gift and not told the others, but he used it on Penelope without permission. This was a violation of their most sacred law. Yep, right up there with no time travel. And wearing pants at the summit table. *Okay, maybe that last one isn't sacred, but it should be.*

Penelope turned and headed for the door. "I need to go after him. I need to talk to Zac—"

"Penelope, it's not real. Zac used his powers on you and likely has been doing it for a while."

Penelope reached the door, ignoring Ixtab, and pulled the handle.

"Zac isn't the God of Love as we suspected, he's the God of Temptation," Ixtab blurted out. "And I'd bet my best pair of flip-flops, he compelled Kinich to want your blood more than anything on the planet."

"I did what you asked, Cimil. And not only didn't it work, but Ixtab discovered us." Zac stared out the tinted window from the back of the limo at the passing cars, talking into his phone.

"Hmmm. That does sound like a furry pickle," Cimil replied.

"This isn't a fucking joke! I've lost her. And I'll be tried for treason. This is all your fucking fault. Why the hell did I listen to you?"

"Roberto! The microwave is beeping!" Cimil cleared her throat. "Sorry, Zac, my potpie is ready. Where was I?"

Cimil was so damned lucky he didn't know where she was. Otherwise, he'd go there now and squeeze the life right out of her.

"Let me think. I've lost the only woman I've ever loved!" Zac bellowed. "That's where we fucking were! And after seventy thousand years, I finally discovered my gift only to face banishment. Oh yeah. And they'll strip away my powers!"

"Banishment? Strip power? That sounds awful. What the heck did you do?" she asked.

She was going to play the "I'm Stupid" game, was she? "I'm going to kill you, Cimil. And then, when you get a new body, I'll kill you again."

"Now, now, brother. Calm down. You don't see Minky getting in a tizzy when things don't go her way."

"Minky is a unicorn." *Strangle, strangle, strangle her*...

"Shhhh...She might hear you. Minky thinks she's a vampire who turns into a bat. How else would she be able to fly? Anyhooooo, the truth is that I didn't want to tell you."

"Tell me what?" he asked.

"The truth. I didn't want to tell you the truth."

"Which is?" he asked reluctantly.

"Roberto! Potpie! Now!" Cimil barked and then returned to her conversation. "You think a vampire with that sort of hearing would get that the microwave's beckoning him to bring me my savory snack."

"Cimiiil? Truth!" Zac growled.

"Truth? Truth? Oh, shucks. Where did I put it this time? Hold on, brother. Now let me see...Oh, look! I found an original bionic man doll!"

Zac heard clanks and crashing in the background.

"Where the hell are you, Cimil?"

"Popping tags with Roberto," she replied.

"Popping what?" he asked.

Cimil growled. "You shame Macklemore—I'm at a thrift store. Where else would a goddess find a microwave for her potpie and new pair of pink hot pants? And a Lee Majors doll! Score!"

Zac felt his face simmer with red-hot anger. "I'm going to hunt you. Then I'm going to rip out your—"

"Truth! I found it! Here it is. The truth is that everything is going according to plan," she said.

"You mean I won't be tried for treason? I still have a chance to win Penelope away from that prick of a brother?"

"No. Not that plan. The other plan."

What the fuck? "Mind explaining." Now Zac wanted to retch.

"Yes. I mind. But I will tell you this: everything will work out as it should, brother. Now, do you remember when I told you to make sure you had a safe place to hide and to tell no one of its whereabouts? Where is it?" she asked.

"I'm not telling you anything." No. He'd never trust Cimil again. And if it was the last thing he did, he'd make her pay.

"Fine. Be that way. Where's the love? Seriously. All right, go to your hiding place and stay there until you are found."

"Who's going to find me?" he asked.

"Well, I am, silly," she replied. "Do you think I'd let you get away with what you've done? Tootles."

"But I did what you—!" The call ended and Zac had the distinct feeling that he'd just been duped into doing Cimil's evil handiwork. Maybe he should go to his brethren and confess immediately before things got any worse. Wouldn't they understand this situation? He couldn't help that he loved Penelope, and he'd be damned to simply stand by and watch that son-of-a-bitch Kinich break her heart over and over again.

Gods fucking dammit. This situation was beyond screwed. Because now Penelope hated him.

"Driver, to the airport, please. The international terminal." Zac would never forgive Cimil for this. Ever.

Trece

Ixtab entered Kinich's bedroom and groaned with frustration at the sight of Penelope stretched across red satin sheets next to an immobile and much improved but still slightly battered body. With her long dark hair braided and the floral dress she wore, it looked as though she planned to take Kinich for a picnic the moment he woke. Obviously, Penelope would be the fried chicken. And the potato salad. And apple pie.

"You shouldn't be in here," Ixtab barked. "It's been three days now, and he might wake up at any second. And remember, until we break Zac's handiwork, you're still Kinich's favorite treat."

Penelope didn't move from Kinich's resting form. "I'm not leaving." She lovingly stared at his bruised face.

How could she look at the man like she wanted to ravish him? He was a mess.

Yes. No thanks to you. Ixtab winced. Why was she always causing everyone around her so much pain?

"Penelope, I want you to know that I'm really sorry about this. You, Zac, Kinich. Especially Kinich. I didn't want to let him fall, but—"

"You don't need to explain. You did what you had to do and saved Antonio. Kinich will survive."

"Yeah. Lucky for him that moving truck broke his fall." *Ouch. That really had to hurt.*

"What matters is that we'll get another chance. I'm just glad Viktor and my mom decided to take a vacation from Euro Disney to come check on me." Penelope paused. "That sounded weird, didn't it?"

Yes, it had sounded weird. But these days, weird was the new normal. And she was right; it had been one hell of a crowd control job—sixty people's memories had to be wiped. And then there was that whole saving Kinich and Antonio thing. So, yeah, bet your sweet, icky vampires she'd been happy they had stopped by for a visit.

"How's Antonio doing, by the way?" Penelope asked.

Ixtab shrugged. "Still asleep. Viktor thinks I messed up the transformation because I touched Antonio right before he drank the blood." She scratched her temple over her dark veil.

Ixtab still couldn't comprehend how she'd touched Antonio without preparing herself or saying her chant. And then—*wow!*—there'd been that very odd thing with their souls, lights ebbing and flowing from one to the other. Perhaps it had been due to the stress of the situation. Stranger things had been known to happen when it came to her gifts.

Well, she wouldn't risk contact again. Vampires clearly weren't immune to her powers. Case in point, Kinich. And it was just as well, because vampires were revolting—

except for her brother, of course (poor, poor Kinich), who was only temporarily revolting because he looked like a giant heap of steak tartare. *No thanks to you.* But all other vampires? Ick. They were dead, and she hated death. Well, not hated it exactly; however, to find death attractive? Nope on that. Seriously. How could humans be so obsessed with them? Vampires were lepers. Worse than lepers.

Zombie lepers with missing limbs. Ixtab shivered. She liked humans. Alive, full of light and warmth, and she especially admired the ones who laughed. Francisco had been that way. His laugh had been contagious. It was the reason she'd fallen in love with the mortal.

And the reason he died.

Ugh! Stop that. You're like a lame one-woman execution squad who keeps firing on herself.

"So, what will happen to Kinich when he wakes up?" Penelope asked. "Will he still want to kill himself?"

Ixtab shook her head. "I don't think so. Although I don't have experience with vampires, and Kinich is the first I've ever tried to cleanse. I believe I extracted all of the bad juju." Ixtab looked at her watch: 4:44 p.m. The winter sun would set in one minute. "Shoot. I need to go. I want to be there when Antonio wakes up—if he wakes up—and you really can't stay here alone. We need to figure out how to break Kinich from wanting your—"

"I'll stay with her." Penelope's mother stood in the doorway. Like usual, she wore something light and cheery. Today it was white leather pants, white suede boots, and a white cashmere sweater. She'd nailed the ex–angel vampire look.

"Just be careful," Ixtab warned. "I'll be back in a few—"

Suddenly, Kinich flew from the bed and tackled Penelope.

"Kinich!" Ixtab shrieked as Penelope's mother jumped on Kinich's back, but he was too strong. He chomped down on Penelope's neck, and she screamed in terror.

An agonizing wail burst from Kinich's mouth and flames exploded from his lips. He dropped to the floor, taking Julie down with him.

Holy shit.

Within seconds the flames died, but Kinich lay writhing in pain.

Ixtab stripped away her veil and handed it to Julie.

Julie paused for a moment and gaped at Ixtab.

"Here. Press it to Penelope's neck." Ixtab wiggled the veil in front of Julie's face.

Julie blinked and then turned her attention to Penelope and inspected her neck. "It's just a scratch. Are you okay, baby?"

Penelope burst out with hysterical laughter, tears pouring from her eyes.

Lips charred and resembling two lumps of coal, Kinich sat up. He stared at the wall like he'd been thumped over the head with a flaming sledgehammer.

"Mind telling me what's so funny, Penelope?" Ixtab asked, catching her breath and seriously trying not to freak. Yes, gods freaked. More often than any one of them would ever admit.

"He can't drink my—my—oh, God, it's just so funny!" She rolled from side to side on her back. "He can't bite me. I've got sunlight flowing through my veins. I'm Kryptonite!"

Ixtab scratched her head and exchanged glances with

Julie. All this time, Penelope had been right; Kinich couldn't hurt her. The Universe had seen to that. How was it possible that a quasi-mortal got one leg up on her in the "right department"?

Penelope stopped laughing and looked at Kinich. Potent beams of fury radiated from her eyes toward his.

"Well, I'm sure you two have a lot to catch up on." Julie scrambled to her feet and looked at Ixtab. "Let's give them some privacy."

"But— Uhh...is it safe to leave her alone?" Ixtab asked.

"I think the question is, is it safe for him?" Julie replied.

"You son of a bitch!" Penelope dove straight for Kinich and began pounding his chest with her fists, causing tiny bursts of fireballs.

Hopefully Helena and Niccolo had ample fire insurance for the building.

Ixtab made for the door behind Julie while Penelope let loose with a verbal avalanche of "How dare yous" and "You damned idiot! Don't you ever leave me again!" and "What the hell were you thinking becoming a vampire?... I'll kill you myself if you ever pull that crap again" and "How could you bite me! Jerk!"

Ixtab followed Penelope's mother out into the hall and closed the front door.

"I heard screaming from upstairs." Viktor rounded the corner, panting. "What's going on? Does the fucking drama ever stop around here?"

Julie chuckled. "Kinich bit Penelope and got a dose of sunshine. Now she's giving him a dose of her mind."

Viktor smiled, pulled Julie into his arms, and bent over

to lavish her neck with kisses. "This is excellent news, my love. I adore happy endings."

"Oh. Me, too," she said with a breathy voice. "Did I tell you that ex-angels specialize in the art of happy endings? My tongue is really—"

Ick. Ick. Ick. Vampire love. Ick.

Number six: watching vampires kiss is like watching two corpses make out.

"Sorry to interrupt your ewy-gooey undead moment, but how's Antonio?" Ixtab asked.

The shift in Viktor's eyes from sky to navy blue said it all: not good.

"Christ. Is he dead?" Ixtab asked. "I mean, I know he's dead—or undead—whatever—but is something wrong? Shouldn't he be awake?"

The look on his face told her that he hadn't a clue. Once again, Ixtab's own darkness filled her cells. Why did the thought of Antonio not surviving affect her so strongly?

Because we need him to open the portal and save your other stupid brother and Helena's ex–vampire hubby so we can kick the Maaskab's rear ends once and for all.

Yes. That must be it.

"I don't want to give you false hope, but I believe Antonio still has a chance," Viktor said. "I do not see any signs of true death."

Julie squinted at Ixtab as if trying to see behind her veil. "You okay, honey?" She reached for Ixtab, but Viktor swatted her hand away.

"Do not touch her. Ever. She is poison, my love," he said.

"Viktor, honey," Julie protested, "that was very rude. Besides, I saw her without the veil, and she's really—"

"No," Ixtab interrupted, "it's true. I am poison. I'm

a monster. You shouldn't ever touch me." Ixtab held out her hands to drive the point home. Her skin was gray. *Disgusting.*

She turned toward the stairwell. "I need to go out for a few hours. Call me if there's any news of Antonio."

Antonio felt a burning sensation in his eyes. Fire. They were on fire! As was his entire body. He rolled to his side in agony and landed on the hard floor with a thump. The bright light above blinded him. *Wait. I can feel my... eyes?*

He jumped to his feet and slammed his back against the wall, his head whipping from side to side. He was in his bedroom. "*Caray.* I can see."

Not only that, but he could hear and smell and feel the tiniest of vibrations in the air. He ran to the window and threw it open. "*Sí!* I can see!" He sucked in a lungful of cool evening air. He tasted the city on his tongue—hot dogs roasting on the corner, the rose-scented perfume of a woman walking her dog nineteen stories below on the sidewalk, a couple sipping hot chocolate in the park just across the way.

"I'm back. I'm fucking back!" he bellowed from the window.

And I'm hungry. Really damned hungry. And what the hell was that exquisite smell? He breathed deeply. Ocean. Car fumes. A bakery. Garbage. And...

Vanilla laced with daisies.

His eyes scanned the sidewalk below. This was pure amazing. Even in the waning sunlight, he saw the faces of pedestrians and...

Vanilla and daisies. Yes. The smell radiated from the woman who'd just turned the corner out of sight. *"Mierda!"*

He scrambled into his closet, threw on a pair of jeans, boots, and a black sweater. Not that he felt cold. No. He felt fucking brilliant!

Heart racing, he fled from his apartment and down the stairwell. Each step he took, he luxuriated in the fluidity and strength of his body. He moved like the wind on steroids. His body felt invincible and strong and larger than life all at once.

What the hell was going on? He vaguely remembered the bizarre dream of the woman and the strange conversation of the man with the deep voice who spoke of vampires.

Almost to the ground floor, Antonio stopped in the stairwell. "No. Hell no. I'm a vampire?" He inspected his hands and rubbed his face and neck. His skin felt tingly and alive. He didn't feel dead.

He placed his right hand over his heart. There was nothing.

"Diablos!" He jumped back to escape his own chest. "What the hell?" He began recalling his neighbor, the one who attacked him and sliced through his neck. Antonio rubbed the spot, but there was no trace of any injury. His memories then flashed to the woman who'd been at his side as he bled. She was the same woman—vanilla and daisies—who'd come to the hospital and touched him. His heart jolted to life and began to thump like a team of galloping horses in his chest. The overwhelming urge to find her washed over him.

"What the hell are you waiting for?" No matter how

absurd the situation, the one thing he knew, the *only* thing he knew, was that he needed to find her. He had prayed for his vision to return if only to see her face. The face of an angel. She had to be because she'd saved his life. Twice.

He raced through the lobby, out the front door of the building. He moved with such speed that the...*humans*? *Caray*. Was he truly calling them humans now? As if they were something altogether different and his brain had already accepted a concept his erratically beating heart had not.

He rounded the corner and caught her scent. A sharp pain jabbed at his gums and the coppery tang of blood coated his tongue.

Holy Santa Maria! No puede ser. He put his hands over his mouth. *It can't be.* He'd popped out a fang! A *pinche* fang, like a *pinche perro*! Two of them! Not only that, but Antonio began to salivate, too. He'd never smelled anything sweeter than that scent of daisies.

His new razor-sharp vision—*you mean, fang-sharp vision, don't you?*—caught the inky blur of black cloth slipping into an alley. He rushed to the mouth of the backstreet and was about to announce his presence when he spotted the woman cloaked in its shadows. She lifted a tabby, much like his beloved cat Simon, and held it to her chest as she spoke to it. "There's a good kitty. That's right..."

He smiled inwardly; she, too, loved animals. The woman must have been very distraught after killing his cat. *An honest mistake, no doubt. Because surely such an angel would never kill an innocent creature on purpose.*

He poked his head around the corner once again, but she'd disappeared.

Confused, Antonio slipped into the alley. His sensitive ears picked up every sound, but there were none to be heard; it was as quiet as a library on Friday night. Slowly, he moved through the garbage-strewn passage. Large Dumpsters marked every dark doorway, and empty wooden pallets were heaped in random piles. Antonio then noticed the alleyway hooked right and connected to another long side street with an outlet. As he followed along, the eerie silence chilled his bones, but what he witnessed next chilled his heart.

Several rats lay twitching on the ground alongside the orange cat—dead orange cat with half a rat sticking from its mouth, like it had choked on the thing. A man, wedged in the corner between the wall and a large green Dumpster, lay with a shard of jagged glass sticking from his throat. The smell of blood filled the air.

Antonio approached the man who wore dirty black jeans and mud-caked boots. His army-green jacket smelled of something odd, some sort of burned material. *Chemicals?* Drugs perhaps. But his blood...

Antonio cupped his hands over his salivating mouth. "No. You are vegetarian. You do not believe in killing for your food."

He crouched in front of the man. "Who did this to you? Hold still, I will call for an ambulance." Antonio reached in his pocket. No cell phone. *Diablo.* "I'll be right back."

The man gurgled, "The woman." He pointed down the alley and promptly expired.

No. His beauty? His vanilla-and-daisies angel? She did this? She killed these poor animals and this man? *Impossible.*

Antonio followed the trail of her scent to another alley

ten blocks away. The sounds of the city—cabs, horns honking, pedestrians talking on their phones—roared in his ears. Headlights blazed down the street like shooting stars. Everything felt exaggerated—brighter, louder, the smells much more potent.

He approached the alley cautiously and peered around the corner. Death. It smelled like death mixed with that sweet perfume. Suddenly, he saw a shadow moving toward him. He ducked into a doorway as she passed by in a ... *Morticia Addams costume? What the hell?* "Who *are* you?" he said more as a criticism rather than a question.

"Shit." The woman turned. She froze and held her hand to her veiled face. "Oh my gods, is it really ... you?"

Who did you expect? Cousin It? "Who the hell are you?" he asked again.

The woman took another step forward, and he instinctively wanted to bolt. Something about her terrified him, disgusted him.

Her hands, reeking of death, reached for him. He pushed himself flatter against the wall. "Don't fucking touch me."

"Of course. I don't know what I was thinking." Her arms fell to her side, and there was a long moment of silence as they studied each other.

What was she? Why did she wear that awful veil over her face? And why did he feel the strangest urge to touch her.

"You shouldn't be out alone," she finally said. "Not on your first night."

"Who are y—"

Her phone rang—*the Death March*?

"Hold that thought." She held up her index finger and

then dug through her brightly colored purse to retrieve her cell.

"I bet you're missing someone," she said to the other person.

Antonio heard every word coming over the earpiece as if he himself held the device. The voice was one he recognized—the man from his dream. The one who did not want to make him a...*vampire*.

The cold, hard pieces of his new reality clicked into place. He really was a vampire, which meant...everything was ruined! His plans to decipher the tablet and open the portal, to save his brother, his plans for his own freedom. Yes, he had thought he was fucked when he'd lost his sight, but now he was irrevocably screwed. There was absolutely no hope. He'd become the one thing he vowed he'd never be: a killer like his father. "You did this to me, didn't you?" He scowled.

The woman's veiled head lifted, and he knew she was looking at him. Hell, it felt like she was staring right through him.

"I'll make sure he gets back. Bye." She ended her call and dropped the phone in her bag. "Yes. I had Viktor turn you, but there was no other choice."

She'd had him turned into a monster. A vampire for fuck sake! This couldn't be happening. This couldn't be! She'd destroyed his life. *Caray!*

"There was another choice!" he yelled. "Death! And trust me, that would have been better."

"You don't understand—"

"Do you have any...*any* idea what you've done? Do you? *You* are a demon from hell! You've single-handedly destroyed my life, everything that I care about! Everything, goddammit!"

Wanting to shake her by the shoulders for what she'd done, he reached for her, but she jumped back.

"Don't touch me! Don't ever touch me!" she reprimanded.

She had said the same thing that time he'd run into her by the elevator in his building. She'd told him that he disgusted her.

He stepped back and held up his palms. Blinding, raging fury engulfed him. He needed to get away from her before he did something he regretted.

He turned and ran as fast as his new vampire feet could carry him.

Catorce

———

Penelope pounded and pounded and pounded until her fists were raw with blisters. Kinich simply stood there and took it. So many hours and days she'd wept and cried over losing him, over his not loving her enough to overcome his urge to drink her blood, but she hadn't wept nearly enough. Now those bottled emotions came gushing out like an unstoppable tsunami.

After a few minutes, she lowered her head to Kinich's chest and released one final sob before fisting his charred white T-shirt and wiping her eyes.

"Are you done now, my sweet?" he asked.

She felt a strong hand run down the back of her head and trail down her neck.

"Yeah, I think so." She sniffled.

"Good." Kinich scooped her up and deposited her recklessly on the bed.

"I'll be right back."

Before she protested, he was gone. "Hey! Where are you going?"

She heard the refrigerator open and then slam shut. He went for a snack? Right in the middle of her epic melt-down? Dammit. She wasn't done yet. And he had this coming. No, it wasn't his fault that Zac had put the temptation whammy on him, but Kinich had done plenty of other pigheaded crap to deserve a good tongue-lashing. For starters, he'd made a risky plan that involved rolling the dice with Roberto the Ancient One, which landed Kinich in Vampire Land. Then he'd refused to see her, to trust her, when she'd known in her heart they were meant to be. All the while, she'd been left alone with Zac to rule the gods. And pregnant! And trying to stop the end of the world!

I mean...seriously!

Penelope marched from the bedroom, through the living room—*yikes, someone really needs to talk to Helena about these decorations. Gloomy much?*—to the kitchen, where she found Kinich, shirtless (*oops, guess I ruined it with all those fireballs*), wearing only his drawstring pajama bottoms, chugging.

Penelope swallowed hard and took in the heavenly vision of the behemoth male standing before her. Nearly seven feet of pure, hard, immortal muscle, with smooth, slightly golden skin—nowhere near as tanned as before, but nevertheless completely yummy—endless ripples of abs, biceps flexing as he tilted his mouth up, drinking from a plastic pouch.

She would just pretend he sipped punch and allow him to continue because right before her eyes, Kinich's body filled out, the bruises on his glorious broad back fading into nothing. His caramel-brown hair returned to its full, glorious length, filled with those streaks of gold she loved so much.

Kinich withdrew the bag from his mouth and glanced at her. "I told you to stay put." He swiped another bag from the counter, tore off a corner, and threw his head back once again, chugging deeply.

"No, you said you'd be right back."

Kinich made one last suck, threw the pouch in the trash, wiped his hand across his mouth, and then stared at Penelope like he wanted to sip her next.

She took a step back and held out her palms. "Whoa. I thought we established you can't dine on me."

He lowered his gaze to her breasts and scratched his stubble-covered jaw. "Says who?"

Wow. Had he just filled out another two inches in his biceps? Even when Kinich was the God of the Sun, he had been big and strong and freakishly desirable. But now...? He was frigging colossal and a whole hell of a lot sexier.

Put that man on a package of underwear!

Instead of pouncing as she secretly hoped, he turned his back and plucked a bottle from the cupboard. *Red wine?* He didn't bother to remove the cork. Instead, he snapped off the neck and guzzled straight from the jagged opening.

Okeydokey. I see we're going to have to reintroduce proper manners to Kinich.

He finished off the bottle, slammed it down on the counter, turned toward Penelope, and licked his full lips.

Oh, hell. Did he just get more handsome? It was difficult to pinpoint exactly which part had improved, but his body looked as though it had been refined by da Vinci's

brush and Michelangelo's chisel to create flawless definition in every bulging muscle.

She looked up at the ceiling. "Really? Really? You've
got to be joking. That's not fair."

"Now," he growled, "where were we?" He stepped
forward, and the hungry expression on his intensely gorgeous face was augmented by the fact that his turquoise
eyes shifted to a very deep, dark brown.

Oh, Christ, he was going to attack her. Penelope took a
step back. "You can't—"

Before she blinked, Kinich had her against the wall.
His thrusting tongue was hot as it pushed inside her
mouth, but thrusting hips were hotter.

"Gods, I missed you, woman," he said with a breath
that filled her lungs with the most potent, delicious smell
ever. Dark spices, tropical citrus, male, lust... *Ohmygods.*

"Really? Really?" She looked up at the ceiling. "'Cause
he didn't smell yummy enough when he was just a god?"

"Who the hell are you talking to?"

She shrugged. "No one. Are you taking me to bed now?"

He smiled, and for the first time in weeks, Penelope
saw the deity she'd fallen in love with. The one who
secretly helped forgotten children, the one who'd sacrificed himself to save her, the one she had been born to
love and comfort even in his darkest hours. She brought
her hand to his cheek, savoring his masculine roughness,
and soaked him in. She couldn't believe they were actually standing together in the kitchen, their bodies pressed
together. Happiness and triumph washed over her.

"Just my luck, I'm finally a vampire, and the sifting
dimension is closed." The Maaskab had locked it up—
that's how they'd managed to capture Guy, Niccolo, and

the others. "We'll have to do it here; the bed is too far away."

His head dove straight for her neck. She flinched and then relaxed as she felt his hot tongue suck on the base of her neck. Her body took exactly two seconds—two—to ignite. Goose bumps covered every inch of her skin, her nipples tightened to sharp, little points, and heat flooded between her legs.

Oh, gods, he feels so incredible. Better than she remembered. Better than anything on the planet. Being with him felt like being whole again—with a whole hell of a lot of extra man now included.

She watched from the corner of her eye as he tugged down his pants and pulled himself free.

Lord, he was magnificent. Thick and long and solid. Images flashed in her mind of the last time they'd been together. It had been the kind of sex that could turn a woman into an addict. Because from the moment he enters, every nerve ending floods with endorphins and goes into a euphoric shock, pleasure ripping through every inch of her body. No. A woman could never walk away from a man like that. She could never forget that kind of sex. Unless she were drugged by Cimil as part of her evil master plan, as was the case for Penelope's first time with Kinich, which was the reason she was now knocked up. A long story.

She sighed into Kinich's needy, hot lips. Then, like magic, she found herself stripped of her dress, underwear, and bra. She glanced down at the shredded pile of clothes on the floor. "Sneaky vampire. How did you do that?"

He didn't reply, but simply covered her mouth with his and pressed his naked body against hers, allowing her to enjoy the feel of his hardness and warmth against her skin. Gods, he felt so good, so unbearably good. "What are you waiting for?" Hadn't she suffered enough?

He replied by securing her legs around his waist and positioning his hard, pulsing cock at her slick entrance. Penelope felt her body tense, recalling the last time he'd taken her. The pleasure of his large cock had not come without a small price of pain, but it had been worth it.

Instead of pushing inside, relieving her of the aching tension, he began rubbing himself between her folds, using the wall behind her to hold her in place.

Oh, she remembered this dance. It was her favorite steamy memory of Kinich. She'd relived it hundreds of times. Alone. How sad.

Not anymore.

"Oh, gods, that feels so good," she panted. He kissed her hard and continued rocking himself against her, massaging her bud with the silky head of his cock. So much heat. There was so much heat. "I think I'm going to— ohmygods, please..." *Yes. Yes.* "No! Wait!"

Kinich quirked an impatient brow.

The power now housed inside her would make any nondeity rather uncomfortable, and that went double for a vampire allergic to sunshine.

"Remember what happened last time?"

He held up a small ring on his index finger. "Black jade. I had it made just in case."

She blew out a breath. Thank the gods for her smart, strategic-thinking ex-deity. The jade would blunt her powers. She hoped. Because, dammit, they'd waited long enough.

"If it hurts, just stop," she said.

He smiled a little wicked smile. "Ditto."

He stared into her eyes and pushed.

She clenched her teeth as he worked his way inside, pushing in and pulling out, slowly filling her inch by inch with his girth. Christ, had he grown down there, too?

"Look at me, Penelope. I want to see you."

She opened her eyes and stared at Kinich's exquisitely handsome face. The cheekbones and muscled jaw, the caramel-colored brows, and thick lashes adorning turquoise eyes.

"Gods, woman, you feel so hot. So tight. I'm not going to last."

Relief flooded Penelope. They were compatible and the black jade was doing its job. They were finally together. "I love you, Kinich."

Kinich barreled down hard, using the wall behind her to drive deeper. With each sharp, delicious jab of his cock, she felt his fangs scrape her neck, driving her to dig deep into his broad back with her nails. He pounded into her with every ounce of pent-up lust, and she took him, knowing he needed it just as badly as she did.

"Yes. Harder. Harder," she moaned. Her insides knotted with sweet tension. She would never get enough of this sexy, powerful, deliciously large male.

Kinich made one final thrust and groaned toward the ceiling as her orgasm exploded and her body clenched around his twitching cock. She clawed him closer, wanting the moment of their joining to last longer, to never stop feeling their breaths move in synchronization, to forever feel the pounding beats of their hearts.

Kinich held her tightly as she felt the last of his release with several gentle pushes and groans.

"Oh, gods, Penelope." He lowered his sweat-covered forehead to hers. "That was worth every fucking minute of hell." He kissed her in a wet, sloppy, lazy kind of way that told her she'd just worn this behemoth vampire out.

"I love you, Penelope," he whispered.

She smiled. *Finally. Thank the gods, he finally said it.* "Can we do that again?"

"That was only a snack."

Quince

He called you a demon from hell! From hell! "And nice job, Ixtab," she scolded herself. "You lost him! Dr. Van Brainy Vampire is somewhere on the loose in the world. Gone." Yes, she'd managed to "misplace" the only being on earth who could help unlock the portal.

Reason number eight—or is that number seven? Dammit. I'm losing count. Reason number whatever: they are so damned fast! It's completely annoying.

After he'd gone running off into the night, she'd circled every back alley and every park she could think of, sniffing for death. Aside from the usual—a few poor lost souls whose time had come naturally—there were no signs of rampant death or a wild, hungry vampire on the loose.

Almost dawn now, Ixtab returned to the penthouse to face the ridicule of Viktor. At least her sister Fate wasn't there to rub her nose in this fiasco.

She pushed open the front door. Kinich and Penelope

sat in a love seat near the window making out like two horny teenagers, and Viktor and Julie stood next to the bar sipping red wine, laughing.

Ixtab sighed. *Here goes.* "I lost the physicist."

Viktor smiled. "You lost who?"

Ixtab set down her enormous handbag on the floor and sank on the couch. "I know. I'm a complete loser. I can't do anything right."

"Honey," Julie said. "What are you talking about?"

"Antonio. He got away. I looked everywhere for him, but—"

"Ixtab, he's out on the balcony with Fate," said Julie.

"He's here?"

Viktor smiled, then nodded. "Yes. And aside from not being hungry—pretty damned strange for a new vampire—he's fine. We've spent the night getting him up to speed on our world."

Ixtab pointed toward the open French double doors that led outside. "You mean— he's there? Now? With my sister Fate?"

Again they nodded and exchanged glances. "She came to check up on you and the tablet."

"Oh." Well, that was just peachy. *Yeaaah.* Fate was probably digging her perfect paws into Antonio, no doubt wiggling her sweet, little tanned behind at him and showing him her bows and arrows, too.

Not that I care.

Right on cue, one of Fate's infamous giggles seeped into the room from the outside terrace.

Ixtab dug her pink nails into her palms. That was Fate's seduction giggle. No, she'd never taken a lover, but she collected admirers like insomniacs collected tchotchkes from the Home Shopping Network. She had over a million likes on Facebook and double that amount of followers on Twitter.

Bitch.

Julie stepped toward Ixtab only to be jerked back by Viktor.

Julie sighed impatiently. "Honey, she's not a rabid dog. She's one of His divine creations." Julie looked at Ixtab. "One of His beautiful creations."

Ixtab shrugged. "Only on the outside."

"Someone's got the pouties today, huh?" Julie said.

"Maybe."

"Oh, honey, I've seen your face and looked into your eyes. You're about as beautiful as they come. Don't ever doubt that."

Darn angels. Always so nice and uplifting. Phooey. "I'm going to get some rest."

"Antonio says you are to meet him at eight a.m. sharp in his lab," added Julie. "He needs an assistant that can work around the clock and won't die if he makes a mistake."

"I'm sure Fate will happily volunteer for the job."

Julie made a little wiggle with her brows. "No. His explicit instructions were to have *you* help him."

He wanted her help? Why? He'd called her a demon. He'd blamed her for turning him into a vampire, and then ran away, all of which left her feeling absurdly wounded.

"Should I tell him you'll be there?" Julie asked.

"Yes. I'll be there." Because the truth was, she wouldn't be able to stay away even if she wanted to.

January 17. Time: 8:00 a.m.

After a very long, hot shower and three failed meditation attempts, Ixtab had finally given up any notions of this meeting with Antonio going smoothly. Simply thinking of being in the same room turned her into a nervous Nellie. Or was that giddy goddess?

Sigh. Why would a vampire have such an impact on her? She had no clue, but one thing she knew for certain was that she couldn't wait to see him again.

Ixtab raised her hand and knocked lightly.

"Come in." Antonio's voice filtered through the thick wooden door.

Ixtab peered inside his small but bright and clean lab with two small mad-scientist workstations—beakers, rats, terrarium, some computer equipment—in each corner, and a large stainless steel table in the center of the room.

"The front door was open," she said.

She spotted Antonio sitting on a stool at the corner of the table wearing only a plain white tee and faded jeans. With his short, dark, skillfully mussed hair and five o'clock shadow, he was, he was ... *Sigh.*

When human, he looked like perfection, but now he looked like a refined, heavenly treat, like he'd been worked over with supernatural man enhancers that took his already too perfect body—broad chest and strong, lean everything—and filled him out in all the right places. His spine now held a perfect posture that would never, ever, ever deteriorate with time and made him appear taller, more imposing. Yes, before he'd been the most exquisite mortal she had ever laid eyes on. But now? Now he was the most exquisite male—mortal or otherwise—to exist.

Reason number whatever…Ugh! Not fair. Stupid, gorgeous, icky vampire!

"Come in and close the door." His angry eyes flashed her way, then back to his notebook, and for that instant, Ixtab felt like a pathetic, needy creature craving his attention.

She carefully shut the door.

"First," he said, looking at the scribbles on his pages, "what the *diablo* is the story with the Morticia getup? Get rid of it—it's a distraction. Second, no more secrets and lies. I know what and who you are; your sister told me everything."

If he knew who she was, then why did he speak to her like that? Perhaps ass kickings were his thing. And how had he adjusted so quickly to his new state? Most mortals took years to accept what they'd become and to reach their full a-hole vampire potential. Not this guy. He looked like he'd settled right the hell in.

"Anything else?" She parked her fist on her hip.

He looked up from the notebook, and though he could not see her eyes, she felt as if he were looking right through her.

"Yes," he replied. "If you ever cross me, I'll quit. I don't like you. I don't care if I save the world. I'm not a deity, and I hope to fuck I never become one. You will do what I say, when I say, and you'll like it. You'll sleep— if your kind ever fucking sleeps—and eat—if your kind ever fucking eats—when I say. Then, when this is all over, you will give me the gift of never letting me lay eyes on your disgusting, veiled face again."

Ixtab felt like she'd been pummeled by a torpedo. "Whoa there, Sparky. First, what's with you and the swearing? And second, what did I ever do to you?"

"Didn't you hear a word I said on the street?" he asked.

He'd said a lot of things. Most of them not very nice, which meant she'd already compartmentalized them in that vacuous place inside her brain where she put everything she would prefer to forget. "Not really."

Her reply visibly sent him over the edge.

"I'm a vampire because of you." He jumped from his seat and punched the wall, sending half of it crumbling into the other room. *Uh-oh*. Helena would be pissed. More repairs. "You! God fucking dammit. You have no idea what you've done."

She'd kept him alive. End of story. "I don't understand," she said.

"Like I give a shit if you do. Let's get one thing straight: you promised to never leave me."

Where the hell was he going with this? He couldn't possibly hold her to that deathbed promise.

"And?" she asked.

"And as long as I live, you belong to me—a lowly, *disgusting*, pathetic vampire."

Was that what this was all about? He wanted to punish her by making her his little Igor punching bag. And that comment...jeez. Sounded like someone had a bruised ego.

"This has nothing to do with me calling you 'disgusting' the morning Kinich attacked you, does it?" She hadn't meant it; she'd simply wanted him to stay away from her.

"I'm angry because you had me turned. You have no idea what you've done."

Ixtab's rage finally bubbled over. "Oh, but I do! I saved you. And if you want to be angry with someone, why aren't you angry with Kinich? He's the one who attacked you." Actually, that wasn't right, either. Kinich only attacked him because he'd been whammied by Zac.

"Hate him?" Antonio seethed. "For being a vampire, a slave to his bloodlust? He had no choice. But you..."

Oh, good. At least he wasn't holding a grudge against Kinich. That was something. As for her turning him into a vampire, there was no other choice. Why couldn't he get that through his thick, backward man skull? And where did he get off treating her like an old, chewed-up shoe? Him. An icky, yicky vampire. Well, he had another fang coming!

"What I do not understand is why you would do so when you think so little of us?" he said with a hint of regret.

"Huh?" Ixtab's rage sputtered out. Was that hurt in his beautiful green eyes? It was hard to tell with him up there and her down there. She'd need to start wearing heels.

"Your sister Fate told me how you loathe my kind," he said calmly. "You think we are an abomination to this world."

True. But damned that Fate! Why would she tell him? *Stupid cow.*

"I can't help how I feel. Vampires are bottom-feeders." *With exception to Kinich, Julie, Viktor, and Helena, of course.*

Before she blinked, his large hands clamped her shoulders and a spark of dark energy released from her body.

"No! You can't do..." A split second passed but nothing happened. Once again, he didn't show the faintest sign of yearning for death, and once again, she found herself frozen, mesmerized by him.

"How? How can you stand to touch me?" she croaked.

His olive-green eyes drilled into her. "Who the fuck knows? Who the fuck cares?"

I do. Oh my gods, I do!

His eyes went wide, and he looked at his hands and then released her like yesterday's garbage.

"I-I..." Ixtab turned to leave before she had a complete meltdown right in front of him. Or hugged him. Or cried from confusion. Or kicked his man truffles—*Are they milk chocolaty brown like the rest of him?* Or something very, very bizarre in between. The Universe had to be playing a cruel, cruel joke on her. Her entire existence she'd longed to simply touch another being. Not kill. Not save. Simply...touch. For no other reason than because she wanted to feel connected to the world. Her entire existence, she'd watched mortals go throughout their day, unaware of how lucky they were—an embrace, a pat on the back, shaking hands...a kiss. Such simple gestures. Imagine a life without these things. Imagine how lonely and disconnected from the world one might feel.

So after eons of near isolation, the Universe finally decided to listen and granted her wish? Like this? In the form of an icky vampire who hates her guts? And who reminded her of the single most painful moment of her life?

Well, thank you, Universe! Getting your own stand-up comedy show next? A special on HBO perhaps? 'Cause... har-fucking-har, lady! Ixtab's anger took the steering wheel. Unfortunately, she couldn't take it out on the Universe, so that left her with...

"Find another pooch. I am the Goddess of Suicide. I answer only to Death, and guess what? He doesn't want you. You're not good enough."

Antonio's beautiful green eyes flickered to black. "*Muy bien.* You want to play hardball? Then kiss your world good-bye, Ixtab. I know I'm the only one who can crack the tablet's code. Without me, humanity perishes. How do you like those *manzanas*?"

He knows I'm compelled to put humans first?

Dang it! Checkmate.

"Fate told you, didn't she?" *Going. To. Kill. Her.*

His wicked smile produced a little dimple on each side of his mouth.

"Oh, you can guess again, mister, if you think flashing those adorable little dimples will bend me to your will. I don't care if you are the hottest card-carrying member of the penis club—I've gone seventy millennia without a man. I'm immune to your drop-dead gorgeousness!"

He looked at her with a blank stare. "Seventy thousand years without getting laid?"

Oh, pita chips! Ixtab cupped her veiled mouth. "Well… uh, I meant…" *Shit, shit, shit.* "…Without a boyfriend. Of course I've *had* a man." *To dinner. Once. Change subjects! Anything to escape this conversation.* "Fine. I'll help you! What would you like me to do, Dr. Dracula?"

His smile faded away. "Don't call me that."

Hit a nerve did I? "Sorry. I meant"—she made her hands into claws—"maaassster," she slurred, doing her best impression of Igor.

A twitch of a smile flickered across his lips, but his frown quickly rebounded. "You are completely childish, you know that?"

And just like that, the anger between them dissipated like a wisp of steam. Hands down, this was the oddest situation ever. Odder than the time Cimil started a pumpkin rodeo—she'd claimed that the squash weren't getting their fair share of fun—and odder than the fact that random good-looking men always seemed to bump into her (and then meet their demise).

But this one... this one is still alive. And she couldn't deny she wanted him to touch her again. And again. However, that didn't mean she wasn't pissed and wouldn't have to teach him a lesson or two on how to behave with a goddess.

Sounds exciting.

"Childish, huh? Since I'm a deity, you think I'm supposed to act like a crusty, old know-it-all? Where's the fun in that? Don't let my immaturity fool you; I'm ancient. I'm deadly. And if you cross me again, I'll..." *Oh, drat. What would I do?* "I'll do something baaad."

He tilted his head to one side. "Are you done?"

"Uh...yeah. I think so," she replied.

"Good." He placed his hand on her back and moved her toward the table. "Because we have a portal to open."

Ixtab's eyes went wide beneath her veil as his touch sent waves of intoxicating bliss through her body. Oh, gods. What was happening? And what was she getting herself into?

She hadn't a clue, but there was no doubt in her mind she was already knee-deep.

Dieciséis

⌐

"No, *caray*! This is not working!" Antonio threw his pen at the wall—one of the still standing ones—and it stuck in the plaster like a dart.

Clearly he hadn't grasped the magnitude of his strength yet.

"Don't panic, Dracula. Just move to the next one." Ixtab poked him lightly on the arm. Over the last ten hours, she'd touched him every chance she had. She still couldn't believe it. She'd touched him dozens of times and nothing bad had happened! Another living creature! And he was still alive! Slightly irritated, but alive.

While he had been working on the tablet, conducting experiments, she'd done some tests of her own. She now knew that when they made contact, dark energy did indeed flow out of her body into his, but he simply seemed immune to it. This was so...*awesome!* Better than the time Cimil allowed her to ride that prize pumpkin! *Okay, that was a lame comparison.* Nonetheless, this was the most exciting thing she'd ever experienced!

She poked him again and smiled. Her cheeks cramped from grinning so darn hard.

"Stop that." He'd glance at her, half glaring, half perplexed.

"What?" Smile. Big smile.

He frowned and then returned to his work with such intense focus that she couldn't help but wonder what was really in this for him? He behaved as if solving the mystery of the tablet was the end of the world.

Because it is?

Okay. Yes. But taking the worry to a level ten was the job of a deity. Not a ... well, new vampire.

She passed him a sheet of paper with formulas. "Try this one." Poke.

"It's not going to work," he said, not lifting his head.

"You haven't even tried it."

"No. I mean the poking. You can't annoy your way out of this," he replied.

Who says I want to? "I have no idea what you mean?" Poke. *This is so wonderful.*

He growled. "You are a very, very strange woman."

"I'm a deity. We invented strange." *I can't stop.* She reached out her hand, but he caught it midair.

"Next time you do that, I'll break your neck," he growled.

"Has anyone ever told you that you're oodles of fun?"

His green eyes turned black. "No."

"Have you ever wondered why?"

"No. Now pass me the other file—the one with the red label." He pointed to the stack on the edge of the large table.

"Say please," she said playfully. *Gods, I feel drunk! At least, I think this is what drunk feels like. I will need to consult with Belch.*

Perhaps you're happy!

Yes. Maybe this is what being happy feels like!

He shot her a hateful look.

"No, not saying please?" She smiled and passed the file anyway.

Despite all her goofing around and his belligerent disposition, Ixtab had to give the damned brilliant man kudos where kudos were deserved; he was on to something. He'd figured out that the tablet reacted to energy fields (no surprise there given everything in the Universe is comprised of energy); however, he had hooked up his laptop to a homemade box that contained a complex system of diodes and amplifiers. The little box could mimic and transmit almost any energy pattern—a frog, a cat, a flower, just about anything. With the experiments he'd been conducting, he had already narrowed the list down to ten catalysts and validated his data with live tests. Now, he believed, it was simply a question of sequencing the energy patterns correctly to trigger the tablet's power. So far, however, he'd managed to get the object's surface to vibrate, but nothing more.

"No. Dammit. I'm missing something." He sat on the tall stool and hunched over the table, pressing his forehead against the cool stainless steel surface. His lean, wide back stretched the fabric of his T-shirt, and Ixtab couldn't help but notice how the broad shoulders tapered down into a tight waist before presenting a perfectly shaped ass. The shape of the muscles were like two round globes of manly assiness.

Assiness? Not even a word, goddess. She shrugged. *I like it. Assiness fits.*

"Perhaps if you ate?" she suggested.

Antonio rolled his forehead against the table. "I'm not hungry."

"You're a new vampire. Of course you're hungry—"

His head snapped up. "No. I said I do not want to eat."

"Eventually you will need to eat something, or you will go mad, perhaps kill an innocent mortal."

"Doubtful," he snapped. "I do not eat meat. I never have, and I never will. The thought of drinking human blood disgusts me."

Ixtab gasped. "A vegetarian vampire?" Oh. This was a disaster waiting to happen.

He scowled at her. "I do not believe in killing. And if I ever had to kill someone or something, I certainly wouldn't enjoy it like *some* people."

Had that been a jab?

"You think I go around killing people for fun?" she asked. Normally, thems would be fightin' words, but she was in such a good mood that nothing could sour it. Not even a grumpy, gorgeous— *Wait! No! Icky! Oh, hell... gorgeous vampire. Damn this happiness rocks. Everyone should try it!*

"Yes," he said. "I believe I also used the word 'enjoy.' I saw what you did to that man in the alley and to those animals. You murdered them without a second thought and skipped away like you'd been to a fucking party."

Happiness starting to go...

"I don't kill—"

"Don't try to deny it; your sister told me everything. You are the Goddess of Suicide." He stood and towered over her, fuming with contempt.

Getting weaker...

"Yeah, but—"

"You were cruel and cold and heartless during my darkest hour in the hospital. Now I know why; you enjoy watching others suffer and taking their lives."

"Okay. Maybe a little, but it all depends on the person. And who the hell are you to judge me? You...*man tart.* I bet those women you use might have a thing or two to say about your compassionate side. Or lack thereof."

"Sleeping with women and giving them pleasure is not a valid comparison. And did you just admit you enjoyed watching me suffer when you found me in the hospital?" he asked bitterly.

Hmmm... "Maybe I enjoyed watching you suffer a little. You were being pretty damned cranky, and if I recall correctly, you even wanted to throw away your life."

"Maybe I was *cranky* because *someone* killed my cat!" He pressed his body against hers.

"I said I was sorry about the cat! Okay? I'm sorry. He came out of nowhere!"

"What kind of person kills someone's cat while they're in the hospital? Blinded in an accident?"

"I can't bring back your cat, but at least you have your sight again. And look! You still don't appreciate the second chance you've been given. Can't you just be happy?" Though he was ten inches taller and outweighed her by a good hundred pounds, she pushed back with her body, refusing to lose any ground in their battle of the wills. After all, she was a goddess and he, only a lowly, yummy...*Wait! No!* Icky vampire. Dammit, if he didn't feel warm and hard and masculine in all the right places. She'd never had such delicious contact with another. This was better than that damned ride at Euro Disney all the vampires loved. This was better than bagging ten rapists in one night. This was—*gasp!*—better than a 50 percent off sale on cotton floral prints at Fabric Land! *Knees don't buckle. Knees don't buckle.*

"This isn't a second chance," he yelled. "I am a disgusting, goddamned vampire!"

"Yes. You are! Be happy!" she screamed back.

"Wait. You think I'm disgusting?"

Hell no! Not even a little! "You said it, not me," she replied.

"Let us just see what's under that veil, shall we?" He swiped for it, but she caught his wrist and growled. "Nobody touches the veil, Bub..." Goddammit, the contact was euphoric. Tingles and shivers banged their way through her body. The bliss of touching another living being, without it being...well, work related, was sinfully enjoyable. It felt like she was having sex with her hand. *Errr, not sex with my hand—'cause that's really no fun after seventy thousand years—but sex through my hand.*

She squeezed his wrist a little harder and made a tiny groan. Thankfully, he was too darn busy glaring with those olive-green eyes and snarling with those beautiful lips to even notice.

"What are you hiding under there, Elvira?" he whispered. "Or is it *Jeepers Creepers*? Is your face mangled and twisted? Do you wear that to keep the children from screaming?"

Ixtab stood on her tiptoes and leaned into him. She couldn't pass up a chance to soak in more of his deliciousness. And was that...? Oh yes, it was. Ixtab's eyes practically rolled inside her head as she felt his slightly firm cock against her stomach.

Does he even realize?

Ixtab almost lost it right there, and by lost it, she meant tear off her clothes and throw herself at him shamelessly. She even wanted to remove the veil and show him her face. Could she do it? Betray her vow?

The tablet began to vibrate on the table, and both their heads whipped in its direction. Antonio glanced back at Ixtab's veiled face, then down at their bodies pressing tightly together. His face suddenly turned bright red.

Oops. He just realized.

He stepped away and turned toward the tablet, giving her his back. "Leave," he snarled.

"But I—"

He went for his microscope. "Leave. Go find someone to murder, Morticia."

Ixtab growled under her veil. Not because he'd insulted her—hell, maybe he had every right to be mad. Who knew? But her brain felt like it had been scrambled, leaving her completely disoriented. It must be something about touching him. Yes. Perhaps she *was* drunk. That would explain why she'd gone from loathing the man to being completely and utterly... *Oh. My. Gods! I've gone mad! I'm lusting after a vampire!*

She headed for the door and heard Antonio hiss under his breath in disgust as she left.

Diecisiete

Hoping the crisp winter air might clear her fuzzy mind, Ixtab stood on the penthouse balcony looking out across the lights of the city.

Dammit, could this situation be any more confusing? She actually wanted him. Him. A vampire. As in, would chew off her own leg for another chance to touch him. How could this have happened?

And oddly enough, it was nothing like the feelings she'd had for Francisco. Not even close. This felt like someone had injected her with a giddy love potion that turned her heart into a quagmire of flutters and odd palpitations every time she simply thought of Antonio. It was completely overwhelming. And irrational. And scary. And fun. And exciting. And dizzying.

She took a deep breath.

There's got to be a reason for this. Some... rational scientific explanation. A chemical reaction perhaps?

Fancy fudge! No it's not. I like him. Really, really like him.

No! It cannot be.

Well, it doesn't matter how you feel. He hates you. Loathes you!

Did he truly think she went around killing random people for fun? How could he possibly believe such an idiotic idea? It was true she enjoyed hunting those with dark souls who plagued humanity with their evil ways. Who could resist such entertainment? Rapists and those who abused children were an especially nice catch. And the animals she often used in a pinch—well, she tried to find ones with diseases or that were nearing the end of their furry little lives. The way she saw it, they would die soon regardless, and before they departed this world, their lives served for the higher good. Of course, the poor people who ran over the suicidal squirrel, cat, or dog didn't appreciate their sacrifice, but the world was full of such imperfect situations.

For him to think she simply went around enjoying her job? She hated her job. It was hands down the worst deity gig on the planet. Hell, even Máax, her banished brother, aka the One No One Speaks Of, had it better. And as for those she killed by accident, there was only remorse. She had the veil to prove it.

"Everything all right?" Julie appeared at her side staring with one of her soothing, angelic smiles.

"Sure. No. Maybe. Okay, it's a disaster."

"Are you speaking of the tablet or the physicist?" Julie questioned.

"Both, I guess. We can't seem to keep from wanting to tear each other's heads off." She sighed. "You'd think a creature with my years would know how to handle a male."

Julie laughed. "Wisdom is gained through trial and error, and you haven't had experience with either. Not when it comes to men, anyway."

"I must be making up for lost time—not that I want 'experience' with an egotistical, whiny, icky vampire." *Lie, lie, lie.* "Oh, sorry. I didn't mean you. You're not icky. Neither is Kinich. I suppose Viktor and Helena are pretty nice, too, now that I think about it. But the rest..." She made a sour face under her veil. "Icky."

"So you find Antonio... 'icky'?" Julie asked.

Ixtab sighed. *No. Not in the least. I find him intriguing and irresistible. In an icky sort of way. Of course, I don't appreciate him treating me so rudely. That's a little uncalled for. Maybe.* "Actually, I think I like him."

Julie smiled. "Oh, Ixtab. That's wonderful."

Ixtab sighed. "No. It's not. He hates me for having him turned into a vampire. And the ironic part is that he's the only creature on the face of the planet I can touch. He's immune to me. Even more ironic is that he's the spitting image of the man I once loved and killed." How odd. Confessing this dreary little fact about Francisco wasn't nearly as hard as the time she'd told Kinich. Of course, she'd never told him the gory details.

"Interesting," Julie replied with a little too much levity. "Sounds like fate playing its hand."

Ixtab hissed.

"Oh, not your sister Fate, but divine fate—it's much more precise and intelligent. Not that I don't like your sister."

Ixtab shrugged. "Wouldn't care if you didn't. She's no

friend of mine." *Neither is Antonio—which I don't get. Can't he see I saved his life? Twice?* "You think we'd at least get along."

"I never had any sisters, but perhaps if you spoke to her," Julie said.

"I meant Antonio. But Fate...? The only thing that could induce me to forgive her would be her public admission of being a complete fraud and jackass. Even then, I still might need to see her suffer in a volcano for a few thousand years."

"Whatever she did must've been pretty bad," Julie said.

"Ruthless is more like it. The one thing I've learned is that nothing is forever, including being the Goddess of Suicide. A rotation of powers will come, and then we'll have to see where the chips fall. Until then, I get the chair with the pointy nipples. I get to taste and feel humanity's darkest moments. I get to be hated by egocentric, brainy vampires."

Julie looked out past the horizon. "He doesn't hate you, Ixtab. If he did, you would not be foolish enough to have feelings for him. Love doesn't work that way."

Whoa there! "Who said anything about love? I'm strangely attracted to him in a highly irrational, addictive, euphoric sorta way, where I might possibly cease to exist if I never see him again, which is the textbook definition of lust. Not love. Besides, he made it clear he doesn't wish to see me again."

"I'm sure he doesn't mean it," Julie argued. "He's been through a lot, and now he's got the weight of the world on his shoulders."

"Actually, that's his enormous ego," Ixtab replied.

"Have you seen the size of that sucker?" Ixtab spread her arms to demonstrate. "Needs its own blinking lights and Wide Load sign."

Julie smiled like a first-grade teacher with an MBA in patience. "Is it really that? Or is he simply a man who's been drawn into a difficult situation and needs your help, your compassion? Look at all he's been through."

Damned angels. Always so, so, so ... right!

"I want to show him compassion, trust me. If you only heard the things he said, you'd understand that the situation isn't salvageable. He truly, truly hates me. Perhaps deservingly so."

Julie chuckled. "Then ask yourself why he rejected Fate's help repeatedly and demanded you instead."

Oh. "He rejected her?"

Julie nodded. "She tried all night to convince him to work with her—he is quite the catch, you know—but when he said no, she was so miffed, she stormed out and hasn't returned."

Maybe he rejected her because he wanted to torture me. He admitted as much.

Ah, but he did "respond"—clears throat—*to you, so maybe she has a point.* Ixtab's stomach fluttered with joy, recalling his very masculine response to their bodies touching.

Piff. Probably some vampire hormonal reaction. After all, vampires were notorious for their prolific erections. *He'd probably get excited if a cucumber salad looked at him the wrong way. Vegetarian vampire! Really? Who ever heard such ridiculousness!*

Ixtab smiled under her veil. Actually, the thought of him sucking down carrot juice made him that much more attractive. He wasn't a killer like she was. "All right. What do I do?"

Julie shrugged. "You're the deity; take the high road and apologize for whatever it is you've done. I'm sure you've had plenty of practice with that over seventy thousand years."

That would be a resounding *yes*. Especially if one happened to be referring to the unintentional slaying of beloved pets.

"Okay. I'll do it. How do I look?" she asked Julie and held out the flowing hem of her very drapey dress.

"Um...um. You look very...mysterious?"

"Excellent!" *Better than morbid.*

"I did not mean the *good* kind of mysterious," Julie said politely.

"You didn't?"

"Have you considered a new look?" she asked.

No. Not at all. The clothes kept the world safe; they reminded Ixtab to always be careful and prevented people from getting too close. The "freaky" factor to her look was critical. "What did you have in mind?" Ixtab asked.

"How about something a little more modern? More revealing perhaps?"

"I don't think I'm ready to give up the veil."

"Then take one step and change something else." Julie's eyes swept over the dress.

Ixtab pondered the advice. "I supposed I could buy something new once the stores open—I've always wanted to try some of those undergarments I see humans wear."

Julie lifted a brow. "You've never worn underwear? Or a bra?"

She wasn't human, so her body didn't really sweat or get dirty in an underwear sort of way. And her breasts were eternally perfect. The only reason she'd have to wear undergarments would be to please a man, which had never really been a part of the equation. "No. I go commanda."

"Okay, then. Panties would be a great place to start."

Dieciocho

The next morning, Ixtab entered Antonio's quiet apartment and anxiously pressed her ear against the laboratory door. Despite what she'd said to Julie, apologizing wasn't easy; although given her flair for mistakes, she considered herself an expert. Just as she might consider herself an expert at being cruel when she felt the recipient deserving. Yes, there had been a truth to what Antonio said. She had enjoyed his suffering on the day they'd met so perhaps she deserved his distrust and anger. She'd seen him as nothing more than a man floozy who looked like someone she'd once loved, and she had wanted to punish him for it. That was a mistake for which she now felt sorry.

Here goes nothing. She opened the door to his lab and found him sitting in his usual spot. "You don't need to kill to drink blood, yanno. The bagged blood is donated by perfectly healthy living people who stay that way after leaving their deposit." She held up a bag of blood. "Yummy. Yummy. O negative in my tummy."

Antonio paused in his writing for a moment, but did not look up or acknowledge her presence.

"Boy, tough crowd tonight," she said.

"It's morning," he grumbled.

"True. Did I ever tell you the one about the Spanish vampire physicist and the Goddess of Suicide who were tasked with unlocking a portal to another dimension in order to stop the destruction of the planet?"

He didn't even crack a hint of a smile, but dammit if he didn't look gorgeous. And not because he'd gone and showered or shaved or anything like that. Oh no. The man had a good centimeter of black stubble covering his angular jaw, his usual stylishly mussed hair was completely disheveled, and he'd removed his T-shirt and replaced it with a black apron that exposed his corded biceps and barely covered his well-formed pectorals.

Ixtab's mind sputtered; he was simply too divine to be true. Gods, she couldn't think or breathe or remember her damned name. How the hell would she be any use to him in this state?

"I'm waiting," he said flatly, scribbling away.

"They were totally fucked."

His head snapped up, and he glared at her. "That wasn't funny. Not even a little."

"I'm the Goddess of Suicide. What do you expect?"

He chuckled and returned to his formula.

He laughed? It was a proud moment.

"So. Can I interest you in a bite?" she asked.

His eyes darted up, not completely reaching her face, then back to his writing again. "No thank you."

Had he looked at her breasts? She had worn her low-cut black dress that hugged her upper torso and then flared slightly at the hips. She'd also made sure to put on her shorter veil, the one that landed just below her shoulders, specifically to show off her newly elevated bustline. Not that the girls had sagged before, but this contraption she'd purchased scooped them up and pushed them together. "Men of this era really like intermammary sulcus?" she'd asked the fitting room clerk, thinking this fad had gone out in the 1700s.

The woman had simply stared.

"Yes, of course. That's a silly question." Ixtab rotated in the mirror viewing her curvy, five-foot-eight frame. "You don't think it makes my breasts look like a tiny butt?" Ixtab had asked.

The woman shook her head and assured Ixtab the garment would be worth every dime. She'd even convinced her to purchase matching pink, lacy "boy shorts," insisting it was "all the rage with the men." Ixtab still wasn't sure why boys would want to wear pink lace or why men would wear the undergarments of boys when there was no room for their "man junk," as she'd heard the youth called it nowadays.

Antonio's eyes returned to Ixtab's chest for a brief moment, as if he were struggling not to look, but couldn't resist.

Oh. He did it again! Yippee!

Her joy then stumbled and tripped. *Oh, pita chips.* The clerk hadn't told Ixtab what to do after the bra had done its job of attracting attention.

Maybe I am supposed to show him my breasts? She suddenly wished she'd paid closer attention to the mating rituals of humans. Yes, yes, she understood the nitty-gritty basics; however, the finer details? It had seemed like a waste of time given the unlikeliness of ever having any nitty-gritty.

Hmmm... She'd seen a few movies where mortals pretended to talk about one thing, but were really talking about sex. Perhaps she should give that a go.

Clear throat, shoulders back, and... "You're sure you're not *hungry*?" She placed the bags on the table in front of him.

"I wouldn't say that," he said plainly.

"Perhaps a little *taste* might make you feel better."

"No amount of blood will make me feel better," he stated bleakly.

Okay. That didn't work. Perhaps he missed the cues.

Or perhaps you should just show him your boys' underwear?

Yes! She reached for her hem, then caught a glimpse of sadness flickering in his eyes. *Oh, hell. Good job, goddess.*

Abort seduction ploy. She mentally sighed. "What will?"

"Are you offering your help?" he said as if he secretly desired it.

His undertone of desperation clawed at her insides. Gods, it was the damnedest thing, but his despair suddenly felt like her own. And not only did she feel uncontrollably compelled to help him, she also felt something pulling them together. Could it be fate?

Yes. Perhaps this was fate—the good, universal, intelligent fate, of course. Not that horrible snooty, "too good for you" sister of hers. Could this crazy, strong, sophisticated man, tinged with a feral darkness and armed with razor-sharp intelligence, be the answer to her prayers? There was only one way to find out.

Show him your panties?

No, you idiot! Your heart. Show him your heart.

A rush of courage washed over her, compelling her to open up. "I've never told anyone this," she blurted, "but I wear my veil as a punishment for the innocent lives I've taken." *There. I said it.* "To be clear, I do everything in my power to save people, but I can't stop killing a few by accident. Including someone I once cared very deeply for. I've never forgiven myself."

He crossed his arms and studied her with his dark green eyes. "Why are you here, Ixtab?"

"Why do *you* want me here?" she asked.

"Who says I do?" He got up, stepped around the table, and took several steps toward her.

"You. You told Fate you wanted me here."

"Maybe I just didn't want her."

Ouch. "I'm sure I deserved that after I killed your cat. And I did enjoy watching you suffer—just a little. And I'm sorry. I'm also very sorry for having you turned into a vampire. At least part of me is because it's not what you wanted. The other part of me couldn't be happier that you're still alive."

He questioned her with his eyes.

"Because of the saving humanity stuff," she added quickly. "Obviously, I could never be into you—a vampire." She poked him in the arm. "Much." *Gods, that felt good!*

He studied her with his cold eyes. "You're like an infuriating child, you know that?"

True. So true. A slightly infuriating child with panache for death. "I've actually been told I'm a basket of fun. My sister Cimil says they should supersize me."

Gods, why had she said that? This wasn't the time for stupid jokes.

His full lips made a hard line. He turned back toward his table, sat on his stool, and began typing into his laptop. "My *pinche* luck."

What the hell is that supposed to mean?

Patience, Ixtab. He's been through a lot.

"May I ask you a question?" she said calmly. "You clearly aren't happy about being a vampire, so why continue working on the tablet? Why not let the world end? That could solve all your problems."

"Like you, I answer to another power."

"Oh, do you answer to chocolate-covered donuts, too? Sometimes they call out, 'Eat meeee.' Then it's all over; I must obey."

Gods dammit! I did it again. What the hell is wrong with me?

He slowly shook his head. "Are all deities so insane?" he grumbled.

Yes. But . . . "Call me after you've lived seventy thousand years without anyone to share it with," she snapped. She had her brethren, but they were all as miserable as she was, for the most part. "Sorry—I didn't come here to pick another fight. I came to apologize for my lack of compassion toward you. And now I'm offering my help, if you want it."

He lowered his head and let out a sigh. "I don't know. I don't know anything anymore. It feels like my life . . ." His voice trailed off into deep contemplation.

Don't you do it. Don't you dare crack a stupid joke!
"What? Feels like what?" *Good job.*

"Would you stop talking? I'm trying to..." He looked down at his laptop.

Stop? Did she come equipped with that setting?

She looked at the man slouched over his notebook in front of her. *Oh, gods... you've only made things worse!* The heaviness in his shoulders tugged at her heartstrings. If only she could do something to ease his pain, but she was so bad at this. She didn't know how to connect with him—or anyone, really.

Ixtab moved behind him and pressed her body and cheek against his bare back. "I am sorry," she said quietly, placing her hands around his waist over the apron.

Antonio sucked in a sharp breath and jerked his spine straight. "Why do you keep touching me?" he said in a low, deep voice.

She sighed. "I don't know." Then she inhaled his scent, fully expecting him to pull away, but he didn't.

Several moments ticked by, and she noticed that his heaviness began to lift, replaced with a heat that sieved through his skin and into her body. She felt their lights spark and tingle as they began to mingle. Her own heart began to thump in time with his.

Gods, what was happening to her? She instantly knew she would never get enough of this, of him. She was addicted.

She removed her hands from his tight waist, and then ran them up the bare skin of his sides, savoring the slope of his broad back.

She felt Antonio's chest expanding and contracting at an accelerated pace, but he remained still as her hands moved under his apron, exploring the velvety, hard ripples of his abdomen. Gods, he felt so delicious, so perfectly firm and smooth, so masculine. She leaned into him a little harder, enjoying the feel of her breasts and stomach against the heat of his back. Gods, she'd never wanted a male like she wanted him. The way he reacted to her touch, almost like he needed it as much as she did.

Her hands moved slowly up his washboard abs and glided to his muscular, firm pectorals. They were so sensually male, so hard, though not as hard as the two tiny nipples she found. She explored them with the ends of her fingers, wanting nothing more than to feel them on the tip of her tongue. Would he let her touch him like that? Kiss his perfect chest, lick his insanely muscled stomach? She would have to remove her fortress of black fabric to do so.

Could she let him see her face, her body? Expose herself to him?

Yes, yes, she could. She'd let him see everything. She'd do just about anything to feel his entire naked body flush with hers, because if touching him with her hands felt this good, she could only imagine the pleasure of having him on top of her, writhing between her thighs, inside her.

"Antonio." She folded her veil and placed a light kiss on his shoulder blade. "I want to show you something," she whispered. She kissed him again, savoring the tiny shivers she coaxed from his body each time her lips touched his smooth, bronzed skin. Gods, she would enjoy this. She slowly began moving her hands down, down his chest, down his stomach—

He released a low groan, and he shifted on his chair, widening his legs.

"Gods, Antonio. What you do to me," she whispered and

then slid her hand to his groin. Her fingertips grazed the moist tip of his erection protruding from his waistband.

Antonio groaned again and then suddenly spun around, knocking Ixtab square in the jaw with his elbow.

She heard a loud crack and felt the floor leap up and smack her on the back of the head. *Ouch. That hurt.*

Antonio stared down at Ixtab, who appeared to be unconscious. *Santa mierda!*

"Ixtab! Ixtab!" She was out cold.

Dammit! He'd have to be more careful with his new strength. He'd already torn two shirts, cracked the sink in half brushing his teeth, busted two doorknobs, and ripped open three pairs of button fly jeans—each time when he'd thought of Ixtab. Not like he had a fuck of a clue as to why he had that reaction toward her. The damned goddess pissed him off and mocked everything he held sacred. She was crass and lacked the fragile femininity he adored in his usual fare of one-night stands. But Christ almighty, if he didn't find Ixtab's smell the most addictive scent known to man—err—vampire. And her touch...? *Dios*, he'd never felt anything so fucking arousing in his entire life.

"Ixtab. Are you all right? Ixtab?" *Shit.*

He hovered his ear above her mouth. At least, he thought it was her mouth. Not that he could see her face.

Her breath was shallow at best.

Santa Maria. He grabbed her wrist to check for a pulse. Yes, there was a faint, slightly irregular beat—*caray!* A soft wave of throbbing tingles wrapped its way up his arm, over his shoulder, and spread through his body.

Joy. Light. Euphoria. Warmth.

Unable to pull away, he closed his eyes and allowed the sensation to saturate each corner of his body and mind. She was like a drug. A delicious, sensual drug that he now recalled tasting earlier when she'd touched him during their fight. Only then, he'd mistaken it for vampire adrenaline.

Now, come to think it, the sensation felt eerily similar to when she'd touched him in the hospital and the other time when he lay there dying.

This could not be a goddess of evil and death.

So what was she?

He slowly lifted her lacy veil, trying not to stare at the two firm breasts cloaked by snug black fabric. He swallowed hard.

As she lay there completely still, he realized he could make out the full outline of the body she tried so desperately to hide. She was actually quite lovely. A long, lean form with a small waist and curvy hips. And he already knew she was perfect in the breast department.

Of course, she was a goddess. Why wouldn't she be perfect?

Her sister, Fate, had painted her out to be a monster. A killer. And Ixtab had admitted freely that she was.

So what did the face of this killer truly look like? He slowly lifted the veil. One inch. Then another. A smooth neck with light golden-brown skin revealed itself. No. It wasn't the pale, corpse-like flesh he'd expected; it was simply beautiful.

He glanced down at her hands. He'd never noticed them, but they, too, were a soft, creamy mocha brown. As if she spent her days in the Mediterranean, sunbathing. *Lovely.*

He lifted a little further, his heart racing with anticipation, with morbid curiosity, with hope.

A chin. Perfectly rounded to a small point and made of the same silky skin on her neck. Then...*Dios mío, lips*...

Words of blatant, ungentlemanly lust stuck in his throat. Two full, sexy lips stared back at him, mesmerizing him with their voluptuous perfection. Did they feel as silky as they looked? He leaned in close and ran his fingers over her lower lip. They felt like rose petals, soft and velvety little pillows. He placed a small kiss on her mouth. Heaven. Kissing such soft lips felt like heaven.

His mind instantly panned south, imagining how her other soft and tender spots might look and how he might enjoy kissing those, too. His fangs suddenly popped from his mouth and his shaft burst through the buttons of his jeans.

Christ. Now he finally understood why vampires wore leather pants. He'd have to order a pair or two immediately. In the meantime, his long apron would have to do.

He lifted a little bit more to see the rest of her face, and then...

"Ixtab!" She simply dissolved into thin air, leaving nothing behind but a pile of empty black lace and a very sexy set of pink, lacy lingerie.

Diecinueve

"What do you mean, you 'lost Ixtab'?" Kinich stood in the doorway of his apartment with a white towel wrapped around his waist, smelling of sex and woman. A really hot woman. Literally. The smell of sunshine seeped from his every pore.

"Lost. As in . . *Coño*, she fucking vanished. Is this one of her powers?"

Kinich scratched his head and stepped aside to allow Antonio to enter. "How hard did you say you hit her? And what's with the apron?"

"I haven't ordered my leather pants yet."

"Ah. I'll give you the name of the local tailor. We get a bulk discount, and he does excellent work—triple stitching in the crotch."

"Fantastic." Antonio sank down on the black leather couch and dragged his hands down his face. "*Santa Maria*. I hit her so hard she crashed to the floor like a bag of rocks. I'm not used to this new strength."

Penelope, with her dark hair appearing as though it had been teased in every possible direction, scrambled from their bedroom wrapped in a pink Hello Kitty bathrobe.

Antonio raised a quick brow.

"What?" she squabbled. "I borrowed it from Helena's closet upstairs."

Wasn't Helena the current ruler of the vampire race? This strange, new world he'd been sucked into was farcical.

Kinich looked at Penelope with the utmost adoration. "Antonio says he lost Ixtab."

Penelope stifled a laugh and then turned sheet white. "The Maaskab aren't back, are they?"

"Maaskab? You mean the evil priests we fight?" Antonio asked. Fate and Viktor had spoken to him about the "situation." And one might presume it was the reason he'd decided to continue on with his work. But no. It was her. The haunting woman from his dreams who appeared the very first night he possessed the tablet. Only now, now that he didn't really sleep, he heard her voice each time he closed his eyes, pleading to end her agony. And dammit if he didn't feel drawn to her—like she pulled him with invisible threads attached to his soul. There was simply no denying that he was destined to meet this woman, whoever she might be.

So what did this . . . *thing* with Ixtab mean?

"No," Kinich replied. "The Maaskab have not returned. We haven't seen any aside from Emma's grandmother since the last battle. Our physicist here says he accidentally hit Ixtab, she passed out, and then she disappeared."

Kinich and Penelope exchanged several rounds of awkward glances.

"What?" Antonio asked.

"I believe you killed her," Kinich replied.

Killed her? "It was only a thrust with my elbow, for Christ's sake."

"Lucky hit, vampire." Kinich shrugged. "You must have cracked her neck."

"Isn't she immortal?" Antonio argued.

Kinich snickered. "Oh yes. And when she returns, she's going to be pissed. And not pissed in a mortal female kind of way where she throws her shoes at your head." He looked at Penelope.

"Hey!" She took a swipe at his arm. "I was really mad that day, and you weren't being a very nice Sun God."

Kinich pulled her close and kissed her nose. "No, I wasn't. And you may throw your shoes at me anytime you like. You look extremely beautiful when you are venting." He kissed her deeply. "And you are even more beautiful carrying my child. By the way, I cannot wait to find out the sex. If it's a girl, I would like to call her—"

Antonio cleared his throat.

Kinich glanced at Antonio. "Are you still here? Shouldn't you be looking for a place to hide, vampire?"

"Do I want to ask why?" Antonio groaned.

Without pausing from her ogling, Penelope replied, "Aside from being the bringer of self-imposed death, Ixtab is also known as Ninlil, Xochipili, Xilonen, Inguma, though the Basque thought she was a he, and—"

"You've been studying, my little Sun Goddess." Kinich beamed at Penelope.

All these—oh, hell, what did Americans call it?—goo-goo eyes were making him sick.

"Yep. I'm finally on the book of Inuit, Akych," she said.

"Very good. Yes. Akych is the name for Sun God."

"Would you two stop with the incessant mutual admiration and tell me why I need to hide? It was an accident. I didn't mean to hurt her."

Kinich laughed and released Penelope. "That will not matter. A weaker, lesser being killing a deity in his or her immortal form is akin to giving a public bitch slap."

Weaker? Lesser?

"Like all deities," Kinich continued, "Ixtab's Achilles' heel is her ego. But her anger is by far her biggest flaw. Unfortunately for you—and the rest of us—she is the goddess in charge of happiness, flowers, natural seasoning, sport, winds, grain—"

"That doesn't sound so terrible. In fact, those sound very nice." *And explains why she smells so great.*

"And," Kinich added, "nightmares, strangulation, hangings, and toothaches. Fate was the last person to kill Ixtab by accident. And her return brought with it five days of global windstorms; three months of every game around the planet ending in a tie—the Germans and Latin Americans almost lost their minds; a plague of horrible toothaches and nightmares; a shortage of cardamom and cloves—the people in India and the UK were very unhappy without their curry; and the disappearance of daisies for an entire decade."

Antonio scratched his unshaven jaw. "Not that I wish the world to be afflicted with the absence of a Super Bowl winner or subjected to flavorless dishes, but that doesn't sound so devastating."

Devastating was that he'd hurt—*estúpido!*—killed Ixtab. Killed her while she was doing that thing to him with her body and driving him mad in the most sexual of ways. Accidental or not, it was a terrible feeling. And there was nothing he could do about it.

Ironic. Ixtab was just telling you this is why she wears a veil.

And you mocked her, didn't you, coño?

Pinche karma.

"I said," Kinich clarified, "that's what happened the last time she died. The time before that, she'd been refereeing an arm-wrestling match between K'ak and Belch at the edge of a volcano. The two had been fighting over a small misunderstanding having to do with a llama."

Did he want to know?

No. He really, really didn't.

"And so," Kinich said, "the gods demanded they settle their dispute according to our laws."

Arm wrestling at the edge of a fucking volcano?

"But Belch stumbled, ran into Ixtab, and she fell in." Kinich shook his head. "Not one flower bloomed in the Western Hemisphere that year. And without flowers, no food. It was one of the worst famines ever to hit the planet."

"I thought the gods couldn't harm us humans?" Antonio asked.

"Not on purpose," Penelope pointed out. "And don't forget, you're not human anymore."

Dios mío. Antonio dropped his head into his hands. "It was a goddamned accident."

"Don't worry," Penelope said. "She won't kill you—yet—because you're too important to mankind, but she will make you and everyone else suffer." Penelope cleared her throat. "As Ruler of the House of Gods, I order you to grovel. Immortal-style. Maybe you can defuse the situation."

Kinich chuckled. "Immortal-style! You really have been studying." He kissed her hard. "I love the way you take charge, woman. You're going to make an excellent mother. And it is so goddamned sexy."

"Thank you." Penelope glowed.

"What am I missing?" Antonio did not like the sound of this "immortal groveling."

"We keep a plane at the airport," Penelope said. "You should make it to Bacalar in time to meet Ixtab at the cenote."

"Why the *diablo* do I need to go to a cenote? And what the *diablo* is immortal groveling?" he asked.

"While most cenotes are merely ancient Mayan pools," Penelope replied, "some are portals of the gods. They are also where a deity's light is sent when they lose their mortal shell. From there, a deity can go back to the gods' realm or decide to regenerate another body. I'm pretty sure Ixtab's going to opt for the new body to kick your ass. Get packing, and I'll have the instructions for immortal groveling ready on the plane."

"What about the tablet? And my work?" Antonio asked.

"He's right," Kinich said, "we cannot afford to lose time."

"He'll have to bring it with him," Penelope decided. "We can have the Uchben set up his lab and a secured communication line at Niccolo's villa on the lake. It's only a few miles from Ixtab's favorite cenote."

Again, Kinich glowed with male pride. "I am the luckiest male on the planet to have such an intelligent woman so well versed in the ways of our world. Niccolo's is a perfect place to grovel."

"It is also helpful that Ixtab and Antonio will be removed from any large populations—in case she loses her temper," Penelope added.

Santa Maria.

Veinte

"Save me, Antonio. You must hurry. Time is almost out."

"I'm trying, but I can't find you." Antonio scoured the empty, dark room with his hands. "Please, tell me who you are."

"You cannot allow distractions to come between us, Antonio, between our destiny," the woman's angry voice echoed in his head. "You must stay away from the goddess."

"I don't understand. Why?"

"I speak the truth." Two wide eyes the color of a tropical ocean plowed through his mind. "Even the stars and the moon know I speak the truth—"

Antonio's lids flew open, and he braced himself on the arms of the airplane seat.

Diablos! Now his dreams were mad at him, too? And the odd part was that the woman had never said anything about Ixtab before. Why would she be telling him to stay away?

Perhaps she is jealous. Perhaps she knows the goddess is nothing but trouble. Hell, a person only had to get within a mile of Ixtab to see that. One thing was certain, if he didn't set the mystery woman free soon, he would go mad. First, whether he liked it or not, he had to deal with a very irate, deadly goddess who happened to wield the power of...*natural seasoning*?

He shook his head and glanced at his watch. There was still one hour until touchdown.

He pulled the folded list from his pocket and stared at it with utter disgust. This immortal groveling had to be a joke.

Then again, from what little he knew, deities were the epitome of bizarre as were the vampires they mingled with. He felt like he'd been thrust into a modern episode of the *Addams Family*—Ixtab being Morticia, of course.

Does that make you Gomez?

Caray. Antonio shook it off and went back to the list. *Joder.* This wasn't right. *I cannot do these things. I cannot.*

You must, you idiot. There is no other choice. Especially given the timing of the accident. He couldn't get that moment out of his mind, the way she'd touched his body and pressed herself to his back. Her heat, the sexual tension she created and then released with the mere stroke of her fingertips.

Antonio shifted in his seat, recalling how she'd grazed the tip of his cock with her hand.

He adjusted his throbbing erection and looked down at it. "Don't you have something else to do?" He'd tried several times to relieve the ache himself, but that only made him think of Ixtab, which only made his cock harder.

Shit. What was happening to him? First blind, then he'd died and turned into a vampire, and now he was addicted to this goddess—who, he might add, wore a very unattractive outfit to hide herself and might actually look like a gremlin. What else could possibly get in the way of fulfilling his destiny and opening the portal?

How about killing Ixtab and immortal groveling?

"What. The. Hell!!" Ixtab exploded from the cenote, her brand-new body nude, dripping wet, and trembling with anger. She was tempted to go back to her realm just to torment the vampire—from there she could use the full array of her powers to rain a fury of hell on his immortal ass—but nothing felt more satisfying than delivering justice in person. And justice there would be. Because no one, and she meant *no one,* snubbed her out like that. She'd opened herself to him, showed him comfort, she'd worshipped his body! And what was his response? He killed her! A vampire actually knocked her block off.

The cloudless evening sky burst with a round of violent thunder and rattled the jungle with its tremors.

Ixtab scaled the deeply cracked wall of the slick, algae-covered cenote and balanced on the edge. She squeezed the stale water from her long dark hair while glaring at the squawking toucans above. "You think this is funny?" She looked out into the dark jungle. A hard wind whipped through the air. "This is war. And the vampire's gonna pay."

Ixtab marched forward and tripped over something large, landing with a face-plant in the moist, leaf-covered dirt. She flipped on her bare bottom and sat up. There, in a standard grovel position with his face pointed toward the ground and arms extended straight forward, was a large man dressed in black leather pants and white tee. A lone shopping bag from Nordstrom sat on the ground to his side.

Well, look what the undead cat dragged in. "Antoniooo," she growled.

"Yes, goddess. I have come to throw myself—" He paused and fumbled with a sheet of paper in his hand, sliding it under his face without lifting his head. "I throw myself at your mercy and ask your forgiveness. To atone for my grave error, I have brought you this gift of fresh clothing and have prepared to make the appropriate sacrifices and offerings." He paused again and glanced at the paper. "Oh Divine One."

What the pita chips? Ixtab marched over and swiped the bag. "No peeking." She slipped on the black dress— a nice little soft and stretchy cotton number that was straight all the way down and slightly formfitting—and a soft silk black veil that hit right beneath her chin. This was a definite upgrade from her usual punishing outfit reminiscent of a widowed Italian grandmother, straight from the back pew of the *Godfather*. But given the circumstances, she would wear the offering gladly. Better than traipsing around the jungle with her rear end hanging out. Although she did have a fabulous rear. Stonehenge, after all, had been *erected* in its honor.

Now, as for this unexpected display of groveling...

"What gives, vampire?"

"What do you mean, Oh Divine One?" he asked.

She narrowed her eyes. "Get up. Tell me why you're here and why I shouldn't smash you into a thousand bits with my pinkie." As if she could. Compared to the other gods or a vampire like Antonio, she was as physically strong as a chicken. With the flu.

Antonio unfolded himself and rose to his feet, causing Ixtab to nearly fall off hers. In his snug black leather pants—*oooh, triple stitching. Nice*—and white tee stretching across his thick, muscular chest and upper arms, he looked like a god—only a very sexy version. Gods weren't that sexy in her mind—too perfect. But Antonio's towering height; deeply entrenched, raw masculinity; rolls of manly muscles; and hard, deep green eyes were more divine than any male walking the earth. Oh yes. If he were a deity, this man would have a pyramid built in his honor. Maybe two.

She cleared her throat. "Had a little makeover, did you?"

Antonio ran his large hand through his wild, short hair. "Penelope insisted I cut my hair on the way to the airport." His icy gaze fixed on Ixtab's breasts, which were prominently displayed via the low-cut neckline and snug fabric. "To please you," he added with a deep voice that held a hint of an itch. An itch Ixtab wanted to scratch.

Bahhh... Ixtab's insides nearly liquefied.

Wait, he killed you. And by now, all of your brethren will know about it—damn that Twitter. You will endure a good solid five hundred years of taunting after being taken down by a vampire's elbow. Stupid, icky vampire! I will squash you for this!

She didn't know what stung more, the humiliation or his rejection.

"You came all this way to show me your haircut and bring me a dress? 'Cause if you did, I can tell you right now, it's not enough." She raised her hand. What should it be? A hundred-year fang-ache? Maybe burn off his arms with a concentrated dose of chili peppers? The arms would grow back. Eventually. And he didn't really need them to complete his work on the tablet, now did he?

"Whoa!" He held out his hands. "I came to perform the ritual of immortal groveling. That's why I'm here."

Immortal groveling? Ugh. That was so last baktun. That stale, old ritual was Fate's idea and entailed nothing more than sacrificing a large animal in the deity's name, followed by a feast of the god's favorite dishes. Ixtab didn't even like meat. Unless you counted vampire ass as meat.

"And in exchange for your forgiveness and leniency, I will..." Again he glanced at his paper.

Ixtab swiped it from his hands and read the list.

1. *You will wash the goddess's feet, rub them with essential oils, kiss her toes, and then paint them pink.*
2. *At no time during the period of groveling, will you wear a shirt or call her by name. "Oh Divine One" shall be used.*
3. *You will prepare her favorite dish, and when you serve her, you will walk only on your knees.*
4. *You will write and recite a poem about the smallness and insignificance of your manhood while belly dancing with a sword balanced on your head.*
5. *And finally, you will offer your body to the goddess for a night of pleasure.*
6. *If by dawn you have not pleased her, you are to offer your pancreas.*

She could scarcely contain her laughter. This sounded like the groveling ritual Cimil had proposed way back—minus the clown flogging and unicorn rodeo. It had gotten Ixtab's vote—minus the clown flogging—but Fate had convinced everyone to take the high road. *Piff! Fate... such a goody-goody.*

"Who gave this *sacred* ritual to you?" Ixtab asked in her most serious voice.

Antonio bowed his head. "Penelope and Kinich. They said if I did not come in person and do these"—he swallowed something sticking in his throat. *Perhaps his pride?*—"things, that you would unleash a global plague or famine."

Oh no. She had no intention of doing that. Not that she ever would. On purpose, anyway. Well, there'd be no accidental disasters today. Whatever public shame she would endure for being whacked by a lowly creature of the night would be well worth it; watching Antonio humiliate himself was going to be fun. *Payback is such a... well, I'm not a bitch. But the argument has been made that I am cold, reckless, and deadly. Creadly? Yes, that's it. Payback is a creadly.*

"I'll think about not smiting humanity. Now, get to the groveling!" she barked.

Antonio bowed his head and gestured with his arm. "This way, Oh Divine One. I have a Jeep waiting for you down the path."

Ixtab smiled and sauntered past, but then her smile turned to a frown. What would she do when he got to number five?

Oh, Ixtab. What the hell are you talking about? He's an icky vampire. As if he could ever tempt you.

Yes. But he's a sexy, icky vampire I can touch and who makes me...tingle. The urge to touch him was suddenly overwhelming. Maybe the joke was on her.

Panic, fear, and anger set in. Panic, because she was in new territory. What if he really offered himself to her? She'd never been with anyone, and he was quite experienced. Fear, because she realized how much the idea pleased her. Anger, because any advance on his part would not be genuine. He'd been tricked into it, believing that having sex with her would avert a global catastrophe.

Well, she wouldn't accept his offer. She was too good to take a peace-offering sex handout from an icky vampire. She was a goddess. An ancient, immortal soul of divine origin. That's right. She was like royalty of the Universe.

Who really, really wants to be liked for being herself.

You idiot! You sound like some mortal teenager pining for the captain of the football team.

She gave herself a mental flogging. It didn't do the trick; she still wanted him. And wanted him to want her back.

Oh, boy, I'm in trouble...

Which meant so was he. Everyone knew Ixtab was bad news. *Creadly...*

⁓

Antonio felt uneasy. Extremely uneasy. At first, because he wasn't sure what the deadly goddess might do to him. But then...he'd seen the goddess naked. He didn't mean to look, but when she fell, he'd stolen a glance of her body—sleek, muscular, tanned, and curvy—laid out on the ground. Gods save him. At least he hadn't seen her front. That ass was enough to push him over the edge of sanity. Smooth golden skin over two perfectly shaped mounds with a crease cutting across the tops of her back thighs, separating those silky legs from that blissful ass. Oh, gods, there was no way she could be a monster.

Could she? Or had she lied about the reason she covered her face?

Santa Maria. If only he hadn't killed her, he would have seen what hid behind the curtain.

Yes, coño, *then you wouldn't be with her now.* And whether he liked to admit it or not, a tiny part of him felt insanely satisfied to be near her, the two of them alone, to see her alive and well and full of her usual piss and vinegar.

Santos, the woman is death personified. He and death had a long, long history. The take away? Not the best of amigos. Nor would they ever be. Lately it seemed that fate had it out for him. First by making him a vampire, which he was determined to not let change who he fundamentally was at his innermost core and deter him from fulfilling his destiny, and then by tempting him with the female who not only killed, but also seemed to enjoy it on some level.

Perhaps you are overthinking the situation. She does not reciprocate any sexual desires you have for her. Or, should I say, if she had any, that is now over.

In fact, what started out as a very successful groveling ritual had turned down a dark, murky path filled with cobweb-covered potholes, rotting vegetation, and venomous snakes. Ixtab's disposition, for no apparent reason, shifted from mild irritation to outright hostility the moment they got into the Jeep.

The night now set upon them, he shifted gears into second and wound down the dirt road through thick, impenetrable jungle as the GPS instructed. He'd been told by Penelope that everything would be waiting for them upon their arrival. The Uchben had a garrison nearby and would see to it that the lakeside villa was cleaned, stocked, and ready for them.

He pulled into the gravel driveway lined with tiki torches. Unable to drive any farther, Antonio turned off the engine, but didn't dare look at the goddess in her tight black dress. Who knew how much longer his leather pants would hold? "Guess we're here."

"Great. I love walking barefoot. If I'm lucky, I'll find a nice juicy slug or scorpion to greet my toes."

Caray. He knew he'd forgotten something: her flip-flops. He'd left them on the plane. Ironically, she liked her flip-flops loud and sparkly. Who would have guessed?

He turned off the headlights. "I planned to carry you, Oh Divine One," he whispered. "Your feet"—*which I'm about to scrub like a lowly servant*—"should not touch the ground."

Ixtab turned his way. "Piggyback? You expect me to ride piggyback on an icky vampire?" she spat.

This groveling crap was awful. An insult to every molecule of testosterone in his body. If it wasn't for the fact that he'd hurt her while she was rubbing the tip of his—

He cleared his mind. *Don't think of it. Don't think of it...* His erection had finally abated, and gods only knew how long that would last.

"Yes, Oh Divine One," he replied. "You will ride me." *Christ. Did I really just say that?* "I meant, piggyback, of course."

"Ugh! Fine." She opened her door and turned away, waiting for him to pick her up from the passenger side.

He exited the vehicle with a sigh, walked to her side, and turned his back to her. "Get on."

"Get on?"

"Oh Divine One," he added.

First, he felt Ixtab's hands clutch his shoulders. Next, her body slammed into his, and she wrapped her legs around his waist.

He quickly braced himself against the Jeep and held back a lusty groan. Gods be damned, the sensation of this goddess touching his body was torture. And beyond any pleasure he'd ever known. The mere feel of her breasts pressed against his back was enough to make him bust his zipper again. Thank gods he wore his new leather pants with the triple stitch.

"You okay, vampire?" Ixtab whispered in his ear with a breath that heated his lobe and shot right down to his shaft. "Or am I too much for you to handle?"

He gave his head a little shake, righted himself, and stood straight. "No. Just fine, Oh Divine One." He sucked in a lungful of restraint and marched down the torch-lit path, trying to think of anything but Ixtab's body—her most intimate parts included—pushed against him. No, he would not think about the fact that her dress was hiked up well past her upper thighs and she wore no panties. He would not think about how her voluptuous breasts jiggled against his shoulder blades with each step or how the silky skin of her arms and legs rubbed against his new, overly sensitive vampire skin and filled him with a euphoria that could only be described as the world's most addictive supernatural narcotic, which took away his hunger along with his darkest thoughts and filled him with strength.

Oh, gods. He suddenly found himself fiercely desiring step number five—offering himself for a night of pleasure—which scared the hell out of him. For starters, Ixtab's sister had said she was a monster. So what sort of face truly lay beneath that veil? If her lips were any indication, she had to be beautiful.

But the sister hadn't said, "She's a little homely and might someday grow out of it." No. She'd said, "monster," which meant heinous. Repugnant. Shockingly ugly. Did Ixtab's face reflect images of the thousands of souls she'd taken? Or perhaps her features were marred with a horrid disfigurement. Why else would she want to hide it? Surely shame wasn't the real answer. Second, despite what his rock solid dick said, his heart knew what it felt. He believed in fate and having a destiny; his destiny was opening that portal. His destiny was ... *her*—the woman from his dreams. He could feel it with every fiber of his being, and with each passing minute, he knew only holding her, saving her, taking away her pain would bring peace.

To prove his point, Antonio closed his eyes for a moment and instantly heard her words filled with desperation, "The stars and the moon know I'm telling you the truth. Why won't you listen, Antonio? Stay away from her ..." Then those haunting eyes stared back at him from the walls of his eyelids.

His raging of lust instantly abated. *That's right*, idiota. *Now think about the weather—or ... fucking stars and the moon! Whatever it takes to get on with this night, so you can continue your work.*

Whatever happened, he needed to ensure the goddess would not accept any offers of pleasure for the evening. Not that it should be a problem; she already thought of him as a despicable creature. She'd said so herself numerous times. Her earlier actions prior to the accident must have simply been one of her evil tricks intended to torture him. That's right. She admitted she enjoyed watching others suffer, watching *him* suffer. She'd likely intended to work him into a sexual lather and then skip away. And he would not allow himself to fall for that trick again. No matter what his body said.

"The place is an improvement over the New York winter weather, is it not, goddess?" He glanced up at the brilliant, starlit, tropical sky. Gorgeous. "Reminds me of the night with your sister."

She dug her heels into his sides like a rider spurring a belligerent horse.

"Ow. What was that for?" he asked.

"You spent the night with my sister?" she growled. "Which one? Fate?"

She had a sore spot for her sister, did she? He made a mental note—could come in handy later. "Your sister Cimil, actually. We spent a very...interesting evening in Mexico together when I found the tablet." Yes, it had been interesting. And by interesting, he meant disturbing. She continually rambled on and on about the understated joy of treasure hunting at garage sales. Then she froze in midsentence and made little circles with her hips as if spinning an invisible Hula-Hoop. He juddered.

"Oh. Cimil." Ixtab's killer heel grip relaxed.

Apparently she didn't see Cimil as a threat. Another mental note.

After several minutes of marching down the narrow path lined with thick-leaved plants and small torches, they arrived at an arched entryway with a wrought iron gate. He set the goddess down and tried to ignore how she felt when she slid down his back.

He pulled out his sheet of paper and punched in the code. The gate unlatched, and he pushed. Inside was a lush garden, spacious courtyard with an illuminated fountain, small fire pit, and soft music playing—Spanish guitar— from hidden speakers. He approached the elaborate stained-glass front door and entered. It reminded him of his family's beach home back in Spain. Warm sandstone-colored tile, wide-open living room leading out to what appeared to be a long torch-lit dock, and an indoor fire pit in the middle of the room with a giant stainless steel extractor. The muggy tropical air wasn't the least bit cold, but the fire looked warm and inviting nonetheless.

Antonio glanced over his shoulder at Ixtab. *Weather, weather, weather. Think weather. Think of the woman in your dreams. Think stars and moon. Think of anything but Ixtab's smell...* "The bedrooms look to be in that direction if you'd like to freshen up." He nodded to her right.

"Thanks." She sauntered away but toward the door leading to the dock instead. She slipped her dress over her head, offering him another glimpse of that perfect ass and the unveiled waves of long dark hair flowing down her back.

He sucked in a breath. *"Ay, mujer. Que picosa."* This time he looked without shame, drooling over her tanned, perfectly shaped ass and lavishing many impure thoughts upon it. Thoughts involving warm oils and his hands.

He made a little groan as she disappeared outside, then adjusted himself. Yes, thank the gods for leather pants and triple stitching.

Why is it, that moments of profound clarity—epiphanies, if you will—come at the most inopportune times? The ride to the villa had been one of those, and now Ixtab needed to think. Really, really think.

She sprinted toward the sanctuary of the cool lake water she'd swum in since she was a mere sprig of a goddess one human year old.

The coolness of the fresh water instantly refreshed her bare skin, but she wished it could do more than wash away the stale scent of the cenote on her body. So many years she'd lived. So many damned years watching people evolve. They lived, they loved, they felt pain and triumph, they failed and succeeded. Then they died. The irony was that watching the humans live their lives and the world evolve didn't make her feel like a part of it. To the contrary, she felt left behind. An outsider. Completely alone. Ultimately, like her brethren, she simply stopped evolving and growing as a living being. What was the point? There was no one to share it with.

One might think having thirteen brothers and sisters for eternity might provide some form of comfort for *this*. She couldn't quite call *this* a life, now could she? During the drive to the villa she realized that "siblings" or not—they weren't truly related, after all—her seventy thousand years of existence didn't come close to offering the same amount of joy one human being experienced in a single lifetime because she didn't have love. Not true love.

Not from a man who saw her soul, her light—ominous thunderclouds and rainbows included—and loved her for who she truly was. Thinking about Antonio offering himself to her as part of that stupid prank had made her realize that.

Her head broke through the water's glassy surface, and she stared up at the stars and the full moon. She sighed and glanced longingly toward the dock of the villa. Creator almighty, she felt drawn to that male, but she didn't want one night. She didn't want just sex, even though the newborn possibility of this intrigued her. No. She wanted more. She wanted to be hit over the head in love. She wanted to evolve. She wanted to grow up and then grow old with someone. She wanted to know she was the center of someone's universe. She wanted... a real life.

Just once. Just once. Just once.

The revelation stunned her. Perhaps because she'd spent an eternity burying these desires. Perhaps because she had spent the last two hundred years punishing herself for Francisco's death, believing he'd been the one for her. But had he been? What she felt for Antonio was so very, very different. With Francisco, she felt drawn to him, yes. She admired how he held the dying in his arms and showed them selfless compassion. His kindness was what she loved. However, Antonio... Deep breath. Her feelings left her mind and body spinning in a state of utter chaos. She craved him completely. He made her want all of those crazy things she'd never have: love, family, a life together... All of them impossible for someone like her, a goddess who trafficked dark energy.

If only she could change.

You?

Piff! Yeah, right. That's like asking a skunk to stop stinking. Her role was her role and that was that. It didn't matter how sad she felt about it.

Then another epiphany hit her like six tons of immortal bricks. Perhaps that was why Antonio was really there: to offer a chance. *To prove you are capable of compassion and good, to open the portal and help put the Universe back on its feet. Perhaps he is your ... catalyst for change.*

"Is he my ... spark?" she said quietly under her breath. Why else would the Universe create a man whose destiny was to become a vampire—*hearty enough to withstand my touch*—who looked like the mortal she once loved. Why else would the Universe throw them into this situation?

No, the thought was silly. The Universe didn't care about her, she was merely its slave. A slave without the right to hope for anything. Yet she did. Making her a fool. A simple, lonely fool. The resentment threatened to consume her.

She ducked under the water and swam and swam and swam until her humanlike body demanded oxygen, causing her to break the surface.

"Ixtab!" she heard Antonio call, his voice echoing from across the calm waters of the lake. Oh, how she loved the sound of him saying her name. "Ixtab!" he called out again. "Where'd you go?"

She released a long, slow breath and swam toward the dock, the darkness concealing her from his view. "I'm here, vampire. And you are to refer to me as Oh Divine One or have you forgotten?"

He dropped a towel on the dock, grunted, and stormed back inside.

I know how you feel ...

Ixtab toweled off and found one of the many well-appointed bathrooms, each furnished with the opulent luxury only the infamous Niccolo DiConti would obsess over. She showered with scented soaps and fruity lavender shampoo, and then blow-dried her waist-length hair, all the while thinking about Antonio and how badly she wanted her assumptions to be true.

And the only way to find out is to speak with him, openly and honestly. Yes, she was not a child. She was a grown goddess, thousands of years old and afraid of nothing.

She entered the attached bedroom   a modern, luxurious suite with the large vampire-sized bed covered with down pillows and white silky sheets. Laid out were several shopping bags. She opened them up and found black dresses and a veil and...a pair of black lace panties?

Penelope must've purchased these, because no way had the vampire gone out shopping, but what had Penelope been thinking? Ixtab held up the panties and inspected the miniscule scrap of fabric with curiosity. "How can anyone claim these are underpants?" She threw them over her shoulder. "Might as well go commanda."

She shrugged on a dress similar to the one she'd worn earlier, only this one was a bit shorter, cutting off right above the knees. Once again, the veil was a sheer, silky black and came down to her chin, not nearly long enough to cover her thick, waist-length tresses.

A heavenly, chocolaty smell saturated her nose, capturing her attention. My favorite dish! Deities didn't need to eat, but that didn't mean she wouldn't drop her panties—if she'd worn any—for a chocolate caramel soufflé.

Ixtab found her way to the kitchen and her eyes locked on a shirtless Antonio standing behind the chef's island among an explosion of mixing bowls and flour. The air whooshed from her lungs as she took in all of his muscled male glory—arms, chest, and neck lightly dusted with cocoa powder.

His olive-green eyes flickered with the unmistakable look of . . . hunger?

He then grumbled and dropped to his knees. All but his thick head of dark, messy hair disappeared behind the chef's island. "Ready for the ritual to commence, goddess?" he growled.

She snickered. Oh, this groveling would be the death of his poor male ego. *Good. That'll teach the beautiful man to crack my neck. He should learn to be more gentle.*

Even though she'd already forgiven him. "You may rise, Antonio," she conceded.

She blinked and he was standing again.

"Ah. I see you are beginning to master your speed," she said.

His eyes set firmly on her. "But not my strength, so you might want to avoid standing behind me. Or anywhere near me."

That wasn't what she wanted. At all. In fact, far too much time had passed since she'd touched him and now the craving gnawed at her.

Barefoot, she sauntered over, cleared a small spot on the counter, jumped up, and took a seat. "You'll have to be more careful then, won't you?" she said, facing him directly.

He shook his head and crossed his brawny arms over his perfect chest. Ixtab ogled him shamelessly. His skin—

smooth, firm, and tan—with endless cords of muscles looked so inviting. Yes, it had been far too long since she'd touched him. She ached for that euphoric pulse of energy rushing through her veins. She realized how truly addicted to him she'd become, but somehow, that only excited her all the more. She loved the feeling of their powerful connection.

"I want to touch you," she whispered. She could've simply done it without saying a word, but she needed to know if he craved her touch, too.

Towering over her, his gaze turned from hungry to downright carnivorous. He stepped a little closer and dropped his arms to his sides. The invitation sent her pulse soaring.

Slowly she reached out and ran the tips of her fingers over his collarbone, luxuriating in the feel of him as he watched.

"Why does your touch do that to me?" he asked as if astonished, pleased, and suspicious all at once.

She snapped back her hand, but he caught it in his, waiting for his answer, piercing her with his deep green eyes. She couldn't speak being this close to him, touching him. Smelling him was better than she'd remembered. Was it possible he'd become more desirable?

"Wh-what d-does it do to you?" she stuttered.

He slowly took her hand and laid it flat over his heart, his gaze never breaking from her obscured face. "It does all sorts of things."

Ixtab's head swirled. "L-l-like"—she swallowed—"wh-what?"

"It feels like a warm fire igniting in my veins," he said in a low, deep voice. "It fills me and yet leaves me hungry, wanting more. And it does…" Still holding her hand to his warm chest, he stepped nearer and pressed his lower torso against her closed legs. "This."

Ixtab made a little jerk and gasped as she felt his warm, hard cock against her knees.

Her heart began to thump wildly in her chest, and the heat rushed into her belly, continuing deeper. Oh, gods, she wanted him to part her legs and slide himself between her thighs. Her body lit up knowing that the only thing between them would be a pair of leather pants.

He brushed his warm fingertips over her collarbone, as she'd done to him. Oh, gods, she could feel his hot breath on her skin. She wanted him to touch every inch of her body.

He licked his lips and slid his hand through her curtain of hair and caressed the curve of her bare neck. "Your lips," he whispered, and bent his head just a little farther so that his mouth was directly over her ear, "were so soft and warm when I kissed them."

He'd kissed her? "When?" she asked, barely unable to keep from panting.

"While you were out cold, before you disappeared on me," he said softly, seductively.

She shuddered as her body pulsed and throbbed in the most delicious places. Had he looked at her face, too? "What else did you see?"

Still cupping the side of her neck, he moved his other hand under her veil and began stroking her lips. "Just these." He lightly nuzzled his face against hers before placing his hand over her chin. "And this." Then down the front of her neck. Was he trying to drive her mad? "I want to see the rest."

Take off her veil? Let him see her face?

Yes. She wanted this, too, she realized. She wanted him to see her. She needed him to gaze into her eyes and see her soul, to know if he might accept her for who she truly was.

This is it.

He gripped the edge of the fabric and began to pull.

The alarm buzzed behind him, and she suddenly jerked away from him.

His eyes instantly filled with irritation, and he stepped back, breaking their contact.

Oh no. Did he think she was rejecting him? "Antonio, I-I..."

He turned away and shut off the alarm. "I've set up your... your toe-worship station in the living room," he grumbled.

Toe-worship station? Penelope and Kinich had really gone overboard with the groveling instructions.

"Antonio, I want to—"

"I'm an idiot," he hissed under his breath.

"What? No, I—"

"I'll be there shortly," he said coldly.

Why wouldn't he let her explain? Because if he did, he'd hear how his touch was the best thing she'd ever experienced. He'd hear how she wanted more, but simply needed a moment to work up the courage to take off her veil. Because it wasn't just a veil; it was her armor, her penance, her way of thwarting the undeserved admiration of others.

"Very well, vampire." She left the room feeling mildly deflated. *Gods*, she was so *bad* at this whole intimacy thing! She completely came apart around him like a total fool!

She wondered down the hall to the opulent living room,

her mind spinning. She needed him to listen, to know her story: why she hid her face, how he looked exactly like Francisco, and how he could touch her when no one else could. She would tell him how he filled her with hope.

But how did one start such a conversation with a...

Damned stubborn, bossy vampire! She huffed. Didn't he know how hard this was for her? She had no experience with intimacy, physical or otherwise; it was completely unknown to her.

She rounded the corner into the living room and nearly tripped. A freshly lit log crackled in the fire pit, and white candles sprinkled every corner of the room with warm, flickering light. A pile of neatly folded, white, fluffy towels had been stacked next to an overstuffed armchair placed near the fire, along with a steaming metal tub of water that beckoned to her feet.

He'd done all this for her? None of this had been on the list.

Okay. Breathe. Breathe. You're a goddess. You can make him listen. You are strong. You are strong. You are... so lame! Stop acting like a child.

She sat in the chair and carefully dipped her toes in the water. The smell of roses instantly penetrated her nostrils, and she threw back her head. Every woman should be given the gift of immortal groveling. At least once a year. And with a man like Antonio—fiercely masculine and obscenely handsome. *Who is completely peeved at you!*

"Enjoying yourself?"

Ixtab looked up, but didn't see anyone.

"Down here, Oh Divine One," Antonio said petulantly.

"Oh, for heaven's sake, call me Ixtab."

"Yes, Ixtab," he said with a slow, deliberate pronunciation of each letter of her name and then flashed a fiercely carnal look her way.

She swooned right then and there. How could she say anything coherent when he looked at her that way?

She swallowed. "Antonio, I know you don't trust me, and I keep making a huge mess of everything, but I-I..." She fumbled with her words and tugged at her neckline. It was getting very hot in there.

Without breaking his raw gaze, he dipped his head, fished her feet from the tub, and pushed it aside. He wrapped the left foot in a warm, soft towel and firmly grasped the right. "Close your eyes."

"No. Wait," she protested. "You don't need to do this..." Her words trailed off as she became lost again in the sensation of his touch. Her nails dug into the padded arms of the chair. His hot, rough hands gently stroked her heel, but it felt as though he stroked her entire body. *Is this why so many human women get pedicures! Wow. Have I been missing out.*

"Close your eyes. Relax," he repeated briskly. This time she noticed his low, scratchy voice. *Ummm.* There was that itch again.

"I don't want to close my eyes. I want to..." *Oh, gods, that feels incredible. What was I saying?*

"Whatever pleases you," he said coldly, his strong fingers began gently working each toe. Oh, this was too much. Not only was he touching her, but also the sensuality of his hands was a sultry bliss. She stared down at his bare chest with its chiseled definition, the firelight behind him illuminating his muscular biceps—large biceps that flexed while his hands caressed and massaged her foot. The sight of him was more erotic than she could bear.

An unintentional groan escaped her mouth.

Antonio froze and looked up at her veiled face.

Dammit. She was making a fool of herself. He'd been tricked into this groveling scheme, forced to touch her. That's not what she wanted. She wanted real. She wanted...him.

Okay, it was time for that talk. She snapped her foot away. "That's enough. Antonio, there's something—"

He swiped her foot and placed it firmly between his two hands. "I'm not done yet," he growled.

Again, she snapped her foot away. "No. I think you are."

His eyes lit with fury. "What? Not good enough for you? Is a disgusting vampire defiling the sanctity of your toes?" Again, he grabbed her foot.

"What? No. I only want to—"

He rose up on his knees, placing himself firmly between her thighs, and pushed her back in the seat. "I flew all the way down here to grovel for your pompous, arrogant ass over something that was an accident. So, I dare you to insult me again. I dare you to move another inch, Oh Divine One, before I've completed this foot rub."

Why wouldn't he let her speak, for gods' sake? And why was he making her own immortal groveling so damned hard?

"Or what?" she seethed.

His eyes said, *I double-triple dare you to find out!*

Dammit, she didn't want to fight with him. She wanted to talk. She wanted to know if her heart, her soul, should dare to dream that Antonio might be the Universe granting her wish.

Let him finish the foot rub. Maybe he'll calm down and

then you can talk. She grumbled like a petulant child and relaxed in the chair, signaling her submission. He sank back on his heels, grabbed the bottle of oil to his side, coated his hand, and spitefully jerked her foot directly in front of him.

He slathered each toe and then her heel and ankle. When his strong hand reached the lower calf muscle, he looked straight up the line of her leg and froze. She watched as his eyes zeroed in, right on her.

Oops. She snapped her legs shut as his gaze turned from a deep olive green to charcoal black.

Uh-oh. A vampire with black eyes only meant one of three things: hungry, angry, or inconsolably horny.

In her case it had to be...Well, it had to be...*He just looked at your womanly pride and joy. But he couldn't possibly...*

She tried to retrieve her foot but it was in vampire lockdown.

His head dipped and he placed his warm mouth forcefully over her pinkie toe. A tiny squeal involuntarily escaped her mouth followed by his groan.

"You liked that, did you?" he said in a gravelly voice. His mouth moved to her ankle and sucked. "You like having a disgusting vampire touch you, don't you, Ixtab?"

Chest heaving, hands gripping the armchair for dear life, she replied, "I don't think you're disgusting—" She felt the faint scrape of a fang brush her lower calf as his hot tongue and mouth massaged their way up another inch. "I think you're— Oh, gods." Every touch, every miniscule point of contact felt like exquisite, little convulsions rocketing through her body. After thousands of years of being deprived of physical contact, every inch of her skin lit up with sensual explosions. She gripped the chair even harder.

"Say it. You think I'm what?" he asked with that heavy voice saturated with sex. One strong hand slid its way up her inner thigh while his mouth and tongue slowly worked their way up the inside of the other leg.

"Very...very..." She clamped her eyes shut and felt his sharp teeth scrape their way a little higher.

"Very what?" His hot breath bathed her inner thigh. Then one hand moved another inch and then another until she felt their roughness brush over her sensitive flesh between her legs.

She bucked lightly and her nipples hardened to sharp points. "Oh, gods." *Naughty vampire.* No one had ever touched her like that. Ever. And the most arousing thing of all was how he took control. No shame or shyness. No permission asked. He simply did what pleased him. Gods be damned, but now she knew what she'd been missing out on all these thousands of years. In her wildest dreams she would never have imagined.

"Very sexy," she finally answered with a breath.

"Good," he replied and then ran one hot finger down the middle of her slick valley. "Now, show me how much you like me."

Show him? Show him? If she did that, she would be grabbing that thick dark hair of his and riding his face like a drunk cowgirl who'd found the last bronking bucko on the planet.

His mouth worked an inch closer to her sensitive bud, and she knew only a moment of contact would be required. He withdrew his hand to make way for his mouth in the space she'd narrowly allowed him. *Oh, gods...*

She glanced down to see the most erotic sight she'd ever witnessed. His one hand had reached down to free his hard cock from the confinement of those hot leather pants. She couldn't see his manhood, but she saw the unmistakable, rhythmic pumping of his hand.

Holy deities of sex and sin, he was pleasuring himself to the view of her.

"Tu flor de mujer es tan exquisita." He groaned.

Had he just called her womanly bit an exquisite flower? Her mind swam in an endless, delicious mess of sexual images displayed before her.

The exact moment his mouth covered her flower, his free hand slid up her torso and clasped her breast over the fabric of her dress. With his large, firm touch he massaged her breast in time to the expert strokes of his delving tongue and pumping hand.

Holy deities of ancient Babylonia, she'd never experienced such a sensation.

"Don't stop. Ohmygods. Don't stop."

His silky, hot tongue dipped and stroked and glided over the tiny bundle of sparkling nerves. They coiled with delicious tension. "Oh, gods, don't stop."

His hot, panting breath quickened with each tiny jab of his tongue. "Never. You taste so delicious. So fucking sweet."

"Yes. Yes." She was centimeters away from experiencing that wave of mind-crippling nirvana. She rocked her pelvis against his tongue. "Holy stars and moon, Francisco!"

He stopped.

She stopped.

Every creature on the planet stopped to tsk in her general direction.

Shit. Shit. Shit. Did I call him Francisco?

"Did you just say... 'Holy stars and moon, *Francisco*?'" He scowled.

Yes... Yes, I did. Shit.

Before she could say a word, Antonio was gone.

Oh no. Oh no...

Maybe there was such a thing as second chances. But what she now needed was a third.

Veintiuno

"What do you mean, you 'lost' Antonio?" Penelope asked from the other end of the cell phone.

Ixtab paced across the giant gourmet chef's kitchen, glaring at the perfect little chocolate caramel soufflé. "Stop mocking me. Okay? It was a perfectly innocent mistake."

"I'm not mocking you," Penelope replied. "I'm confused."

"I was talking to the soufflé." Ixtab turned her back on the dessert, which served as a sad little reminder of how she'd wrecked the entire evening. "What's there to be confused about? I lost him."

I really, really lost him. The one male in the Universe who'd perhaps been born for her.

"How does one 'lose' a vampire exactly?"

"Well, we were...um...Antonio and I were—"

Penelope squealed on the other end of the phone. "I

knew it! I knew it! You do like him! And I could tell he's totally into you, too. The way he pretends to hate you, it's so fifth grade. So how was it? Did you?"

Ixtab cringed as she heard Kinich's deep voice in the background over the phone.

"I think they did it," Penelope told him.

"Did she keep the veil on?" Kinich asked.

"I don't know. Let me ask," she replied to him.

Ugh! Idiots. "Yes. I kept the veil on, but we didn't have sex." *We might've if I hadn't screwed it up.* Worst of all, she'd humiliated him. Now he would never trust her, and she would suffer an eternity without knowing what they really meant to each other.

"Why not? Were you too afraid? Because my mom told me what you look li—"

"I called him by another man's name," Ixtab blurted out. "In the heat of the moment."

"Oh, that's bad," Penelope replied. "She called him another man's name," she repeated to Kinich, who began laughing hysterically in the background.

"Glad you find this funny," Ixtab barked.

"Ssssh, honey. Let me finish talking to her." Pause. "Sorry, Ixtab. I'm listening."

"Good. Because he left and took the tablet with him."

"Maybe he's on his way back to New York," Penelope offered.

Ixtab shrugged and turned around. The soufflé still sat there on the large granite island, still mocking her with its giant chocolaty goodness. "I checked with the Uchben. They haven't seen him."

"He probably took a commercial plane."

Ixtab's phone beeped. "Hold on." She pulled the device

from her ear and saw a text. It was from the Uchben chief. *Crapola.*

She returned the phone to her ear. "The Uchben tracked him through Customs. He got on a flight to Spain."

"I guess you're going to Spain, then. Would you like me to text you the immortal groveling instructions?" Penelope offered.

"No, thanks. I've got it committed to memory."

"Ixtab? I know I don't have to say this, but we need him."

Silence. "I know." There were less than eight months left to open the portal. "What I don't understand is how you can be so calm and so happy."

"I have faith. And I have Kinich."

"So, you don't believe the end is near?" Ixtab asked.

"No. I don't. Because you are going to fix this. That portal will open; we will get our warriors back and win. There is no other possible outcome."

Ixtab wished she were as confident as Penelope. But in all her thousands of years, she'd never seen the cards so stacked against them. Most of all, she'd never seen one of Cimil's prophecies be wrong; although now, they all understood that Cimil couldn't truly see the future—she merely spoke to the dead, who apparently lived in another dimension where time ceased to exist, which was an entirely different conundrum altogether. Still, she'd never seen Cimil once be wrong. If she said the world would end before the autumnal equinox, then it would.

Ixtab sighed. "I'll get the vampire physicist back." *Somehow.* Maybe she was making this into a bigger deal than it was? She'd only called him by another man's name. It was an honest mistake. And once she explained the reason behind it, he would understand. *Or perhaps he will find it disturbing that he looks like the lost love of your life and believe that's the only reason you want him.*

Then again, Antonio had fared well with all of the oddities thrown his way. Extremely well. Magical tablets, vampirism, deities. Nothing seemed to faze him.

Except you...

Somewhere in Europe...

Giant, furry pink suitcase in hand, Cimil skidded on her red platform shoes into the ultra-baroque-style living room of Roberto's vampire lair. "Honey!" she screamed. "Have you seen my pony?"

There was no reply. "Roberto! Pony! Now!"

Again, no reply.

Cimil stomped her foot. "One would think a vampire might have better hearing."

Cimil turned and slammed into a tall, cold wall. "Ugh! I hate it when you sneak up on me like that. Have you seen my pony? It's time to go, and you can't be late. You must be there when the portal opens and make sure nothing goes wrong!"

Roberto didn't respond.

Cimil sighed. "I know they're expecting *me*, not you, but that doesn't matter."

Roberto blinked.

"Of course, I'm worried," Cimil replied. "Ixtab has to get sucked in with the incubus, and the Maaskab cannot leave. The events are all tied together and there's a point zero-zero-zero-zero-zero-zero-one chance that the physicist will fail. Got it?"

Roberto, with his black eyes and equally black hair, shook his head slowly. Then again, Roberto seemed to do everything as if he had all the time in the world. Which they didn't. That clock was ticking, and there was no room for errors. Not this time.

"Gasp!" She shook her finger at him. "You ate him! Didn't you? You ate Mr. Mylittle!"

Roberto shrugged casually.

"Dammit!" Cimil smacked him on the chest. "I told you to stop eating my pets—except for the clowns. They're okay, but fangs off the others!"

Roberto simply stared.

"Oh, don't you give me that look," she quibbled. "It was no honest mistake. You knew that pony was special. Hell in a bicycle basket! We'll talk about this later; we'll miss our plane! Grab the luggage, would you?"

Roberto dipped his head and followed her out the door.

No, no room for mistakes now. Everything was going according to plan, and it was up to her to ensure things stayed that way.

Veintidós

Antonio's family lived about an hour northwest of Barcelona in one of the oldest winemaking regions of Europe near Vilafranca del Penedès. The area also held the distinction of housing the Santa Maria de Montserrat abbey, home to the world's oldest, functioning printing press and the sacred Black Madonna. Ironically, it had been the monastery Francisco belonged to. Maybe that's why Ixtab hadn't visited this place for centuries and opted to spend most of her time in densely populated cities that provided plentiful distractions from her woes.

As the town car wound up the tree-lined hillside, neat little rows of skeletal, hibernating vines blanketing every visible mile, she couldn't help but remember how the world once looked. Life was so much simpler before its taming. For humans and for deities.

Really now? Back then, only the most powerful and wealthy of humans were entitled to a good life free from starvation, tyranny, and oppression. And modern medicine, well, what a horrible misery life was for the masses before its existence. There was a time, not so long ago, that mothers watched their children die from the flu. They were lucky if a few survived to adulthood. Yes, everyone struggled. As for deities, well, back then, life wasn't a box of assorted doughnuts, either, now that she really thought about it. Unlike her other brethren, her power of releasing one's soul from darkness required a more...personal touch, one might say. Long journeys over oceans on rickety wooden boats, weeks on horseback or by foot, it could take twelve months to travel from the portal in Mexico to eastern Europe or Asia.

Funny how one always yearned for the past, simpler times, but conveniently forgot the difficulties. That was her problem, really. Wasn't it? She lived in the past, a made-up, perfect past with Francisco. But it didn't exist. It never had. And now she was throwing away something real for a fantasy. Yes, there was a reason she called out Francisco when Antonio had been touching her so intimately. In her heart, she truly hadn't let go. What she needed to do was live in the present. Not the past, not the future where one hopes for better days ahead, but the present. Because now is all anyone truly has.

Okay, well right now, *you need to get your groveling speech ready.*

Right.

Ixtab flipped open the manila folder she'd been carrying in her bag and thumbed through Antonio's file once again. Penelope had supplied it several weeks ago, but for some reason, she hadn't given it much thought. It was one of the more fascinating mortal family histories, with generations of royalty dating back to the 700s. What struck her as odd, however, wasn't their exaggerated wealth—they had more money, land, and assets across the globe than the world's largest company—but that over the last several centuries, they'd stayed out of the limelight. No political ties, no newspaper articles, no Oprah specials. And humans were obsessed with such powerful families—the Kennedys, the English royal family, the Gates, the Wiggles—but the Aceros were an unknown.

Ixtab gazed out the tinted window of the backseat. Though the day was sunny, the cold seeped through the glass. Or maybe something else caused the chill in her bones. As the car passed the open gates, with the name Acero in wrought iron proudly arched over the lane, she distinctly felt the growing presence of a dark energy. Her teeth began to chatter.

"Le subo la temperatura, señorita?" asked the driver.

"No, gracias." He could raise the thermostat to one hundred and it wouldn't make a lick of a difference. For whatever reason Antonio came here, she now knew it wouldn't be good. No mortal, or immortal for that matter, would want to come here. *Yet this is his home? He grew up here?*

The car traveled along the hillside overlooking acres of slumbering vines below until they reached another gate, this one closed. The driver pulled up to the intercom and lowered his window.

Before he spoke, the spiked iron gates slid open, creaking and whining the entire way as if setting the scene for a horror movie about to unravel.

Damn. This place was creepy. And *this* coming from the Goddess of Suicide.

The car pulled forward to an empty, gravel-covered, circular driveway. The large three-story home—a simple Spanish-style with tiled, arched doorways and wrought iron balconies with flowing red vines—had to be a hundred-plus years old.

The flutter of a curtain from the top story window caught Ixtab's eye, but the face quickly shrank back into the shadows. Ixtab's heart plucked away at an unsteady rhythm inside her chest. Why was she so nervous? Was it the darkness she sensed or the fact that she was about to see Antonio?

She slipped from the car and grabbed her bag from the Uchben driver, who of course knew the drill. *"Gracias. Y quédate cerca, por favor."*

The driver nodded and indicated he'd stay in the nearby town. Good. Who knew how long she would be here. Five minutes or five weeks. Whatever it took to make things right with Antonio.

She walked up and rang the doorbell, but no one came. They'd already seen her arrive, so why not? Did Antonio simply think she'd scamper away?

She waited another moment and decided to open it herself. Heck, she was a deity. *Leave the social norms to the humans.*

"Hello?" The oxidized hinges of the thick wooden door creaked as she stepped inside the dimly lit entryway with a vaulted ceiling. The floor was tiled with faded blue and reddish-brown Moroccan tiles, and to each side, a grand tiled staircase curved up to a landing.

She dropped her bag next to the large potted plant and gazed up. "Hello?" she called out.

A burst of warm air collided with her face and sent

her mind spinning. The aroma carried memories with it. Powerful memories. The smell of roasting chili peppers and dried flowers from the market in Santiago where she'd once strolled with Francisco. The smell of rosemary and lemons—Francisco always smelled of the tonics used to bathe the sick.

Dammit, goddess. You have to let go! You will lose Antonio if you don't.

"May I help you?"

Ixtab jumped.

A petite woman with one lazy eye and dark hair pulled back, wearing a traditional maid's uniform, appeared.

"I'm here to see Antonio," Ixtab said.

The woman's one good eye scrutinized Ixtab's draping, black outfit.

"It's all the rage in Paris," Ixtab said dryly. "Let me know if you want me to hook you up. But I warn you, prepare to be mobbed by flocks of nude male models."

The woman narrowed her one good eye. "I am Kirstie. Follow me, please."

That seemed like an oddly peppy name for such a sour-looking woman. "Fine, your loss, Kirstie; I can't seem to keep the hotties off me." *Of course, they all die, but who's asking?*

The woman led Ixtab up the right-hand staircase to where the landing expanded into a great room with Saltillo tiles, a large fireplace, and a sitting area that connected to a long hallway with large windows to one side and arched doorways leading to other rooms. "Wait here, please."

Ixtab took a seat on the soft white sofa and watched the strange woman disappear down the hallway.

Antonio appeared out of nowhere. "Why the hell are you here?"

Christ! Ixtab jumped again. What was with these people sneaking up?

Ixtab looked at Antonio and instantly melted. A barrage of emotions and sensations washed over her. One out of the three was naughty.

Number one: Not naughty. Seeing Antonio again instantly loosened that horrible tension constricting the flow of energy in her chest. She could finally breathe again, and her heart fluttered away at a cheerful pace as if it were clapping and jumping up and down, overwhelmed with jubilation.

Number two: Not naughty. She couldn't help but take notice of how tired Antonio looked. It saddened her because she knew this was her doing. She'd chased him away, wounded his pride. He was the one person in all the world she'd give anything to make happy, yet she'd done the opposite.

Number three: Naughty. Her girly goddess parts started a little square dance. Despite his worn appearance, he still looked delicious. He'd ditched the sexy leather pants for a pair of his trademark faded jeans and a navy-blue Hollister tee that one might accuse of being one size too small. Not Ixtab, however. At the first moment possible, she'd find a lame excuse to get him to reach for something, somewhere on a very high shelf, which would allow her a peek of his sleek, sexy lower abs that she already knew included a manly trail of dark hair leading the way to a very wonderful place.

Stop that. You came to grovel and come clean with him. This is your chance.

"You still haven't eaten, have you?" she asked.

"You came all this way to nag me?" He crossed his thick arms over his wide chest.

"No. I came to..." *Beg you to forgive me.* "...Talk. Can we go somewhere more private, Antonio?" She knew that creepy Kirstie lurked in the shadows, listening.

Antonio's deep green eyes narrowed. "You remembered my name. How gracious of you, Oh Divine One."

Ixtab's entire face tightened with the jab. "I deserved that. I know. But if you could give me ten—or fifteen— actually, given my age and the length of the story, I might need sixty minutes. Each day. For a week."

He frowned and made a little "no way" grumble.

"Please? Besides, if you don't hear me out, your cougar fantasies may never come true."

He gripped his waist with one hand. "A seventy-thousand-year-old isn't even close to '*cougar.*' You're more saber-toothed tiger."

Touché. "And yet, I wager you to find a female of legal age purer than me." She raised her eyebrows. "Pure as the driven snow, and more eager to melt than Thanksgiving turkey."

A flicker of amusement danced in his eyes. "Sorry. Not into poultry."

"How about gravy?" she asked.

"No."

"Ah yes. A vegetarian. Pumpkin pie, then?" Yumm... who could resist?

"Not hungry."

Okay. This conversation had taken a very odd culinary detour and was heading for a dark cavern filled with lonely, cold nights.

She sighed, reached out, and placed her hand on his bulky upper arm. How she'd missed touching him. Gods, it was euphoric. "Please. I don't want to talk about holiday dinners. I just want a few minutes. Listen to what I have to say, and then I'll leave if you like. It's important."

His harsh expression instantly softened. And dammit if she didn't see the bags under her eyes disappear. Or had she imagined it? It was as if he'd suddenly transformed into a vision of vampire health. Even that hard line of lips now held a hint of curve on one side.

Ixtab yipped on the inside. *He's happy! He's happy to see me!*

"My quarters are this way." He bowed his head and gestured toward the hallway. "After you."

She passed him and felt his eyes burning into her. "I see you've reverted back to your original costume," he said.

She smiled brightly. "Just wait until you see what I haven't got on underneath."

That ought to shut him up.

It did.

How the hell did she know he'd be there? Hell, not even *he* expected to be there. Five minutes after he'd left the villa in Bacalar, unsure he'd ever be able to bear the sight of the goddess again—because surely her "slip" had been meant as a slight, intended to put him in his place for what he'd done to her—he had received the call and then gotten on the next flight out.

So why the hell had she come? Was it to insist the humiliation ritual continue? If yes, the goddess had another thing coming. She could bring down a rain of locusts or peppercorns or…*whatthehellever*, and it wouldn't change his mind. He was done with these ridiculous deities because his fucking time was up. With that one phone call back in Bacalar, everything in his world had changed; the day he'd spent a lifetime fearing had finally arrived, and now nothing mattered. Only opening that portal.

He followed her into his room, a large suite toward the back of the estate on the third floor overlooking the vineyard. Though he hadn't been home in over six years, they'd kept it ready. It was a sign his father knew this day would come and he'd return. "You cannot negate your duty any more than you can the Acero blood flowing through your veins. Doesn't matter how far you run, there isn't anywhere I can't find you."

But Antonio, from the moment he'd understood what it truly meant to be an Acero, hoped he'd find a way for him and his brother to escape the path so many had taken before. He had much higher hopes for their humanity.

Antonio shut the door behind him and scrutinized the woman draped in bulky layers of black lace. By now, however, he'd learned not to judge an Ixtab book by its Ixtab cover. Underneath the facade of a woman resembling an old-world widow from Italy was an ancient, immortal female with a tongue as sharp as a sword and equally capable of taking down a man. And from the first moment she'd touched him, he realized her hold over him was slightly more dangerous; he was addicted to something within her.

And I hate her for it.

Not only was she distracting him from his fate, but

she'd humiliated him. Called him Francisco of all the goddamned, *pinche* names in the world. Perhaps it served him right; what had he been thinking becoming intimate with her? *She's nothing but an evil goddess.* A distraction who pleasured in his suffering from day one. *A monster. Just like her sister said.*

He crossed his arms and leaned against the door, putting as much distance between them as possible. "All right. We are somewhere private. Now, speak. Why the *diablos* are you here, woman?"

"Woman?" It had been eons since anyone had called her that.

His eyes narrowed. "Cut the *mierda*, goddess. Are you here to humiliate me further?"

Ixtab's eyes surveyed the sparsely decorated room. A large bed and a sitting area, no personal belongings— similar to his apartment in New York. It was as if he rejected the notion of having a real home. Why?

"No," she said, "I don't want to humiliate you. I'm here because I want to tell you that—"

"I have every intention of unlocking the portal," he interrupted. "So you've wasted your time coming here if it was to convince me to continue my work."

His vampire sass began to boil her blood. "If you cut me off one more time, I swear I'll ... sizzle your man junk with an assorted array of spicy seasoning. I came to apologize. And because I thought you might need my help."

"Actually"—he dropped his arms and walked toward the large glass double doors leading toward his private

balcony—"I made significant progress last night. Alone."
He yanked open the doors and stepped outside.

The winter sun hit him directly in the face, but he
didn't shirk away. How strange. He seemed to bask in the
warm rays like a mortal. Normally, vampires avoided the
sun, given how it drained their power.

He glanced at her from outside. "You've got ten minutes. Then you need to leave."

Grrr...

Deep breath. Patience...

Ixtab blinked and followed him outside. "All right. But
no interrupting. Got it?" He didn't reply so she took it as
a yes and began telling Antonio about the man she once
loved. Two hundred years ago she'd found him, a Benedic-
tine monk who had forsaken his family to travel the world
to help the destitute, the lost, and the sick. "It wasn't what
one might expect or see in a corny mortal movie," she
explained. "A fatal illness had ravaged Chile. Most hard-
hit was Santiago, and those who remained were stricken
with grief. I worked day and night, helping to clear out
their darkness so that those who lived could move on.
Everywhere I went, I saw him. The poorest of neighbor-
hoods, the makeshift hospitals, the churches where the
living gathered to mourn. He was everywhere, fearless,
holding the hands of the dying until their time came. I
watched from a distance at first, but after a week, I could
not ignore him. Something about his light drew me in."

Ixtab held back a sob. She'd never told anyone the entire
story—not even Kinich—and now, reliving it brought her
back to that exact moment in time. Fresh as yesterday.

"He and I became friends—more than friends, really. I
wanted him. He wanted me. But I knew being with a man

wasn't possible. Still, he insisted we were meant to be together. He begged me to kiss him, touch him, and swore there was nothing to fear; fate had brought us together. Though I didn't tell him I was a goddess, I did tell him I was . . . different. Poison. He didn't care. His conviction, his willingness to leave his life behind for me"—she looked into Antonio's intensely focused eyes—"was so strong that I believed he was right." Ixtab made a pathetic little shrug. "Until he touched me. Before I realized he'd been wrong, he'd made it to the cupboard and swallowed rat poison. I did everything I could, but he died."

Ixtab held her breath for several moments before she finally gathered the will to tell the next part of the story; he looked like Francisco.

She took a deep breath. "This is why—"

"I get it," he interrupted. "You've got a history. A painful one. And you still love this man. So let me ease your suffering from believing you need to put me out of my misery and let me down easily. I'm not interested in you."

Ouch. "You're not?"

"No." His gaze was cool and sure. "The other night was nothing more than a fulfillment of an obligation for your silly immortal groveling ritual."

Double ouch. He'd only made a move on her because he felt he had to and not because he wanted to? It was exactly what she'd been afraid of.

Ixtab mentally crumbled underneath her veil. "I see," she muttered.

He cleared his throat. "And though I'm very sorry for what you've been through, for your loss, you're not the only one who has a past filled with painful secrets."

"Such as?"

"If that were any of your damned business, I would have told you by now."

Reason number nine—somethingorother that vampires are icky: they can be so damned cold for no apparent reason.

Ugh! Well, she'd had just about enough of that. "Mr. Icky Vampire, may I remind you that you're speaking to a deity. And while I realize your brain may be running at half steam because you've yet to feed and that you're angry about the little name slipup, if you speak to me like that again, I *will* punish you."

Antonio stepped in and closed the space between them. "Be my guest," he snarled.

H-h-he's daring me? Me? "Don't say I didn't warn you..." Ixtab reached out, intending to give him a little taste of something she liked to call...an Ixtab spanking: a hint of chili pepper. In his nether region. After all, what was the use of being the goddess of natural seasoning if you couldn't deploy the power of the chili pepper on command?

But as she reached, Antonio caught her hand. He stared down at her, fuming. Several angry moments passed, him studying her. Her studying him.

"What's really under that veil, Ixtab?" he whispered. "What are you afraid of?"

"Why are you *really* so angry at me?"

"You first," he growled.

Gods, he was gorgeous. The way his upper lip with that pronounced dip in the middle twitched when he was mad. The way those deep green eyes flickered to black as he lost control. The way the pulse in his neck visibly strummed away. She loved seeing him so full of...life.

What an odd thought. Vampires weren't full of life. *Antonio is.*

"I'm not afraid. I'm a goddess. I fear nothing." *Except perhaps losing you...*

"Really, now?" A resentful laugh bubbled from his lips. "Prove it. Take it off."

Could she let him see her? Yes, she'd already determined that she wanted him to look into her eyes and truly see who she was on the inside. She wanted to know if he was her mate, because standing before him, she now knew she wanted him with every spark of her immortal light.

"Remove it yourself," she said, lifting her chin.

He didn't hesitate for a moment to grab for the lace. But just as he began to tug, he stopped. His face turned pale.

"What are you waiting for?" she said.

He didn't respond.

"Are you afraid you'll hate what you see?"

He dropped his hand and stepped back. "I need to go and see my father." He turned toward the door.

"Wait."

He stopped in the doorway, but didn't turn around. She watched him take several breaths. "I'm not afraid," he said, "that I'll hate what I see—it's the opposite. And right now, I cannot afford any distractions. Too much is at stake."

Ixtab's pulse quickened with his admission. He considered her a temptation? She felt the rush of hope gushing through her veins.

Yes! Disco dance!

And the feeling in her chest was a sure sign that her heart had finally healed. Dare she even believe the

Universe cared about someone like her, that she, too, deserved to be happy and have love?

An odd tension filled the air, and she sensed the dark thoughts spinning over his head like a tornado of despair. What was he afraid of?

She walked over and placed her hand on his back. Gods, she couldn't get enough of this, of touching him. "Why? Why are you *really* afraid to see me?"

Finally, he let out a sigh. "You should know that one of the reasons I'm working on the tablet is because the woman I am destined to be with is on the other side of that portal. And while I admit I feel a certain... attraction for you, I know it isn't real. You are not her." He walked away, leaving Ixtab there to digest those words all alone.

Veintitrés

⌐

Antonio's words felt like a hard kick to Ixtab's gut. *Woman? On the other side?* Why hadn't he ever mentioned this? *You dramawhore, Universe! How could you?*

Antonio couldn't possibly be destined for another female. Could he? It didn't seem right. Not when the connection between them felt so powerful, like the Universe herself had forged it with the strength from her very own heart.

Ixtab couldn't decide if she felt angry or heartbroken. Or both. *Both! Vampires Are Icky reason number ten: because they're like tumbleweeds; they'll roll on top of anything!*

Ixtab walked over to Antonio's neatly made bed and sat down. Her heart sagged. None of this made any sense. How had the woman gotten there? How had he met her? How did he know that this woman was destined to be his? Why would the Universe bring Antonio into her life only to give him to another?

Dammit! She couldn't accept this. How could she have lost him already? Had she been wrong about her feelings?

Yes! Because you're an idiot! A complete idiot! Of course, he doesn't want you. You. Are. Not. Destined. To. Ever. Love. The Universe hates you. She always has, and she always will.

"You're not my brother's usual type. Although it's hard to tell with that outfit you're wearing," said a deep voice.

Ixtab turned her head and instantly felt the room swirl in such a way that indicated her humanlike body might go into shock—ironically, the same thing happened the last time she was in Spain. But that was because she'd stupidly tried to assist a large crowd of people hell-bent on killing themselves. Unfortunately, the bulls had already been set free. Who knew the beasts loved black lace?

Well, this time her body wasn't suffering from a blow to the ribs, but from another blow to her heart, mind, and soul. Because when the Universe decided to roll with a doozy—i.e., producing the most improbable outcome thinkable—well, the bitch had flair. *Fucking Universe.*

Ixtab slowly rose to face Antonio's brother.

"Let me guess," he said, "Antonio didn't tell you about me?"

Ixtab cleared her throat. "No." The word still came out scratchy.

The man bobbed his head and produced an arrogant smirk. A beautiful, arrogant smirk. "Yes. He's learned the hard way that telling women he has an identical twin isn't the smartest move."

Ixtab shook her head slowly. "N-n-no. I suppose it's not." *How could you, Universe? How? You made two copies of Francisco? Come! On! Goddamned, dramawhore!*

Wait. Hold your whoreses! This situation could no longer fall into the quirky-way-of-the-Universe category. There were two men who closely resembled the man she once loved and snubbed out? This situation had officially become an "Oh, hell no!" Something unearthly was going on.

But what the heck was it? She didn't have a crumb of a deity inkling.

Hmmm...Cloning?

No. Francisco died long ago before any technology existed to store DNA.

Hmmm...

Space aliens were stealing her memories and using them to create people suits to live inside?

No. The gods had put a stop to that little cluster of a situation last year, after those Cimilites (yes, yes, they named their damned planet after her—*idiots*) were discovered. One would think such an advanced civilization would have been more careful to not get caught. *And know that there's only enough space in the Universe for one Lady Gaga.*

No, *señor*, something else had to be going on. What was it?

Ixtab sighed and looked the man over. He was absolutely gorgeous. The same dark green eyes, powerfully built frame, and olive skin. Only this identical version had delicious waves of dark, jaw-length hair, wore plain khaki pants and a white polo. He was also warm and full of life.

Human. Ixtab sighed. He was lovely.

"Oh, gods," she whispered. "Please don't tell me your name is...Francisco."

Antonio's brother laughed. "Yes, it is. How did you know?"

Well, that explained the man tantrum Antonio had in Bacalar.

He walked over to Ixtab and held out his hand. "My family calls me Franco for short. Francisco is what we call my father."

Ixtab's pulse thumped away at a million immortal miles an hour. *His father?* Okay. Her goddess alarm went to DEFCON one. This situation screamed supernatural conspiracy, though she couldn't figure out what could possibly be happening.

She looked at Franco. Yes, he was identical to Antonio in every way. Would she be able to touch him, too? The possibility tumbled loudly in her head like a pair of sneakers in a dryer. Then she looked down at Franco's outstretched hand. She knew she shouldn't, but she felt entranced, as if in a bizarre dream or an alternate universe. She slowly lifted her hand to shake his.

"Don't fucking touch her." Antonio moved quicker than the eye and swiped Franco's arm away.

Ixtab's moral compass snapped into place. *Holy crap.* What had she been thinking? She cupped her hands over her veiled face. "Ohmygods, I'm so sorry."

You're in shock. Yes, hot-man shock. Oh, please don't let me see doubles. Please don't let me see doubles. Of the doubles. Because that would be a little too ABC Family teen special.

Franco turned and snarled at his brother. *"Qué? Qué me dijiste?"*

"You heard me." Antonio bellied up to his brother and growled in his face. "Don't," he said in a low, quiet, menacing sort of way. "Touch. Her. Don't *ever* touch her."

Franco laughed. "Calm the hell down, *coño*. I'm not

going to steal her from you." He looked at Ixtab and studied her as if attempting to decipher if what lie hidden beneath the shroud was worth competing for. Then he flashed a wicked little smile and added, "Yet."

Uh-oh. That meant, "Game on." Ixtab stepped back, waiting for the boy explosion. And shockingly, some sick, twisted part of her wanted to block out the perturbing details of the situation and instead focus in on a little fantasy involving mud. Goddesses had their pervy little twin fantasies, too.

"You'll have to excuse my brother's poor manners," Franco said. "I'm afraid we have a long history with women. If you're staying for dinner, perhaps I'll get the chance to tell you all about it."

Ixtab felt oddly annoyed. She didn't want to hear about any other women in Antonio's life.

"She's not staying," Antonio growled.

"I'm not?" Ixtab retorted.

"No," Antonio replied.

"Says who?" she asked. "Last time I checked, I superseded you on the evolutionary totem pole." And she wasn't going anywhere until she got to the bottom of whatever the hell was going on.

Antonio's eyes narrowed and his face turned a pissy shade of red.

"I'll leave you two lovebirds to quarrel alone." Franco winked at Ixtab. "I hope we meet again."

"Don't count on it," grumbled Antonio, watching his brother leave.

"Why the *hell* didn't you tell me you had an evil twin?"

Antonio studied her. "He's not evil."

"Well, he doesn't seem like the nicer version of you."

Antonio rubbed his brow. "He is angry with me for not being here sooner. That is all."

"Okay. So he's not your evil twin. Point for Antonio. Now why the hell didn't you tell me about him?" she asked.

"Why would I?"

"Well…well, I guess— I don't know. Normally humans tell everyone such unique tidbits about their lives. They can't help it; it makes them feel special."

Antonio shrugged. "I'm not human; I'm a vampire."

"Don't start. Why were you hiding this? What aren't you telling me?"

"I'm not hiding anything." His body went rigid.

"Then why are you suddenly cloaked in a cloud of bloated cockiness? For the record, bloated cockiness is the same as cockiness, but without the legitimacy factor. Kind of like when a really stupid person tells you how they rock at *Jeopardy!* when you know that isn't the case."

Anger simmered in his eyes. "I'm *not* hiding anything. And I do not appreciate your questioning my integrity."

"Oh. Look at that. You just moved up the ladder to defensive cocky. Why do men always do that? Instead of simply owning up when they've been caught lying, they behave as if they're at a cocky poker game. I'll see your defensive cockiness and raise you to colossal cock," she said in a deep mocking voice. "Oh, well then, I'll see your colossal cock and raise you…." Ixtab burst out laughing.

"What's so funny?" he growled.

She exhausted her chuckle while he glared. "Oh—I made a joke! Get it? I'll see your colossal…oh, never mind. Where was I?" She cleared her throat. "Oh yeah. You're totally hiding something."

"Am not." He stepped forward.

"Are too." She stepped forward, leaving an inch between them. She could smell his sweet breath and feel his energy seeping into her veins. Gods, she wanted to kiss him.

His head dipped an inch, as if he were thinking the same, but then he stopped and turned to leave. "I need to go see my father."

She grabbed his arm. "You just went. Stop running and tell me. Why didn't you ever mention the woman? And your twin? I know something is going on, something bad. I can sense it in the air." He didn't respond but once again, she felt the fear and suffering building inside him. "Maybe I can help."

"My father is dying, and there is much to settle before he moves on."

So that was why Antonio was here. "I'm sorry." She stroked his arm, not knowing if it was to comfort him or fuel her need to touch him.

"So am I."

Of course. It was never easy for anyone to lose a parent. This had to be weighing heavily on his soul, and here she was poking the bear, picking a fight with him during his time of need. Gods, she was such a bitch. "Is there anything I can do?"

"I wish you could. But no."

"Are you sure? If the cause is something dark." She swallowed, knowing this entire place felt poisoned.

Antonio shook his head and she could swear she saw his eyes tear up. She'd never seen a vampire cry over anything. They were too tough. They were numb. They were like those little calluses on the edge of her big toe that no amount of pumicing could remove.

"How long has he got?" she asked.

"Not long. A few days, perhaps."

"Your mother must be heartbroken," she said.

"My mother died after giving birth to us, so it's just me and my brother now."

"If there's anything I can do, say the word," she said. "I never had parents, but I know it can't be easy to lose him."

"I'm not worried about losing my father. The bastard can rot in hell for all I care."

Whoa! That was unexpected. "I'm not following."

He rubbed has hands over his face. "I have to go. If you need anything, ask Kirstie, our maid." He stopped and looked at her, his gorgeous olive eyes filled with distress, a distress that spiked her heart. "Ixtab?"

"Yes?"

"I must open the tablet tonight."

"You're not going to tell me why, are you?" she asked.

He shook his head no.

Ixtab watched Antonio leave. Nothing about his situation felt right. Nothing about it made any sense. It was hands down the oddest situation she'd ever been in. Even stranger than the time Cimil threw a chocolate fondue party—for the record, there were no strawberries or cake for dipping; there was only…Cimil. But as bizarre and painful as this situation had become, nothing was worse than the hollowness burning inside. She could no longer deny that she felt something for Antonio. And it killed her to know that he wanted this other woman.

Who was she?

Reason number eleven: vampires are really good at keeping secrets.

She had to know what was going on before that portal opened, and there wasn't much time. She scratched her itchy veil. The answer seemed to be staring her right in the face. Perhaps if she got away from the darkness of this house, she would be able to think clearly.

She picked up her phone and called for her chauffeur.

Veinticuatro

⌒

"Hola. Me llamo Ixtab, pero mis amigos me llaman Ixy."
Ixtab stood before a group of roughly twenty people sitting on steel-gray foldout chairs in a small room toward the back of the village town hall. The dingy yellow walls were blanketed with fliers, including a shocking amount of missing persons photos—mostly women.

It had taken Ixtab's driver over thirty minutes to find the nearest AA meeting—or anything-A meeting—however, Ixtab's fuzzy head had benefited from the afternoon drive through the historic town.

"Hola, Ixy," the group replied.

"Hola. I know I've compelled everyone in this room, so it's not as if you have a choice in the matter, but I do want to thank you for being here. I've got a lot on my mind." She began telling the nearly comatose crowd all her woes, including the odd bit about the look-alikes: Francisco, Antonio, and his twin. Yet divulging the facts

didn't help her sort out this mess in her head as she'd
hoped. Too many pieces were still missing.

"So, any clues?" she asked.

A few random grumbles came from the group, and
then, "If you ask me, *señorita*, you should stay away from
that house and that family. They are cursed and everyone
knows it." Ixtab took a good look at the man in his eight-
ies wearing thick glasses and a moth-eaten sweater.

"Cursed? What kind of 'cursed'?"

No one responded. And this was why the art of compelling rocked. "Tell me now. I command you," she said
directly to the old man.

"They say the father is possessed by the devil. He
steals the souls of young women." The old man pointed to
the wall and then went on to say that the police had inves-
tigated the family many times over the decades. Dozens
of missing women had been traced back to the estate, but
each time the charges were dropped without explanation.
"Any policeman who goes into the house never remem-
bers ever being there."

Red goddess flag!

Speaking of compelling, is that what Antonio's father's
been doing? *Crap.* Could he be a vampire, too? But then,
why was he dying? *No.* That didn't make any sense. Perhaps it was the case of an overly superstitious people.
These small towns loved their spooky legends.

In any case, Ixtab already had to check out Antonio's
father on the top of her list. Whatever was going on—the
dark energy in that house, Antonio's obsession with the
tablet, his twin—she'd bet her favorite red flip-flops that
the father was the key to everything. "Thanks everyone,
this noodling session was really helpful."

She was about to leave but had a last-minute thought. "Hey, can I ask you guys another question?"

No response.

"I command you to nod."

They nodded.

"Thank you. You're a fantastic group of people. I really mean that." Ixtab talked through her rather confusing feelings for Antonio, as well as the fact that he'd said he was meant for this other woman.

"So, what do you guys think? What should I do?" Ixtab asked. "Be honest," she added, compelling them to speak the truth.

"You must tell him, and for God's sake, take that stupid curtain off your face. It looks like you're going to give a puppet show on your head," said the elderly man.

Okay. Maybe the compelling thing wasn't all that great.

"Just...take it off? Like that?" she asked.

Everyone nodded.

"Now?"

Maybe they were right; she'd been wearing the damned thing for a few centuries. At first, she'd said it was to pay penance for the horrible things she had done and to keep the world at arm's length. Perhaps the real reason was that she was a coward. She'd used the veil to keep everyone away, not because she feared for them, but because she simply feared becoming attached to anyone only to lose them. Yes, perhaps her sister Fate had been right. Ixtab was a coward. The funny part was that it took a vampire to show her that.

She looked down at her toes. Though it was winter, she wore her pink flip-flops and her toes were painted her favorite pearly pink. She chuckled at herself. What *was* she doing wearing this ridiculous costume? This wasn't her. In fact, all this time, she'd never been able to give up the sundresses and sandals she wore underneath.

I never could let go of who I am on the inside.

She loved laughter, though she clearly sucked at making jokes; she loved warm, sunny days and watching flowers bloom. She loved how she could create happiness by removing the darkness from a poor soul's heart—a young mother with depression, a spouse who'd lost his or her partner, or a kid who felt left out in life. She loved that she could make their pain simply vanish and allow them to see that tomorrow was another day filled with hope and the possibility of a good life, a happy life.

No. She wasn't death or darkness or evil. She was good. She was also complex and imperfect. *Like any one of the Creator's creatures.*

She looked up at the eager faces before her. "Actually, I love happiness. I adore it!" Yes. Happiness was her biggest power. Her true gift. Why hadn't she ever seen it before? From this moment forward, she would be known as the Goddess of Happiness. Okay, sure, she would still need to do something with that negative energy she extracted from nice people, and that meant the unlucky country-club members would be stricken with the urge to jump out a window or something of the like, but that did not discount the fact that she saved many, many deserving souls.

She reached for her veil and stopped. Could she do this? Show these people her face? Yes, it was time to move on and turn over a new leaf.

"Go ahead," said a nice woman with a red sweater and a bright smile. "We are waiting."

"Okay, here goes." Ixtab slid off her veil and murmurs of approval erupted from the crowd.

"You see," said the woman, "that wasn't so hard. Now was it?"

Ixtab shook her head. "It feels good." She took in the sensation of being bare and exposed. How would it feel when she showed herself to Antonio? What if he still chose this other woman? "What if he doesn't want me?" she mumbled.

"Love is always a risk," said the elderly man. "But a life without love is a life not worth living."

Wise words.

"All right. Time for me to face him and whatever else awaits." She stopped. "Oh, and...everyone here now hates alcohol—so you're free to live a happy life if you choose—and you'll forget I was ever here. 'Kay?"

The crowd nodded absently with smiles plastered on their faces.

Goddess of Happiness strikes again!

Thirty minutes later, Ixtab arrived back at the estate, but there were no signs of anyone. She'd returned the veil to her head, wanting Antonio to be the first to see her, and right now, it was time to have a chat with Antonio's father.

Ixtab went upstairs and heard a small rustle coming from the hallway. She followed the noise and saw one of the doors ajar. She pushed on the dark-stained cherrywood, but found the room empty. Empty of people that was.

Ixtab sniffed the air. It was a large study with dust-covered, floor-to-ceiling shelves filled with antique leather-bound books. To one side of the room was a large desk—also made of stained dark wood and equally old as everything else in the study. Yes, though innocent looking enough, darkness stuck to everything.

Ixtab's eyes roamed the shelves. From the look of the books' ages, they'd been purchased at the time the estate had been built. She plucked a copy of the *Divine Comedy* off the shelf and thumbed through the pages, then replaced it. *Amateur...*

The faint sound of voices shouting began pouring into the room. She spun around and noticed the sounds came from the other side of the bookshelf. She leaned in, realizing there was a hidden room.

The yelling grew louder, and though the voices were muffled, she heard Antonio speaking in Spanish to another man who sounded weak and old. *His father.*

"You fucking bastard," Antonio said. "You can't do this to us."

"I can, and I will," the man replied. "It is the way of our species."

Species? What the hey?

"You've lived more centuries than you can count; perhaps it's time for el Trauco to die—you wouldn't be missed by anyone. That I can promise."

The man laughed. "This coming from a vampire. Why don't you come and see me in a thousand years and tell me if you're ready to give up *your* life?"

"I am nothing like you. I would rather die than take the life of my child to survive."

Ixtab crept away quietly. This was like an immortal Spanish soap opera. A mystery woman trapped on the other side of the portal? El Trauco—why did that name sound familiar? Antonio's father's comment about species? Vegetarian vampires? Okay—that part was more like a Haight-Ashbury immortal soap opera, but still. Could things possibly get any more confusing?

Ixtab went downstairs to her room and dialed Penelope on her cell.

"Ixtab. Thank the gods!" Penelope yelled. "Why haven't you been answering your phone?"

"I was busy," she replied.

"You were having sex with him?"

I wish. "Not that kind of busy," Ixtab grumbled.

"Oh. Sorry to hear that. Did you at least get him back to work?"

"That won't be an issue. There's another problem," Ixtab said.

"Let me put you on speaker." There was a pause and then Penelope asked, "There. Can you hear me?"

"Yes." Ixtab rolled her eyes. "I can hear you..."

"Good. Kinich is with me. We're listening."

Where should she start? "Well, first of all, Antonio didn't go to Spain to run away from me."

"Oh! That's great!" Penelope responded.

"He came here because his father is dying."

"Oh no. That's horrible."

"But he hates his father, so he's not sad about it," Ixtab added.

"Is that horrible or good? Because it sounds like a little of both," Penelope said.

"I'm not sure," Ixtab said, "which is the reason we need to talk." Pause. "Kinich, are you listening?"

Ixtab heard a rustling in the background and then a "Heeeey!" from Kinich that sounded like someone had taken away his favorite toy.

"Sorry," said Penelope, "he was kissing my tummy. He's listening now."

Resist. Resist hating them for their sickly, sweet

cuteness... "I overheard a conversation between Antonio and his father. They were yelling about him taking the souls of his children, and I most definitely heard the word *species* thrown in there along with the name el Trauco. What the hell is el Trauco?"

There was a long silence before Penelope chimed in. "El Trauco is a mystical creature from Chile that preys on innocent young women and impregnates them."

"How did you know that?" Ixtab asked.

"I've got an iPhone. Hello. Sometimes you deities are so old-school."

Ixtab pulled her phone from her cheek and stared at the device. *Oh yeah. I guess I could have Wiki'd that. I am pretty lame.*

Then her mind began to jam the improbable into place, forcing the pieces of the jigsaw to fit together. *Gasp!* This couldn't be. This just couldn't be. *Hate you dramawhore Universe! Hate, hate, hate you!!*

Feeling the blood pool to her feet, she scarcely managed to eke out, "I'll call you later." Ixtab hung up and flopped faceup on the bed. There was no way! No way!

Yes way.

It was the only explanation that made sense. The darkness, the missing women, the look-alikes, and finally, Antonio's obsession with the tablet.

Poor, poor Antonio. All this time, *this* is what he'd been up against? Gods, why hadn't he told her? And now that she knew, what would she do about it?

First, you need to find out how. Yes, how? Because never in a million years would Ixtab have seen this coming. It was simply...impossible.

Ixtab followed the foul stench of death and decay through the house back to the study and to what had to be Antonio's father's hidden bedroom, or lair as some creepy creatures liked to call it. It reeked of everything in this world she despised—the absence of joy or life—and the malevolent energy was so powerful that it doubled her over the moment she touched the faux bookshelf slash hidden door. Or maybe it was the pain of her past catching up with her. Or perhaps the disappointment she felt, because if her assumptions were true, then Antonio's arrival into her life had nothing to do with destiny or fate or the Universe giving her another chance. It would simply be the result of a terrible oversight by the gods.

Feeling that her heart might actually burst from sadness, she trembled as her hand gripped the wooden shelf and pulled. *Gods dammit, please don't be him. Please don't be him…*

The hidden door creaked open and the obscure room, with its thick, black velvet curtains and mahogany furniture, looked more like a dreary tomb.

"Quién es usted?" The old man, who wore a burgundy bathrobe with gold trim, sat up in his bed.

Ixtab's heart nearly shriveled up into a ball of despair and anger. Yes, his face was thin and his eyes a dull, hazy gray, but the resemblance to Francisco—and Antonio and Franco, for that matter—was undeniable.

But how? How? On the very godsdamned day she'd finally put the past behind her? On the very day she'd realized she no longer had to be the Goddess of Suicide, but could be something more, something better—the bringer of happiness. Noooo! She refused to believe it. Re. Fused! Why did the Universe insist on punishing her?

Ixtab's knees began to tremble violently and adrenaline coursed through her humanlike body, making her feel like she might actually explode from the shock.

How . . . ?

"Mind explaining why the hell you're not dead?" Gods, how she wanted to hurt him. How could this be?

He narrowed his cataract-covered eyes. "I recognize your voice. It is very, very familiar. Who are you?"

"Who am I? Who am I? I've spent two hundred years mourning your death, punishing myself for killing you! And you ask, 'Who am I?'" Oh, gods. Now she would never remove the veil. She felt so . . . so ridiculous!

"Ixtab," he whispered. "Is that you?"

"You bet your ass it's me! And how the hell didn't I know?"

How had he gotten past her radar?

He slowly rose from the bed and wobbled his way toward her. "Please, let me see your face. I've dreamt of you for so long."

"Stop! Just stop! Don't pull that crap on me! Wait. Maybe I should just kill you. Again!" She reached for him, but he did not move away, causing her to pause.

"Go ahead," he said. "You would be doing this old incubus a favor."

Well, in that case, she wouldn't touch him. There'd be no favors for this despicable, disgusting vile creature. Not today.

"Please, touch me," he said, his voice sounding like a rickety, old fence. "If I die, I will move on to my next body."

Ding, ding, ding!!! Five-alarm goddess bells screamed in her head. "We got rid of your kind centuries ago. How? How is this possible?" she asked.

It had taken the gods a few decades to exterminate the incubi, but they'd done it. So they thought. The key had been finding and destroying the incubi's portals into the human world—which ironically turned out to be a handful of sulfuric hot springs near present-day Las Vegas.

"How?" the demon cackled. "Obviously I hid. Quite successfully, I might add."

"Your bodies don't last," she argued. Unlike the gods, the soul of a demon is corrosive to their humanlike shells. Over time, they wither away and die. And without their portals, the demons weren't supposed to make new bodies or be able to travel back to their realm, leaving their souls simply in limbo for all eternity. That had been the plan, anyway.

Unless... "You found a way to make hosts?" she asked.

He smiled and displayed his brownish-yellow teeth. "More like...offspring. Your sister Cimil was more than willing to help me for the right price. I like her; she's quite the evil one, isn't she?"

Cimil? Oh no. This was bad. Really, really bad. She'd been the one in charge of exterminating the demons to begin with. And what did he mean exactly by "offspring."

"Are you trying to tell me—"

"Exactly! Francisco, the *original* Francisco, was one of the first. It was fate that I took over his body after you'd fallen in love with him. The way you looked at me with your adoring eyes—I'd never experienced such pleasure and knew I had to have you for my own. No matter how long it took. I am on body number eight, by the way."

Dirty, rotten bastard took Francisco's body and pretended to be him? Poor, poor Francisco. He had been a kind, selfless, purehearted man. He hadn't deserved to have his life stolen like that.

"For the record," she spat, "that look of adoration wasn't meant for you."

He flicked his wrist in the air. "Are you certain about that? Are you certain a tiny part of you didn't see me for who I truly was during those few days we were together? Because if I recall correctly, you said you loved me."

Oh, gods, she had said it. But she'd thought she was talking to Francisco and not some horrible, disgusting demon. Why hadn't she noticed the change? How could she have been so blind?

Ixtab hit pause to digest what it all meant, then hit a cold, hard wall. Who could possibly make sense of all this? The man she once loved had his body hijacked by an incubus who'd survived the banishment of his race with the help of the deity who was supposed to have killed him: Cimil. Cimil also helped him figure out how to find new bodies to live inside. And to top off Ixtab's crap fiesta, she now had genuine feelings for another of the demon's offspring, but Antonio believed he was destined to be with portal woman (species unknown). All the while, they were supposed to be figuring out how to open the portal so they could free Guy and Niccolo in order to prevent the apocalypse—prophesied by Cimil.

Don't forget, the entire vampire army is on furlough in Euro Disney and we're sitting ducks until they return. Which they wouldn't do until Niccolo was free and able to amend the law.

The entire situation was bizarre and unbelievable

enough that only one explanation existed: Cimil. Yes, all sick-and-twisted signs pointed to this being her handiwork.

"Ya. That kooky Cimil." Ixtab chuckled sarcastically. "She's a wacky, evil goddess, that one. Always surprising everyone with her fun little pranks. So, what was her wacky price to let you live?"

He smiled again. His tongue was a grayish green. She wanted to yack. "Let's say I had something she wanted. A useless relic I came across during my travels."

Relic? He can't possibly mean... "It wouldn't happen to have been a tablet?" It wasn't a question, but a realization.

"No," he replied quickly.

"You're lying, aren't you?" Demons were notorious liars.

"Yes."

Crapola. "And now you're telling the truth, aren't you?"

"No."

Ugh. So frustrating. "You just lied again, didn't you?"

He smiled. "Yes."

How could she have possibly said, "I love you," to this...horrible, frustrating, icky demon? How? How? How? Oh, gods, she'd never forgive herself. The humiliation would haunt her for another two centuries.

The worst part was how she'd been so judgmental of vampires! She'd actually thought they were icky. But this guy? Hell, there was nothing lower or more disgusting on the planet. She needed to put an end to him.

Vampires rock! Reason number one: they are not incubi.

But isn't Antonio an...?

Oh no. No!

"So, Antonio is really your..." She cleared her throat. "...Son?"

"Yes. But he's not a true incubus."

Oh, thank heavens. I'm still getting over the whole liking vampires thing.

"My offspring are mostly human," he explained, "with just enough of my DNA to provide my light a happy safe home for a while. Cimil was also kind enough to throw in some magic so my male offspring continue to look like Francisco. I know *you* enjoyed my face, so I kept it for you."

Oh, yippee. "You wouldn't happen to want to tell me how you do it?" *Because I'm so going to put an end to your shenanigans.*

"No."

This time, she knew he told the truth; demons loved to keep secrets.

"How about giving me some reason not to Tweet my peeps the deets?" she asked. "I could have your sons locked up and prevent you from making more Franciscitos. When your current body goes, you'll have nowhere to hide."

He chuckled with victorious, evil glee. "Do you really think Antonio and Franco are my only children? I have others, *many* others; although they are female—not my preference—but I could survive, if need be."

"Please don't tell me your daughters also look like Francisco because that would be so very wrong."

"Ixtab, I'm wounded. Do you truly believe I am *that* cruel?" the incubus asked.

"Um. Yeaaah," she replied. "You're a demon. Remember?"

Hack, hack. "Excellent point," he replied.

Well, nothing she could do about a bunch of ugly, burly, part-incubus chicks running around the planet, although she was curious to see what a family reunion might look like.

Ixtab shivered.

In any case...dang it! This demon was good at risk mitigation. It was almost like he'd anticipated this.

Cimil! "Cimil knew this would happen and warned you, didn't she?" Ixtab asked.

"No." His eyes glowed with psycho joy.

Ugh. He just lied again.

Hate. Demons. Hate them.

"I understand why you might be angry with me," he said, "but know, after you 'killed' me, I couldn't not come to you and reveal myself even though this is what I wanted. I loved you—I still love you. And Cimil promised if I did as she asked and remained patient, this joyous day would come."

"This day? As in...our happy reunion?" *Ick, ick, ick... is he serious?*

He nodded eagerly. "Yes. Fate has brought us together, Ixtab. And now it is time for us to be happy."

"But you drain the life from young women for food. Sometimes you screw them as an appetizer. Why would I want to be with you?"

"Oh, now," he replied. Hack, hack, gurgle. "Is it really so terrible that I enjoy the pleasures of the flesh or that I must feed to survive? You didn't seem to even notice before."

Ixtab gasped. Oh, gods, what a damned fool she'd been! The day before she killed Francisco—*errr*—killed the possessed Francisco, she'd gone with him to a convent to visit the sick. She'd thought Francisco had been comforting those poor dying souls when in fact he'd been sucking the lives from them to feed. How could she not have noticed what was going on?

Perhaps because you were so desperate for love that you didn't want to see it. She had been just as lonely then as she was now.

"I love you for who you are, my dear g-g-goddess." Hack, gurgle. "I have no delusions of your sainthood and know every one of your dirty little secrets." He whispered, "I even know the name of every male you've killed—by accident, of course."

"How?"

"I've kept an eye on you all these years, waiting for this day. And know, I do not look down upon you. I never could; you and I are alike. We both kill because it is in our nature, our role in the Universe."

How dare he say that! Ixtab wanted to punch the old, shriveled goat in his decrepit face. "I don't enjoy hurting people like you do— Okay, the evil bastards, yes. They're super fun to kill. But not the others."

Ixtab's mind circulated around the multitude of loose strings while the conversation played out. She knew there was so, so, so much more to this story. First, this evil bastard was about to die. So that meant he'd be going to a new body, preferably a male one. *Antonio or his brother Franco. Oh no.*

She needed to think this through carefully. Very carefully. Time to retreat and regroup. "I have to go."

"Are you coming back?" he asked.

She pressed her hands to her temples. "I-I don't know."

"Just answer me this, Ixtab. Why are you here? Why, after all this time, has fate brought us together again?"

Because you are a disgusting pig, your time has come to pay for your crimes, and this goddess has got your number?

"Enlighten me?" she replied sweetly.

"The Universe led you to the tablet and my son. He led you to me. We are meant to be."

Think carefully. Show nothing.

She nodded slowly. "I've been suffering for two centuries because of your death and now I find you alive. It's a bit overwhelming. I need time to think." She turned to leave and reached for the door. "By the way, when will you make the change to your new body?"

"My heart grows weaker by the moment. Not long now. And then I will be young and strong again."

And likely looking for your next demon baby momma. "One question. Why wait until your body gives out? I mean, why not just kill yourself and do it sooner?" Because...ick! He looked awful—patches of missing hair, dark spots on his skin, hazed-over irises. Not that she cared, but surely he did.

He shook his crooked, wrinkled finger in the air. "You always were smart, my dear Ixtab."

Was that a string of drool flowing from the corner of his mouth?

Vampires rock. Reason number two: they never get old and drool on themselves.

"Cimil advised," he explained, "I would meet my demise if I took any shortcuts. My death must be due to natural or supernatural causes."

Interesting... "And what happens to your son when you take his body?"

The old demon shrugged. "His soul goes...*out*." He flicked his wrist casually, as if he didn't know and didn't care.

Vampires rock. Reason number three: they don't eject people's souls from their bodies and take them over like horrible parasitic extraterrestrials.

Ixtab's plastic cackle bounced off the walls. "Of course. Stupid mortal souls—they are so weak and disgusting. Who cares what happens to them?" Ixtab was extremely grateful for her veil because it hid the panic in her eyes. This had to be a dream.

Dreams only happen to mortals. You, my dear goddess, have just had your entire reality chewed on and spit out like a flavorless wad of gum.

Veinticinco

Panting, Ixtab found Antonio sitting on a bench in the garden, gazing pensively at the cloudless night. "Oh, thank heavens! Kirstie said I'd find you here." Ixtab took a seat beside him. "At least I think she was talking to me. It could've been the wall. It's hard to tell which eye is her good one. And why does she always smell like borscht?"

"You came out here to talk about the maid's wandering eye and her addiction to beets?" Antonio's gaze didn't waver from the starlit sky.

"No. I came out for this..." Ixtab socked him three times in the arm, but it had zero impact. "Why didn't you tell me your father is el Trauco, Latin America's most infamous incubus?"

"And that would have changed...what?" he said calmly.

"Well, well...we could've— I'm not sure."

"*Exactamente*. It would've changed nothing. Killing or locking him away solves nothing."

"That's why you were looking for the tablet, wasn't it?" she asked.

He nodded yes.

Of course, he wanted to get rid of the demon and send him far, far away to another dimension, and the tablet was the key.

Oh, gods. "You should have told me." Ixtab shook her head.

"This is my fight," he said coldly. "No one else's."

"You couldn't be more godsdamned wrong. This mess started long before you were even born."

"Doesn't matter when it started, or by whom, because I'm going to finish it." He looked at Ixtab and the rage in his eyes made her do a double take. *Pita chips! That sure is one hell of a peeved vampire!* She could only imagine the horrible things Antonio had been subjected to. *Poor, poor man.*

"I'm guessing incubi don't get father-of-the year awards," she said.

"No. When I was twenty-two, I brought my girlfriend, Vicki, home for a visit. She'd been begging me for months to visit the vineyard. Though I hated seeing my father— he was always such a coldhearted bastard—I figured we'd barely see him. He was rarely around growing up, or ever. Unfortunately, he was home for the weekend. That night, when I woke, Vicki wasn't in bed. It didn't take me long to find her; I followed the sounds to his study, where he was sucking the life from her body..." Antonio looked away. "Half out of my mind, I attacked and tried to save her, but it was too late. I don't know if it was the need to brag or that he enjoyed watching me suffer, but that's when he told me everything: how he'd done the same to my mother, how my brother and I were merely potential hosts for his next life...So I made a deal. He would take me so that Franco could live, and I would keep his secret—even from my brother."

"So, you began searching for the tablet?" Ixtab said.

"I hoped to send the demon somewhere else before my time ran out. Then all this happened—I was blinded, there was you, and then I became a vampire, removing me from the running to be a host for my father. I failed my brother in the worst possible way."

Lightbulb! "Your father can't use your body because you've changed?"

"Vampires need not apply," he said starkly.

It all made so much sense now. Poor, poor Antonio. What had she done?

"That's why you were so upset with me after the transformation," she said.

He looked at her, his beautiful eyes filled with regret. "I'm sorry for how I treated you; it wasn't your fault I ended up a vampire. At the time, however, I knew it would mean my brother's life—he's the runner-up."

Well, he'd just made opening the portal that much more essential. This demon wasn't going to get his icky incu-paws on another soul if she had anything to do with it.

"I'm so sorry, Antonio." She reached out and stroked his arm. It felt so damned good. "I wonder if this explains why I can touch you—" *And why you're hung like a rhino and the ladies can't seem to keep their frigging hands off of you...* "Incubus feed off the life force of others. Usually they prefer sexual energy, but who knows? You had some of my light inside you when you turned, you're a vampire with a little extra something...there could be a million reasons for how you ended up like you did."

Or just one: This was all meant to happen. You're meant to be mine.

He shrugged. "I've always eaten human food. Until I turned, that is. Then I stopped eating."

No. He hadn't stopped eating, she realized. "Your hunger goes away when I touch you. Yes?"

He nodded. "Yes. Among other things," he said suggestively.

Oh, she so very much wanted to ask about the "other things," but now was not the time to go there, given they had serious issues to navigate. At least, however, the mystery of Antonio's appetite was no longer one of them. He'd been gobbling all of her dark energy, which is why he left her feeling goddamned fantastic every time she touched him! That had to be the reason.

"It's so ironic when you think about it. Here you are thriving from my touch, but it killed your father," she said, thinking aloud. *Yes, must be something to do with his turning.*

Rage sparked in Antonio's eyes.

"What? What did I say?" she asked.

"He was the one you...lo-lo-loved and killed? My father! That disgusting, heartless prick was *your* Francisco?"

Uh-oh. Hadn't she made that clear already? *Ugh. Perhaps I didn't.* "Um. Yes? But let me explain," she said. "I thought he was someone—"

"Stop. I don't want to hear it."

Gods dammit. Why did he always shut her down like that? "It's important you know the truth."

"Right now, nothing matters more than opening that portal. I need to get the woman out."

Oh, the woman… Did he truly believe some stranger was the one for him? Didn't he feel the powerful connection between them? Now that she thought about it, actually, after she'd touched him that very first time in the hospital, it seemed a permanent connection had formed. She continued tasting him on her tongue, his energy. She continued filling with his frustration and despair even without a physical connection.

Ixtab's mind reeled. "You really"—the words stuck for a moment—"want her?"

"Once she's out, she can help us understand how to use the tablet to get to your men. When that's done, I'll make sure my father goes in."

His reply hadn't given her the answer she wanted, but maybe he was simply trying to spare her feelings. Or maybe he was peeved because he'd just found out she had a past with his father. Of course, he didn't know the full story.

Oh, gods. Who can blame him for being upset? What a train wreck. "Antonio, I know everything feels like an episode of *Myrtle Manor*, only not very funny, but I promise I'll do everything I can to help you."

"As I said, the woman will know what to do," he said without even a hint of doubt.

Oh, and I suppose she walks on water and shoots rainbows from her ass like Cimil's unicorn! "And you know all this how?"

"She says so in my dreams."

He dreams with her? Oh, gods… how can this be?

"Well… your plan *sucks*!" she said spitefully.

"Sucks?" he asked.

"It's got so many holes, I could drive an incu*bus* through it."

Antonio laughed.

Dammit! Now? Now he chooses to laugh? "I didn't mean that as a joke. You're banking your entire plan on the woman being there and knowing what to do."

"I know she will be there. And yes, as stupid as it sounds, I believe she will help us find your men and get rid of my father. I believe because I have faith."

Faith? The scientist is leaving it all to... Faith? This was far too important to leave it to that little flake. He might as well light a candle to Chance (another family friend). Hell, throw in a prayer to her sister Fate.

"Okay. Say you're right about the woman," Ixtab argued. "Then the next part of your plan doesn't work; your father knows what you're up to and isn't going to jump in the portal to be banished to another dimension."

"We will surprise him and push him in. My only hope is that he'll never find a way back."

Ixtab looked at Antonio. The light of the moon bounced off the sharp angles of his exquisite face—his jaw, his cheekbones, his thick strong lips. It was then that she noticed how Antonio had a gentle goodness in his eyes that radiated outward. It shaped the angles of his mouth, it brightened the light in his eyes, and it made him tilt his head to one side when he felt concerned. Antonio was simply magnificent. And he deserved to live a happy life. Even if that meant being with another woman. It ripped her heart into pieces thinking such a thing, but it was the truth.

You must truly love him if you're willing to give him up simply to make him happy...

Sigh. No one said being the Goddess of Happiness would be easy.

"I will take care of getting your father inside the portal. You just open it and get the female."

"What about your men?" he asked.

"There won't be time, Antonio. Opening a portal to another dimension isn't like opening the garage door where you can drive your giant incu*bus* in and out as you please." And it wasn't as if his father wouldn't notice the fabric of space opening up right inside his own home. No. If they were lucky, they'd be able to lure the demon to the portal and push him in. If extra–super lucky, they'd do it before the woman got out. If she were, in fact, there.

Antonio stared with his inquisitive eyes. "Why would you give up your plans? I know you and the gods are depending on freeing your men to win your war."

Because she couldn't stand the thought of sacrificing Antonio's happiness. Not after everything he'd been through. Not when she cared so much for him. And not when there was one other little fact. "Cimil has clearly been manipulating all of us, herding us like mindless sheep to this destination. She wants us to use the tablet to free our men, and given her evil deceptions, I'm not so sure this is what we should do." Yes, they might be better off finding another way to free Guy, Niccolo, and the others. She only hoped she was making the right decision.

Oh. Look who's leaning on Faith now!

Shut up!

Antonio continued to stare. Was that gratitude in his eyes? "Why are you still wearing the veil?"

She didn't know. Perhaps to hide her sorrow; she didn't want to lose him to this other woman, yet she certainly didn't want to deny him the chance to save his brother or follow his destiny. There was simply no getting around it. The portal had to be opened. "Old habits, I guess."

He opened his mouth to say something but snapped it shut and stood. "I'll go prepare. Can you have my father in the basement at midnight?"

"Sure." *I'll go to him after I light some candles. Maybe make a call to Fate...*

Because pulling this off would require a miracle. Sadly, the last time she'd seen Miracle, she was somewhere in the Bahamas with Chance.

Veintiséis

⌒

"Are you sure you understand? Don't let anyone see you, and you are only to intervene if the physicist needs help." Cimil popped a handful of Milk Duds into her mouth and chewed nervously, staring at Roberto.

Roberto nodded and then kissed her wrist.

"Gud. Becosh whateber happens, dosh Scabs can't be awowed to go fwee. Got it? We mush start kiwing dem off." Chew, chew, chew. "Gods, I wuv Milk Duds."

Roberto tightened his parachute.

"Shee you in"—chew, chew, chew—"Shedona, baby."

She gave Roberto a push out of the plane's rear door somewhere over Vilafranca del Penedès.

Gods, this was going to be wicked hard. She needed to have everything set just right or Operation Over would be...well, over. Phooey on that! She hadn't carefully planned centuries of events merely to have it all fall apart in the final phase.

Cimil chewed and looked at her watch. She'd need to make a detour to her piggy bank—an ancient temple where she kept her most prized treasures (gold; jewelry; three Thighmasters; Bigfoot; the world's largest pachinko machine; a few spare tablets for the all-necessary time travel and dimensional hopping; magic fairy dust; a flea circus; her collection of Betamax *Love Boat* episodes; and last but not least, a few hibernating armies for that rainy day, aka apocalypse) in Mexico and then head over to Bacalar to ensure all was ready for Chaam's big arrival. According to her calculations, she'd still make it to Sedona in time to meet up again with Roberto, hand off the spare tablet, and then turn herself in. All part of the master plan.

I wonder if I'll have time to hit a few garage sales before I'm imprisoned? A few beanbag chairs might be nice for her jail cell, and she needed a new saddle for Minky.

"I'll jus hab to make time..." Chew, chew, chew.

Yes, because some things were too important to pass up even when the world's fate hung in the balance. Garage sales being one of them.

At a quarter to midnight, Ixtab sat in her room and took one final look at the page she'd written, debating whether or not to put it in the envelope. What good would the truth be for Antonio now? No good at all. Yet she wanted him to know who she really was, not who she used to be: happy. Because of him. He'd freed her soul from the demons of her past—well, sorta. Mentally, the shackles were gone. And now she knew she was good not in spite of her flaws, but because of them. They taught her humility and compassion. They taught her to forgive—mainly herself, but forgiveness nonetheless. She wanted him to know that she'd never loved his father. And as much as it pained her to say so, she wondered if she had truly loved Francisco. Her past felt like an illusion caused by desperation and loneliness. It took meeting Antonio and feeling the powerful bond between them to realize that. Antonio helped her to understand what true love felt like. And she was eternally grateful for it, even though he didn't love her back.

She sighed. What good would it do to know all that? None. If she cared for Antonio, she would not stand in his way to a wonderful life.

She tore up the page, threw it in the trash, and then gazed up. "Please. Just let him be happy, that is all I ask..."

But would the Universe listen this time? She could only hope. Because this plan of hers was insane. Completely insane. And it depended on her ability to lie. For the record, lying never came easy for her, and tonight, she needed to put on the performance of a lifetime.

She shook her head. How had everything gone from bad to messed up to seriously messed up to this? She'd come to Spain looking for Antonio, filled with hope, and found instead her dead lover who wasn't a monk, but a stinking, rotten incubus. Now, she was going to help Antonio and give him up forever to another woman.

Never in a million years would she have seen this coming.

Doesn't matter now, it came. She looked at her watch. *And it's showtime. Antonio is depending on you.*

Ixtab stood and smoothed down the front of her bulky black dress. Gods, when this was all over, she was going to burn these wretched clothes. That is, if she ever made it back to this realm.

"I'm glad you came," said Francisco in a scratchy voice. "I knew you would."

Ixtab walked over to the bed and pulled up a chair next to him. The room smelled of decay, death, and evil.

"Did you now?" Ixtab responded coyly and pulled the dark green blanket up over his chest while crinkling her nose underneath her veil.

He coughed. Drool trickled from the corner of his mouth.

Ick. Just . . . ick.

"Of course. You cannot fight fate." He wheezed his words.

"I fight with her all the time." Ixtab reached over and fluffed the enormous pile of pillows under his neck and head. "Once we were on a pig farm, and I pushed her into a huge pile of poop. It was really funny, actually—but that's beside the point. I'm not here because I've decided to be with you. Yet. I *am* here to ask questions, and the only way this will work is if you tell me the truth."

"Ask away and the truth shall be yours," he replied.

Grrr . . . "You just lied again, didn't you?"

He made an evil snicker that faded into a cough.

"Can you at least *try* to tell the truth?" she asked.

"Perhaps."

Finally! A straight answer. "Good enough. So after you die, you'll take your son's body. Then what?"

"What do you mean?" he asked.

"I mean, how do you expect us to be happy if Antonio is always going to be hunting you? He hates your guts, you know. And he'll hate you even more after you take his brother from him."

"Who says that I will?" the demon questioned.

Huh? "You are taking *Franco's* body, aren't you?" That's what Antonio had said to her in the garden—*"vampires need not apply"*—and that Franco would become the next host.

The demon wiggled his head from side to side and puckered his grayish-pink lips in a noncommittal sort of way.

"Aren't you?" she asked again.

"I admit that had been my original plan, but I believe Antonio will be the better choice. Now that I've learned you are able to touch him and he is immortal—I think I may have found a permanent host."

What? What? Oh. Come on! Why does everything have to be like this? Hate you, Universe! This was horrible. She needed the demon to want to kill Antonio—that was part of her plan. What plan? Well...the one she'd frigging made up somewhere between discovering the ex-love of her life was actually killed by an incubus and that she'd sacrifice anything to save that incubus's son, Antonio—who she actually loved.

"But he's a vampire," she protested.

"That shouldn't matter."

"He seems to think it does," she replied.

"Perhaps he's been misled by a certain...demon?" the demon snickered.

Oh no.

"I do, however"—hack, hack—"believe the transfer may take a little extra help this time," he added.

"Help? What, like a shoehorn or something?" She needed him to talk, to share his plan so she could effectively divert.

He lifted his gaunt hand off the bed and wagged his scraggly finger. "Uh-uh. I'm not telling. You'll simply have to wait and see."

"Don't you trust me, Francisco? After all I suffered because of you? Don't you know how many years I wanted to crawl into a hole and die because I missed you?" *And now I want to do the same, but because you're alive.*

The demon's thin lips formed a hard line. "You do not want to help my son?"

"If you know anything about me, then you know I can't stand vampires. I find them repugnant—I even started a list: They hate sunshine. They drink blood. Oh, I especially can't stand how disloyal they are. For example, your son has figured out how to open the portal, and he thinks I'm here luring you to go to him so he can throw you in. He'd never do such a thing if he weren't a leechy monster."

He studied her. "And you are telling me this because?"

She shrugged. "I'm a goddess who despises weakness, which is why I think your son is a vile bag of useless vampire giblets. You should be ashamed to be related."

He nodded his head slowly. "Yes. He is a disgrace to my bloodline—so much...*kindness and loyalty*—but I still plan to take his body." The demon licked his sticky, putrid lips. "I can't wait to have you in my bed."

Do not vomit. Whatever you do, do not vomit. "That's the problem. You won't have me. Do you honestly think I'd let a vampire touch me, even if he had you inside him?

Haven't you learned anything spying on me all these years?"

There was a long pause. Clearly the demon hadn't thought his plan through. "What are you proposing?"

That you buy this giant, stinky bridge made of pure bull crap I'm about to sell you? "Haven't you asked yourself why I can touch him? It's obviously because your genes have evolved—must be whatever dark magic you used to create your little mini-Franciscos. I touched your other son, too," she lied. "No problem. I bet if I touched you, it would be the same."

The demon blinked. She did not. Not that he could see her, but not blinking was the key to rock solid bluff. "Watch..."

He jerked away, but there was only so far he could go considering his limited mobility.

Ixtab willed her cells to open to his darkness and take his energy in so he'd believe the lie. *Please work, please work, please... Teen uk'al k'iinam. Teen uk'al yah.*

The most vile, horrid, sticky energy poured into her. And though it was only for a brief instant, she had to keep herself from falling over and retching violently on the floor. Only the thought of Antonio's happiness kept her strong.

"Ha! See!" She forced the cheeriness into her voice.

The demon looked confused for several moments, and then a crescent moon grin stretched across his face.

Oh, boy. And to think, all those crusty, yellow teeth could be mine.

"This is truly wonderful. How?" he asked.

"Must be fate. Or you simply rock. Or perhaps both." It had always amazed Ixtab how, despite being the masters of deception, demons were among the easiest species to manipulate. Their arrogance made them all too willing to believe any lie related to their awesomeness.

Demons. So lame...

Ixtab stood and dusted off her hands. "So, let's get rid of Antonio before he causes us any problems." *Please buy my bridge. Please buy my bridge...*

"I do not fear him."

"You should, big boy. He's immortal, smart, and he's hell-bent on getting his revenge. We need to get rid of him. Please? I couldn't be happy knowing his deception has gone unpunished."

The demon reached for her hand—*shit! Teen uk'al k'iinam. Teen uk'al yah*—and kissed it. Like poison from a venomous snake, his vile energy slithered its way up her arm. She wanted to remove her own hand with a cleaver.

"What do you want me to do, my love?" he said, stroking her wrist with his slimy fingertips.

Keep contents of stomach inside. Keep contents...

"He's waiting for you now," she advised. "We go downstairs, and when he opens the portal, I will push him in."

"You are so wonderfully evil, just like your sister, Cimil."

Gods. She still couldn't believe Cimil had been helping this vile creature. There had to be an explanation.

Well, that little gherkin has to wait for another party.

"If only Cimil were here now; she'd be so proud..." Ixtab sighed for effect.

"Then you are in luck, my sweet Goddess of Suicide..."

Happiness, asshole. Goddess of Happiness.

"Your sister is not far," he said, "and with her she brings her delightful friends."

"Cimil? She's coming here?" Ixtab tried to quell the parade of panic marching with drums and tambourines, refusing to be ignored.

"Why, yes. I told you I anticipated moving into a vampire's body might be a bit tricky, so I asked for her help."

Oh, crap. Cimil would see right through her. Ixtab had to hurry. "Funtastic! I've been dying to see her."

"And the Maaskab are already here," the demon added.

"Here?" *Oh, gods, no ...*

"Yes. They came to assist with the transfer, too, since this is their magic. They are staying in the guest villa. Should be quite the party tonight."

Maaskab? The fucking Maaskab are here? Here? Hate you, dramawhore! Hate you!

"Oh, honey. That's great!" She clapped with nauseating enthusiasm. "I think the Maaskab are so misunderstood. Why can't the other gods let them do their thing? I mean, really ... the world would be such a boring place without evil."

Oh. My. Gods. No wonder she'd felt so much darkness when she'd arrived. It had overpowered her from a half mile away. *Breathe, goddess, breathe. You can do this ...*

"My sentiments exactly. I have a brilliant idea." Hack, hack. "You could have sex with me after we deal with Antonio. I am sure my heart will give out, and then I can be inside Franco's body for our second round." He licked his scaly lips, which donned the color of a rotting corpse.

Oh yes! Just what I've always wanted: sex with Gollum. My precious ...

"Oh. That's a lovely plan, my love. Fate has been so kind to me, bringing you back into my life."

The demon snapped his finger. "Help me up, Ixtab. Let

us pay a visit to Antonio and his tablet. His demise will be my wedding gift to you."

Married? Insert dirty fork in eye now. "Married? Oh, Francisco..."

He reached for her hand and gave her a proud, beaming...hack, gurgle, hack. "Take my hand, woman."

Oh, gods, not again. Teen uk'al k'iinam. Teen uk'al yah. She'd need to touch Antonio soon—to lighten her load—or she wouldn't make it. Her body was very close to full capacity.

Veintisiete

"This better fucking work," Antonio mumbled to himself as he tested the circuit board one last time. Last night, he had isolated three distinct energy patterns, and the moment he had begun to cycle the current through the tablet, its center dissolved into a vacuous spiral. He watched the tiny opening grow a few more inches before the board shorted out, but he knew he'd done it. He only hoped that tonight he could get the portal to open all the way and for a duration sufficient enough to accomplish his goal.

Antonio looked at his watch and then glanced at the door. Dammit. Where was Ixtab? It was time.

Part of this plan still didn't feel right. Yes, he needed to rid his family of the demon once and for all. It was his duty. And yes, he felt in his heart that the woman he saw each time he closed his eyes was connected to him in a way that would never be explained by science or logic or anything rational. Yet he couldn't help but want to go to

Ixtab and run away with her. The attraction he felt, despite not knowing what she looked like, was...epic. He'd never felt such a carnal craving for a woman.

Yes, but she'd said herself that the love of her life, the one she hadn't gotten over, the one she thought she killed, was your father! How could she love that...pinche monster?

But how much could she love him if she were willing to help send him away? Perhaps not much. Perhaps she, too, had been deceived as surely thousands of women had over the demon's lifetime, including Antonio's very own mother. No, he shouldn't hold Ixtab's mistake against her.

But where was she? He looked at his watch. Midnight.

She'll be here. Have faith... He pushed Run Program and stepped back. The tablet began to vibrate with a loud hiss.

"Well, well. I've underestimated you, my son. I'll be very sorry to see you go."

His father and Ixtab stood side by side in the doorway, Ixtab gripping the old demon's arm. A surge of jealousy scorched his veins. How could she be touching him?

He looked at Ixtab. "What is going on?"

She shrugged. "Sorry, but your father and I have reconciled. And now that I can touch him, well, what can I say? I'm a sucker for a sex demon. Vampires...not so much."

She—she still loves him? How?

"I trusted you," he screamed. The noise coming from the tablet was deafening, as if the plates of the Earth were grinding together.

"No, asshole. We trusted you!" she screamed back. "You were supposed to open that portal and free our men, but all along you wanted to find some slut on the other side."

"So this is a punishment for that? For her?" Antonio couldn't believe Ixtab had deceived him. Her sister had been right; she was an evil monster.

Antonio's heart did not want to accept what his rational mind presented as the truth. Yet there she was, holding his father's arm and clearly taking his side—she'd tipped her hand and told the demon everything.

The wind in the room kicked up.

"Punishment for her?" Ixtab howled. "As if I care who a disgusting, weak vampire has the hots for. I've been reunited with my true love, and you're a threat to him. So time to go."

Ixtab turned away from Antonio and toward his father who, even in his emaciated state, was a head taller. She slipped off her veil and shoved it at his chest. "Hold this, my love!" she screamed over the loud noise.

A crack blasted through the air, and the tablet completely disappeared, creating a small wind tunnel in the center of the table, where a pale, delicate hand shot out.

Holy shit! Antonio gripped the hand and began pulling. If he were going to die or be banished to another realm, at least he'd save the woman.

A euphoric jolt coursed through his body when two hands gripped his shoulders from behind. Then he felt a pair of lips brush against his ear. "Hurry, Antonio. Get her out," Ixtab whispered.

Ixtab had been faking it? His mind surged with adrenaline. He wanted to spin around and see her face. He wanted to hold her. He wanted to kiss her. But dammit, he had to get rid of this demon!

"Oh no you don't!" Ixtab screamed. "Get your icky vampire ass inside that portal."

Antonio felt a gentle push on his back as Ixtab faked a struggle.

Another hand popped out. He gripped both of the woman's wrists and pulled. An elbow, a shoulder...

"Get your incu-ass over here, Francisco, and help me. He's too strong!" Ixtab screamed and grunted, pushing gently on Antonio's back.

The woman's face appeared in the hole. Two dark eyes filled with fear. Long dark hair. A delicate pale face with freckles on her nose.

Who the hell is she?

"Pull," the woman screamed frantically, "I'm almost out!"

The voice! He recognized the voice. But this was not the same face he'd seen again and again and again in his dreams. This was not that woman! Her eyes were completely different.

"Who the hell are you?" he bellowed above the noise, as he grunted and tried to free the woman from the grasp of the portal. At the same time, he felt an arm reach around his neck. The flesh was icc-cold. His father. This was it. Antonio gave one last yank, and the woman popped out, the force throwing her against the wall. He felt the arm around his neck tighten, pushing his head toward the portal.

Now it was time to get rid of this demon once and for all.

He grabbed the offending arm and turned his body. Those hazy, evil eyes stared through him as Antonio saw the faces of every soul his father had taken. So many innocent lives staring back at him.

Antonio grabbed the demon's upper arms and the two

began wrestling, each one trying to push the other into the portal. The old demon was much stronger than he looked.

Antonio glanced at the portal; the noise was beginning to fade. *Shit.* "It's about to close!"

Two golden-brown hands reached up from behind the demon and pressed against the sides of his saggy neck. Antonio watched as his father's face turned bright red, causing him to scream.

The demon fell to the side, and Ixtab threw herself over him, toppling the demon toward the portal's entrance. Just as its gravity took hold, the demon reached out and gripped Ixtab's arm. Her entire body jerked toward the portal's entrance.

Oh, hell! Antonio dove for her other hand and caught it as her body slipped inside.

He looked down at her face and staring back were two of the most hypnotic turquoise eyes he'd ever seen. They were bright, nearly translucent, framed with thick black lashes.

The woman. She's the woman? Why had he been seeing Ixtab's face while hearing this other woman's voice?

Yes, these were the catlike eyes he'd seen over and over again in his dreams. The entire time, it had been Ixtab's face in his visions! And her face was a breathtaking image of beauty. Two full lips, sculpted cheekbones, arched black brows framed with flowing brown hair. As he stared into her eyes, the world seemed to stop spinning around him. The noise, the wind, the chaos ground to a halt.

"You," he whispered. "It's you..."

He'd simply never seen a woman more beautiful in his life.

She smiled with a certain knowingness and joy that could not be articulated with words.

"Let go, Antonio," she said. "Be happy. For me."

What?

Her eyes shifted from side to side. "The portal is closing. Let go. Be happy!"

Had she lost her mind? "No! You promised you would not leave me." And what the hell was with this "happy" crap? He began to pull her arm. The wind and noise screamed in his ears.

"For fuck sake! Be happy, I command you!" she screamed. "Let go! He's got my other wrist."

No. He couldn't. He couldn't let her go. "Never."

"Why do vampires have to be so stubborn? The portal is closing! And you need to run before they come."

Run? Run from whom? He ignored her and pulled again. Her other hand reached out and gripped his, but instead of firming up her grasp, a searing hot pulse surged through his arm like hot lava.

"Happy!" she screamed.

"Goddammit, no!" he roared. Unable to hold on, his hand released her, and he watched her face disappear into the black hole right as the portal snapped shut.

"No!" He threw himself over the tablet. "Ixtab!"

She was gone.

His mind flew into a raging panic. "Fuck!" He would simply open it again and go after her. "You're not leaving!" He turned toward the edge of the table, but his equipment was gone. He spun in a circle and looked around the room. The entire place was empty. The portal had sucked everything in. "No! Fucking hell!"

"You can't open the portal again, anyway. The demon will come out," said a quiet voice.

A woman in a dingy white cotton dress, with little red

flowers embroidered on the hem, stared back with large dark brown eyes from the corner of the room.

"Who the hell are you?" Antonio barked.

She dusted off the front of her dress. "Miss Margaret O'Hare. Now, grab the tablet; we need to get the hell out of here!"

He stormed over, lifted her by the shoulders, and shook her. "I'm not taking you anywhere! Not until you tell me how to get Ixtab back!"

Gods help him, he would torture this woman if he had to.

The woman, whose eyes filled with contempt, was about to speak, but she stopped. Her gaze gravitated over his shoulder. "Oh, horsefeathers!" She looked at Antonio. "You want to know how to get Ixtab back? Put your game face on, vampire. It's showtime."

Antonio slowly turned his head.

What the... hell?

Veintiocho

⌐

The three men, if they could be called men, stood just inside the doorway of the small makeshift basement lab. And while Antonio had witnessed many horrific things in his life, these creatures were far beyond his wildest nightmares. That said, he didn't have time for this bull crap because Ixtab was all that mattered. He'd fucking had her all along, and he'd let her go. *How?*

"What are they?" He pushed Margaret squarely behind him.

"Maaskab," she replied.

These were Maaskab? That night in Helena's penthouse, Ixtab's sister Fate had described them as powerful, evil priests. He'd envisioned men in black robes sacrificing rabbits and chanting spells in Latin over a cauldron. Fate had completely left out the part about their rancid bodies being covered in odoriferous black grime and their hair being ropes of foul dreadlocks dripping with blood. And their sizes... *mierda del diablo.* They were beasts bigger than any creature he'd ever seen.

Well, he could give a shit about their size because gods only knew what that sadistic bastard of a demon could be doing to Ixtab. "What the fuck do you want?"

The largest of the creatures stepped forward and pointed its vile, blood-crusted finger at Antonio. It wore nothing more than a loincloth made from some sort of animal hide and a necklace full of human thumbs.

Or are those big toes? Christ... what a pinche *pack of* locos.

"Give us the tablet." Its voice sounded like nails screeching across a chalkboard.

Antonio looked down at the shimmering artifact lying on the floor beside him. Like hell he would. He'd rather die than hand over the only means to getting Ixtab back.

He placed his foot on top of the tablet and slid it a few inches back. "Pick it up, Margaret." He had no clue if he could trust this woman who'd come through the portal, but clearly she was his best bet in the room.

He felt her move, even though his eyes stayed locked on the dangerous creatures, thinking through his options. Not many. They were in the basement of the house, and the only way out was through them.

"The tablet is mine," Antonio growled.

The creature studied him with its soulless eyes—black irises surrounded by blood red. "Cimil promised it to us in exchange for helping the incubus. Where is he?" it growled, red spittle projecting from its mouth.

Cimil? The goddess who led him to the tablet in the first place?

"Don't let them have it," Margaret whispered from behind. "God only knows what they'll do with it."

No one, and he meant no one, was getting the tablet. Even if he had to drink these bastards to keep it. *Gulp, gulp, motherfuckers.*

There are three.

Sí, that is a pinche problema.

He quickly assessed. Could he use his speed to run past them? It was worth a try, because if he stayed there, he'd end up fighting them anyway.

Time to go.

He twisted and grabbed Margaret, clutching the petite woman like a football under his arm. They made it two steps before something plucked them out of thin air and whipped them to the cement floor. Antonio heard Margaret scream as his head smacked the ground, stunning him.

He opened his blurring eyes. *Caray!*

One of the creatures stood over Margaret and pulled a long, bloody dagger from its waistband. It raised the dagger over Margaret's chest.

She held out her hands. "No! I am your king's mate! I am your queen!"

The gargantuan creature paused and studied her for a moment. Whatever impression Margaret had hoped her words might have failed. The creature raised its knife and plunged. Antonio leaped and grabbed the Maaskab's arm, stopping it a centimeter from her chest. The monster's eyes widened and moved to Antonio's face.

That's when Antonio felt it: the darkness inside the evil priest. It snaked up Antonio's arm, seared its way into his flesh, and sank into his veins. He'd never felt anything so vile, so void of life, so horrid. And it tasted . . .

...Fucking delicious! More...

The creature sank to its knees, leaving bloody tracks down its throat as it clawed and struggled to breathe. Antonio drank it in, feeling the creature's energy sate his hunger and fill him with power. This was nothing like Ixtab's sweet touch. This was like eating meat. Raw, bloody, delicious meat.

"Watch out!" Margaret screamed, scrambling from the floor toward the sanctuary of the corner.

An arm reached around Antonio's neck and squeezed. He released the first creature and latched on to the new attacker with his hands. Delicious, succulent, dark energy poured in. How could something so horrid taste so good?

The creature dropped to the ground, lifeless.

Antonio looked up, ready for another meal, but he found only Margaret staring in wonderment. "How did you do that?"

Antonio looked around the room. He wanted more.

Margaret pointed toward the door. "The third one fled."

Antonio closed his eyes and savored the sensation coursing through him. In all his years, he never could've imagined that killing something for sustenance could feel so magnanimous, so damned good, like he'd been born to do it.

No more soy milk for you.

Okay, except perhaps for the chocolate kind; that shit is good.

Panting, he stood and leaned his heavy frame into the wall, shaking his head. "Are you all right?" he finally asked the woman.

"Yeah. I think so."

"Good. Now mind telling me who you are," he said.

"Margaret O'Hare. I already told you that."

Like that even came close to fucking explaining it. "Let's start with the basics—why did you tell that creature you are its queen?"

She produced an awkward laugh. "Because I am?"

Great. I just freed the Maaskab queen. Well, at least they didn't seem to like her much. That was something.

Killing time on the plane and catching up on her important secondhand eBay shopping, Cimil held up her phone and looked at the text message from Roberto. "Oh, thank the gods." She sighed with relief. The incubus and Ixtab were sucked into the portal as she'd hoped.

Sweet. Any Maaskab get away from the Dr.? she texted.

Roberto: Just one. I ate him.

Ewww . . . was he chewy?

Roberto: Yes.

Yeah. She'd eaten a Maaskab once when she'd run out of Milk Duds. There was such a thing as too chewy and the Maaskab were it.

Cimil: And the flock of Scabs hanging out in the guest villa?

Roberto: Ate them, too. Was hungry.

Cimil cringed. "Jeez. No kidding."

That's a good vampire. See you in Sedona for the handoff.

Then he could start rounding up all the vampires in Euro Disney for the final phase of Operation Over. Because little did anyone know there was really only one ruler of the vampire army, and that was their maker: Roberto.

Roberto: I love you my little cuddly ball of death and destruction.

Cimil: XOXO, Baby

"What do you mean you 'lost' Ixtab?" Penelope asked on the other end of the phone.

"Lost. As in fucking gone!" Antonio screamed, pacing across his bedroom.

"Was that before or after the Maaskab attacked and you ate them for dinner? By the way, that is quite possibly the most disgusting meal I've ever heard of. Way worse than those cactus larva tacos Belch keeps raving about," she said.

Yes. Yes, it was. And he'd do it again in a heartbeat. "I didn't eat the Maaskab, I drained their souls for sustenance," he explained.

"Wait. So you didn't drink their blood?" she asked.

"No. I am a vegetarian; I don't drink blood." *But I apparently drain dark energy from living creatures and turn it into food.*

What the hell have I become?

"I'm not following," she said. "Can you start over again? Go to the part where you say you killed Ixtab *again*."

"I didn't kill her…" Which was good because Ixtab would never forgive him if he ever did that again. "…We opened the portal, and she was sucked in with my father," he explained.

"The demon? She got sucked in with the demon?"

"Yes. She sacrificed herself," he replied.

"Oh, that is so sweet. She must love you."

Ixtab? Love him? He'd be lucky if she spit in his general direction after all of the crap he'd pulled on her.

Antonio snarled at himself.

"Well, she must," Penelope argued. "Don't panic. The most important thing is you didn't let the Maaskab get the tablet. We can still reopen the portal and get her back."

"We can't," he said. "The portal sucked in all of my equipment."

"Then build more equipment," Penelope said.

"It will take months!" he screamed. *Calm down,* coño. *Calm down.*

"No. It won't. Besides, we don't have months," said Margaret, who stood behind him listening to the conversation and picking through a pile of clean clothes the maid Kirstie had brought to his room. No doubt they smelled like borscht.

"Who is that talking?" Penelope asked.

"That's why I'm calling," he said. "She came out of the portal—she says she knows how to reopen it on her own, but she's demanding to see the gods first."

"Who is she?" Penelope asked.

"She says her name is Margaret O'Hare," he replied. "She says she's your brother's mate, Backlum Chaam's mate."

"Hold on," Penelope said and then screamed for Kinich.

"What's wrong?" Antonio could hear Kinich panting in the background. "Is it the baby?"

"You're so sweet. Gods, I love you." Penelope repeated the conversation to Kinich.

"A mate? Chaam? I wasn't aware of him finding one," Kinich grumbled in the background.

"She's demanding to speak with us," Penelope explained. "All of us. Do you think it's a trick? I mean, she came out of that portal; she could be another demon. What if this is a Maaskab trick?" she asked.

"Let me speak to her," Kinich barked over the phone into Antonio's ear.

"They want to speak with you." Antonio held out the phone, but Margaret simply stared, unsure of what to do.

Antonio activated the speaker. "Go ahead. They're listening."

Margaret walked over and screamed hello into the phone.

"Chaam never mentioned a mate," Kinich said. "Can you prove what you say?"

"Proof? No, I don't have proof," she screamed.

"You don't need to yell," Antonio whispered.

"Oh. Sorry." Margaret blushed. "I don't have proof, but I can tell you this: your sister Cimil is behind it all. Chaam turning evil, killing those women, the creation of the Maaskab and the Obscuros. She's the reason your brother Zac compelled you and had you try to kill Penelope."

There was a long silence on the other end of the phone. "Why didn't you tell me?" Kinich asked.

Apparently the question was directed at Penelope, who simply stuttered. "It's t-t-true." "Your brother Zac is the God of Temptation. He used his powers on you so that you'd be tempted by my blood," she said regretfully. She blew out a breath. "He also used his power on me so I'd leave you and marry him."

Antonio was grateful not to be in the same room with

them because Kinich's fury could be felt halfway around the world, and at this moment, Antonio had about all the rage he could manage given the situation with Ixtab.

"I see," Kinich said. "Antonio, the Uchben will be there within the hour to take you to our plane. Bring the woman to Arizona immediately. I want to hear what else she has to say and so will my brethren."

Antonio hung up the phone and looked at Margaret who returned to picking out clothes. "All right. The gods have agreed to meet with you, now tell me what you know."

"I need to bathe. Do you have a powder room?" she asked politely.

"You're not going to tell me anything?"

"Powder room?"

That was a no. *This woman may not make it alive to Arizona.*

Veintinueve

⁓

Antonio fought desperately not to throttle the mystery woman calmly sitting across from him on the private plane. From the moment they'd hung up the phone with Penelope and Kinich, she'd stopped talking.

Sure. Six goddamned weeks, the woman doesn't shut the hell up. "Save me. Save me!" And now he couldn't get her to speak one syllable worth a damn. He wanted to know how she'd been able to communicate with him. Why had he seen Ixtab's face but heard this woman's voice? Why did she want to speak to the gods? What was on the other side of the portal? Was Ixtab safe? Every time he asked a question, she'd simply replied that there'd be no answers until she had what she wanted.

Rage and panic, coupled with the powerful surge in energy he felt from his rather large snack, made him feel like he might actually lose his fucking mind. *You will get her back. You will save Ixtab...*

He returned to his seething. And glaring. And stewing. "I saved your life," he blurted out.

"And you have my gratitude," Margaret replied with a cold stare.

"You have a sick way of showing it. What do you want? Money? Revenge? Just tell me what the hell is going on, and I'll get you anything you want."

"Right now, I'd like a strong drink. Whiskey."

Whiskey? She wanted whiskey?

He pointed toward the bar in the back of the plane. "Help yourself."

She popped out of her seat, seemingly oblivious to the fact he might actually rip off her head before they made it to Arizona.

Antonio slid his iPad from his leather backpack, mumbling furiously while his e-mails loaded.

After the attack, while his maid saw to Margaret's "powder room" needs, he'd carefully wrapped up the tablet, preparing it for transport, and jumped on ordering new equipment to be delivered to Arizona. He calculated it would take one month to rebuild the simulator. He prayed Ixtab would be all right until then, wherever she was, because he'd never forgive himself if he lost her.

But what will happen if you open the portal again? If his father were to escape, they'd be back to square one; the demon needed a new body. On the other hand, he couldn't live without Ixtab. He needed her. No, perhaps *need* was too casual of a word. A man could say he needed clean socks or a cold beer on a hot day. A man could claim he needed a good fuck or new lawn mower. *Need* wasn't the correct word to describe what he truly felt. Ixtab had infused herself with his heart and soul. Without her, he felt like a hollowed-out shell of a man who might never have the urge to take another breath or fight another battle or give a shit about anything ever again in this world if he didn't get her back. He didn't *need* Ixtab. He'd cease to exist without her.

And how the hell had he been such an idiot to not see she was the one? From the moment they'd met, he'd been drawn to everything about her—sharp edges, horrible humor, the tenacity of a pit bull. Holy hell, she was magnificent. And then there was her beauty. It was hard to imagine that beneath the awful black shroud hid the most divine female to ever walk the planet. Deeply bronzed skin; full, sumptuous lips; long, flowing dark hair; and a set of piercing eyes that could stop any man in his tracks.

Christ, he'd wanted her so badly even before he'd known what she looked like, which was a testimony to the powerful connection between them. Yes, that night in Bacalar—touching and kissing her body so intimately— had been the most unexpected, pleasurable experience of his life. He could only imagine what it would have been like if they'd been able to finish what they had started. But his lust didn't come close to the depth of emotion he now felt for her.

He'd never have another sane or happy moment again without her.

He had to get her back.

Though would she want him after everything he'd done so horribly wrong? He'd refused to listen to her countless times, he'd unjustly directed his frustration and anger toward her when she'd simply been trying to help him, and he'd thrown this other woman in her face after she'd told him about the most painful moment of her life. Then... she still sacrificed herself for him.

Gods, he was such a coldhearted bastard. He'd let his hatred for his father and fear of losing his brother consume him.

He could only hope for a chance to make amends. Yes, whatever it took, he would find a way to get her back without freeing his father. *Perhaps the gods will know what to do. Because this Margaret woman sure as hell isn't going to help me.*

He looked at Margaret, who seemed lost in her own thoughts, and then at his watch. They were still two hours away. He went back to his e-mail, hoping for a short distraction. There was a note from his brother, who was on a business trip to Los Angeles and none the wiser that his life had been on the line or that their father was a demon and had been sucked into a portal. Antonio would have to explain everything when the time came.

Then Antonio saw that one of the parts he'd ordered for the circuit board was out of stock. "Son of a bitch," he seethed. "Eight weeks for one *pinche circuito*!"

"I wouldn't bother, yanno."

He looked up at Margaret, who stared with intense dark eyes, sipping a glass of whiskey. "What do you mean?" he asked.

"The equipment can't open the portal. It never could."

"What do you mean?" he asked again, this time scathing.

She turned her gaze out the window.

She wasn't going to answer.

"What did I ever do to you?" he asked.

She didn't respond, but that wouldn't stop him from giving her a piece of his mind.

"You nearly drove me mad while I tried to free you. Do you have any idea what I went through? Do you? I went blind. I had my throat ripped out and died. I turned into a vampire and killed—yes, *killed* a goddess, who, by the way, happens to be the woman I love and have now lost! Lost saving you! So if you think for one moment that I won't hurt you to get her back, you are mistaken."

She glanced at him, her face a vision of tranquility. "I know you won't believe me, but Ixtab getting sucked into the portal was never part of my plan."

"Then help me get her back. Tell me how to reopen the portal," he demanded, standing over her.

She glared fearlessly with her deep brown eyes. "Do you think I'm an idiot? You think I'm going to tell you anything before I have what I want? I've waited over eighty years, watching the man I love suffer." She looked out the window. "You'll get your answers, Antonio, when I have justice for Chaam."

"What if the gods don't give you what you want?" Whatever the hell that was.

"Then it's simple. You will not get Ixtab back."

Like hell he wouldn't.

Near Sedona, Arizona

Two hours later, the sky swirled with brilliant shades of blazing oranges and reds as the plane touched down just after sunrise on the dusty airstrip at the Uchben base. For a few moments, Antonio imagined it was a sign that the heavens were filled with contempt for his having let Ixtab slip through his fingers. And they had a right to be angry with him.

You fool.

The soldiers, who'd flown the plane, wasted little time ushering him and Margaret into a black Hummer and getting them to the estate a few kilometers away, situated atop a hill. Antonio had never been to this part of the country, but it looked exactly as one might imagine. Large cactus jutting from the ground like thorny sentinels, watching over miles of open sandy-brown dirt, the sharp angles of the buttes off in the distance, the straggly dry vegetation scattered across the desert floor like confetti after a big parade. Somehow the barren surroundings only made Antonio feel more anxious. This was not the sort of place he imagined his fate being decided.

The vehicle pulled up to the imposing, arched entrance of the sandstone-colored adobe home.

"This way. Everyone is waiting in the summit room," said a soldier in a Scottish accent. He wore his red hair in a long braid and was dressed in black military garb. He didn't wear any insignia but seemed to be in charge. "And I ken put that in the vault fer ya." He reached for Antonio's bag, which contained the tablet and his notebooks.

Antonio held on; knowing the Maaskab were after it, he wasn't so sure he wanted to let the tablet go. "I don't think I caught your name."

"Gabrán. They call me, Gabrán." The man's voice was filled to the brim with don't-fuck-with-me tone. Antonio approved and handed over the bag.

They followed Gabrán inside, down several long hall-
ways, through the estate and finally to a set of enormous,
hand-carved double doors. A loud ruckus radiated from
the other side.

Antonio heard Penelope's voice. "Shhh. They're here."

Gabrán opened the door and there, standing around a
giant stone slab table was a group of very odd-looking circus types—a tall man with long silver hair down to his
ankles, wearing a giant jade headdress; another man with
a large round belly, wearing nothing but a pair of white
underpants; another woman had an enormous beehive
atop her head; and a few others who were ready to attend
a costume party. If it weren't for Penelope and Kinich
standing at the head of the table—who he'd already met,
along with Fate—Antonio would have believed that these
were not in fact deities, but people who'd escaped from
the insane asylum.

"Is that a burro with a sombrero standing in the corner?" Antonio asked the cold-faced soldier holding open
the door.

"'Tis," was his only reply.

Diablos. Qué locos. "After you, Ms. O'Hare." Antonio
gestured to the woman, who now wore a plain baby-blue
sweater and a denim skirt his Kirstie had given her. She
looked like she should be attending classes at college, not
orchestrating an epic blackmail of the gods to free her
"king." Of course, nothing ever appeared as it should in
this world.

"Maggie, call me Maggie." She smiled at Antonio,
though he was in no mood to smile back.

"Hello, Maggie. I'm Penelope Trudeau and this is—"

"I know who you are." Maggie's eyes swept the rooms

as she held out her palm, signaling for silence. "Kinich, Belch, K'ak, Fate, Bees, Akna, A.C., and that lady—I forget her name."

"How do you know who we are?" Kinich asked.

"I've been trapped inside that portal since 1934," Maggie replied. "And though you could not see me, I saw just about everything from the realm where I was trapped."

Belch chimed in, "Did you see this?" He sprang from his chair and showed everyone his backside.

"Yes! We've all seen it!" everyone screamed.

With a satisfied grin, Belch sat back down in his throne and returned to his jumbo martini glass—the kind most people used as a decoration to hold candy and such.

Penelope cleared her throat. "My apologies, Maggie. Please continue. Why have you requested an audience?"

Maggie's dark eyes shuffled around the faces in the room. "As I explained on the phone, Cimil has betrayed you, all of you. Not only am I here to set the record straight and demand justice, I'm here to ensure you free my mate, Chaam."

A collective gasp erupted.

"Then you've wasted your time, woman," replied Kinich. "He will never be freed. He is evil."

"Yes. He is. But it's not Chaam's fault, nor does he wish to be; that's why"—Maggie looked right at Antonio—"Ixtab is going to cure him."

Hisses and objections filled the room.

Maggie slapped her hand on the rough stone table. "Enough! My patience ran out decades ago. You will listen to everything I have to say. You will free Chaam and you will punish Cimil."

"If you've been spying on us, you...*pest,* then you are aware we do not take orders from mortals," Fate pointed out, cleaning her nails with an arrowhead she'd plucked from her quiver.

"Then you won't see Ixtab, Guy, and the others again," Maggie said.

"Silly mortal, we have the tablet." Fate sighed her words as if she were much too important for this conversation.

Gods, what a snotty woman. How had Ixtab put up with her for seventy millennia? He'd only been in Fate's presence a collective hour at best, and already he wanted to lock her in a closet. In fact, her snobby attitude was the reason he'd rejected Fate's repeated pleas to assist him in his lab when he had met her in New York. Sorry, but he liked his women with a little humility. He liked Ixtab.

Maggie shook her head. "You're all idiots. The tablet can't free your men; while they are trapped inside another dimension, it's a Maaskab spell that holds them there. You must free Chaam and make the trade with the Maaskab if you want them back. But you must cure Chaam before you do it or he'll return to his evil ways. Ixtab is the only one who can help him, and I'm the only one who knows how to get her back." She looked at Antonio. "Like I said on the plane, you're welcome to rebuild your equipment and try, Mr. Acero, although I can guarantee, you will fail. There is only one way to invoke the tablet's powers."

Antonio's mind ran with that statement. He remembered the portal opening at the precise moment Ixtab had entered the room with his father. Was there another variable?

"We will not free Chaam," Kinich declared.

"Fine. Then our conversation is over. And so is everything else. You! Your baby." She pointed at Penelope. "Everything! Because I can guarantee that this path you're on, the path that Cimil created, is leading us all to a very, very bad place." Maggie turned to leave.

"Wait," Antonio said to Maggie and then looked at each of the gods. "Ixtab is your sister. Isn't she worth a few minutes of your goddamned precious time?"

Penelope gently stroked Kinich's arm. "He's right, my love. Let's hear Maggie out."

Kinich grumbled, but accepted.

Penelope moved to the side and gestured toward the large throne at the head of the table. "Sit, Maggie. We're all ears."

Maggie looked around the table, and Antonio couldn't help but wonder what sort of insane story she was about to tell. For the record, prior to meeting Ixtab, he'd thought his world was pretty damned strange. On the outside, he looked like a rich playboy from a privileged Spanish family, who owned the most prestigious wineries in Spain. In reality, his father was a monster who killed women for sustenance, including Antonio's own mother. Antonio's public and private lives couldn't be more contradictory or bizarre. That's what he believed, anyway, until he became a vampire—the least eventful part of this story—who loathed the thought of drinking blood before finding out evil Mayan priests made a tasty snack. Add that Ixtab, the Goddess of Suicide—a damned ridiculous title for such a lovely creature—was the love of his life and trapped with his demonic father in another dimension. *Sí. Pretty fucking strange.* Yet somehow, he knew they were only getting started as Maggie cleared her throat and lifted her chin.

"About eighty years ago," she said, "I accompanied my father, an archaeologist, on a dig in southern Mexico. It was a terrible time in our lives; my mother had passed away only a few months earlier, and unknown to me, my father had become obsessed with bringing her back. Also unknown was that the tablet he'd discovered"—Maggie looked at Antonio—"was no coincidence. Cimil planned for him to find it and made sure he believed it could resurrect the dead."

"Can it?" asked Penelope.

Maggie nodded. "Yes. It can, though not the way you think; the tablet has the ability to open portals to other points in time in addition to other dimensions. So if one wanted, they could go back and save someone before they die. The problem is returning. The portal only stays open for a short while. So if one doesn't carry another tablet or have someone to reopen the portal from their point of origin, they might not return. That said, my father never got far enough to figure any of that out. He died before he had the chance to open it."

"Did Cimil kill him?" Penelope asked, appearing horrified.

"No. Chaam did." Maggie dropped her head and appeared to be struggling not to cry. "My father had been missing for several days, and I'd been searching the jungle for his excavation site—he'd kept it a secret. Then I got lost and, unfortunately, bumped into a very angry jaguar. When I ran, I fell and hit my head. That's when Chaam found me.

"At first I thought I'd lost my mind. He told me he was

a god, and while I didn't believe him initially, every time we touched, I saw things. Visions. It took less than one day before I realized the truth; we were meant to be. He knew it, too. But what we didn't know was that our meeting was all part of Cimil's plot."

Antonio now began to feel anxious. There were simply too many parallels to his story, including Cimil's direct involvement with his finding the tablet, which ultimately led him to Ixtab.

"The details aren't important," Maggie explained. "However, Chaam eventually found my father. He'd gone mad and was about to kill a young woman—a friend of mine named Itzel. Chaam was forced to kill him, and Cimil made sure I was there to witness everything."

"Why would Cimil want all this to happen?" Kinich asked.

Good question. Because apparently whatever Cimil was up to definitely involved him and Ixtab, too. Bottom line, he didn't like where this was going.

"Because the events triggered the portal, which sucked me in," Maggie explained. "Then Cimil told Chaam I'd died only to make him suffer more. Everything she did was so his bond with the Universe would sever. Then she got inside his head and made him do horrible, horrible things, including trying to end the world—which she's still planning to do. That's what this is all about! Everything she's ever done was always about this."

Antonio found it very difficult to believe that finding the love of his life, Ixtab, would in some way contribute to the end of the world. No, something felt very . . . off.

"Do you have proof of anything you're saying?" Kinich asked. "Your accusations are extremely serious."

"I have another witness." Maggie turned toward the door of the room and pointed. "Máax saw everything, too."

The entire room gasped.

"You!" Fate screamed. "How dare you bring him here! He is not to be spoken of by anyone! He is dead to us!" She turned her back.

"Who the hell is Máax?" Antonio didn't see anyone.

"Máax is just another victim in all this," Maggie exclaimed. "How many deities will you allow to fall victim to Cimil? Huh? First Máax, then Chaam. Even Kinich and Zac. How about when you were imprisoned inside your own cenotes! Seventy years! While Cimil roamed free. Why can't you see? She's been playing with everyone. Listen to Máax. He will tell you the truth! He's incapable of lying!"

"Who the hell is Máax?" Antonio demanded loudly.

"He is the God of Truth," Maggie replied.

"No! He no longer bares that title," Fate barked. "He is the One No One Speaks Of. He broke our most sacred law. He is dead to us. Banished forever."

"Enough!" Kinich commanded. "We will listen to what Máax has to say. We need to know the truth."

"You are no longer a deity, brother. You do not command us," Fate said to Kinich.

"Yes, he does!" Penelope chimed in. "He is my husband. He and I are bound. Therefore, we are one and now share the role of Ruler of the House of Gods."

"I love being a deity. This is getting interesting." Belch poured another martini and leaned back in his chair with a giant grin.

Interesting? Interesting is what one might say about a person with two thumbs on one hand. This was a fucking circus. And they all seemed to be sharing the same god-damned delusion, fighting about someone named Máax who wasn't there.

"When did you marry?" asked Bees sweetly.

Penelope blushed. "Yesterday. We stopped over in Vegas on the way here. We wanted to wait to tell everyone since there's so much going on."

"That is lovely news," Bees said. "Have you registered yet?"

"No. We haven't had the chance," Penelope replied.

"How about a llama? Everyone needs a llama," Belch offered with projectile spittle.

"Are you people for real? You're like children on a sugar bend," Maggie said. "Can we please get back to the conversation?"

"*Puta madre!* I couldn't agree more," Antonio added impatiently.

Penelope cleared her throat. "Sorry. That's how they roll around here. I guess it's rubbing off on me. Yes. We would like to hear what Máax has to say. Where is he?"

Máax's deep voice rang out across the room. "I am here." Penelope jumped out of her skin.

"What the hell?" Antonio said.

"Máax was banished and therefore invisible," Kinich stated calmly.

Yes, a pinche loco *circus, complete with invisible clowns.*

"The girl speaks the truth," Máax said. "I have witnessed Cimil's actions."

"Traitor," Fate hissed at Máax, paying no attention to what he was trying to say.

"I did what I must. I do not regret it." Máax's deep voice held no intonation, no emotion, no room for debate.

"What did he do?" Penelope asked Kinich.

"Time travel," Kinich replied. "And vows he will do it again."

"Okeydokey, then," said Penelope. "Is he really incapable of lying?"

Kinich nodded yes.

"What next?" Penelope asked.

"You must free Chaam, and Cimil must be stopped." Maggie turned to Antonio. "I will tell you how to free Ixtab, and in exchange, she will cure Chaam."

Antonio wasn't sure he liked Maggie's plan. Not only did this Chaam sound dangerous, but opening the portal and freeing Ixtab only solved one problem. The other fact remained that his father had gone in with her.

"What about Guy, Niccolo, and the men?" Penelope asked.

"Once Chaam is free," Maggie stated coolly, "the Maaskab will remove the hex; they will free your men. They want to fight you like Emma's grandmother said."

"Cimil convinced them this was their path to victory," Máax added.

"Then it's settled, we free Chaam," Kinich stated.

"It must be put to a vote," Fate stated dryly. "Despite how Chaam became evil, the fact remains that he did many terrible things and is, in fact, very dangerous. Releasing him is a risk and there is no guarantee Ixtab will be able to cure him."

Penelope sighed. "I understand that, but if we can cure him, it could be the turning point for us; we'd have the Maaskab leader on our side. No war. No apocalypse. Done. Over."

"You all assume," Fate said, "that the apocalypse will be brought by the Maaskab. But that is not what Cimil predicted. She said the end was coming, not by whose hand."

"Who else could it be?" asked Penelope.

Fate picked a piece of invisible lint from the front of her white dress. "That is for fate to decide."

A loud groan erupted.

Penelope rolled her eyes. "All in favor of freeing Chaam and hunting Cimil?" Belch, K'ak, Fate, Akna, Bees, and A.C. raised their hands. "And Kinich and I vote yes, too."

"I will volunteer to bring in Cimil," A.C., God of Eclipses, said in a dark voice.

"That won't be necessary."

Everyone gasped and turned. Standing in the doorway was Cimil and a vampire. A very, very pale vampire who looked as though the thought of living one more second might bore him to death.

Maggie instantly lunged for the goddess, but an invisible hand reached out and held her back. "Her time will come, Margaret. Do not waste your efforts on her," Máax stated calmly.

Cimil, who wore what appeared to be a pink-checkered square-dancing outfit, smiled. "Máax, sweetie. So glad to *see* you!" She burst out laughing. "Get it?" She turned to her vampire who made no reaction whatsoever.

"Yeah. I know. It's totally true," Cimil replied, though he hadn't said anything.

"Cimil, what do you have to say for yourself? Did you

turn Chaam evil? Have you been plotting the end of the world?" Kinich asked.

"Is that all you've got on me? 'Cause, I can tell you right now, *my* list is way longer." She looked at her vampire. "Right, Roberto, baby?"

Roberto, who wore a black cape, red satin shirt, and leather pants, nodded at Cimil and then swooped out of the room with a twirl of his cape.

"Tootles!" Cimil chuckled and shook her head. "Vampires. They're so dramatic with the whole entrance and exit thing. Did you notice? His cape is completely wrinkle-free. I'm getting really good at ironing. Aaahh... domestic bliss at last."

"Cimil!" Kinich screamed. "Yes or no?"

Cimil jumped and then smoothed down her straight red hair. "Yes. It's true. Every word. Before I say anything else, I demand a lawyer and fair trial. And a fruit basket. But instead of fruit, I want it filled with bagged blood. It's for Minky, my unicorn. You do allow unicorns in prison, right?"

"A.C.? Can you deal with her?" Penelope asked.

Antonio blinked and suddenly Cimil was on the floor, sawing logs, her pink petticoat a tangled mess around her waist and her shiny, pink hot pants on display.

Kinich nodded at his brother A.C. "Thank you. Do you mind taking her to our special holding cell?"

A.C. bowed his head. "My pleasure. I've always wanted to use my gift of sleep to shut her up."

"Well, that was certainly unexpected," Penelope mumbled to no one in particular, then looked at Maggie. "I'm sorry, Maggie. Truly sorry for what you've been through." She looked at Antonio. "The tablet is in the vault, so whenever you're ready, let us know."

"I'm nowhere near ready," Antonio replied. "We cannot release Ixtab without risking that *jodido demonio* from escaping as well." Gods, this was the most infuriating situation, because there was nothing he wanted more than to get Ixtab back. There had to be a way to do it without freeing that bastard father of his.

"Oh! Man! I looovvvee this channel. It just keeps getting better and better." Belch poured yet another martini and burped.

"You're vile," Bees hissed.

"Christ almighty." Kinich shook his head.

Penelope reached out and stroked his forearm. "What, honey? What's the matter?"

He grumbled and then sucked in a breath. "The only deity capable of dealing with a demon is Cimil—the underworld creatures are her domain."

A collective "Oh, crap" rang through the air.

"Checkmate!" Belch clapped and then roared with laughter, smacking his hand on the table. "Oh, gods, Cimil is a riot."

Penelope ignored Belch, as did everyone else, and looked at Maggie. "You can go now. Ask the soldier outside to have someone show you to a room."

"You're not letting Cimil go, are you?" Maggie asked.

"No. We'll find another way to deal with the demon," Penelope replied.

"I want your word." Maggie looked around the table. "I want everyone's word or no deal. And for the record, I'm not telling you how to open the portal until Chaam is free."

"For this to work, doesn't Ixtab need to be there when we release him?" Penelope asked.

"Guess you'll have to take the tablet to Mexico then and open the portal outside Chaam's prison. Won't you? Do we have a deal—yes or no?"

"Yes," Penelope stated.

Treinta

⌒

Antonio waffled between fury and panic as the powerful yet clearly insane deities debated what to do next. It
seemed that Cimil was an excellent chess player, but by
no means was this checkmate.

"We must strike a deal with Cimil."

"No, No deals."

"Then let the demon out. We'll catch up with him
later."

Their words flew through the air so quickly that Anto-
nio had a difficult time keeping up with the conversation.
One deity would start a sentence, another would finish.
They went around and around like an angry pair of cats.

"Stop!" Antonio barked. "If you let my father out, he
will need a new host. That host will be my brother. Not
acceptable."

Penelope, who seemed to be the calmest out of the
group, stood and paced at the back of the room. "I will

talk to Cimil and see what she wants in exchange for her help with the demon."

"No," Bees said. "Her crimesss are unforgivable. No dealsss; this is what she wants."

Penelope held out her hand. "I know. But we're talking Cimil here. Maybe all she wants is a chocolate chip cookie or a ride on her unicorn."

"Good point," said Bees.

"I agree," Fate said. "Let's see what she wants."

"I want to be there," said Antonio. His father could not be allowed out and Ixtab had to be saved. If Cimil was the only one who could make this happen, he sure as hell wouldn't leave the job of convincing her up to this wackypack.

"Are you still here, vamp-ubus?" Fate scowled at Antonio.

"Vamp-ubus?" asked Antonio.

"Incu-pire, then?" Fate offered.

Antonio simply stared.

"Well, I must call you something, and vampire slash incubus is much too lengthy," Fate explained.

"How about Antonio, for fuck sake," Antonio growled. These deities were unbelievable. How had Ixtab remained sane living with them all these centuries?

Fate glanced at the ceiling, pondering. "Antonio Forfucksake? I don't get it."

"Enough!" Antonio screamed. "My woman's life is on the line. Can you people—deities, what fucking ever—please focus?"

Bees chuckled. "Do all Spaniards swear so much? You put the Demilords to shame."

"Wait," Fate asked, gasping. "*Your* woman? You mean Ixtab?"

"Are you deaf?" Antonio replied. "Yes. Ixtab is mine. Does this present an issue for you?"

"Oh!" Penelope squealed. "Congratulations, Antonio. I knew it would work out for you two."

Fate grumbled something about vampires being disgusting.

Kinich cleared his throat. "Eh-hem."

"Fate," Penelope said, narrowing her eyes, "I've always wanted to say this: stop being such a bitch and shut your pie hole." Penelope grabbed Kinich's hand and kissed his cheek. "I love you." She looked at Antonio. "And you are very welcome to listen in when we talk to Cimil."

Antonio bowed his head. "Thank you. I hope this mess doesn't get any more complicated."

"You havvven't been arounnnd very long"—Belch chuckled—"havvve you?" He raised his glass into the air. "'Cause you haven't seen anything yet."

After a short drive back to the Uchben base, where the plane had landed earlier, Penelope and Kinich took Antonio to a small building toward the edge of the compound. For the most part, it looked like your everyday administrative office—lobby, glass conference rooms, cubicles—with the exception of one thing: two large soldiers with automatic rifles standing on either side of an elevator bank toward the back.

Antonio felt his ears pop when they reached the negative twentieth floor—twenty stories belowground.

"What is this place?" he asked.

The elevator doors slid open, and they stepped out into a dark hallway lit with red lights.

"This is where our operations are housed," Kinich explained. "There's a control center; a bunker large enough to house tens of thousands of people if needed; a hospital, training facilities, and, of course, weapons."

"Don't forget the mall, honey," Penelope added. "And the restaurants— Oh, if you're into beer there's a great pub. They have a thousand different beers."

"Some other time perhaps," Antonio replied politely. He wondered if they had any fare of his liking. A nice Maaskab or two to suck the life out of; he was getting a little hungry.

"This way." Kinich gestured toward a set of doors with a keypad on one side. He punched in the numbers and the door clicked. "This, of course, is the back entrance to the underground complex. We keep the holding cells separate from everything else."

Antonio entered what looked to be a rather large prison block with three tiers of cells on all sides, overlooking a caged guard station in the middle of the ground floor. Armed men in black were posted in every corner. "How many prisoners are in here?"

"Right now," Penelope said, "about a hundred. This is where we keep detainees until we decide what to do with them—rehabilitate, put on trial, or, in the case of Belch, keep him confined until he promises to put his pants back on. He once spent a month in here."

Kinich chuckled. "He never was a fan of clothing."

This was a very odd, odd group of beings.

"Hi, guys."

All three turned and saw a young redheaded woman sitting outside a cell.

"Emma!" Penelope embraced the woman who looked

like she'd seen better days—deep circles under her eyes, hollow cheeks, and a melancholy smile. "This is Antonio Acero. Antonio, this is Emma Keane; her fiancé is Guy Santiago, also known as Votan, the God of Death and War."

They shook hands briefly, and now more than ever he felt the sting of being unable to open the portal and rescue the trapped men. "I'm sorry about the situation and not being able to free your fiancé—"

"It's all right, Antonio. Penelope already told me everything Maggie said. I know we were barking up the wrong tree." Emma spoke as though she'd already lost hope.

Penelope reached out and held her hand. "We'll get him back, I promise. In fact, that's why we're here." Her eyes flashed toward the cell in the far corner.

Emma looked like she understood. "Good luck with that."

Antonio suddenly caught a mental whiff of something delicious. "Hmmm..." There standing on the other side of the bars, where Emma had just been sitting, was an elderly woman in a blue jumpsuit. Her head had been shaved and her skin looked like it had been scrubbed raw. Her black-and-red eyes drilled into him and he couldn't resist licking his lips.

Emma flashed a glance over her shoulder. "Are you drooling over my grandmother?"

He nodded yes.

Emma hissed. "Seriously?"

"Emma's grandmother is a Maaskab," Penelope explained. "We're holding her until the next summit meeting so we can discuss a cure for her."

"Hey! Hey! Over here! You're late!"

"Ah. There's Cimil," Penelope said with contempt. "I'll be right back, Emma. Wish us luck..." She gave Emma a quick hug and whispered, "It will all be over soon."

Would it be? He wasn't so sure.

Antonio and Penelope followed Kinich to a large cell in the corner.

Cimil stood on the other side of a thick glass window, waving. She wore hot-pink pajama pants and a pink bathrobe. Her flaming-red hair was pulled into pigtails. Hannibal Lecter had nothing on her.

"Can I just say, for starters"—Cimil pulled up a giant fluffy beanbag chair and plopped down right in front of the window—"this is the best vacay ever! I love winning stuff."

Penelope, Kinich, and Antonio exchanged glances. She couldn't be serious. Could she?

"Cimil," Kinich said with a stern warning in his voice, "we need to talk, so cut the shit."

Cimil popped open her robe and flashed her T-shirt: "Shit is my middle name. Except on Wednesdays when I speak Klingon, then it's baktag."

"Funny, Cimil. Very funny." Kinich placed his palms against the glass and leaned in. "What do you want?"

Cimil smiled, her bright turquoise eyes twinkling. "*Moi?* Want something? You came to see me. So what do *you* want?"

Kinich narrowed his eyes.

"Well, I suppose I do want *something*," she said. "A new pony would be nice. Roberto drank mine; he thought it was an offering. I'd also like world peace. Or whirled peas. Either-or. Both are fun. And then there's that little matter of—"

"Enough!" Antonio could take no more. "If you say one more ridiculous, fucking thing, so help me, I will break through this glass and pluck out your eyes."

Cimil sprang from her beanbag chair, clapping with excitement. "Oh! Pluck, Pluck, Eyeball is my favorite game!" She looked at Penelope. "It's like Duck, Duck, Goose ... but with eyeballs!"

Antonio slammed his fist into the glass, but it bounced right off. He'd kill this deity if it was the last thing he did.

"Don't waste your strength, Antonio," said Kinich. "The glass in these cells are deity reinforced—unbreakable."

"But Cimil is a deity. Can't she use her powers to get out?"

"The cells are also warded. No energy can permeate the cell. Nothing gets in or out." He pointed to a small speaker embedded in the wall to the side of the glass. "Not even sound; we use an intercom system."

I guess it's her lucky day, then.

"Cimil," Penelope said sweetly, "please? I'm sure you already know why we're here. So what do you really want?"

Cimil froze; her face, expression, and eyes went blank.

Penelope snapped her fingers. "Cimil? Hello?"

Cimil's eyes moved to Antonio. "I'm not going to help you with the demon."

Antonio growled. "Why the hell not?"

Penelope touched Antonio's arm signaling for him to give her a chance. "Cimil, we know you must want something. So spit it out," she said.

Cimil's gaze was nearly catatonic. "I want a fair trial."

"And what do we get in exchange?" Antonio asked.

"Nothing. I will not help you with the demon."

"Why not?" Penelope asked.

"Because you don't need my help. You simply need to choose."

Antonio felt the blood drain from his face. "Do you mean I have to choose between Ixtab or my brother's life?"

"Or perhaps your own." Cimil winked and sat down in her chair, her gaze utterly vegetative.

Penelope snapped her fingers again. "Cimil? Cimil?" She looked at Kinich and shrugged.

"Gods dammit, answer me!" Antonio demanded.

"She's done talking," Kinich said and pulled him back.

"What the hell do you mean, 'She's done talking'? I'm not done." No, he was just getting started. "Open that fucking cell."

Kinich flashed his palms. "Trust me, if I believed letting you take a few bites out of Cimil would help the situation, I'd let you in there. But she is a deity."

"So that means she does not need to pay for her crimes?" Cimil had lured him to the tablet and the tablet had taken away Ixtab.

"No, Antonio, it means she's immortal and there's nothing *you* can do to harm her. She will get what she deserves. The gods will see to that," Kinich said, his turquoise eyes turning to a deep, dark gray.

Cimil mumbled, "Everyone will get what they deserve."

What the hell did that mean?

Antonio ran his hands through his hair. This was going nowhere fast and he was no closer to getting Ixtab free. Perhaps it was time to take matters into his own hands.

No more Mr. Nice-ubus. Or was that . . . Mr. Nice-u-pire?

"What the hell are you doing here?" Maggie hissed through the open doorway, holding a fresh towel to her body.

"Relax. I only came to talk," Antonio said.

"I'm done talking. At least until it's time to free Chaam." She pushed the door closed.

"Wait." He wedged his foot in the crack. "Please... I am." *Qué joder.* "I. Am. Begging you."

Margaret stared up at him for a few moments and then sighed. "All right. Come in."

"Thank you."

Margaret disappeared through the bathroom doorway without a word.

Antonio entered the spacious bedroom and sat down in the small sitting area in the corner.

"Everything here"—she emerged from the bathroom wearing a robe and a towel on her head—"is incredible. Did you know they have a computer screen in the bathroom that can play music, control the temperature of your bathwater, give a weather forecast, and make phone calls?"

Yes. The wealth and opulence of the deities put even his family to shame, although his father had been more into the sort of luxury that attracted females: a yacht in the French Riviera, the penthouse suite in Monte Carlo, private planes. If his father weren't a life-sucking, cold-hearted demon, he might actually consider the guy fun—during his earlier days, anyway. His prior lifestyle of drowning his sorrows and bedding women no longer interested him.

Now there was only one woman he wanted to bed. And the irony was he couldn't have her.

Not yet, anyway.

Maybe never, she might not forgive you even if you do free her.

"It must be hard adjusting to the changes," he said.

She sat across from him, a demure look on her face. She was actually quite lovely now that he looked. Pale skin, freckles on her nose, wide brown eyes. It was difficult to believe she was over one hundred years old.

"Being back isn't as bad as you think," she explained. "I didn't have any family apart from my father, so in a way, I'm returning to what I left behind: nothing. I suppose it was a blessing not having to worry about anyone while I was trapped. Except for Chaam, anyway."

"How is he?"

Sadness filled her eyes. "I don't know. I can't see him now that I'm free. I only hope we'll reach him in time—and that Ixtab can cure him."

"About that," he said. "I need to tell you there's a problem."

"Horsefeathers. They're letting Cimil out, aren't they?"

Antonio shook his head no. "She refused to help me. If we open that portal, my father will be released. His body is about to give out, which means he will require a new one, and he intends to take my brother's. Obviously, I can't let that happen. I won't give up his life for Ixtab's." Dammit. This situation was impossible.

"No. You're wrong, Antonio," she said. "I heard him speaking to Cimil—I kept a very close eye on her—he intends to take *your* body."

His body? A vampire? "I didn't think that was possible. Are you sure?" he asked.

"I heard the conversation a day before you showed up to your father's house. He believes that Ixtab belonged to him. He wanted your body so he could finally be with her. That's why the Maaskab were there, to help with the transfer—in exchange for getting the tablet back, of course. Could you imagine? Maaskab with the ability to time travel? They'd be able to do anything they liked."

Antonio was no longer listening to Margaret. Because now the cold truth of the situation had just turned into an inhabitable tundra of despair. He could save Ixtab in exchange for his own life. He would be the next host, not his brother, if the demon got out.

"Are you all right?" Margaret asked. "Antonio?"

He nodded slowly. "I didn't know." He looked up at her. "I didn't know he wanted me." *So that's what Cimil meant when she said I'd have to choose.*

"I'm sorry."

"At least I no longer have to choose between her and my brother. If the choice is giving up my life to save her, then I choose her. I will always choose her."

Margaret's eyes teared up. "You're a good man, Antonio."

Not anymore...Now, he'd be a dead man—or cease to exist, anyway—and leave behind the only person he'd ever truly loved without having the chance to tell her.

"Margaret?"

"Yes?"

"How do I open the portal?"

She stared for a moment, clearly thinking over her response. "I think we should wait until we're in Mexico. When Chaam is released, we open the portal for Ixtab. Otherwise, I have no guarantee they'll free him."

Antonio stood up. "Ixtab will make sure that Chaam is freed, Margaret. She would not double-cross you because she's good. I've never met anyone like the woman—so willing to sacrifice herself for the happiness of others."

Funny. Now that he thought about it, why was she the Goddess of Suicide? Ixtab wasn't depressing or morbid. She was sexy, quirky, and strong. She was happy and wanted nothing more than the same for others. And wasn't happiness one of her gifts? So why wasn't she the Goddess of Happiness? *Caray*, if they got through this, he'd lobby the gods for a name change. She didn't deserve such a horrible title.

Margaret's eyes reflected her concern. "I don't know."

"Please, Margaret. Please tell me how. I know you want Chaam back, but you have to remember this mess is Cimil's doing, not anyone else's. Now she's behind bars, and the truth has been exposed. It is over. You've played your hand and done your part. Now the rest of us need to do ours."

"I can't risk it," she said.

"Do you want me to beg? Because I will. Whatever it takes." He lowered himself and kneeled on the floor in front of her.

Margaret hissed. "Stop. Don't do that. You're breaking my heart. I'll tell you . . ."

Antonio sprang from his seat, grabbed her shoulders, and picked her up to embrace her.

"Whoa, there, vampire." She wiggled in his arms. "I think"—she grunted her words—"you're forgetting how strong you are."

"My apologies." Antonio set her down.

She secured her robe and smiled. "To open the tablet, you must make a sacrifice."

"Sacrifice?" *Diablos*. He'd have to kill someone?

"And it must be in the name of true love," she added.

Qué? "You know that sounds like a fairy-tale cliché, don't you?" His mind started formulating how a sacrifice made specifically in the name of love would have any scientific bearing. Simply put, the tablet's atoms reacted to external stimuli and energy patterns, so could this mean that love, an emotion, had its own frequency?

"Yes. But it's true," she said. "It's how I ended up trapped. My father had been trying to open the portal, hoping to bring my mother back from the dead. He was about to tear out Itzel's heart—he must've translated the word *sacrifice* on the tablet and thought killing someone was the key to its power—when Chaam found him. I know my father was mad, his soul past the point of redemption, which meant Chaam was obligated to kill him on the spot for the good of humanity. That's their law. Then I showed up, and Chaam had to choose between killing my father right in front of me or serving his duty. Somehow, and I don't know how, but Chaam resisted his hardwiring to put his duty first. He broke his bond with the Universe to save me from the pain of watching my father's death."

"You said he killed him anyway."

She nodded. "Yes. Chaam's decision, his sacrifice to negate his duty opened the portal, but it didn't change the fact that my father had turned evil. My father went for Itzel's heart. Chaam stopped him just in time."

"I am very sorry to hear that." It seemed like a senseless tragedy. One that he hoped would not go unpunished if Cimil had truly been the instigator. But that was a task for the deities to deal with. Right now, however, he needed to rescue Ixtab, who had sacrificed herself for him. Did that mean she loved him? Because the portal had definitely opened.

His heart suddenly warmed at the idea. *Could she truly love me?* After everything they'd been through, it would be a miracle. *And make it all worth it.*

She shrugged. "What's done is done. Chaam deserves a second chance."

"We will make sure he gets one. Right now, I need to go and get Ixtab back." He turned to leave, then had a thought. "Margaret, you said that you could see and hear everything from the other side of the portal."

"Not everything all at once, but it allows you to watch whomever you choose. Quite the superspy tool, if you ask me."

Antonio smiled. When they'd met, Ixtab had told him she was a spy. "Ixtab can hear me now, can't she?"

"Probably. If she's with the demon, then so can he."

Good. He had something to say to both of them.

Treinta y Uno

Antonio stopped by Penelope and Kinich's room to advise them of the change of plans—he would open the portal immediately. Of course, he heard nothing but loud animal-like grunting and howls so he'd opted for advising one of the Uchben soldiers. The plan was simple. They'd open the portal inside a holding cell at the prison and pull Ixtab out. If the demon was freed in the process, the cell—which Kinich said could contain any being—would prevent the demon from going anywhere.

Except your body. Yet that was a chance Antonio was willing to take; this had to end and Ixtab *would* be freed. And if doing so meant he needed to sacrifice his life, then so be it. Even better if it resulted in that demon's eternal incarceration. He only hoped he might be given a few precious moments to simply hold Ixtab again and tell her how he felt. However, if the cards were not in his favor...

He slipped outside and looked up at the starry sky. So

many nights he'd stared up at the stars, wondering where his fate might lead him, wondering the purpose to all his struggles and suffering. None of it seemed to make any sense then, but now it did: everything led him to her.

"Ixtab, if you're listening, I want you to know I am sorry for not seeing who you really were. I was blind when we met, blinded by my fear—fear of losing my brother, of failing him. I believed that saving Margaret was my only way out. What you don't know is that it was your face I saw. It was your eyes I dreamed of and saw every time I closed my eyes. It was you, Ixtab. Always you. So if I do not get a chance to say this in person, I want you to know that I love you—you were meant to be mine. And whatever happens, I'm grateful for finding you."

He paused, a small piece of him hoping he might hear a reply or any sign that his message had been delivered. There was nothing but silence.

"And Father, if you're listening. I don't care how many lifetimes it takes, I will send you back to hell. You'll not win, not against me."

The wind howled, sounding as if it contained voices—shrieks and wails. "Yeah. Fuck you, too."

Alone in the prison cell, Antonio laid the tablet on the cold cement floor and stared at the thing. This was it. Time to set everything right and make sure the demon never harmed another being again.

His plan was simple. Open the portal and pull Ixtab out. Once she was freed, the guards were standing by to extract her from the cell. He only hoped he could do so before the demon emerged. Because once it was freed, this cell would never be opened again. Yes, the demon would stay here until the end of time or until the gods could find another way to deal with him.

"What now?" he asked Margaret through the glass. Behind her stood Kinich; Penelope; the woman he'd met the prior day, Emma; and a dozen soldiers dressed in black.

Margaret shrugged. "Do you have something to sacrifice in the name of true love?" Her voice echoed through the speakers and bounced off the sterile walls.

He nodded. "Yes."

"Well?" she asked.

He couldn't reveal his plan. Not when Ixtab might be listening in; she'd never allow him to sacrifice himself to save her. "I can't tell you, but I'm ready to make the sacrifice," he said.

"Try thinking of your offering," Margaret suggested.

He did that and once again nothing happened.

Kinich and Penelope exchanged worried glances.

"It's a Maaskab relic," Maggie said. "Everyone knows the Maaskab use dark magic, which is highly unpredictable. Keep trying."

He did. He thought about the portal opening and the demon taking his body. He thought about seeing Ixtab's face again. Nothing happened. *Mierda.* "Fuck this. I need to get my equipment up and running."

Margaret pressed her palms against the glass. "I already told you, that won't work. Dammit! Try harder. Chaam is almost out of time!"

"What do you mean?" Kinich asked her.

She looked up at him with teary brown eyes. "I mean that if you don't let Chaam out of that prison soon, we won't be able to cure him. He's poisoned with evil, and it's been eating away at his soul. There's almost nothing left of it—he'll end up just like my father."

She looked at Antonio through the glass. "Keep trying."

"Something isn't working," he explained. "It's useless."

Then Margaret's pale face lit up. "No. It's not useless. You can save Chaam. You can gobble up the darkness inside him. I don't know why I hadn't thought of that before."

She wanted him to drain the dark energy from Chaam as he'd done to those Maaskab? Antonio mulled it over. Chaam was immortal, so there was no risk of killing him. "But that doesn't get Ixtab back," he stated coldly.

A cackle erupted from somewhere in the complex. It sounded like Cimil. "Peekaboo! I can't see you!" she screamed. Of course, she couldn't see them because they were in a separate cell toward the back of the prison. "Peekaboo . . . can't see you!" Cimil hollered again.

Batshit loca.

Maggie's head whipped toward the sound and then back in Antonio's direction. "I have a solution."

He waited.

"You'll have to trust me, Antonio, but I figured out how to get Ixtab back without risking the demon being set free."

He hoped Cimil hadn't been her inspiration because that would be bad. Very, very bad given Cimil's legendary panache for lying, cheating, and causing death and mayhem. Add that Maggie had already proven she'd do almost anything to free Chaam . . .

"No," he said. "Your trust ran out the moment Ixtab became your sacrificial lamb," he told her.

"Antonio," she said, "why would I double-cross you? You're the only one who can save the man I love."

She had a point, however...

"You're asking me to go to Mexico, have the gods free this evil deity Chaam, attempt to cure him, and then simply trust you'll be able to open the portal and free Ixtab while dealing with the demon?"

She nodded. "Yes."

"Y el puente apestoso?" he said.

"Huh?" She quirked a brow.

"And the stinky bridge?"

"Okay. Thanks for translating. Once again, huh?" she said.

"You are trying to sell me a bridge made of bullshit. No?" he said.

Maggie's nostrils flared. "Haven't you learned anything? I. Am. The *only* one here you can trust." She glanced at Kinich and Penelope. "No offense, but saving Chaam isn't on the top of your list."

"The loss of my brother in our lives has troubled me deeply," Kinich said. "We are not of the same blood and bone as human siblings, but the deities are connected by something much greater: the Universe." He looked down. "I have felt the loss of Chaam's presence. Deeply. As have we all. And there's nothing I would not give to have my family whole again."

Well, that was one hell of a guilt trip. Now Antonio had to save this...*Chaam*. He couldn't deprive a family of the chance to save their brother. Not after everything he'd gone through to save his.

He closed his eyes and said a silent prayer that Ixtab would come back to him. "I will help Chaam."

Kinich gave him a look that needed no words. Gratitude. "I'll let the Uchben down in Mexico know we're coming. Let's get you on a plane."

"I will—" He saw Maggie making a beeline for the door. "Where are you going?"

"I'll see you on top of the temple! With Ixtab! Don't worry!" She disappeared out the door.

Christ almighty. He couldn't believe he was actually putting his fate, his destiny, in the hands of this strange woman who'd popped out of the portal.

Antonio couldn't help but feel like a rat running through the maze, every turn, every twist just part of some bigger plan.

"You okay?" Kinich asked. "You look pale all of a sudden."

"I'm not sure, but I have the distinct feeling that none of this is happening by chance."

"Welcome to my world," Kinich replied.

Treinta y Dos

~

Twelve Hours Later. Ten Kilometers North of Bacalar, Mexico

Antonio could not believe that such a short distance from an innocent-looking, sleepy lakeside town, nestled in a lush tropical forest, existed a large Maaskab structure, where a deity of epic evil proportions stayed incarcerated. Then again, why the hell not? Compared to what he once believed, the world was nothing but one giant illusion.

He still digested the shocking facts, scientifically impossible facts he'd learned of from Kinich on the plane ride down. For example, not only were deities and vampires real—not so strange, he supposed, given his heritage—it seemed the immortal races were mimicking the humans and undergoing their own genetic evolution. In other words, they, too, were turning into one giant melting pot: ex-deity vampires, ex-vampires who were

now demigods, fallen angel vampires, the human offspring of an angel who now housed the power of a deity
(Penelope), offspring of deities who were mortal (Payals), and children being born of parents from the various
combinations. It made him wonder what his and Ixtab's
children might be like if they should someday be so lucky.
Could female deities even have children? he wondered.

*Half incubus-vampire, half deity. Now that would
be interesting.* Especially considering Ixtab's multitude
of abilities: happiness, seasoning, toothaches…death.
*Gods, I hope we don't have a daughter; her mood swings
might be a threat to humanity. Then again, a tiny Ixtab
would be…simply adorable. And you'd never have to
worry about the boys touching her.*

Hmmm…

"*Bueno.* So, you're trying to tell me that no one comes
here? No one knows about it?" Antonio asked Kinich.
The noon sun glimmered off the shiny black pyramid
before them, blanketing the structure with blurry waves
of gaseous heat.

"The Maaskab built this place and we took it from them
in a battle. The grounds are heavily warded with their
magic. Humans intuitively stay away," Kinich replied.

"Don't planes fly overhead and see it?" Antonio asked.

"The wards make them believe they see only jungle,"
Kinich explained.

"And where did the Maaskab go?" he asked.

"Many were killed in our last battle," Kinich responded.
"The rest are in hiding, waiting patiently for their next
opportunity to attack. I'm sure they are watching us now,
though I'm also sure they'd think twice about engaging;
this place is heavily guarded by Uchben."

Antonio heard a trickle of doubt seeping into Kinich's voice and glanced over his shoulder. A very tall barbed wire fence ran the perimeter about fifty meters back from the base of the pyramid. Frankly, if these Maaskab were as powerful as everyone said, he couldn't see how a bunch of humans, i.e., the Uchben, and a fence could stand against them.

"So how the hell are we getting him out of there?" Antonio asked. Was there a door or secret tunnel?

"There is an opening at the top of the structure. It's a straight drop down deep inside the pyramid where Chaam is held." Kinich pointed to the soldiers who expeditiously unloaded pulleys and ropes from the Jeeps they'd arrived in and carried them up the face of the pyramid.

Antonio also noted a large cage. "Deity reinforced?"

"Yes," Kinich responded. "Just in case we are unable to cure Chaam."

Not a chance. Gods, I'm fucking hungry...

"Who's going inside to get him?"

Kinich looked uneasy, a fact that did not sit well with Antonio, but at this juncture, a little bout of nerves was no match for his determination.

"I will go," Kinich replied. "This is why I asked Penelope to stay behind with Emma. It would make her very uneasy to witness what I am about to do."

Probably a wise choice given the high concentration of evil vibrating through the air; it was no place for a pregnant woman.

"I think I should go down and attempt to cleanse him before bringing him up," Antonio suggested.

Kinich scratched his golden-brown stubble, and his eyes flickered from turquoise to gray for a brief moment.

"No, he may be conscious, and given his state of mind, he may resist you. I have a better chance of pulling my brother out."

But the evil energy, even from outside, was extremely potent. "What will happen if you're exposed to whatever is inside?" Antonio asked.

"I'm sure a few minutes of exposure won't be fatal. Plus, I will have you and Ixtab to help me if anything happens. Yes?"

Antonio only hoped that Margaret would keep her word and deliver Ixtab as promised.

A caravan of black Hummers pulled up on the dirt road and stopped. Antonio immediately recognized the deities unloading from the vehicles. The man with ankle-length hair and the enormous headdress (*that fit in the car, how?*), the lady with the beehive hat, the one who seemed drunk (though he wore a toga today), Fate, and a few others whose names he didn't remember.

"And I have them," Kinich added, jerking his head toward his brethren. "They'll make sure nothing bad happens."

"You are certain you don't want me to go in?" Antonio asked.

"You simply need to focus on your part: draining the darkness from Chaam's body once we emerge."

One of the soldiers called for Kinich. About twenty men at the top of the pyramid had erected a triangular structure with a pulley system. Kinich grumbled. "Wish me luck."

Antonio hesitated to follow. Where was Margaret? She'd said she would have Ixtab freed before Chaam came out.

Gods dammit. Please come. Gods, he'd never felt so anxious or desperate in his entire life.

Antonio spun around, taking in the eeriness of the jungle skirting the base of the black jade pyramid. There were no animals, no birds, nothing but complete silence.

A gentle wind blew across his face. It smelled of daisies and vanilla. "Ixtab?" He looked toward the sky and treetops.

No response.

Was she watching him now? He closed his eyes, longing for the vision of her that once haunted him, but nothing came. No, if he wanted to see her again, he'd have to put his faith in fate. Not Ixtab's sister Fate—horrible woman—but the fate ruled by the Universe. So where the hell were Maggie and Ixtab?

"You coming?" Kinich called out from above.

"*Sí*, I am coming." Antonio climbed the large steps, feeling the energy radiating from deep within its bowels. He could not imagine being inside such a dark, overwhelming place, although his stomach disagreed and grumbled loudly. Well, at least he was hungry, because he had a feeling he was about to eat a very large meal.

Atop the pyramid, Antonio observed Kinich tying back his long golden-brown hair and then hooking on his harness. There was no fear or hesitation in his movements, which made Antonio think that perhaps after so many millennia of existing, there was little left that scared such beings. It was odd to think that someday he, too, might be thousands of years old. He could only hope to have Ixtab at his side for every moment of it.

Kinich positioned himself over the mouth of the black hole and winked before jumping feet first. The soldiers, all large men, held the rope easily and allowed its length to slide at a steady pace through the pulley system, down into the well-like structure.

After a minute, the rope slacked in their hands.

"Kinich has reached the bottom. He will pull on the rope once he's ready," said the largest man with cropped dark hair, who didn't speak much, but seemed in charge given the way the men watched his every move.

"How long?" And dammit! Where the hell were Margaret and Ixtab?

"Should take a minute. He only needs to hook the other harness under Chaam's arms," said the soldier.

Antonio glanced down the face of the structure where twenty or so men stood at attention next to the deities who appeared to be...*bored?* The deity wearing the toga played thumb wars with the beehive lady.

Antonio shook his head. No. He would never fully understand these creatures.

A minute ticked by, then another. Antonio's cell phone vibrated. *Caray.* He slipped it from his pocket. Penelope. He had to answer.

"Is he okay? Please tell me he's okay," she said.

"He's still inside the pyramid; I'll call you the minute—"

"That's the signal, men! Pull!" the Uchben leader yelled.

Diablos. This was it. "I'll call you as soon as it's over." Antonio hung up the phone and slipped it back into his pocket. As the rope came out of the hole, Antonio noticed how it had changed color, as if covered with some sort of black powder.

Finally the top of a blackened head emerged, but was

it Kinich? Or Chaam? The men pulled again and the top of the second man surfaced. The two were harnessed together. Both were large and covered head to toe in soot.

The men quickly pulled them out and lay them both on the ground. Antonio hurried to the first man and brushed the black powder from his face. It was Kinich. The darkness immediately began to crawl inside Antonio's fingertips. It was thick and sticky like molasses in his veins.

Qué sabroso. Delicious.

Kinich groaned. "That's enough. Save my brother."

Antonio stepped over Kinich and examined the other man. He was large, if not larger than Kinich.

Time to eat!

Antonio rubbed his hands together and placed them on the man's shoulders. The taste was palatably different. This was caustic and vile, nothing like the others. Antonio wanted to pull away, but found himself unable. He began to choke and hack, feeling his own soul violently protest the invasion. *Oh, gods. So much pain, so much destruction...*

Suddenly, something slammed him into the cold stone platform. Antonio couldn't breathe, couldn't see, couldn't speak.

"What the hell were you thinking, huh? Stupid, icky vampire!"

Ixtab placed her hands on either side of Antonio's cheeks, pulling away the toxic poison. *"Teen uk'al k'iinam. Teen uk'al yah. Teen uk'al k'iinam. Teen uk'al yah."*

Despite his body twitching and trembling violently, he was still the most gorgeous, magnificent male she'd ever laid eyes on. "That's right, Dr. Incu-pire, just relax. I'm here now."

His eyelids fluttered and his irises slowly faded back to their magnificent olive green with specs of gold and golden brown.

"Is it you? Are you really here?" Antonio mumbled.

She nodded. "Yes, my sweet man. I'm here." *Through a miracle of all miracles.* Still holding his face, she leaned down and kissed his lips. They were soft and warm and the most heavenly lips she'd ever touched. And if they weren't in the process of dealing with a very horrible situation, surrounded by a large group of soldiers, she would be ripping off his clothes and taking him right there.

Antonio groaned.

"Oh. Please don't make that sound. It's giving me very naughty thoughts at a time when you are incapacitated and vulnerable, which is only fueling my urge to take advantage of you in very naughty, publically inappropriate ways."

"Don't let me stop you." He grinned.

Ugh… you have no idea what that does for me to hear you say that. "I'd like that, but…" she glanced at Chaam lying immobile on the ground. "I have to help him."

"No," Antonio protested, unable to speak above a whisper. "Whatever is inside him isn't like the others."

"You made a promise," Maggie pleaded, running up the steps to the platform. Her red, pale, freckled face was covered in sweat and tears.

"Dammit," Ixtab scolded Maggie, "I told you to stay down there with the others."

The Maggie girl paid her no attention and dove straight for Chaam's limp body.

"Ugh. Thanks for listening to the goddess. You're a real treat." From the moment Ixtab had arrived back in Sedona, compliments of Máax's expertise in both tablets and time travel—something she'd need to deal with later—this Maggie girl had been blubbering and apologizing and blubbering some more. She was a complete wreck.

Ixtab removed her hands from Antonio and leaned down to whisper in his ear, "I have to do this."

She stood and walked over to Chaam. His large frame was lying curled into a ball on his side, and Maggie blubbered over him, petting his cheek. "Ohmygods. Hang on. Just ... hang on," she said over and over again.

"No, please, no," Antonio grumbled. "I can't lose you. I love you."

Ixtab's mouth fell open. "Do you have any idea how long I've waited to hear that?" She beamed. "I love you, too, vampire."

"Then don't do this," he mumbled. "Just help me up; I will cleanse him—"

"No," she interrupted. "I am truly immortal and cannot be killed. You are not." Although deities *were* vulnerable. Case in point, Chaam, her beloved brother. The sort of darkness that gravitated toward a deity wasn't the same for a human, vampire, or Maaskab. This was a thousand times more potent. When she'd once tried to heal Cimil of her insanity, not only had Ixtab failed, but it felt like her body had been injected with acid. Then two hundred years later, she awoke. Yes, bad deity juju was some seriously strong stuff. Despite the odds, she had to try. She had to. Maggie and Chaam had been wronged, and though Ixtab wasn't responsible, it was the right thing to do. It was what she hoped her brethren might do for her if the situation were reversed. Her only comfort was knowing Antonio was now immortal. Hopefully, he'd be there when she woke up.

Here goes nothing…

Ixtab placed her hands together, said her prayer, and then kneeled to place them on Chaam's back. In the first few moments, she felt nothing, but then the floodgates of dark energy opened. She tasted so much pain, so much despair. Her light jolted inside her mortal shell, as if wanting to flee from the heinous monster invading her body. Then came the screams and blood and agonizing pleas of his victims. So many faces, so young, so horribly murdered. Ixtab reminded herself that such things, such hideous atrocities were not of his doing; he'd been possessed. Inside Chaam, there was a kernel of goodness fighting to resist every evil act, every violent moment, but the darkness inside had been too strong.

Ixtab drank his pain, drank his darkness, and allowed herself to fill until she tasted Chaam's light running clean.

She snapped her hands away and stared at her palms. Her skin was dark gray. Gods, how did she still manage to stand?

"Is it over? Is he all right?" Maggie asked, kneeling down and stroking Chaam's cheeks.

Chaam groaned and cracked open one turquoise eye. "Bobcat, is that you?" he whispered in a raspy voice.

Maggie burst into joyful tears. "Yes, your bobcat is here."

"Ha! I did it! I did it!" Ixtab did a little dance and then crouched down next to Antonio. "I'd kiss you right now, but you look like you've just gone to the all-you-can-eat ninety-nine-cent buffet. Are incu-pires supposed to be that shade of green?" She smiled.

"Are goddesses supposed to be gray?" Antonio mumbled.

"I'll be fine; just need to find a place to dump this bad juju." Too bad Antonio was out of action. Maybe she could off-load onto a few trees until she located country-club members.

"Chaam," Maggie said, stroking his soot-covered forehead, "you're safe now, my love." She kissed his lips repeatedly and cradled his head.

Ixtab had never felt so happy. Antonio was safe, albeit green, and Chaam was cured. Ixtab looked at the soldiers who were still poised in a strike position in case things went south with Chaam. "Well, don't just stand there! Get Chaam loaded into a Jeep and to the airstrip."

"No," Chaam grumbled. "We cannot leave."

"What?" Maggie said frantically. "Honey, we need to get you out of here."

"Help me sit up." His voice was scarcely a whisper. Maggie lifted his head and helped him up. "The Maaskab will never let you leave here with me."

"But Chaam. We can't stay here, it's too dangerous," Maggie argued.

Chaam looked at her pale, sweet face. "Maggie, my love. It's okay. I am their king; they do not know what's happened here and will not hurt me. And we must let the others leave safely."

"Honey, they could be watching us now. They'll know," Margaret argued.

"Then you and I will put on a nice show for them to see. Get ready to run; we are going to fake a getaway," he commanded.

Kinich, who'd been helped up by two soldiers, pulled away and crouched in front of Chaam. "Brother. You don't need to do this. We've got plenty of men—"

"No!" Chaam barked. His soot-covered face and glowing turquoise eyes made him appear like a creature of the netherworld. "There will be no fighting. I will not have Margaret's life risked. If I stay, the Maaskab will let you all leave in peace—I will see to it." Chaam blinked. "What the hell happened to you, Kinich? Are those fucking fangs?"

Kinich grinned to display his incisors more clearly. "They are nice, yes?"

Chaam blinked again, but did not reply.

"There have been many changes, including my mate, Penelope, who is carrying my child and now co-ruling the House of Gods," Kinich added.

Chaam smiled, clearly believing that was a joke. Wait until Chaam made it to the next summit meeting.

"Go. All of you." Chaam looked at Margaret.

"I'm not leaving you. Not now. Not ever," she protested so vehemently that her body trembled violently. She looked like she might punch him in the man-fritters.

Chaam frowned. "I will join you in a few days, I pro—"

"No!" she screamed. "I'm not leaving you. And if it's safe for you, then it's safe for me because I am your queen."

Ixtab giggled. Margaret was perfect for Chaam. She had the right amount of sweet, the right amount of sour. "I suggest you listen to her, brother. Margaret doesn't seem like the type to back down."

Chaam pulled Margaret down into his lap and kissed her deeply.

"Let's get the fuck out of here," said Kinich. "This place gives me the heebie-jeebies. Oh, by the way, brother, make sure your fucking Scabs release Guy and the vampires—that was the deal for setting you free. And I'd stay the hell away from Guy if I were you until someone's had a chance to fill him in."

Chaam broke the kiss and winced. Obviously, he remembered all of the terrible things he'd done, including trying to kill Guy's mate at one point.

"It's not your fault, Chaam," said Margaret. "It was Cimil."

Chaam nodded. "I know, but the things I've—"

"No. We're not doing this right now." Margaret kissed him again.

"She's right, Chaam," Ixtab pointed out. "We really should get the hell ..."

"Ixtab?" Antonio had been sitting on the ground next to Ixtab, but now hovered over her. "Ixtab? Ixtab! Are you all right?" he screamed.

"How did I get on the ground?" She felt her body becoming heavier and heavier as if being pulled to the Earth's inner core.

Antonio's dark green eyes drilled into her. "Don't do this, Ixtab. Don't go ..."

His voice faded into nothing as the screams and howls of Chaam's victims consumed her until she was nothing.

Panic. Pure fucking panic. Ixtab's skin had turned a ghastly shade of gray, almost like she'd been spray-painted the color of a storm cloud. Then he noticed black spider veins spreading over her face and arms.

"Help her!" Antonio looked at Maggie, Kinich, Chaam, and the soldiers. No one stepped forward. "What the fuck is wrong with you people? Help her!"

Kinich's face filled with torment. "Antonio, we cannot touch her, only you can. You can help her."

Caray!

"Listen," Kinich added, "we need to leave here now. I sense the Maaskab are near, and as Chaam pointed out, we do not want a fight on our hands. It's not the right time."

Antonio stared down at Ixtab's immobile face, his heart torn in half. "I can't lose her," he whispered.

"And you won't. But now is the time to be strong, vampire." He felt Kinich's firm grasp on his shoulder. "We must go."

Antonio slipped his arms beneath her body, instantly feeling the darkness slither through his skin and making its way into his veins. *Hmmm. Tastes kind of . . . nutty?*

Treinta y Tres

Ixtab snuggled against the masculine warmth at her side and savored the sensation of being completely enveloped in a sweet male scent. She nuzzled her face against the source of the heat. Gods, it felt like heaven—smooth and firm. All man...

Cue Marvin Gaye song now. Sexual healing, I want.. sexual healing... la-la la-la...

"Ummm..." she groaned, never wanting to leave this dreamy place filled with luscious, sensual energy.

She felt a warm hand run down her back and pull her closer into the soothing heat, which she now realized ran the length of her body.

"Umm..." she groaned again. *Best dream ever.*

Upgrading now: "Unchained Melody"...

Sigh.

How about, "Bump Uglies"?

Yeah, The Krabbers rock. Ukuleles are magical.

"You like that, do you?" a deep male voice whispered in her ear. Her mind began to slip out of the foggy paradise. But she didn't want to leave it. Everything felt so good.

"*Mahalo* . . . Yes. I like it," she mumbled, not bothering to open her eyes. "More."

The hand slid from her back to her backside. A firm hardness pushed into her belly. Her naked belly. *And a naked hardness?*

Ixtab opened her eyes slowly.

"I'm glad to hear you say 'more,' because more is exactly what I had in mind." Antonio's green eyes and hungry smile greeted her.

Yes, best dream ever . . .

She blinked and stared at his stunningly handsome face—thick, dark lashes; straight nose; well-defined cheekbones; and sultry, full lips in the shape of a heart. And though there was an exquisite perfection to him, his black stubble and strong features made his appearance fiercely masculine. Then there was her favorite part . . . *that deep olive skin against his green eyes.*

"You're breathtaking, you know that?" she said and lifted her hand to his face.

"Nowhere near as breathtaking as you," he said.

"How would you know? You've never really seen me," she replied to the dreamy vision of Antonio.

He smiled. "Now you've put me in the unfortunate position of sounding like an appalling pervert because I've done nothing but look at you for one week straight." He kissed her lips softly. "Every." He kissed her lips again. "Single." Another kiss. "Inch."

"Really?" she asked, unable to keep from panting

gently while her body worked itself into a quiet, sizzling frenzy.

"Oh yes. Well, almost every inch." This time he kissed her with an urgency that sent the blood rushing between her legs. His heated tongue slipped inside and massaged hers with his own. She'd never been kissed so deeply, as if he were making love to her lips. "There is one place I didn't go. Saving the best for last, I suppose."

His hand slid underneath the silky sheets, over one breast, down her body. His head then disappeared and she felt him tugging at the only garment she wore. *Panties?*

"Oh!" The soft touch of his fingers ran over her sensitive bud. "Ohhh!" His warm and silky mouth came next.

"Oh my gods." There was no preamble, shyness, or modesty with this male, but why would there be? He was just the sort of male who was used to taking control in the bedroom and well versed in the art of pleasuring a woman.

Lucky, lucky me!

His warm, smooth tongue glided over her with a languid, sensual pace—the pace of a man who clearly savored the task. She felt a little scrape of his teeth and her body snapped to. *Wait.* She looked straight up at the ceiling, realizing suddenly that this wasn't a dream. This was the room she stayed in at Kinich's estate.

She sat up and threw back the covers. Antonio's adorable face was nestled between her thighs. "What's going on? What are you doing?"

He flashed a devilish smile. "What does it look like?"

Licking me like a naughty Tootsie Pop? "No. I mean, why we naked in bed together?" And... oh, gods, had she really just stopped that delicious man from doing that delicious thing to her body? How stupid was she?

He shrugged his brows, his grin widening. "One of your sister's ideas." He crawled up and hovered over her body, his face directly above hers, his thick-muscled arms flexing and straining as he held his weight off of her. "She recommended more skin contact to help extract the dark energy from you faster." He lowered his hips enough to allow his erection to press against her tingling, pulsing entrance. "I think being naked in bed with you for a week was far more draining on me than you. Although now that I've been fed so well, I think I might recover."

Yes. What *would* he do with all that energy? And hadn't she been about to say something very important?

He dipped his head and kissed her forcefully.

Oh! Yes! I had questions... What were they? So many thoughts mulled around in her head like an expectant father waiting for a cigar. What had happened to Chaam? Were Guy, Niccolo, and the others set free? And how had she lived her entire existence not knowing this pleasure? The pleasure of being with someone she loved, of his mouth covering hers, the smell of him filling her nostrils, of his stiff, warm cock pressing into her.

The anticipation barreled over him. Antonio lowered his body on top of hers, placing himself firmly between Ixtab's thighs. He began writhing, rhythmically rubbing his erection between her legs. He dipped his head to her neck and kissed. "Your breasts against my chest, the feel of your soft skin, your taste—I've never experienced such sinful pleasure."

He moved his mouth back to hers and ran his hand between their bodies, positioning himself just so. "I can't wait a moment longer," he whispered in her ear.

She turned her face placing them nose to nose, realizing in an instant that this was it. And she couldn't have wanted it more.

He thrust his hips sharply forward with a loud groan. His thick shaft penetrated deep inside and released that delicious tension clinging to her inner muscles. Her eyes fluttered as she took him in, exploding with shivers and heavenly waves of sensual bliss, while he pumped himself into her, hard and fast.

He lifted his chest, using one hand to hold himself up and the other to grab the nape of her neck. "Look at me, Ixtab. Open your eyes."

And she did.

Ixtab had never felt anything more erotic than watching Antonio's face, the fierce gaze of his eyes as he pounded his hard shaft into her, using her body to sate his savage sexual hunger, as their lights, their energies mingled and danced, their minds intertwining. Images began flooding her mind—the sensation of his cock sliding in and out of her tight passage; his large, rough hands cupping her breasts and the feel of her taught nipple on the tip of his finger. The glowing warmth of love in his heart.

They were sharing each other's thoughts? *Yes, he is my mate. Without a doubt.*

And she wanted him to know how sexy he was, how his body—those deep, rippling abs; powerful biceps and chest; the strong, thick legs—quenched a primal female thirst she'd lived with for tens of thousands of years. And how his soul filled her heart. *Gods, I love you...*

Continuing his relentless rhythm, he dipped his head. "Yes. I heard that."

Oh, gods, don't stop, don't stop. I'm so close...

"And that. But I forbid you to come. Not yet. Not without me."

What?!

"But I-I-ohhh..." She couldn't think. "I'm going to..."

Antonio pushed his large frame forward, and groaned.

Come...

He poured himself into her, and her entire body ignited with erotic tremors. She gripped his shoulders as wave after wave of intense, blinding orgasms racked her body.

And I thought ukuleles were magical... Wow.

After the moment passed, Antonio slowed to a leisurely pace, rocking his hips against her. He kissed her with his love-swollen lips, and though hers felt raw and battered, nothing felt more delicious than the taste of him on her tongue, the feel of his beard on the edge of her mouth.

"Gods, I can't believe how sexy you are, Ixtab," he said.

I can't believe I just had sex. Seventy-thousand-year-old virgin no more! Yes!

"How was it?" he asked, smiling.

She shrugged. "You were okay, I suppose. But you might have to try again. Just to get it right."

"Oh, you really shouldn't have said that." He flipped her over and placed his hands on her hips.

She laughed. "What are you doing?" *Gods, I hope it's what I think...*

"May I remind you that I'm part incubus and a vampire. Both were built for hard, hot sex. And we never tire." He thrust deeply into her from behind, causing her to gasp. "And we are extremely competitive."

Gods, you were so worth the wait...

Four Hours Later

Antonio pulled Ixtab close to his body and tucked the sheet under her shoulder. Hands down, that had been the best sex of his life. And in some strange way, bedding her answered questions he'd had about himself for many years. For example, he'd always known that his appetite for sex was insatiable and that his incubus blood gave him the instincts to master any woman's body. They always walked away glowing and sated, as if they'd spent the entire day at the spa being pampered. He, on the other hand, simply felt empty. Unsatisfied. Hungry for more.

With Ixtab, however, it had been completely different. Not only did she sate his sexual thirst, but she left him in a euphoric state. Bliss. She was his bliss, mind, body, and soul. He would never get enough, not for a sense of lacking, but for a sense of pure joy.

He kissed her forehead and studied her features. Wide catlike eyes that shimmered with every shade of turquoise and green imaginable. Full, sensual lips. Deep bronzed skin. She was nothing shy of exotic—the sort of woman men would kill for, men would die for. "I love you," he said quietly, unused to the sound of those words coming from him. In fact, apart from his brother, he couldn't recall ever saying them to anyone else.

Ixtab gazed up at him with her wide eyes. "And I love you. Now it is time for us to talk."

Yes. It was. But Antonio feared having this conversation because the truth may mean the end to them both.

Treinta y Cuatro

"So, what happened?" she asked.

Antonio sat up in bed. "Maybe this should wait another day; I don't want to ruin what little time we may have left together." He slipped from the bed giving her a glimpse of his perfect, tanned ass and powerful back muscles. *Gods, even his butt crack is perfect.* She sighed.

"Where are you going?" she asked.

"To take a shower." He padded toward the bathroom.

"Wait!"

He froze.

"What's going on?" The negative energy spiked off the charts.

Without bothering to turn around, he asked, "Did you do it?"

"What? Did I do what?" She truly had no idea what he spoke of.

"Time travel," he said in a quiet voice.

So that's what this was about? Time travel?

"Well, yeah. I guess I did. But—"

"Fuck." He dropped his head and then stormed off to the bathroom.

What the hell?

Ixtab leaped from the bed and followed him. He was already in the shower turning on the water when she entered.

"Antonio?" She slipped inside the Italian tiled stall.

He shoved his head under the extra-large showerhead and leaned into the wall.

"What is it?" she asked.

"Fuck. Fuck. Fuck," he said.

What was going on? "Antonio! What?"

He spun around. "It's prohibited, Ixtab! Prohibited. You will be punished." He turned his face once again toward the water, but she could see the muscles flexing in his neck.

Oh. Now she understood. "Antonio, it's okay—it's not what you think."

He hit the wall, cracking several tiles, and then turned and grabbed her by the shoulders. "Like hell it's not. I just got you back, Ixtab."

She shook her head and smiled. *Sweet, sweet, vampire.* "It's okay, Antonio. I time traveled, yes, but when the others hear my story, I promise there will be no punishment—not for me or for Máax." And even if they did punish her, so what? It would be banishment so she'd no longer have any powers and be forced to live in the human world for eternity. Big whoop.

"Máax?" he asked.

She nodded.

"Máax is responsible?"

Again, she nodded. "Margaret knew that Máax had used the tablet before. So when the portal wouldn't open, she went to see him, hoping he'd tell her what went wrong—why it wouldn't open for you. The truth was, nothing had gone wrong. I simply wasn't there."

"What do you mean?"

"Máax did know how to use the tablet—he was banished for using it to time travel. Anyway, he took the tablet from Kinich, opened the portal, and went back to the moment I was sucked in. He brought me straight back to the moment he'd left."

It was a little confusing when she thought about it, but basically Máax had hopped inside the portal, grabbed Ixtab, and pulled her forward in time. So by the time Antonio tried to open the portal and make an offering in the name of love, she was no longer on the other side of the portal. The tablet didn't react because his request of it made no sense.

When she arrived in the future, to the moment that Máax opened the portal—well, Antonio, Kinich, and the others had already left for Mexico, but she and Margaret weren't far behind. Pretty damned cool when she thought about it.

"And my father?" Antonio asked.

That was the best part. "Máax obviously knew I'd been sucked into the portal with him."

"And?"

Ixtab shrugged. "Máax was waiting for him the moment he entered. Seems your father's head fell off and only corporeal beings can pass through the portal and enter the physical world. Oops."

Antonio's stern expression relaxed. "*Perdón. Pero...* You are saying you didn't choose to time travel?"

She shook her head no, smiling.

"And my father will never return?"

She shook her head. "No. His light cannot come back to this world. To be honest with you, I wish it could."

He made no attempt to mask his disapproval. "Why?"

Ixtab chugged down a resentful breath. "Because he's a complete bastard, and I'd like nothing more than to squeeze the life right out of him." She looked at the floor. "Máax told me that his last words were, 'Tell Ixtab I sent them all. I sent them to remind her that there could never be another.'"

"What did he mean?" Antonio asked.

Her mouth turned down and her eyes filled with tears. "I'm not 100 percent sure, but I believe he was behind a good portion of the random men who 'accidentally' bumped into me and died. I think he wanted me to suffer, to be miserable without him. For that, he should be punished. Instead, his light roams free in some other dimension. Where's the justice in that, Antonio? Where, for gods' sake?"

He pulled her into his arms. "Have you learned nothing, woman? Nothing at all? The only thing that matters is that we are together now and that I will not lose you. Ever."

"No. Never." She wrapped her arms around Antonio's neck. "Not as long as the Earth remains."

"Wait." He looked at her with mild concern. "So what happened to the tablet?"

Ixtab shrugged. "Máax said he had some unfinished business."

"Then let him have it." Antonio kissed her hard and pressed her back against the cool tile, which, at this point, felt soothing given how hard her poor body had been worked over by his earlier. Yes, she was a deity, but he was pure virility. He lifted her up and guided her legs around his waist—hard, perfectly sculpted with diagonal rivets sloping toward his erection.

Gods, she would never get enough of him. Hot water dripping from his hair and brow, the shower's steam rising behind him as if he were a god, he thrust forward. "Gods, I love you," he said.

She closed her eyes, savoring the feel of him entering her. Only this time, this time he knew they had all the time in the world; she could feel his calmness, his unfiltered passion for her. Heaven.

Treinta y Cinco

Ixtab wore her favorite pastel yellow dress with white daisies and spaghetti straps, and for the first time in a very long time, she entered the summit chamber with a glorious smile on her face. Perhaps because Antonio held her hand and hadn't let it go for hours, even as she'd gone out on her morning jaunt for souls in need. In fact, he seemed to enjoy the outing more than she had. A woman who volunteered at a battered women's shelter had been having a rough go of it lately after her husband died. And Ixtab, for the first time ever, performed the cleansing ritual as the Goddess of Happiness, which had made her even happier. Of course, Antonio had an instant snack. It was simply amazing how he converted dark energy into food. It meant that Ixtab could help so many others now that she wouldn't have to spend her time looking for country-club members. They were truly the perfect team—in love, in work, and in play.

Antonio and Ixtab made their way to the table, but what she saw stopped her in her tracks. "Who did this?"

Penelope and Kinich smiled. "We thought you deserved a new chair."

This one had several symbols carved into its stone back: a chili pepper, a sunflower, a giant happy face. Ixtab sighed. "Thank you, everyone. That's the nicest gift I've ever had." She proudly took her new throne, and Antonio stood behind her as Penelope initiated the meeting.

"All righty, everyone. I call this summit of the gods to order."

Penelope took roll call. Aside from Ixtab, present were K'ak, Fate, Belch, Bees, A.C., Akna, and whatsherface, the Goddess of Forgetfulness.

Missing were Cimil—still in deity jail—Zac, Máax, Chaam, and sadly, Guy. Ixtab's heart grew heavy. She avoided her impulse to reach for Antonio for comfort. Some pain simply needed to be felt. Instead, she raised her hand. "Penelope. Before we start, has anyone heard from Chaam and Maggie?"

Penelope looked down at her hands. "No."

Hell. It had been over a week already. "How about Guy?"

"Did someone call my name?"

The deities' heads swiveled toward the entrance. Guy stood in all his enormous deity glory, wearing tattered, dirty clothes, glowing like a kid who'd just found a ten-dollar bill.

Kinich immediately went to greet him with a hug. "It's about fucking time. Where the hell have you been?"

"We were freed this morning," Guy replied, "somewhere north of the pyramid; we were simply spit out into the jungle and had to hike to a phone so the Uchben could retrieve us." Guy looked him over briefly. "Are those fucking fangs, brother?"

"Nice to see you, too," Kinich replied. "Where's Niccolo and the other men?"

"Niccolo is with Helena and his daughter—he couldn't wait to see them. The others went straight to Euro Disney to join the rest of the vampires—the damned strangest thing if you ask me, but strange seems to be the order of the day lately." He directed his comment at Kinich's mouth. "As for me, I'm here because I can't find Emma; she's not in her room."

Ixtab smiled. "She's in prison."

Guy's expression dropped off a cliff. "What the hell? Who is responsible?"

Ixtab quickly added, "She is there visiting her grandmother."

Guy stared and his eyes filled with tears. Tears! Votan, God of Death and War, had tears streaming down his face! Hell just froze over!

"Y-y-you mean..." he blubbered. "Emma's grandmother is not dead? I didn't kill her?"

No doubt because he'd gone toe-to-toe with the old woman in the last battle, Guy believed he'd killed Emma's grandmother, which would have put the world's biggest rift between them. The irony was that no one ever survived a fight with Guy and lived to tell. *Except for Granny! Oh! This is going to be so much fun messing with him!*

"Not only that, brother," Ixtab said proudly. "Emma has a little surprise for you."

Guy wiped the tears from under his eyes. "What?"

"Guess you'll have to go ask her. You'll also be happy to know that I'm no longer the Goddess of Su..." Guy was gone faster than you could say "happiness."

"Never mind..." Ixtab smiled at Antonio. "I really wish I could be there to see the expression on his face when Emma tells him she's having a baby," Ixtab said.

"And that Emma's grandmother is cured," Antonio added.

"What?" Penelope asked.

"Emma came to see us this morning and begged Antonio to suck out the bad juju from her," Ixtab said.

"Weren't you afraid you'd kill her?" Penelope asked Antonio.

"I sipped slowly and there was plenty of goodness left in her soul." He made a sour face. "The good juice tastes awful."

"Emma must be so happy. She gets back her grandmother and man on the same day. Gods, I just love happy endings." Penelope sighed. "Okay. Where were we?" She looked around the table.

Ixtab slowly raised her hand. She didn't want to do it, but what had to be done had to be done. Cimil harmed so many, including the ones she loved. "We must discuss Cimil's fate."

Penelope nodded solemnly and wrote it down. The deities unanimously agreed.

"I would like to bring the topic of our brother Zac to the discussion floor," Kinich grumbled. Everyone raised their hands and Penelope recorded the votes.

"We must discuss Máax. He has broken the sacred law of no time travel," Fate said.

Ixtab snarled. "No. I do not agree. Máax only did so to save me so that I could save Chaam, and therefore Guy and the others."

Fate looked at Ixtab. "Did he or did he not time travel?"

"Yes. But—"

"Is it not a violation of one of our sacred laws, one that requires a review?" Fate asked.

"Yes. But—" Ixtab tried to reply.

"Was he under the influence of an evil power that forced him to break our laws?"

"Enough, Fate," Penelope barked. "Honey?" She looked at Kinich.

He nodded. "Yes. We must discuss the facts—a sacred law has been violated, and it is the rule."

"Frigging insanity!" Ixtab threw up her hands. "He's already been banished and made invisible. He's been denied any comfort or companionship for eternity. There's nothing left to punish him with."

"Not so," Fate replied. "We can entomb him for eternity."

"I hate you, Fate."

Fate smiled. "Ditto."

Ixtab looked at Kinich and Penelope, who shook her head. "I'm sorry. We have to follow the rules and at least discuss the matter according to our laws."

For the next hour, Ixtab hung her head as the debates continued and voting concluded. Unfortunately, there wasn't getting around what would come next. The laws they'd created to maintain a balance of power and protect humanity from themselves were now playing against

Máax. Ironically, these were the same laws that would bring justice to Cimil and Zac.

Ixtab felt Antonio's comforting hand on her shoulder as verdicts were recorded, and more than ever she was thankful she wouldn't be facing this next chapter of their history alone. How had the gods arrived to such a sad place? Yes, many good things had happened, too: Everyone was free, and of course, Ixtab had finally had her two wishes granted. After seventy thousand years, she was no longer the Goddess of Suicide. And she now had the most perfect male on the planet to share her life with. Yes, the Universe had been good to her. Finally.

And yet dark times were coming. Very dark times. Despite what anyone said, Cimil had prophesied the end of days, and Cimil was never wrong. Ever. To make matters worse, the gods would have to face this challenge with their loyalties divided. Because there wasn't a deity in the room who would not give their immortal soul to fight for one of the gods facing justice, herself included. She'd do just about anything to ensure Máax wasn't punished.

"Time to read the decrees: Zac will be tried for treason," Penelope said, tears running down her face. Ixtab knew they were tears of regret, not of pity for Zac. What he'd done to her and Kinich was unforgivable. "I hereby order Zac to be hunted and brought to the gods for justice. If found guilty, he will be stripped of his powers and banished to the mortal world for eternity."

She paused with a heavy sigh. "Máax will be tried for violating our sacred law of time travel." Penelope continued tearing up, and Ixtab couldn't help but join her. Not even Antonio's comforting touch soothed her sadness. "I hereby order Máax be found and brought to the gods for justice. Because this is not his first offense, if found guilty, Máax will be entombed for eternity." Penelope swallowed.

"Go on, honey. You're almost done." Kinich squeezed her arm.

"I decree that Cimil will be tried for twenty counts of treason, fifty violations of our sacred laws—including aiding an incubus—two hundred counts of murder by the hand of Chaam, and the possible slaughter of hundreds of thousands of innocent mortals at the hand of the Maaskab and Obscuros, whom we believe she created."

"Don't forget the torture and imprisonment of ten naked clowns," Fate added.

"They got free," Belch argued.

"Okay, we'll let that one slide," Fate said.

Penelope continued reading the decree. "If found guilty, Cimil is to be stripped of her powers and banished to the human world where she will be entombed for eternity."

Belch made a chuckle.

"What's so funny?" Ixtab asked. None of this held even the slightest spark of humor. Máax being put on trial was a travesty. And the fact that Zac and Cimil had done such awful things was nothing but a tragedy for everyone. At the end of the day, even though the gods weren't biologically related, Zac and Cimil were her family and possibly losing them—even if in the name of justice—felt terrible.

"You want to know what's so funny?" Belch slapped his knee, chuckling like a...well, drunken fool. "Haven't you idiots learned anything?" Belch looked around the table. "Wait for it...wait for it..."

"Wait for what?" Penelope said, a tremble in her voice. The doors flew open with a gust of wind.

Belch slapped his hand on the table. "Checkmate! Gods, she's good."

THE PAUSE (not the end)

Hi all! Once again, a giant "Thank you!" to everyone who's supported this series. I hope the agony of waiting for this sequel was worth it. By now, you've probably figured out that we're almost to the end of the Accidentally Yours series. Just one more novella (*Accidentally... Cimil?*) and then the final book (*Accidentally... Over?*). OH NO!!!!

And don't forget, if you liked this story, please be sure to click those happy stars on the etailer's website, drop a LIKE, or write a review on Goodreads. (I still do a little disco dance when they are good.) I also have a mailing list for updates on upcoming books (visit www.mimijean.net) and a fun reading group on Goodreads called Ask Mimi Jean Pamfiloff, if you'd like to chat/ask questions about the books. And, of course, there's always good ol' Facebook, Twitter, and e-mail!

Hope to hear from you!

Mimi J.

P.S. Mean people still suck! ☺

Roberto, the Ancient One, has had his eye on Cimil for four thousand years. He's been patiently waiting for the day to make her his forever—but can Cimil's wild heart ever be tamed?

Please turn this page
for an excerpt from

Accidentally ... Cimil?

One

3000 BC (Give or take a few centuries. Who the hell's counting?)

The day started like any other. A typical day in the life of a goddess. An ancient, lonely, bored-out-of-her-immortal-skull goddess.

I opened my mind to my brethren, listened to their thoughts—*yawn*—felt their worries—*trivial*—and contemplated my otherworldly navel until I decided where my talents were most needed in the world. On this day, that meant checking in on my brother Kinich, God of the Sun, whose self-imposed exile was seriously getting on everyone's last nerve.

Especially mine.

Don't get me wrong; I was also worried. What affected him affected all of us. We were connected. Brethren, of the same light. And we all tasted his pain, which is why I can say ... *What a big baby!*

Yes, yes it sucked to be a deity, a slave to mankind's well-being with no end in sight, no hope of finding true love or of having a life, but that was the gig. How many millennia did it take to sink in? Apparently, for Kinich, more than two. Or three. Or four. It was time to bring him back to our realm, time to take his place among us.

So I hopped into the portal which spat me out in the usual place—a cenote in Mexico—summoned Minky, my trusty unicorn, and dashed off to Giza, Egypt, where Kinich was hiding out. Like I said, a typical day.

Jealous? Well, don't be. I haven't gotten to the real story, yet.

Cue jazz hands and waffly waves of air for extended flashback ...

It all started when I arrived at the small, dusty market. Normally, this section of Giza bustled with camels, caged birds, and those other stinky animals—humans—but on this particular day, the place was a ghost town. When I asked Minky to do a quick sweep of the city, she immediately reported back. The masses were gathered outside the pharaoh's palace for a big speech. Naturally, we went to check it out, and that's when I saw *him.*

Hello, man-candy!

As I stood at the foot of his great temple, the desert sun glistened off his rippling abs and deeply tanned, bare chest, his golden staff gripped in his large, powerful hand (yes, yes. I mean a real staff! Not his man-trinket. Jeez ...). In typical pharaoh fashion, he had a razor-thin beard—more like a sculpted five o'clock shadow—along the very edge of his jaw and an elaborately braided goatee, which we shall call a pharaoh-tee. 'Cause this hottie was no goat. He was more of a huge frigging viper in a man's skin—deadly, powerful, with a barbaric gleam in his eyes. He wore a tall black-and-gold headdress that on any other man would scream "Please kick my ass," but on him, it looked pharaoh-licious.

I licked my lips and watched with sheer fascination as his dark eyes drilled into the crowd, daring anyone to step forward and defy him. I shivered from the raw potency of his male strength. And when our eyes met for the briefest of moments, it felt like being hit with a bolt of lightning. Naughty, dirty, lightning.

Who. Is. That? I thought. Yes, yes. I knew he was the king. But who was he really? What made him tick? Why did he glow with an intoxicating inner light that drew me in like a multi-family hut sale? (The BC version of a garage sale, but with pelts, used stoneware—yes, yes, made from real stone—and the occasional old donkey.) Point was, something about him was utterly irresistible. Why?

Inquiring immortal minds want to know...

Immortal minds also wanted to know what it would take to knock that pretty, pretty man off his pretty, pretty pedestal. I wanted to own him. I wanted to bend him to my will and have him begging me for attention. I wanted to *break* him.

Now, before you judge, my precious little people-pets, I'll refer you back to the earlier part of my story. The part where I tell you I am ancient, lonely, and bored. I can't help who I am or that when I see a mortal such as him, it feels like receiving a shiny new toy from the Universe herself.

And Auntie Cimi wants to play.

I elbowed the bald man to my side, standing with me among an ocean of loyal subjects who'd come to listen to their pharaoh publically decree that from this day forward, Egypt would be a united people.

"Tell me," I said in the man's native tongue, "where does your king spend his nights?"

The man's *shendyt*—a simple pleated, white linen skirt—and golden armband told me he was a slave. One who belonged to the king, perhaps serving food or providing entertainment.

The human didn't answer, but instead stared nervously. I got that reaction a lot. Sometimes I wore my hair bobbed, sometimes long and wild as it was today, but it was always flaming red and equally as uncommon as my pale skin and turquoise eyes.

Thank the gods that mortals can't see Minky. I gripped the slave's shoulder and stared deeply into his eyes. "Tell me your name."

The man blinked several times. "Adom."

Adom. Means "receives help from the gods." It's his lucky day!

"Adom," I said, "you will tell me everything you know about your pharaoh, and in exchange, you will be free. Forever. You will be transported anywhere you like and given a purse of gold coins."

The man nodded slowly and pointed north.

I am a good goddess. I am a gentle goddess. I am a patient goddess. I will not turn him into a dung beetle. "You'll have to be more specific," I said.

"T—t—temple of the Sun. Temple of Ra."

Hmmm...How ironic. I'd actually come to Egypt looking for a real live Sun God. Of course, Kinich didn't really hang out in temples, given he pretended to be a commoner. A seven-foot, golden-haired commoner with turquoise eyes. At least his tan fit right in.

"Is your king married? Got a girlfriend? What kind of music does he like? Ska revival? Dubstep? Oh, wait! I know—'80s love ballads!" I had to imagine a male as beautiful and strong as the pharaoh had hundreds of willing women at his beck and call. And what better music for a Stud-gyptian like him than Journey?

Adom shook his head no. "I do not understand your words."

I sighed. That was my problem; no one did. Probably due to the fact that the dead constantly chattered away in the background of my mind—sounded like being at a really, really big cocktail party—sharing every memory they'd ever had. They also existed in a place beyond the confines of time. They were from the future and the past, which made it extremely difficult to keep the present straight inside my head.

"Skip the music question, Spanky. Just tell me about his love situation," I said.

"But I am named Adom, my lady."

"Oh, Spanky, have you learned nothing yet?" I smiled sweetly. "Now speak! Or I'll rip off your toenails!"

"My king," Adom explained nervously, "has taken a vow of chastity until he finds his queen. He believes women rob men of their power and will only share his with her."

Oh. Now this just got a whole hell of a lot more interesting. Because if there was one thing I liked more than tasty, powerful mortals (and playing with them like a cat plays with a mouse), it was a challenge.

"So if he *were* on the prowl," I asked, "what flavor would he go for? Chocolate, strawberry, peanut butter banana?"

Adom stared blankly, a dribble of sweat streaming from his temple, his shiny brown head reflecting the hot desert sun.

Ugh. "What kind of women does he like?"

"I do not know. I have never seen him with a woman."

Dang it. Curse you, nature! You think you're sooo funny taking the cutest ones away from us girls!

I sighed. "Are you *sure* he would not like me?"

"I cannot say. You are very frightening."

True. So true. But...

"That's not what I meant. Oh, never mind! I will simply have to see for myself. Off with you!" I patted Adom on the head and looked up, up, up at Minky, who was about the size of my pet whale. Of course, Minky only had one head and was invisible. The moment my friend Adom touched her, he would be invisible, too.

"Minky, baby, go with Adom. Once you are out of sight, you know what to do." She'd take him anywhere he liked, and give him as much gold as he could carry. I always kept a few hundred pounds strapped to Minky's saddle. One never knew when one might find a good sale. Or need to bribe a sea turtle. Don't ask.

Minky flailed her head and neighed.

"Yes," I replied. "I'll be in the Sun God suite when you return." I turned to Adom. "All righty! Off you go! See ya, papi." I gave Adom a pat on the tushy. "Fly! Be free!"

Adom zombied off through the crowd with Minky on his tail.

As for me? I had a Sun God to hunt down before my

date with a power-hungry, pious mortal who'd finally met his match.

Damn straight, women rob men of their power. Especially when it came to me.

⸻

Just after midnight, I approached the massive rectangular doorway of the Temple of the Sun. I'd spent the day combing dusty markets, smelling the stench of ripe animal dung, and asking around for Kinich. People knew who he was, but not where, which meant he was likely on another extended nude sunbathing excursion in the desert or off praying to the Creator to make him mortal. Who knew? I'd send Minky out to search when she returned. But point was, I really needed a little fun-time to wash away my pissy mood. This part of the world was blistering, sandy, and the human males did not grant me a "shred of cred" when I told them I'd lop off their hands if they groped me.

For the record, it's seriously no fun lopping off men's hands when they don't see it coming. It's the screaming leading up to the lopping event that makes the punishment magical!

In any case, someone needed to teach these horny sycophants some manners—a topic I planned to bring up with Mr. Hunky Skirt after I hobbled his royal ego and wrapped him around my immortal pinkie. After I determined which ice cream he preferred, that was. Nut delight or soft serve?

Cloaked in a black shroud, I approached the two barechested guards wearing manly micro-minnies and then paused in front of the stone fire pit at the entrance. I gazed appreciatively at the torch-lit, glyph-covered walls. The structure itself was quite impressive. So monumental, in fact, that from a distance, the giant statues of Ra—the Egyptian Sun God—to either side of the grand entryway appeared as tiny figurines balancing oranges atop their heads.

"Evenin' there, cowboys. What are your names?" I unveiled my head and watched the firelight dance in their pupils as they took me in.

"Where did she come from?" gasped the man on the left.

"She must be a creature from bowels of the underworld," said the man on the right.

I shot "Righty" the stink eye before I stomped his toes with my sandal-clad foot. "Oh, now, that was just rude. Do I *look* like I came from a bowel?" I opened my cloak and revealed my very skimpy white halter, busty chest, and little white sarong. I'd made both from panels of linen I'd "borrowed" from a merchant in the market. "Where's the chivalry? Really? I bet you don't get many dates, do you?"

The man trembled and blinked.

"Serenity, big boy. Serenity." I closed my cloak. "Actually, I am the Goddess of the Underworld. And by the way, I'm pretty tired of being mistaken for a man. Osiris? Really. Do I look like an Osiris?"

The two men stared blankly.

"Fine. Clearly we won't resolve this now. Take me to your leader," I said in a deep, ominous voice.

The man on the left lowered his spear and pointed it at my chest.

Grrrr... Time for a little game of Cimi Says. I switched

to my compelling voice and repeated my instructions. If that didn't get him moving fast enough, then I'd simply call upon one of my many other gifts. And let me tell you, I had hundreds of tricks up my proverbial sleeve. Far more than any of my brethren. Pain, compelling, bug-makeovers, physical strength, the ability to sniff out a bargain, speaking all languages, speaking to the dead, nabbing souls, calligraphy, the list went on and on.

What was my secret?

Those Mexican cenotes—freshwater pools we used as portals—were jacked up with the most concentrated, supernatural energy known to god-kind, straight from the River of Tlaloc, which flows between our two dimensions, creating a fabulous superhighway for me and my thirteen brothers and sisters. Now, if you don't know my brethren, I'll fill you in later—they're quite the funky bunch—but the point I'm making is that river has power. Learn to tap into it, and it's a deity Flintstone vitamin, and by deity, I mean me. I'm the only one who's figured it all out. That's why I am undefeatable.

"Right this way," said Lefty. I didn't know if he was a lefty, but he was the man on the left so I christened him Lefty.

The two men led me inside, through a maze of lavishly adorned chambers, and then out to a large private garden. Statues and fire pits lined the stone walkway that led to the steps of a smaller temple where two more guards stood with spears crossed over the doorway.

"She is here to see our pharaoh," said Righty.

The two new door jockeys exchanged glances. "No one enters."

Ugh. I don't have time for this. I pushed past Lefty

and Righty. "Take me. Now," I commanded the two new plebes.

They pulled back their spears but then froze in place with awkward, uncomfortably contorted faces.

Darn it. I brain-locked them. Sometimes it happened. Nobody ever said my powers were perfect.

"Everyone stay put until I return," I grumbled. "And don't let anyone in. I'm sure your pharaoh won't want to be bothered. Unless he's into nut delight, in which case, I'll be right back."

I left the four men behind and entered the temple. "Now, where the hell is my man-cand—" My jaw dropped the moment I entered the spacious sleeping chamber and spotted the king standing outside on his private terrace, gazing up at the night sky, wearing nothing but a teeny tiny, tight little man-skirt. No man-panty lines, either, which obviously meant he was one piece of cloth away from being perfect (aka naked).

Well, hellooooo, cowboy!

His long, black hair, twisted into tiny plaits, adorned with gold beads and thread, cascaded down the center of his deeply tanned, broad back. His smooth skin rippled with powerful muscles, two of which were his hard ass.

I sucked in an equally hard breath. That hard ass was connected to the most gorgeous set of powerful, manly thighs I'd ever seen on a mortal. I could only imagine what hung down the other side.

"Are you going to say something or simply stand there all night staring at my ass?" he said in a deep, calm voice, not bothering to turn around.

"Well, obviously, I'm going to stare at your ass. Why? Do I get a prize?"

From the moment the strange woman entered his chamber he knew she was there. Her energy filled the room like a fragrant oil fills the nostrils.

Of course, he had been expecting her. A prayer to the goddess Bastet never went unanswered when one's heart was true to the deities and of divine origin as was his.

And when the woman arrived, he looked out across the dark, star-filled sky, thanking the deities for delivering his wish: A divine female worthy of his greatness, to worship his strength and power, and to provide him with many heirs to rule after his mortal shell crossed over the glorious banks of the Nile to join the gods for eternity.

"I've been expecting you." He turned, proudly displaying his cloaked but prominently displayed phallus. After all, there was no purpose in hiding his glorious erection. It was a badge of honor, a sign of his superior, kingly virility. And of his desperation to end the self-imposed sexual drought. He'd vowed to the gods to abstain until her arrival, confident they would be pleased by his sacrifice and deliver his request.

They had. Delivered, that was. There were simply a few unexpected turns. Nothing a powerful pharaoh could not handle.

What mattered was that his agony was finally over. He would bed her immediately, this very evening, and plant his seed. The ceremonies and public declarations to appease the subjects could come after he'd had his fill of her silky, pale thighs and seen the sure signs of a new life within her.

The woman's wide, jewel-colored eyes dropped to his

shaft, and drank him in without shame. "Is that a pyramid in your man-skirt or are you hiding my unicorn?"

"You like what you see?" he asked. "Good. This pleases me. There will be no room for shyness in my bed." He reached for her chin, instantly feeling a powerful burst of energy coarse through him. He made a point not to react; he'd been expecting a goddess, after all. He tilted her head and stared down at her. "You are very small, but quite lovely. I could not have picked better myself." *Yes, she will make a fine queen.*

He yanked off his *shendyt* and pointed toward the large sleeping platform covered with the finest pillows and softest sheets known to man. "Now disrobe and lay down so that I may enjoy the pleasures of your divine flesh."

Penelope needs money—lots of it and fast, to save her mother's life. So when an offer to carry a stranger's baby falls into her lap, and with it, a million-dollar payday, she can't say no. But then she realizes just who is fathering this golden child, and things go very quickly from steamy to scorching…

Please turn this page
for an excerpt from

Sun God Seeks… Surrogate?

Prologue

Wondering which screw in her head had come loose *this* time, twenty-four-year-old Emma Keane strapped a parachute to her back in preparation for another fun-filled jungle mission.

"Dammit! Stop wiggling!" she barked over her shoulder. "And that had better be your flashlight!"

Well, actually, it was a cranky, rather large warrior named Brutus strapped to her back and wearing the parachute because she had yet to find time for skydiving lessons.

Dork.

In any case, looking like a ridiculous, oversized baby kangaroo wasn't enough to stop her from making this nocturnal leap into enemy territory—Maaskab territory. She had scores to settle.

Emma sucked in a deep breath, the roar of the plane's large engines and Brutus's growls making it difficult to find her center—the key to winning any battle. And not freaking out.

Funny. If someone had told her a year ago that she'd end up here, an immortal demigoddess engaged to the infamous God of Death and War, she would have said, "Christ! Yep! That *toootally* sounds about right."

Why the hell not? She'd lived the first twenty-two years of her life with Guy—a nickname she'd given her handsome god—obsessed with his seductive voice, a voice only she could hear. Turned out, after they finally met face-to-face, their connection ran blood deep. Universe deep, actually. A match made by fate.

Emma rubbed her hands together, summoning the divine power deep within her cells. One blast with her fingertips and she could split a man right down the middle.

"Careful where you put those," Guy said, cupping himself.

Emma gazed up at his smiling face and couldn't help but admire the glorious, masculine view. *Sigh*. She knew she'd been born to love him, flaws—enormous ego and otherworldly bossiness—and all.

His smile melted away. "Please change your mind, my sweet. Stay on the plane, and let me do your fighting."

"Can't do that," she replied. "The Maaskab took my grandmother, and I'm going to be the one to get her back. Even if I have to kill Tommaso to do it."

Guy shook his head. "No. You are to let me deal with him."

Emma felt her immortal blood boil. She'd trusted Tommaso once, and he'd betrayed her. Almost gotten her killed, too. But she'd known—well, she'd *thought*—it wasn't Tommaso's fault. He'd been injected with liquid black jade, an evil substance that could darken the heart of an angel. That's why, after he'd been captured and mortally wounded, she had begged the gods to cure him.

Then she did the unthinkable: she'd put her faith in him again.

Stupid move.

He'd turned on her a second time, the bastard. Yes, his betrayal—done of his own free will—was her prize on that fateful night almost one year ago, when her grandmother showed up on their doorstep in Italy, leading an army of evil Maaskab priests, her mind clearly poisoned.

"If Tommaso hadn't helped her escape, we could've saved her," she said purely to vent, because she really wanted to cry. But the fiancée of the God of Death and War didn't cry. Especially in front of the hundred warriors riding shotgun on the plane tonight.

Okay, maybe one teeny tiny tear while no one's looking.

"Do not give up hope, Emma." Guy clutched her hand, "And do not forget...whatever happens, I love you. Until the last ray of sunlight. Until the last flicker of life inhabits this planet."

Brutus groaned and rolled his eyes, clearly annoyed by the sappy chatter.

Emma elbowed him in the ribs. "Shush! And how can you of all people be uncomfortable with a little affection? Huh? You bunk with eight dudes every night. That's gross by the way. Not the dude part. I'm cool with that. But eight big, sweaty warriors all at once? Yuck. So don't judge me because I'm into the one-man-at-a-time rule. That's messed up, Brutus."

Brutus growled and Guy chuckled.

In truth, Emma didn't know what Brutus was into or how he and his elite team slept, but she loved teasing him. She figured that sooner or later she'd find the magic words to get Brutus to speak to her.

No luck yet.

Accepting a temporary defeat, she shrugged and turned her attention back to the task at hand. She took one last look at her delicious male—nearly seven feet of solid muscle with thick blue-black waves of hair and bronzed skin. *Sigh.* "Okay. I'm ready," she declared boldly. "Let's kill some Scabs and get my granny!"

She glanced over her other shoulder at Penelope, their newest family member. Her dark hair was pulled into a tight ponytail that accentuated the anger simmering in her dark green eyes. Pissed would be a serious understatement.

Emma didn't blame her. What a cluster.

"Ready?" Emma asked.

"You better believe it," Penelope replied. "These clowns picked the wrong girl to mess with."

Guy frowned as they leaped from the plane into the black night.

Glossary

Baktun: Twenty cycles of the Mayan calendar equal to 144,000 days or approximately 394 years.

Black Jade: Found only in a particular mine located in southern Mexico, this jade has very special supernatural properties, including the ability to absorb supernatural energy—in particular, god energy. When worn by humans, it is possible for them to have physical contact with a god. If injected, it can make a person addicted to doing bad things. If the jade is fueled with dark energy and then released, it can be used as a weapon. Chaam personally likes using it to polish his teeth.

Book of the Oracle of Delphi: This mystical text from 1400 BC is said to have been created by one of the great oracles at Delphi and can tell the future. As the events in present time change the future, the book's pages magically rewrite themselves. The demigods use this book in Book #2 to figure out when and how to kill the vampire queen. Helena also reads it while they're held captive, and learns she must sacrifice her mortality to save Niccolo.

Cenote: Limestone sinkholes connected to a subterranean water system. They are found in Central America and southern Mexico and were once believed by the Mayans to be sacred portals to the afterlife. Such smart humans! They were right. Except cenotes are actually portals to the realm of the gods.

(If you have never seen a cenote, do a quick search on the Internet for "cenote photos," and you'll see how freaking cool they are!)

Demilords: (Spoiler alert for Book #2!) This is a group of immortal badass vampires who've been infused with the light of the gods. They are extremely difficult to kill and hate their jobs (killing Obscuros) almost as much as they hate the gods who control them.

Maaskab: Originally a cult of bloodthirsty Mayan priests who believed in the dark arts. It is rumored they are responsible for bringing down their entire civilization with their obsession for human sacrifices (mainly young female virgins). Once Chaam started making half-human children, he decided all firstborn males would make excellent Maaskab due to their proclivity for evil.

Mocos, Mobscuros, O'scabbies: Nicknames for when you join Maaskab with Obscuros to create a brand-new malevolent treat.

Obscuros: Evil vampires who do not live by the Pact and who like to dine on innocent humans since they really do taste the best.

The Pact: An agreement between the gods and good vampires that dictates the dos and don'ts. There are many parts to it, but the most important rules are vampires are not allowed to snack on good people (called Forbiddens), they must keep their existence a secret, and they are responsible for keeping any rogue vampires in check.

Payal: Although the gods can take humans to their realm and make them immortal, Payals are the true genetic offspring of the gods but are born mortal, just like their human mothers. Only firstborn children inherit the gods' genes and manifest their traits. If the firstborn happens to be female, she is a Payal. If male, well... then you get something kind of yucky (see definition of Maaskab)!

The Tablet: A Mayan relic made of black jade. It has the power to create portals to other dimensions and to another moment in time.

Uchben: An ancient society of scholars and warriors who serve as the gods' eyes and ears in the human world. They also do the books and manage the gods' earthly assets.

Vamp-ubus, Incu-pire: The saucy combination of an incubus and a vampire.

Character Definitions

The Gods

Although every culture around the world has their own names and beliefs related to beings of worship, there are actually only fourteen gods. And since the gods are able to access the human world only through the portals called cenotes, located in the Yucatán, the Mayans were big fans.

The gods often refer to each other as brother and sister, but the truth is they are just another species of the Creator and completely unrelated.

Acan—God of Intoxication and Wine: Also known as Belch, Acan has been drunk for a few thousand years. He hopes to someday trade places with Votan because he's tired of his flabby muscles and beer belly.

Ah-Ciliz—God of Solar Eclipses: Called A.C. by his brethren, Ah-Ciliz is generally thought of as the party pooper because of his dark attitude.

Akna—Goddess of Fertility: You either love her or you hate her.

Backlum Chaam—God of Male Virility: He's responsible for discovering black jade, figuring out how to procreate with humans, and kicking off the chain of events that will eventually lead to the Great War.

Camaxtli—Goddess of the Hunt: Also known as Fate, Camaxtli holds a special position among the gods, since no one dares challenge her. When Fate has spoken, that's the end of the conversation.

Colel Cab—Mistress of Bees: Because really, where would we all be without the bees?

Goddess of Forgetfulness: Um…I forget her name. Sorry.

Ixtab—Goddess of Suicide: Ixtab is generally described as a loner. Could it be those dead critters she carries around? But don't judge her so hastily. You never know what truly lies behind that veil of black she wears.

K'ak: The history books remember him as K'ak Tiliw Chan Yopaat, ruler of Copán in the 700s AD. King K'ak (don't you just love that name? Tee-hee-hee…) is one of Cimil's favorite brothers. We're not really sure what he does, but he can throw bolts of lightning.

Kinich Ahau—ex–God of the Sun: Also known by many other names, depending on the culture, Kinich likes to go by Nick these days. He's also now a vampire—something he's actually not so bummed about, except that the sifting dimension has been closed (something he's always wanted to do) and the love of his life is filled with sunshine. Talk about hot sex . . .

Máax—The One No One Speaks Of: His story is a bit of a mystery, but all will be revealed in Book #5, *Accidentally . . . Over?*

Votan—God of Death and War: Also known as Odin, Wotan, Wodan, God of Drums (he has no idea how the hell he got that title; he hates the drums), and God of Multiplication (okay, he is pretty darn good at math so that one makes sense). These days, Votan goes by Guy Santiago (it's a long story—read Book #1), but despite his deadly tendencies, he's all heart. He's now engaged to Emma Keane.

Yum Cimil—Goddess of the Underworld: Also known as Ah-Puch by the Mayans, Mictlantecuhtli (try saying that one ten times) by the Aztec, Grim Reaper by the Europeans, Hades by the Greeks . . . you get the picture! Despite what people say, Cimil is actually a female, adores a good bargain (especially garage sales) and the color pink. She's also batshit crazy.

Zac Cimi—Bacab of the North: What the heck is a Bacab? According to the gods' folklore, the Bacabs are the four eldest and most powerful of the gods. Zac, however, has yet to discover his true gifts, although he is physically the strongest. Once thought to be the God of Love, we now know differently by the end of this book.

Not the Gods

Andrus: Ex-Demilord (vampire who's been given the gods' light), now just a demigod after his maker, the vampire queen, died. According to Cimil, his son, who hasn't been born yet, is destined to marry Helena and Niccolo's daughter.

Anne: Not telling.

Antonio Acero: Don't want to put any spoilers here, so let's just say he's a hunky, playboy Spaniard with a dirty mouth and a dark secret.

Brutus: One of Gabrán's elite Uchben warriors. He doesn't speak much, but that's because he and his team are telepathic. They are also immortal (a gift from the gods) and next in line to be Uchben chiefs.

Emma Keane: A reluctant Payal who can split a man right down the middle with her bare hands. She is engaged to Votan (aka Guy Santiago) and really wants to kick the snot out of Tommaso, the man who betrayed her.

Father Xavier: Once a priest at the Vatican, Xavier is now the Uchben's top scholar and historian. He has a thing for jogging suits, Tyra Banks, and Cimil.

Gabrán: One of the Uchben chiefs and a very close friend of the gods. The chiefs have been given the gods' light and are immortal—a perk of the job.

Gabriela: Emma Keane's grandmother and one of the original Payals. She now leads the Maaskab at the young age of eightysomething.

Helena Strauss: Once human, Helena is now a vampire and married to Niccolo DiConti. She has a half-vampire daughter, Matty, who is destined to marry Andrus's son, according to Cimil.

Jess: Not telling.

Julie Trudeau: Penelope's mother.

Niccolo DiConti: Ex–General of the Vampire Army. He is the interim vampire leader now that the queen is dead, because the army remained loyal to him. He is married to Helena Strauss and has a half-vampire daughter Matty—a wedding gift from Cimil.

Nick (short for Niccole): (From Book #1, not to be confused with Kinich). Also not telling.

Penelope Trudeau: The woman Cimil approaches to be her brother's surrogate.

Philippe: Roberto's brother. An Ancient One.

Reyna: The dead vampire queen.

Roberto (Narmer): Originally an Egyptian pharaoh, Narmer was one of the six Ancient Ones—the very first vampires. He eventually changed his name to Roberto and moved to Spain—something to do with one of Cimil's little schemes. Rumor is, he wasn't too happy about it.

Sentin: One of Niccolo's loyal vampire soldiers. Viktor turned him into a vampire after finding him in a ditch during World War II.

Tommaso: Oh, boy. Where to start. Once an Uchben, Tommaso's mind was poisoned with black jade. He tried to kill Emma. She's not happy about that.

Viktor: Niccolo's right hand and BFF. He's approximately one thousand years old and originally a Viking. He's big. He's blond. He's got the hots for some blonde woman he's dreamed of for the last five hundred years. He's also Helena's maker.

Match the Quote—Answers

Which Deity Said What?

1. "There's a method to my madness. Yes, that method might be a teensy bit evil and seemingly random, but someone's gotta make life interesting."
   <u>A. Cimil, ex–Goddess of the Underworld</u>
   B. Acan, God of Intoxication and Wine
   C. Zac Cimi, God of (TDD)

2. "Living for seventy thousand years without love is a fate I would not wish on my worst enemies."
   <u>A. Máax, the One No One Speaks Of</u>
   B. Camaxtli, Goddess of the Hunt
   C. K'ak, just…K'ak.

3. "A happy ending awaits us all, but only if we are brave enough to risk everything and have faith it will come."
   <u>A. Ixtab, Goddess of Suicide</u>
   B. Camaxtli, Goddess of the Hunt
   C. Akna, Goddess of Fertility

4. "Don't touch the unicorn. Never, ever touch the
   unicorn."
   A. Cimil, ex–Goddess of the Underworld
   B. The clowns (Cimil thinks they are deities, so that
       counts)
   C. Cimil's unicorn

THE DISH

Where Authors Give You the Inside Scoop

From the desk of Vicky Dreiling

Dear Reader,

I had a lot of imaginary boyfriends when I was a kid. My friend Kim and I read *Tiger Beat* magazine and chose our loves. I "dated" David Cassidy, a yesteryear heartthrob from a TV show called *The Partridge Family*. Kim's "boyfriend" was Donny Osmond, although she might have had a brief crush on Barry Williams, better known as Greg from *The Brady Bunch*. I did a quick search online and discovered that *Tiger Beat* magazine still exists, but the stars for today's preteens are Justin Bieber, Taylor Lautner, and members of the boy band One Direction.

The idea of a big family and rock-star boyfriends really appealed to us. We traveled in imaginary tour buses to imaginary concerts. We listened to the music and sang along, pretending we were onstage, too. Of course, we invented drama, such as mean girls trying to steal our famous boyfriends backstage.

Recently, I realized that the seeds of the families I create in my novels were sown in my preteen years as Kim and I pretended to date our celebrity crushes. As I got older, imaginary boyfriends led to real-life boyfriends in high school and college. Eventually, marriage and kids led to an extended family, one that continues to grow.

In WHAT A RECKLESS ROGUE NEEDS, two close families meet once a year at a month-long house party. As in real life, much has changed for Colin and Angeline. While they were born only a week apart, they never really got along very well. An incident at Angeline's come-out ball didn't help matters, either. Many years have elapsed, and now Colin finds he needs Angeline's help to keep from losing a property that holds very deep emotional ties for him. Once they cross the threshold of Sommerall House, their lives are never the same again, but they will always have their families.

May the Magic Romance Fairies be with all of you and your families!

Vicky Dreiling

www.VickyDreiling.com
Twitter @VickyDreiling
Facebook.com/VickyDreilingHistoricalAuthor

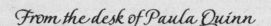

From the desk of Paula Quinn

Dear Reader,

As most of you know, I love dogs. I have six of them. I see your eyes bugging out. Six?? Yes, six precious tiny Chihuahuas and all together they weight approximately twenty-seven pounds. I've had dogs my whole life—big ones, little ones. So it's not surprising that I would want to write dogs into my books. This time I went big: 140 pounds of big.

In THE SEDUCTION OF MISS AMELIA BELL we meet Grendel, an Irish wolfhound mix, who along with our hero, Edmund MacGregor, wins the heart of our heroine, Amelia Bell. Grendel is the son of Aurelius, whom some of you might remember as the puppy Colin MacGregor gave to Edmund, his stepson, in *Conquered by a Highlander*. Since this series is called Highland Heirs, I figured why not include the family dog heirs as well?

I loved writing a dog as a secondary character, and Grendel is an important part of Edmund and Amelia's story. Now, really, what's better than a big, brawny, sexy Highlander? Right: a big, brawny, sexy Highlander with a dog. Or if you live in NYC, you can settle for a hunky guy playing with his dog in the park.

My six babies all have distinct personalities. For instance, Riley loves to bark and be an all-around pain in the neck. He's high-strung and loves it. Layla, my biggest girl, must "mother" all the others. She keeps them in line with a soft growl and a lick to the eyeball. Liam, my tiny three-pound boy, isn't sure if he's Don Juan or Napoleon. He'll drop and show you his package if you call him cute. They are all different and I wanted Grendel to have his own personality, too.

Much like his namesake, Grendel hates music and powdered periwigs. He's faithful and loyal, and he loves to chase smaller things…like people. Even though Edmund is his master and Grendel does, of course, love him best, it doesn't take Amelia long to win his heart, or for Grendel to win hers, and he soon finds himself following at her heels. Some of my favorite scenes involve the subtle interactions between Amelia and Grendel. This big, seemingly vicious dog is always close by when Amelia is sad or afraid. When things are going on all around them, Amelia just has to rest her hand on Grendel's head and it completely calms her. We witness a partial transformation of ownership in the small, telltale ways Grendel remains ever constant at Amelia's side.

Even when Grendel finds Gaza, his own love interest (hey, I'm a romance writer, what can I say?), he is still faithful to his human lady. We won't get into doggy love, but suffice it to say, there will be plenty of furry heirs living in Camlochlin for a long time to come. They might not be the prettiest dogs in Skye, but they are the most loyal.

This was my first foray into writing a dog as a secondary character and I must say I fell in love with a big, slobbering mutt named after a fiend who killed men for singing. I wasn't surprised that Grendel filled his place so well in Edmund and Amelia's story. Each of my dogs does the same in mine and my kids' stories. That's what dogs do. They run headlong into our lives barking, tail wagging, sharing wet, sloppy kisses. They love us with an almost supernatural, unconditional love. And we love them back.

I hope you get a chance to pick up THE SEDUCTION OF MISS AMELIA BELL and meet Edmund and Amelia and, of course, Grendel.

Happy reading!

Paula Quinn

♥ ♥ ♥ ♥ ♥ ♥ ♥ ♥ ♥ ♥ ♥ ♥ ♥ ♥ ♥

From the desk of Kristen Ashley

Dear Reader,

Years ago, I was walking to the local shops and, as usual, I had my headphones in. As I was walking, Bob Seger & The Silver Bullet Band's "You'll Accomp'ny Me" came on and somehow, even having heard this song dozens and dozens of times before, the lyrics suddenly hit me.

This isn't unusual. I have to be in a certain mood to absorb lyrics. But when I am, sometimes they'll seep into my soul, making me smile, or making me cry.

"You'll Accomp'ny Me" made me smile. It made me feel warm. And it made me feel happy because the lyrics are beautiful, the message of love and devotion is strong, the passion is palpable, and the way it's written states that Bob definitely has Kristen Ashley alpha traits.

I loved it. I've always loved that song, but then I loved it even more. It was like one of my books in song form. How could I not love that?

At the time, however, I didn't consider it for a book, not inspiring one or not to be used in a scene. For a long time, it was just mine, giving me that warm feeling and a smile on my face at the thought that there is musical proof out there that these men exist.

Better, they wield guitars.

Now, from the very moment I introduced Hop in *Motorcycle Man*, he intrigued me. And as we learned more about him in that book, my knowing why he was doing what he was doing, I knew he'd have to be redeemed in my readers' eyes by sharing his whole story. I just didn't know who was going to give him the kind of epic happy ending I felt he deserved.

Therefore, I didn't know that Lanie would be the woman of his dreams. Truth be told, I didn't even expect Lanie to have her own book. But her story as told in *Motorcycle Man* was just too heartbreaking to leave her hanging. I just had no idea what to do with her.

But I didn't think a stylish, professional, accomplished "lady" and a biker would jibe, so I never considered these two together. Or, in fact, Lanie with any of the Chaos brothers at all.

That is, until this song came up on shuffle again and I knew that was how Hop would consider his relationship with Lanie. Even as she pushed him away due to her past, he'd do what he could to convince her that, someday, she'd accompany him.

I mean, just those words—how cool are they? "You'll accompany me." Brilliant.

But Bob, his Silver Bullet Band, and their music did

quadruple duty in FIRE INSIDE. Not only did they give me "You'll Accomp'ny Me," which was the perfect way for Hop to express his feelings to Lanie; they also gave me Hop's nickname for Lanie: "lady". *And* they gave me "We've Got Tonight," yet another perfect song to fit what was happening between Lanie and Hop. And last, the way Bob sings is also the way I hear Hop in my head.

I interweave music in my books all the time and my selections are always emotional and, to me, perfect.

But I've never had a song, or artist, so beautifully help me tell my tale than when I utilized the extraordinary storytelling abilities of Bob Seger in my novel FIRE INSIDE.

It's a pleasure listening to his music.

It's a gift to be inspired by it.

Kristen Ashley

♥ ♥ ♥ ♥ ♥ ♥ ♥ ♥ ♥ ♥ ♥ ♥ ♥ ♥ ♥

From the desk of Mimi Jean Pamfiloff

Dear Reader,

When it came time to decide which god or goddess in my Accidentally Yours series would get their HEA in book four, I sat back and looked at who was most in need of salvation. Hands down, the winner was Ixtab, the Goddess of Suicide. Before you judge the title, however, I'd like to explain why this goddess is not the dreary soul you might imagine. Fact is she's more like the Goddess of Anti-Suicide, with the ability to drain dark feelings from one person and redeploy them to another. Naturally, being a deity, she tends to help those who are down on their luck and punish those who are truly deserving.

However, every now and again, someone bumps into her while she's not looking. The results are fatal. So after thousands of years and thousands of accidental deaths, she's determined to keep everyone away. Who could blame her?

But fate has other plans for this antisocial goddess with a kind streak. His name is Dr. Antonio Acero, and this sexy Spaniard has just become the lynchpin in the gods' plans for saving the planet from destruction. He's also in need of a little therapy, and Ixtab is the only one who can help him.

When these two meet, they quickly realize there are forces greater than them both, trying to pull them apart and push them together. Which force will win?

♥ ♥ ♥ ♥ ♥ ♥ ♥ ♥ ♥ ♥ ♥ ♥ ♥ ♥ ♥ ♥

From the desk of Katie Lane

Dear Reader,

As some of you may already know, the idea for my fictional town of Bramble, Texas, came from the hours I spent watching *The Andy Griffith Show*. When Barney, Aunt Bee, and Opie were on, my mom couldn't peel me away from our console television. The townsfolk's antics held me spellbound. Which is probably why I made my characters a little crazy, too. (Okay, so I made them a lot crazy.) But while the people of Mayberry had levelheaded Sheriff Andy Taylor to keep them in line, the townsfolk of Bramble have been allowed to run wild.

Until now.

I'm pleased as punch to introduce Sheriff Dusty Hicks, the hero of my newest Deep in the Heart of Texas novel, A MATCH MADE IN TEXAS. Like Andy, he's a dedicated lawman who loves his job and the people of his community. Unlike Andy, he carries a gun, has a wee bit of a temper, and is blessed with the kind of looks and hard body that can make a good girl turn bad. And after just one glimpse of Dusty's shiny handcuffs, Brianne Cates wants to turn bad. Real bad.

But it won't be easy for Brianne to seduce a little lawman lovin' out of my hero. Dusty has his hands full trying to regain joint custody of his precocious three-year-old daughter and, at the same time, deal with a con-artist television evangelist and a vengeful cartel drug lord. Not to mention the townsfolk of Bramble, who have suddenly gone wa-a-ay off their rockers.

All I can say is, what started out as a desire to give Bramble its very own Sheriff Taylor quickly turned into a fast-paced joyride that left my hair standing on end and my heart as warm and gooey as a toaster strudel. I hope it will do the same for you. :o)

Much love,

Katie Lane

♥ ♥ ♥ ♥ ♥ ♥ ♥ ♥ ♥ ♥ ♥ ♥ ♥ ♥ ♥ ♥

From the desk of Jessica Lemmon

Dear Reader,

I love a scruffy-faced, tattooed, motorcycle-riding bad boy as much as the next girl, so when it came time to write HARD TO HANDLE, I knew what qualities I wanted Aiden Downey to possess.

For inspiration, I needed to look no further than Charlie Hunnam from the famed TV show *Sons of Anarchy*. I remember watching Season 1 on Netflix, mouth agape and eyes wide. When Charlie's character, Jax Teller, finished his first scene, I looked over at my husband and said, "*That's* Aiden!"

In HARD TO HANDLE, Aiden may have been crafted with a bad-boy starter kit: He has the scruff, the tattoo, the knee-weakening dimples that make him look like sin on a stick, and yeah, a custom Harley-Davidson to boot. But Aiden also has something extra special that derails his bad-boy image: a heart of near-solid gold.

When we first met Aiden and Sadie in *Tempting the Billionaire* (and again in the e-novella *Can't Let Go*), there wasn't much hope for these two hurting hearts to work out their differences. Aiden had been saddled with devastating news and familial responsibilities, and Sadie (poor Sadie!) had just opened up her heart to Aiden, who stomped on it, broke it into pieces, and set it on fire for good measure. How could they forgive each other after things had gone so horribly, terribly wrong?

Aiden has suffered a lot of loss, but in HARD TO HANDLE, he's on a mission to get his life *back*. A very large piece of that puzzle is winning back the woman he never meant to hurt, the woman he loved. Sadie, with her walled-up heart, smart, sassy mouth, and fiery attitude isn't going to be an easy nut to crack. Especially after she vowed to never, ever get hurt again. That goes *double* for the blond Adonis with the unforgettable mouth and ability to turn her brain into Silly Putty.

The best part about this good "bad" boy? Aiden's determination is as rock-hard as his abs. He's not going to let Sadie walk away, not now that he sees how much she still cares for him. Having been to hell and back, Aiden isn't intimidated by her. Not even a little bit. Sadie is his Achilles' heel, and Aiden accepts that it's going to take time (and plenty of seduction!) to win her over. He also knows that she's worth it.

Think you're up for a ride around the block with a bad-boy-done-good? I have to say, Aiden left a pretty deep mark on my heart and I'm still a little in love with him! He may change your mind about scruffy, motorcycle-riding hotties...He certainly managed to change Sadie's.

Happy reading!

Jessica Lemmon

www.jessicalemmon.com

Find out more about Forever Romance!

Visit us at
www.hachettebookgroup.com/publishing_forever.aspx

Find us on Facebook
http://www.facebook.com/ForeverRomance

Follow us on Twitter
http://twitter.com/ForeverRomance

NEW AND UPCOMING TITLES

Each month we feature our new titles
and reader favorites.

CONTESTS AND GIVEAWAYS

We give away galleys, autographed copies,
and all kinds of exclusive items.

AUTHOR INFO

You'll find bios, articles, and links to personal websites
for all your favorite authors—and so much more.

GET SOCIAL

Connect with your favorite authors, editors, and
other Forever fans, and share what's important to you.

THE BUZZ

Sign up for our monthly romance newsletter,
and be the first to read all about it.

VISIT US ONLINE AT

WWW.HACHETTEBOOKGROUP.COM

FEATURES:

OPENBOOK BROWSE AND
SEARCH EXCERPTS
•
AUDIOBOOK EXCERPTS AND PODCASTS
•
AUTHOR ARTICLES AND INTERVIEWS
•
BESTSELLER AND PUBLISHING
GROUP NEWS
•
SIGN UP FOR E-NEWSLETTERS
•
AUTHOR APPEARANCES AND TOUR
INFORMATION
•
SOCIAL MEDIA FEEDS AND WIDGETS
•
DOWNLOAD FREE APPS

BOOKMARK HACHETTE BOOK GROUP
@ WWW.HACHETTEBOOKGROUP.COM